STOPPING
for GREEN LIGHTS

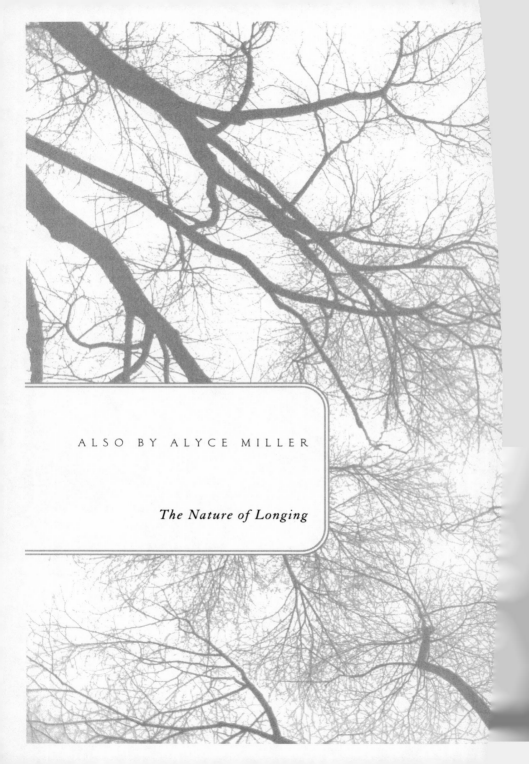

ALSO BY ALYCE MILLER

The Nature of Longing

STOPPING

for GREEN LIGHTS

BY ALYCE MILLER

DOUBLEDAY
New York / London /
Toronto / Sydney / Auckland

PUBLISHED BY DOUBLEDAY
a division of Random House, Inc.
1540 Broadway, New York, New York 10036

DOUBLEDAY and the portrayal of an anchor
with a dolphin are trademarks of Doubleday,
a division of Random House, Inc.

Portions of this work were originally published as "What Jasmine Would Think" in
The Nature of Longing.

Book design by Leah S. Carlson-Stanisic

Library of Congress Cataloging-in-Publication Data
Miller, Alyce.
Stopping for green lights / by Alyce Miller. — 1st ed.
p.   cm.
I.   Title.
PS3563.I37424S76   1999
813'.54—dc21   98-28610
                                               CIP

ISBN: 0-385-48944-7
Copyright © 1999 by Alyce Miller
All Rights Reserved
Printed in the United States of America
February 1999
First Edition
1   3   5   7   9   10   8   6   4   2

I had seen white folks pass on green and therefore assumed the red light was for me.

—*Zora Neale Hurston*

. . . He Was Cool or: He Even Stopped for Green Lights

—*Haki Madhubuti (formerly Don Lee)*

STOPPING

for GREEN LIGHTS

I

When Tish was born, her father named a star for her. Because, he liked to joke, if she ever forgot where she was, she could always look to the sky and find her place again. Growing up, she came to believe in the immutability of the star with her name, out of reach, and visible only at night. The proof, an embossed certificate, lay sealed in a plastic envelope in her bureau drawer among other treasured childhood objects—an old metal gum-machine ring Peachy Stubbs's boy cousin Dev gave her in third grade, a pink and white plastic lanyard from Angela Thompson for stringing a house key, a worn, stuffed cat with crooked eyes her father had brought home from one of his trips. She liked that there were no stars in the heavens specifically assigned to her three younger brothers, Ford, Fisher, and Francis. Maybe, she thought, it was because they were boys and already knew where they fit. Or maybe it was because her father chose to share with her the solace he found in the mysteries of the heavens, knowing they were running out of solutions on earth.

He was a tall, quiet man, with narrow, sloping shoulders, mostly patient and rarely given to temper, but distracted with work. He taught social sciences at the university, and wrote scholarly articles about race and poverty, made up of so many typewritten pages floating loose through the house like dried leaves. Pages of old discarded drafts, lines Xed out, crookedly jotted corrections trapped in the margins, were used for scrap paper, for homework, for doodling, for Scrabble scores, for the private drawings and writings Tish kept in a binder. Sometimes she would write over her father's words with her own.

It was said the two of them looked alike *(You must be Martin Espy's girl)*, though his tight, curly hair was black and cropped close to his head, while hers, a bright wiry red, sprang away from her scalp, thick and startled. Where her eyes held a light gray-sky cast his were earthy brown with yellow flecks. They shared the same broad bridge of nose, and high cheekbones, the legacy, so it was said, of two unnamed Cherokee ancestors no one seemed to know much about.

It had been their routine for years; on clear nights, her father, burdened by the seemingly insoluble state of worldly affairs would summon her into the backyard to consider the stars, and what lay beyond. She tried unsuccessfully to identify the constellations, drawn more to the music of their names than their actual shapes in the sky.

Canis Major, Orion, Pleiades, Little Dipper, Big Dipper.

Up, up, up, she stared at the Milky Way. A million tiny jewels winked down from the corridor of white mist, a place so vast you could get lost just looking.

That was long ago, when things were different. Back then, Tish believed her father knew everything, that the demonstrations and speeches he attended were a sure sign of change. She believed, like her mother, that the work he was doing would make the world a better place.

Back then, the sky at night was full of hope and promise.

"What *are* stars?" she once asked, thinking they reminded her of the gold-foil wrapping on the chocolates her mother put out in cut-glass bowls each Christmas.

"Basically a lot of hot gas. Gravity holds them together."

"What makes them twinkle?"

"Atmospheric dust. Particles. It's an illusion. They're not really—" He paused. "Do they twinkle for you?"

She nodded. He smiled and let it go at that.

What didn't her father know? He understood music, art, history, and foreign languages, odd things like fish and stars, the things below and the things above. Last winter he had even built his own telescope in their basement, grinding the lens himself with painstaking devotion.

That stars were only a trick of hot gas seemed preposterous. Secretly she imagined them alternately as the flickering eyes of some jumbo celestial creature, or the lights of a large and distant city beckoning. After his words faded, and she looked up again, the stars reassuringly became themselves again. Escaped slaves, he liked to tell her, had followed the North Star on the Underground Railroad to freedom. Harriet Tubman had found her way by the night sky and then returned again and again to help others, risking her own life, dependent on stars. If you're ever lost at night, you can always look up to orient yourself, he told her. *First find Orion, then locate the two pointer stars by his belt. There's your North Star.*

What, Tish wanted to know, did the escaped slaves do on nights it was too cloudy to see?

As she got older, on summer nights when heat made sleep impossible, she lifted herself from the damp sheets and went in search of the night sky. Her father, also sleepless, was predictably out back with one eye glued to the eyepiece of his telescope.

Well into her early teens, Tish took for granted the constancy of the sky, trusting the stars and constellations to govern from above with orderly assurance. What you looked for in the sky was there on faith, even if you couldn't always see it. Below, the facts of the world were not so predictable or easily named. The summer she turned fifteen everything changed. What had once made solid sense broke into pieces, and fell like the burning fragments from the meteorite shower she and her father had watched the year before.

II

Tish sat smoking in the backseat of Peachy Stubbs's mother's old finned Fleetwood, circling the Brazil town square. It was irritating, after all the trouble Peachy'd gone to, convincing her mother to let her have the car, that now there wasn't a soul downtown worth seeing. Call it bad luck. Just a couple of stuck-up white senior cheerleaders in bobby socks and uniforms lounging after practice against the windows of Nickles' Bakery and giggling their way through a sack of powdered doughnuts.

What a waste. Tish leaned forward. "Dag, where *is* everybody?" She'd fidgeted all the way through last-period math, full of expectation, imagining how she'd be seen. Flunked a quiz because she couldn't keep her mind on the equations.

From the driver's seat, Peachy craned her neck, then made a left back onto University Street. "This town is so damn dead. Ain't *no* niggas out today."

Wanda Beals, riding shotgun up front, twisted her head around to fix her eyes first on Tish and then on Wanda's cousin Tina, but her words were really for Peachy's amusement.

"Two darkies up front, two lighties in back. Ain't that right, Peachy girl?" It was her way of messing with Tina for being mixed and with Tish for being all the way white. She sucked her teeth hard and self-consciously shaped the edges of her huge ballooning afro with her fingertips. "Turn on the radio. I want to hear some jams." When Peachy fumbled trying to get the station right, Wanda took over, impatiently flipping the dial until it landed on CKLW out of Detroit. Just in time, too. "Hunh! Witch yo' bad self . . ." The volume soared so high it seemed to Tish the clear autumn sky above was about to split right open. "Say it loud, I'm black and I'm proud." Wanda claimed it. "My song, my song!" The heady brass sliced across the bass and drums. Tish got dizzy. Or maybe it was the nicotine from the third Kool Long Tina had lit and passed over. Squinting through smoke, Tish demonstrated a slow, leisurely french inhale. Her bottom lip slackened into a practiced pout, teasing the smoke upward. It looped back through her nostrils in a thick curl.

Tina imitated, but the circle of smoke lost its shape and fanned awkwardly over her mouth and nostrils. She choked, suppressing a cough. A rosy flush crept into her biscuit-colored cheeks. "No, not like that," Tish mouthed, moving to the beat. Confident, she did it again. "Like this." Tina's eyes almost crossed trying to focus on the spiral of smoke now slowly working its way back up her own nostrils. Tish laughed. "Uhn-uh . . . like *this.*"

Wanda turned around in her seat. "Y'all look nasty, like a couple of snorting bulls." She went back to singing, her giant fro bobbing. Her fingers clicked out the beat, each snap landing on the word *black* for emphasis.

"Say it loud," James Brown rasped. Everyone in the car shrieked back, "I'm black and I'm proud."

All summer the song was everywhere, blaring from open windows on the west side of town, from the stone balcony of Afro House on the university campus, from front porches and yards, from strobe-lit basement parties and thumping car radios. It got so it revolved in Tish's head like a 45 on a turntable. She took another long drag on the cigarette.

The same song lit a fire at the first school assembly in early September when a group of black seniors interrupted the pep rally by plugging in a portable record player. "Say It Loud" blasted into frenzied static and drowned out the cheerleaders prancing in red and white, blond voices shrieking, "Go Indians!" Overpowered, they fell out of line, bumped into one another, pom-poms spilling to the floor, faces blanched in shock. It was somber, determined Ollie Jones, president of the unofficial Black High School Student Union, who strode over and seized the microphone, methodically announcing in his deep bass, "How do you spell *Re-vo-lu-tion!*" while raising his fist slowly into the air just like Tommy Smith at the Olympics.

A roar went up. Chaos spread through the bleachers. Black kids rose like a tidal wave and began to chant back, some with fists upraised. The startled principal stormed to the wall and pulled the plug. James Brown wound down a full octave into a low moan. But the chanting only increased. The principal, face reddening, yanked the microphone from Ollie and turned to the screaming bleachers. "Assembly canceled. Return to your homerooms." But he seemed strangely lost in the surrounding black and brown faces, his voice a disembodied echo. As students were herded out by stern-faced staff, a small determined group of black seniors at the top of the bleachers continued to chant "Revolution!" fists circling in the air. Tish filed out with the others, bodies bumping. You could smell excitement in the air. She glanced back, envious. A skinny brown-skinned boy on his way out taunted the shaken cheerleaders, huddled in consternation near the free-throw line. "Yo' man Dr. King is *d-e-a-d* dead, y'all, and the Revolution is here."

Over to one side Wanda and several other black girls had formed a barricade. Wanda's mouth moved, but it was impossible to hear her above the noise. For a moment her eye caught Tish's, and Tish tried to force her way to the side, but the swelling crowd pushed her on through the door. Her heart was pounding. The principal remained at the mike, unleashing a string of Latinates about consequences for perpetrators and transgressors and their infractions and violations: suspensions and expulsions, a mash of polysyllables barely audible above the chanting students, who continued to intone in one unified voice, no longer concerned with rules and consequences. Excited and shaken, Tish eventually wound up in her customary homeroom seat, relegated to quiet on the order of the teacher, who stood in the doorway. With her pencil tip she began to carve the words "Black Power" into the wooden desktop, half daring someone to catch her in the act. She pressed down hard, face burning. How she hated silence. How she ached to jump up and say something startling to the passive white faces now retreating into smug obedience. There was commotion in the hall—shouts and the sound of running feet. A few black classmates arrived, flouncing into their seats, attitudes squashed by admonishments from the homeroom teacher, voices reduced to bitter whispers. The white kids kept their heads bent. Feet scuffed across the floor, books dropped like bombs onto desktops. *Silence!* the teacher ordered. That day Tish thought the heat of her own flesh would incinerate her on the spot. *Burn, baby, burn,* H. Rap had said. Something had changed irrevocably. This went well beyond the wearing of black armbands the week Otis Redding died. It was bigger, more important.

Now James Brown blared from the Fleetwood radio.

"Say it loud. I'm black and I'm proud." They had all memorized every pause, inflection, and hesitation. It was as if the beat pulsed from Tish's own marrow, up through bone and flesh. "I'm black and I'm proud." Although she knew she had no real claim to the words themselves, a flare of excitement shot through her. Her voice rose indistinguishable from the others. "Say it loud . . ."

One more turn around the square in the late October afternoon. People on the street took notice. White people, Tish thought grimly. The loud music thumping and the rattle of the muffler disturbed their quietude. She grinned triumphantly at Tina, who had hot-boxed the cigarette and was now passing it back. They were creating a disturbance for the world to sit up and take notice of.

From up front Peachy and Wanda screamed, "We'd rather die on our feet . . . than keep livin' on our knees. Say it loud!" and Peachy, her funny little acorn head bobbing, pounded on the steering wheel with the heel of her right hand. The whole car rocked.

Peachy had lied to her mother, calling her learner's permit a license. She wouldn't even be sixteen for another three months.

Outside and beyond the rolled-down windows the changing leaves of ancient trees in the square sparkled and shimmered. The old Fleetwood seemed to float on air, like a magic carpet. In the late-afternoon sun everything turned bright and glassy, the sharp light glancing off the old track upended on the edge of the square, where no train had ever traveled. Peachy slowed down for the light changing from green to yellow, and Tish thought how often she'd imagined that the track ascending out of the emerald lawn at a slant was like a ladder to the sky. Sometimes in the summer when thunderclouds rolled in, it looked like something God might have flung down from heaven in anger, or the Devil had shoved up from the fiery inferno below.

But there was no such mystery. The summer before Kennedy was shot, Tish's parents' integrationist group salvaged it from the old rail-road that long ago ran through Brazil and set it up in the square. And Tish's father, Professor Martin Espy of the political science department, convinced the city council to mount a bronze plaque explaining how the track was a symbol of the Underground Railroad, which had run right through Brazil, the last stop before Lake Erie for slaves en route to Canada. Brazil was now on the official register of historically pre-served towns, and some of the restored older houses still boasted secret passages where runaway slaves had once hidden.

Shortly after the track was erected, someone painted *Kill nigers* next to a red swastika across one of the ties. Some well-meaning soul rushed to pour white paint over "nigers," but everyone knew what lay there under the surface. A few days later the *Brazil Gazette* featured a photo of three local businessmen, two white and one black, painstakingly scraping the track clean in a gesture of conciliation and harmony. The caption announced, "Town's historical symbol cannot be whitewashed."

The light changed. The Fleetwood moved into the intersection, and James Brown faded out with "You know me and you can bugaloo . . ." Wanda let out a whoop from the front seat when the next song was "Tighten Up" by Archie Bell and the Drells.

It was rare to get two good (*black*) songs in a row on the white stations. From the front seat, Wanda and Peachy screamed in unison, then turned and laughed at each other for screaming.

In back, Tina, a cigarette perched on her lip, danced up against Tish *(Come on, girl, tighten up)* and they moved shoulder to shoulder, jarring loose the old piece of bedsheet Mrs. Stubbs had carefully pinned across a rip in the fabric. Tish's sweaty jumper stuck briefly to the seat back. Bodies bent, they mimicked the slow descent of horns, then went still as statues for the syncopated pause just before the beat picked up again. Tish timed her movement with Tina's, fists circling in toward their waists, then turning up with the little pop of the wrist right on the beat: "Tighten up." Mentally she was envying Tina's white poorboy, dark leatherette skirt, and cream-colored pointy-toe shoes. She wished she'd worn anything but the old cotton jumper she had on, especially since orange plaid clashed with her hair, and washed out her complexion. Nothing she owned fit anymore, now that she'd added four more awkward inches to her height. Everything about her threatened to come undone—from her unruly red hair slipping and corkscrewing out from under the blue headband to the frayed laces in her brown Hush Puppies.

"Tighten up," Tina sang. The rising smoke spread a thin veil across her face and settled into the delicate sandy mist of her small afro. There was a duskiness to Tina's lightness, the brown flecks in her eyes contradicting the green of her irises, the narrow bridge of her nose fanning into broad nostrils. Tish could almost imagine herself into the riddle of genes that had created Tina, neither white or black, but something perfectly balanced in between. A little of this and a little of that, though Tina proudly remained *black*, make no mistake.

The song ended. The mood in the car shifted.

Wanda announced, "I want me some frozen custard."

The Fleetwood struck out across Division Street toward the 52 Twister a mile north of town.

Wanda slouched. "This is a sho 'nuff dead little town. Ain't nobody out and nothing to do. I can't wait to take my black ass off to college."

College, thought Tish wistfully, looking out the window. It seemed so far away, impossible, even. When she enviously watched the Brazil University students shuttling to and from classes, casually lounging in the green grass on the square, bodies strewn around on sofas in the student union, long hair unkempt, she felt the pull of her own vague desires—to be free.

On either side of the two-lane highway, cornfields stretched as far as the eye could see. If you kept going you would end up at the Cleveland airport. Tish imagined herself there now boarding a plane for some distant place. California. Huey P. Newton and Bobby Seale. She would become a soldier in their army, and never come back. Peachy turned in to the Twister's lot and carefully pulled up to the take-out window. "What'chall want?" Everyone was scrambling for change, emptying pockets, shaking down coin purses. Tish borrowed a quarter from Peachy. "Chocolate . . . vanilla . . ."

The muffler on the Fleetwood rumbled.

"Two darkies and two lighties," Wanda joked again, loudly enough to embarrass the nervous white girl passing out the order in a cardboard carton. *Contempt for the girl's pale skin, the startled look in her eyes.* She shut the window fast, jaw set. Wanda started to mess with her, to ask her if she had a problem, but Peachy set one chocolate cone for her on the dashboard, and said, "Don't trip, girl." She handed back two vanilla cones to Tina and Tish. Wanda pulled out her cheese cutter and began a rigorous assault on her fro.

"Girl, you put that rake in your head one more time," said Peachy, "you gonna be bald as a turkey."

They all laughed. Wanda made a face. She was one of the first girls at school to have worn an afro, and risked suspension. "It's the principle of the thing," she had said staunchly. "This is the way my hair naturally *is*—nappy."

"And don't spill anything on my mother's car seat, *please*," Peachy admonished.

"This ole car is a mess," said Wanda, picking out her hair with one hand and grasping her cone in the other.

Peachy shot her a hard look. "Try telling my mother that," she snapped. "Mama loves her car." They headed back into town, along the outskirts of campus, where university students streamed along the brick paths that angled through the square.

By the upended track, the Fleetwood started to turn, then slowed as Peachy braked to let two brown-skinned senior boys Tish vaguely recognized stroll across. Seeing the girls, they grinned and slowed way down. One of them started pimp walking, right hand in his pocket, left arm dipping low to the ground. "Look at that fool thinking he's so cute," said Wanda. She leaned out the window. "Rodney Pope, you get on out the way, you ain't made of rubber, brother." Rodney grinned and stopped abruptly right there in the street as if struck by lightning. He deliberately angled his head so his tinted granny glasses slid to the end of his nose. Peachy honked and swung around them. They pantomimed shock at such a close call, then beckoned wildly for the girls to come back.

"Rodney is so damn fine," said Tina. "Slow down, let him get in."

Peachy braked. Rodney rushed right over and poked his head in the open window. He took in all four of them in one long gaze. "Mmmmmmnnnn-Mmmmmmmnnn-Mmmmmmmnnnn!" he said. "Damn, but y'all lookin' good." Wanda fell back in her seat. "You need to quit Juanita and come on with me," and she stretched out her arms and shook her big chest in a way that made them all laugh. *Wanda, you so crazy, Wanda stop, girl, you ain't got no sense, why you always wanna embarrass everybody.*

Next to Tish, Tina doubled over in stitches. Up front Peachy revved the motor to make Rodney jump back. He did, but never lost his cool. Wanda blew him a kiss. Keeping a firm grip on the wheel, Peachy pulled way out to avoid a parked car on the right.

A middle-aged white woman stepped unexpectedly into the street in front of them. Peachy hit the brakes. "Now, what is *this* heifer doing?" Wanda thrust her head out the window. She said it loudly enough that the woman turned and stared. Had she actually heard the words or was she watching to make sure they didn't run her down? Tight-lipped, she paused there in the street and marked them with her stare like a curse. But Wanda was undaunted. "Whatchoo lookin' at, woman?" She popped her eyes and leaned out, voice brassy, still laughing. "Am I turning purple or something?" Tish slid down into the seat, half laughing and half praying Wanda would give up. Distracted, the woman tripped against the curb, catching herself just in time. Wanda shrieked triumphantly as Peachy pulled on past.

"Wan-da . . ." Tish warned.

Wanda turned around and made googly eyes. "Yes?" She grinned wickedly. "Listen to Tish, actin' all nervous. Girl, what you so scared of?"

The heat of embarrassment rose to Tish's cheeks.

"Nothin'," she said sheepishly. "I just meant—"

Wanda announced to the air, "Nothin', except that she's riding around with a bunch of loud, black boots." She reached her hand back and snapped her fingers for a cigarette from Tina.

"Go around again," Tina urged. "I see somebody." They began taking inventory: *There goes Rosalynn's brother. He's a freshman in college. No, he ain't, girl, he's a sophomore. There's Juanita. Check her out. That's a boss jacket she's got on. Hey, Juanita! Girl, you seen those bad kicks she had on last week at school? She has some bad vines. There goes Billy Powell—he is so cute for a white boy.*

Tish accepted the last cigarette Tina shook from the crumpled pack and lit it with the lighter Wanda cavalierly tossed back to her. *Come Back Inn*, the name of the club her uncle managed in Elyria, was engraved in black letters. When Tish passed the lighter back up, her fingers grazed Wanda's. In that instant they both smiled, Tish no longer stranded alone in the universe, but part of a constellation.

III

On the east side of town, in their three-story fixer-upper, Martha Espy cast a sidelong glance at the kitchen clock. Outside, the shadows lengthened along Woodland Street. She made a point of asking Tish's brother Ford one more time if he had any idea where Tish was. This was the third time in a week Tish had been late. Very little was lost on Mrs. Espy, who knew ensemble practice never lasted more than an hour. Now another hour and a half had passed with no sign of Tish, and she envisioned various possibilities, including Tish off with some boy. The phone had already rung twice for her, only emphasizing her absence. Martha began fretting aloud about Tish's habitual tardiness and unexplained absences, as she moved about the kitchen preparing dinner. What should she do, she wondered, now that Tish disobeyed her constantly? If it wasn't rolling her skirts at the waist, it was sneaking on eye shadow, or coming in reeking of cigarette smoke. And there were the little lapses of truth and ambiguities, and the sly shrugs, not to mention the lack of consideration, like tying up the phone for hours at a time without a care for anyone else in the family. Hushed conversations, some of them with boys (mostly black) Mrs. Espy knew only by name.

Dinnertime arrived without Tish to set the table, so Mrs. Espy asked Ford to take over. He made a point of assuming the responsibility with exaggerated graciousness, as if to emphasize the difference between his extra-helpful self and his errant sister. Soon Tish's father would arrive from campus, hungry and distracted, and full of details of his day that went on like the continuation of an old list: the in-fighting over a grant, what the dean said, the absence of the department secretary, who was out with bursitis. Then, his face drawn in worry, he would describe to his wife the increasing conflict between militant black students now demanding a black studies department and the administration resisting such notions as separatist. The talk would make them both uneasy, as if a gap had opened they no longer knew how to bridge. *About Tish,* she would say. He would nod vacantly, his mind still on the troubles at school, and try to urge Tish's mother to relax a little about Tish's whereabouts and not worry so much, but Tish's mother would say he didn't understand exactly how exasperating their only daughter had become. Martha would continue to make her point, looking at the clock every few minutes and saying, "Where is that girl?" She worried about her daughter now that there were secrets between them, and Tish had grown moody and spent so much time locked in her room upstairs daydreaming and listening to soul music when she should be studying.

IV

There was a loud snap of Tina's key-chain can opener piercing the top of a red cream soda. Wanda wheeled around. "Dag, I thought you was opening some Colt 45 malt liquor." This got a laugh. "Yeah," Tina joked, taking a swig and passing the can to Tish, "like I'd be drinkin' forties just like those old stumble-bum niggas be hangin' out in the square." More laughter followed by the predictable cracks about winos like old triflin' Pepe Brown or nasty Rudy Prince, who had nothing better to do all day than drink themselves into red-eyed delirium and try out their pitiful, whiny raps on passing college girls. Tish took a swallow of soda and passed the can up to Wanda, who made a point of vigorously wiping off the top with her palm before tossing her half-eaten bag of pork rinds over the back of the seat into Tish's lap, ordering "Don't eat them all." Then Wanda caught sight of one of the university students she knew from the dances she sneaked into at Afro House and thrust her head out the window to call his name and raise her fist in solidarity. She pulled her head back in. "That's Grover," she said, superior in her alliance, "one fine, honest Black Nationalist brother with a strong, beautiful mind."

Wanda's pronouncement created a lightning-quick connection. Grover was framed in Wanda's words, with his gigantic fro and serious expression, striding confidently across the green square with an armload of books: intelligent, rebellious, and studious in wire-rim spectacles. "He sure is fine," Tina agreed, and Tish nodded and murmured, "Can't wait 'til I get to college." How she envied Wanda, always so in charge of herself. Past the bank, past the Memorial Inn, where Tish waitressed in summer to make money for college, past the university art museum, the public library, First Methodist Church, the university auditorium, and back to the block of downtown that ran along the south edge of the square. The muffler on the Fleetwood rattled.

Up front Peachy and Wanda argued like an old married couple.

"Damn, I wish I had some reefer." (That was Wanda trying to sound grown and important.)

And then Peachy: "Girl, what you know about reefer, like you been high more than once." And Wanda countering with "How do you know what I did?"

And then Tish jumped in to point out a sighting of Jasmine and Lamar.

The others' heads snapped around to see. Beyond the leafy trees on the opposite edge of the square, a white Chevy Impala flashed across the intersection in front of the bank heading east. The chrome fender sparkled in the sun, the freshly washed black tires spun. Outlined in the front seat were the distant silhouettes of two afroed heads, aloof and indifferent. Funny how the shape of a familiar car could startle like a well-known face. Lamar's car—it was all over town, sometimes with Jasmine, sometimes without. It was when Jasmine wasn't there that Lamar called himself being slick and was most likely getting into trouble. He was a big flirt, everyone knew, and when he and Jasmine weren't arm in arm in the school hallways, they were fussing at each other publicly. Rumors flew about whether they'd actually broken up or not. They were both seniors, Brazil High royalty, people who mattered. Their every fight and every reconciliation was public knowledge. Most recently Jasmine had slapped Lamar in the hallway for kissing on Elaine White outside the marching band practice room, and he had slapped her back, much to the thrill of onlookers, while Elaine escaped with her uncased flute in hand, terror written on her pretty brown face. Jasmine had screamed and wept hysterically while her closest girlfriends dragged her into the rest room. Later it was rumored Jasmine had to be "contained," and someone else said she'd tried to take "pills." She had been seen leaving school early in the company of her mother. Lamar had looked morose the rest of the day.

"They musta gotten back together," Tina observed.

"They didn't never break up," said Peachy knowledgeably. "They just always fussin' at each other and talkin' that it-shay." Peachy liked to remind them all how she and Jasmine were play sisters, her mother being Jasmine's mother's best friend, and how she was privy to Jasmine's personal business.

"Negro ain't no good, always tryin' to get over on somebody. His shit's done played out," Wanda muttered with knowing irreverence. As if she hadn't made her point, she added, "And Sister's dick-whupped." Everyone erupted into shouts and protestations at Wanda's audacity ("Ooooh, I *know* you didn't say *that,* honey, I *know* you didn't"). She hadn't even bothered to disguise the words in pig Latin, but let them burst in the open, bold as overripe fruit, words that no one else in the car dared speak above a whisper, if at all.

From the back, Tina still laughing said, "Wanda's right. Sister's nose *is* wide open. No disrespect intended . . ."

Wanda shook her head furiously. "Ain't never lettin' no nigga mess with my mind like that."

Murmurs of approval. The Greek chorus of condemnation. There was no misunderstanding what she meant, and Tish knew they must now all be thinking the same thing, that beautiful Jasmine was in the grip of inexplicable passion at its most destructive. Such information made Tish restless, and full of grown-up knowledge. That thing between men and women was indecipherable; Tish's fascination had been provoked in the halls of Brazil High by the fevered looks on Jasmine's face as Lamar pressed and swayed and crooned in her ear, the heat of desire radiating from Jasmine's body in a private moment carelessly made public.

The cigarette Tish begged off Wanda gave her something to do with her hands. She snapped Wanda's lighter closed, suddenly self-conscious of the substance of her own body. She glanced down at her skinny legs, stretched out before her. Not so bad now that her growth spurt had slowed and her calves were filling out, and hadn't Willy Miller leaned over in typing class during a drill of "exclamation point, dollar sign, ampersand" and whispered she was "lookin' healthy"? She inhaled, then blew out an even stream of smoke. It spread out comfortingly, like a web connecting them all.

The light was dropping fast in the sky, the trunks and branches of the trees darkening. Tish didn't even dare consider what time it was. It made her insides jump to think of what punishment her mother was planning and just how mad she would be. Tish began to concoct an excuse. Better yet, maybe she'd just go home with Peachy for dinner and phone from there, explaining she had trouble getting through on the Stubbses' party line.

Imagining her mother's mounting annoyance, the tight mouth and rock-hard jaw, she didn't notice right away the pickup hurtling alongside the Fleetwood. Several Farmers were jammed in the cab, several more seated on the rim of the truck bed. They weren't real farmers, they just called themselves that. They were white boys from school who wore crew cuts, and caps with the names of feed companies stitched across the brims. They went around school terrorizing people they hated—everyone from university types (they called them communists) to the smaller black kids. Some of them even bragged about belonging to the KKK. They were notorious for getting drunk on beer and tearing through campus.

Wanda pointed, "Look, there go those white boys started all that mess last year. Remember? Got Tommy Mosley suspended too."

Tish turned. A miniature Confederate flag flew from the side mirror. Several of the boys stared down with hard expressions. One of them, a senior boy Tish recognized, singled her out. She vaguely knew him as the boy who had threatened to lynch Ford for purposely stepping on an American flag one morning in the foyer at school as part of what he insisted was his "Constitutional right to protest the immoral Vietnam War." Now the boy twisted his face up and slurred something into the air—a kiss? a curse? A big wad of chewing gum spun through the air, hit the window ledge closest to Tish with a thud and bounced off. It had come within an inch of her face. Now the pickup veered dangerously close, and for a moment Tish thought Peachy was going up on the curb and Mrs. Stubbs's car would take a huge dent on the side. But at the last second, the truck roared past, the boys yelling and whooping, and the driver laying on the horn. There it was—the dread word peppering the air in staccato—*nigger, nigger, nigger*—the *r* stinging like pellets from a shotgun. The pickup squealed around the corner heading west.

There was stunned silence in the car, then disbelieving murmurs of

"Did they say what I think they said?" and "No, they didn't. I *know* I didn't hear what I think I heard."

"Goddamnit," said Peachy, who cursed only when she was nervous. Without warning she hit the accelerator. "I'm so sick of this bullshit."

The Fleetwood picked up speed, and Tish felt shock turn to excitement. A moral wrong was about to be righted. She sat up and leaned forward, close to Wanda, who was now urging Peachy on at the top of her lungs.

They were right on the tail of the pickup, and for a moment Tish thought Peachy was going to ram the back end. Several of the boys in back looked down at them with expressions of surprise. They started nudging one another and then laughing. One boy grabbed his crotch and made up and down motions with his fist. Tish felt her adrenaline mounting. Tina began yelling, "Girl, slow down! You're gonna kill us all!" Just as the pickup leaped through the last main intersection heading east out of town toward Christ-Cripple Road, the light changed from yellow to red, and Peachy slammed on the brakes. Hard. They all went forward in their seats, and then flopped back as the car screeched to a halt. Tina grabbed Tish's arm hard and hung on.

"Dag, Peachy! Whatcho doing?"

Peachy didn't answer. Tears gathered in the corners of her eyes. "Fuck this," she said, and let her hands fall helplessly into her lap.

The lights flashing in the rearview mirror signaled the arrival of a police car now pulling up behind the Fleetwood. A collective groan went up in the car. Peachy snapped off the radio. "Damn, it's a white cop, too," Wanda said, craning her neck. She sank down in her seat. "I don't believe this. Peachy, what you almost run that light for?"

They started to fuss. Tish felt herself panic. The first thing she pictured was her name printed in the "Police Blotter" of the *Brazil Gazette* for the whole world to see. The second thing she thought of was how impossible it would be to explain the unfairness of all this to her parents, or how the pickup, now just a faint dot on the horizon, was to blame.

V

Over at the university laundry, Connie Stubbs thrust her arms elbow deep into the industrial washer to pull out another batch of wet sheets. She imagined the Fleetwood was already safely parked inside the corrugated metal carport at home. Her trustworthy baby girl would be straightening up, maybe even running the vacuum over the living room carpet. None of the laundry employees were allowed telephone privileges at work, so Connie couldn't call to check. But each evening when she got home and propped her swelling feet up on the hassock, she contentedly took in the evidence of her daughter's housekeeping efforts. Her nephew Dev, same age as Peachy, might stop over to keep Peachy company, stretched out on the sofa doing his homework, because he was a bookish sort of boy (his teacher called him a math whiz). She secretly worried he was a little bit on the sissy side (what people called "funny"), which is what her husband had also occasionally observed. That's what could happen with a boy too attached to women, whose father had been shot dead when he was just a tiny child, and no man to influence him properly. But she never would have spoken that aloud, and instead was quick to defend him as a good boy, well-mannered and kind, like the son she'd imagined but never had. She loved how he'd drop by weekend nights when all the other boys were off messing with girls or hanging around harmonizing and drinking on the street corner, and how he would sit up with her and listen to music—*her* music—what Peachy wrote off as all that "old-timey stuff," Cannonball Adderley, Earl Fatha Hines, Sarah Vaughan, Eartha Kitt, and velvet-voiced Nat King Cole. Let Peachy go ahead and tease. Connie Stubbs knew good music. These kids nowadays . . . but if truth be told she was proud to have raised three wonderful daughters, two of them full grown now and out of the house with solid lives of their own, and her youngest, now in high school (a change-of-life baby, she had to admit), her appearance a surprise, but her presence a joy. If Connie Stubbs had even for a second imagined, let alone caught those foolish girls riding around acting loud and crazy in her car with the windows rolled down and the music blaring out into the street like a bunch of hoodlums, she would-well-like to have slapped Miss Peaches Denise Stubbs straight into the middle of next week. In truth, she had only threatened on occasion, the words alone enough of a sting; she had never in her life raised a hand to her daughters, never believed that you broke the body to punish the spirit. But it was troubling to see all the mess kids could get into. And Mrs. Stubbs knew full well the kind of trouble that lay out there ready to lure a young girl. She knew about temptation, all the alcohol and drugs out there and so available, not to mention the ways a man could sweet-talk a girl, even a nice girl, and the ruin it could bring. You could see it going on all around you, if you opened your eyes and took a good hard look. People going wrong, headed for disaster. Today's world was even more complicated than when she was growing up. Thank God Peachy was a decent girl, sweet-natured and churchgoing. But, Mrs. Stubbs thought, as she flicked the ends of a still-hot-from-the-dryer bedsheet and lined them up flat and smooth against each other, it always paid to be extra careful. You never took anything for granted. She and her husband, a silent, uncomplaining man who had worked for years now as a skycap at the Cleveland airport, planned a better life for Peachy. Yes, her youngest daughter had opportunities neither of them ever had, and Connie Stubbs, who had barely gotten out of the eighth grade before family demands kept her at home, was going to see that girl get a scholarship to college and go on to a good life, even if it killed her.

VI

The white cop who sauntered up was stocky, with pinkish flesh and a youthful face. Was it curiosity or contempt in the smile? He adjusted his holster before bending down to peer in the driver's window. Wordlessly he passed an icy-blue gaze in a slow pan over each of them. "Let's see who we've got here." As soon as Tish heard the southern Ohio drawl, she felt her heart sink. There was *that look* on his face, the one that certain kinds of white people reserved for dealing with blacks, the way you might look if you were staring at a corpse or a piece of moldy bread. She recognized it from the more subtle grimaces on the faces of certain teachers at school, when their pretenses were shed for a moment.

Her parents claimed such people didn't exist in Brazil, which was so much more enlightened with its history of integration. After all, her parents said, Brazil had always been a haven. Talk of prejudiced teachers was "exaggeration," mention of the iffy attitudes of white classmates' parents written off as wild flights of imagination or misunderstanding. *Why, Mrs. Williams is a lovely person.* . . . Yeah, Tish often muttered, so long as you're not black. It always amazed her how white people assumed that "nice" people couldn't be prejudiced.

Wanda sucked her teeth and exhaled loudly. The cop reversed his gaze and went back over them, taking full inventory, one by one, as if assessing a lineup. His eyes rested on Tina. There was a moment of hesitation, and Tish knew he had briefly mistaken Tina for white. And she knew from the slight pucker to Tina's mouth and the turning away of her head that Tina knew it too.

Eyes riveted on Tish, he asked, "So, where you girls from?"

"From here," said Peachy nervously.

"I was talking to *her*, not you," he said sharply, nodding at Tish. In that moment he had canceled Peachy as if she didn't exist.

Tish answered, "Yeah, I'm from here," but her voice came out oddly feeble. She felt something more was expected. "My father teaches at the university. He's a political scientist." The words fell as if of their own volition from her mouth. Instantly she wanted to scoop them up and take them back, regretting how foolish and pretentious she sounded. Naturally Wanda's head popped around, and she shot back a sharp, unforgiving look.

The cop rocked back on his heels. "What about the rest of you? You sure you're not from up there in Hough?"

Wanda cut in. "You just heard her say we're from here."

The cop never changed expression. "I didn't ask you anything yet, did I? You might want to wait until I do, if you don't want me to take you down to the station and lock you up."

Everyone got quiet.

"Now, if you want to listen to me," he said, drawing on the weight of his authority, "I'll tell you about the traffic laws we observe in this town. Everyone here in Brazil lives by the same rules. I don't make exceptions for anyone, not university, not town, and not colored and not white."

"Shooooot, you didn't need to go and say all that," Wanda snapped. "If you don't make exceptions, why don't you go chase those white boys in the pickup that just did sixty miles an hour through this red light we stopped for?"

The cop's face stiffened, and his smile stretched into tautness. "Miss, if I were you I'd shut up real quick." How he hates us, Tish thought. He slapped the window ledge with the flat of his hand, and then proceeded to walk all the way around the car, making a big point of examining the tires, and pausing at the back and tapping the trunk, before returning to the driver's window. He took out a pad and made notes. Without looking up from his writing he asked firmly for the license and registration, and then extended the flat of one palm.

Tish felt her heart sink. The thrill of the afternoon had evaporated. She watched anxiously as Peachy made a lame effort to search the glove compartment. Her hands were shaking. It was obvious she was trying to stall.

Then Wanda broke in, feigning a proper voice. "Excuse me, Officer, but *I'm* the one with the license. My friend here has her learner's permit. I believe it's *legal* in the state of Ohio to drive with a learner's permit as long as a licensed adult driver is present."

Tina, curled in the opposite corner of the backseat, cracked open one eye as if to say, What on earth is she talking about? Wanda, with the cheese cutter handle protruding rakishly from her fro, dug down in her book bag with a dramatic flourish, making a big fuss searching for her wallet, mumbling to herself. When she found it, she yanked it open and flipped through an inch of plastic dividers, crammed with pictures of nieces and nephews and cousins, and finally extracted a well-worn driver's license. They all knew Wanda didn't drive. Even though she was already sixteen and a year ahead of them in school, she'd never even bothered to sign up for driver's ed because her grandmother couldn't afford the fifty dollars, and the old, leaky Plymouth Valiant that sat on blocks rusting in their backyard was in need of a new transmission. From where Tish sat she caught only a faint glimpse of the license itself, but magically it looked legit, passing from Wanda to Peachy to the cop. He held it out in the receding rays of sunlight. Then, nudged by Wanda, Peachy produced her learner's permit. The cop didn't take that right away, let her stew for a few agonizing minutes. When he finally took the permit, he asked also for proof of registration, never looking at her directly. When Peachy, confidence growing, produced that as well from the glove compartment, he seemed almost disappointed. He took a long, hard look that inspired Wanda to mutter, "Dag, he planning on memorizing the whole damn thing?"

"I need to call this in," he said grimly.

"Do what you gotta do. You ain't gone find nothin'," muttered Wanda, folding her arms across her chest. " 'Cause we ain't did nothin' and you know it."

The cop didn't respond, just stepped back and motioned them all out of the car with his index finger, the way you might summon small children. In a daze, they cooperated, Wanda acting put out and heaving deep sighs, the way she'd sometimes enter classrooms at school, late and daring anyone to do something about it. Exposed like this, Tish felt as if nothing were in her control anymore, and she imagined being taken down to the Brazil city jail, where black kids were always being hauled off, and where anyone passing by would recognize her. Any moment her father could be walking this way home from the university in his black overcoat, swinging his brown briefcase. He would pause, and seeing Tish, what would he do? Tish broke out in a sweat. Dampness gathered in the armpits of her blouse.

"What's your name?" the cop was asking for the second time, impatience in his voice.

"Letitia Espy."

Wanda butted in. "Whatcho asking her for? You didn't ask me, or her, or her—"

"Didn't I tell you to be quiet?" the cop said. Tish could see from his expression that Wanda was getting on his nerves.

He looked at Tish again. "You live around here?"

"On Woodland." Her voice was faint, as if she could make the words themselves disappear. She knew what he was asking and what that street name would signify, just like all the other streets in Brazil named for trees, and she waited to see what he was going to make of it.

"Why don't you just go on home," he said tersely. "Get out of here."

Wanda exploded, hand on her hip. "Why are you gone tell her go on home? You gone let her go, you need to let us all go."

"You keep on mouthing off I'm going to lock you up, Miss Whatever Your Name Is." He shook his finger in her face. She stepped backward, her hand instinctively reaching up in front to shield herself. His expression reminded Tish of a mad cat's, eyes pulled tight and ears flat on its skull. He left his blue eyes fastened on Wanda. Tish saw the hatred there, the disgust. "I don't care what you do down on *your* side of town, but you won't do it on *this* side."

A glance at Peachy's stricken face compelled Tish to speak up.

"Excuse me, Officer," she said, trying to keep her voice steady (though later Wanda would tease her mercilessly about using her "proper white voice," the voice that Tish resorted to from fear, and which she herself recognized as the same one that often emanated from her mother's throat, a voice ringing with authority and privilege), "but some boys in a pickup tried to run us down. I know who one of them is. They came this close to hitting us." She was careful not to say "white boys." And she was careful to look him right in the eye, the way her father had always taught her to when she was addressing an adult. "My friends didn't do anything. They're just taking me home from school, where we had girls' ensemble."

The cop seemed to go deaf again, face hardening. He was giving Tish a chance, playing her off against her friends. He was asking her to save her own skin.

Wanda turned and glared. "Go on, Tish," she said bitterly. "Take your little narrow ass on home." Tish looked at Tina for help, but Tina's eyes were focused on the curb and her mouth was working silently as if she was talking to herself. Peachy began to cry softly. Tish wanted her to stop. Traffic passed. Tish felt them all separating, like strands of hair in a braid, coming undone.

Wanda started dancing against the curb and humming to herself, giving the impression she didn't care about anything, that she was ready for whatever happened and no prejudiced cop was going to get on her nerves. Knowing what she did about Wanda's grandmother, Tish figured Wanda would get all the sympathy and outrage the situation deserved. Esther Beals was the kind of no-nonsense woman who would storm down to the Brazil police station in a hot minute and demand without even the slightest quaver to her voice to know just what they had done to her Wanda and why. Wanda's grandmother wouldn't mince words either—she'd ask, just as bold as she pleased, what business did that white police officer have holding her granddaughter when she was just an innocent passenger in a friend's vehicle going about her business. And she wouldn't be afraid to say the truth about how the cop stopped her granddaughter for being black. She would say it straight to his face, looking him dead in the eye, not glancing away or mumbling the words as if to give him a choice. No, Wanda's grandmother would spell it all out, making it perfectly clear she would brook no foolishness, and if it meant taking the case all the way to the Supreme Court, well, then, Wanda's grandmother could do that too.

Standing there Tish felt the emptiness of her own whiteness. It was what separated her now, even protected her against her own wishes, made the prejudiced white cop set her aside and assert she was free to go.

The first thing Wanda said a few minutes later as they pulled off, license and registration returned, "If it hadn't been for that brother coming along, I'd probably be in the jailhouse now for goin' off on that stupid-ass redneck pig." As luck had it, one of two black officers on the Brazil police force had pulled up as the white cop sat in his car radioing in. There was a long conversation between the two ("Look at brother talkin' shit," Wanda observed, craning her neck), and then the black cop got out and had a word with the girls before he walked back to talk to the white cop again. A few minutes later, the white cop sauntered over and handed back the licenses as if the whole thing had been his idea. He ordered the girls to get the hell out of there, with strict instructions to go directly home.

Once they were a full two blocks away, Peachy pulled the car over, fanning her face with her hand, trying to calm herself. "Wanda, where'd you get a license, girl?"

Wanda seemed undaunted. "It's my cousin Betty's. It's how I take books out of the university library and get discounts at the snack bar. It says I'm twenty-one m.f. 'ing years old."

"But you don't even look like Betty," said Peachy.

"Yeah, but honkies can't tell one nigga from another," Wanda retorted saucily, working the cheese cutter down into her scalp. "And you know that pig wouldn't have stopped us if he hadn't seen ole Tish sittin' up in here."

There were the old innuendos of anger and blame. There was also the matter-of-factness, the stating of the obvious. And that was when Wanda, secure in her own power again, went on gleefully. "Y'all hear Tish actin' like Miss Ann and talkin' all proper to the pig: 'But, Officer, I'm white and you can't arrest me. My daddy is a po-li-ti-cal scientist. . . .'" Even Tish had to laugh at herself. "Girl, you was tryin', though, huh, Tish?" She gave Tish a wink and evened out the edges of her fro with the palms of her hands. To

Peachy she said, "Now get me out of this neighborhood before someone tries to lynch my black ass."

Tish suddenly felt as if she were traveling through someone else's life. Peachy, still rattled, drove way under the speed limit all the way down Elm Street, stopping at intersections that didn't even have stop signs. At the corner of Woodland she asked Tish if she minded walking the two blocks home; she wanted to get away from the east side of town before something else happened.

Tish got out. She watched the receding fins of the Fleetwood bounce over the railroad tracks and eventually wink out of sight. She longed to be part of the conversation in the car. Her chest filled with that familiar desperate, sinking sensation of having come up short. What if in that moment she'd tried to bargain with the cop her friends had read complicity? Her legs turned wobbly as she started up the tree-lined street with its wide front yards and big houses set back from the street. The closer she got to home, the less familiar it all seemed and the more filled with dread she became.

There wasn't time to purge the smell of cigarette smoke from her clothes and hair. She pulled a fistful of green needles from the Fitzsimmons's shrub and rubbed their scent over her face and arms. She would have to fly right upstairs to remove the traces—brush her teeth and change her blouse before her mother got too close.

She searched her mind for a good excuse, something so complicated and detailed as to be impossible not to believe.

As her Hush Puppies hit the front porch, Ford called out, "Tish is here!" Then came her mother's follow-up cry, "Is that you, Tish? Where've you been? When did practice get out?"

Worry and accusation combined in her voice. Then the incriminations began. "I've been worrying about you for over an hour and a half. It's after six. And Angela's called twice looking for you."

The "Angela called" postscript was Martha's way of invoking another witness to Tish's tardiness, someone even more credible than herself—her daughter's best friend of seven years. A small spasm of annoyance seized Tish. Why did Angela have to choose precisely that time to call, and not just once, but twice? She could be so dense sometimes.

Mrs. Espy rounded the corner, tying an apron over her jeans. Her short brown hair was yanked back firmly with a clip. Her blue eyes were stern. She wore no makeup, and Tish was always slightly ashamed of the wrinkles forming at the corners of her mother's eyes and the line now deepening along her forehead. "Did you hear me, Tish? I'm talking to you. I asked where you've been."

But Tish was already running up the steps to the second floor, pleading that she had to use the bathroom. Her mother's voice continued like a distant siren in her head. Her questions were never just the questions asked, but also the ones behind them. Her mother's footsteps pattered into the downstairs hallway, her voice rising up the stairwell, just seconds behind Tish. Mumbling she'd be down in a minute, Tish sped with a sense of urgency past her brothers' room to the sanctuary of her own. She closed her door softly so it wouldn't slam and cause her mother to come demand why. She threw her book bag onto the bed, and yanked her jumper up over her head and off, and began unbuttoning her blouse. Her kneesocks came off easily and lay like two giant caterpillars balled in the corner. Words began to pour through her head with urgency, offering a counterpoint to her mother's voice. Breathless, Tish reached under her mattress, where she kept one of several notebooks labeled *Private* and dropped cross-legged to the hardwood floor. It was a relief to shed her clothes, to sit in bra and panties, and simply be herself. "Skinny legs and all," kids at school teased her. "Biafra baby. Put some meat on your bones." On the inside cover of the notebook, she'd written what all her friends had, calling themselves clever: *If found by person, please drop in mail; if found by male, please drop by in person.* And under that she'd written in all caps and underscored several times: *Nosy people, keep your damn hands and eyeballs off this!*

She turned to a clean page, smoothed it, uncapped a ballpoint pen, and began to write. The contact with the page calmed her. She had filled notebooks with ideas for song lyrics and fragments of poems. From books she'd copied poems she was trying to memorize: Nikki Giovanni, Langston Hughes, Thomas Hardy, Gerard Manley Hopkins, Sylvia Plath. She had even started a play, about a young girl misunderstood by her family. She could use any voice she wanted on paper, even

Wanda's. Her mother's voice grew fainter. "Young lady, I asked you where you've been. You better have an answer, Letitia. Were there boys with you and Peachy? I'm not done with you yet."

VII

The summer before, when Detroit burned, some people swore ash from the fires had floated across Lake Erie into their yards in Brazil. "You can taste it in your mouth," Angela Thompson remarked. "You can feel it clogging up your pores." She stood in front of the bathroom mirror in matching lime-green culottes and shell swabbing her perspiring forehead with cotton pads soaked in Bonnie Bell facial astringent to keep her caramel-colored skin free of shine and pimples. Aretha was on the box, spelling out "respect." Tish could almost taste the grit from the fires. "Black facial skin is oilier," Angela explained. She elbowed Tish in the side. "That's why we don't dry up in the winter like white girls—except our ankles and knees." And they both laughed, Tish leaning into the mirror, searching her own face for flaws.

As usual, Tish and Angela had spent a good deal of that long, hot summer (when they weren't waitressing at the Memorial Inn) playing gin rummy on the front stoop of Angela's ranch house on West Grant Street (Angela almost always won). The cards were just an excuse to look occupied when they were really waiting for boys to drive by and slow down. Occasionally innocuous and boring neighborhood boys like Peachy's sweet but square cousin Dev or old bucktoothed Melvin Goins wandered by to join them up on the porch for a while. Dev was easy, almost like being around a girl, Angela remarked once after he'd gone. "I think he kind of likes you, Tish." Tish shook her head. "No," she said, "we're just friends."

"We've got to get you a real boyfriend, not one of these little silly-ass boys," Angela insisted. And she would run through the list of possible options, boys from school who were unattached. In Angela's company, Tish didn't feel so afraid of boys, but the thought of carrying the conversation all alone made her nervous. She played along, took her cues from Angela, laughed when Angela laughed, frowned when Angela frowned, imitated her confident gestures, learned to say yes and no as if they meant so much more, and make cryptic little noises like "hmmmn" under her breath.

She knew it was Angela who drew the company: her impeccable beauty and the grace and ease with which she granted them a seat on the porch. And then there was always Mrs. Thompson's disarming southern hospitality—"Hello there, how you doin', can I offer you something to drink?"—as she joined them in her Bermuda shorts, trying to stay cool on the padded chaise lounge. She was beautiful in her own way (though Wanda scoffed at Tish for saying so and remarked, "All y'all honkies love that light skin"). Mrs. Thompson's face was the color of buttermilk and she wore her straightened, copper-red hair swept up to the side. If it hadn't been for her broad features, she might at first glance have been mistaken for white.

In the summertime when Mrs. Thompson drove them all over to Curtis Pond, she casually browned herself in the sun while everyone swam. "Mom needs some color," Angela liked to joke. "She's hoping all her freckles run together." But it was no joke to Mrs. Thompson. Color wasn't something to make fun of; lightness was not an advantage she had chosen.

Sometimes Peachy, with nothing better to do, swung by Angela's on foot, and then the three of them, Tish, Angela, and Peachy, would sprawl on the steps, complaining about the humidity and gossiping about people. Peachy and Angela only gently tolerated each other. Behind Angela's back, Peachy called her sadiddy, and Angela remarked how Peachy overpressed her hair—"all that limp, fried mess," she laughed once. But together, in the lengthening shadows, sticky arms and legs touching, Tish greedily drank in the camaraderie, their voices mingling. It made her long for something deeper and sharper, the kind of complex connection you might have with a boy. Like Jasmine with Lamar. Like Wanda yearning for Grover. Tish's own longing took wing at the sound of a passing revved-up engine signaling promise, or the harmony of the Supremes on "Love Child" emanating from the house of an older, more knowing girl across the street. Angela sat mopping the sweat from her face, singing along to the Fifth Dimension (she secretly dreamed of being Marilyn McCoo), awaiting the evening arrival of senior athlete Michael Brown in his Cutlass, whom she was "talking to" now. And Peachy drawing her knees to her chest would sigh and remark it was getting late, she ought to get home. One of the boys on the porch would get up with an air of indifferent duty and he and Peachy would descend the steps into the shadows, Peachy's voice ringing behind them. The boy would walk her home, in a bid for Angela's attention, but Angela would shake her head and say, "Peachy needs to do something to fix herself up, or she will never, ever get a man."

And then it would be just Tish and Angela left, slapping mosquitoes and settling into the habit of their old familiarity. From early on, Tish and Angela had exchanged paperbacks and mood rings, harmonized a cappella, memorized favorite poems and recited them to each other, told secrets, and passed judgment on who was square, who was fast, who was a Tom, who was "cool," and which white girls weren't too stuck up. Sometimes they quarreled with Angela's pesky younger sister, Monica, tried on clothes and fixed each other's hair. Later, they began raiding Mr. Thompson's liquor cabinet, where he housed his Johnny Walker Red and cocktail mixes. It seemed a fair trade-off; Tish had taught Angela to smoke in seventh grade, and last year in ninth Angela had introduced Tish to scotch on the rocks. They didn't drink that often, but when they did it was with conspiratorial pleasure, slowly draining their glasses, then refilling the bottle up to the line with water (Angela had craftily added a little food coloring). They'd curl up in the family room drinking and talking like grown-ups about all the things that mattered. There were times Tish thought of Angela as her double, herself if she were black. It wasn't much of a stretch, really. Their families weren't so far apart. And it wasn't hard to imagine Mrs. Thompson in place of her own mother, an easy substitution, with her own red hair, and the way Mrs. Thompson would put a maternal arm around Tish's shoulder and squeeze her. Tish couldn't ignore the years she and Angela called themselves cousins and mostly got away with it. When they were younger, they even contemplated the fantastic—that somehow through a series of convoluted events Tish might have been Mrs. Thompson's child by Mr. Espy, and then adopted out to the Espys, which might account for why their families had once been so close. They had untangled this possibility with giggles, but later when they'd gotten past the silliness, they began to treat the idea with increasing respect. ("After all, your father is dark for a white man, and your hair is nappy," Angela liked to say, "and you can dance better than any of the white kids.") Tish further fed the tale by reminding Angela of Mr. Espy's spinster great-aunt that everyone said looked just like Lena Horne. "He could be passing, like that woman in *Imitation of Life,*" said Angela with great earnestness. Tish felt the welcome ambiguity collecting its own weight. "Lots of black people do. Lots of white people out there are really black people in disguise. My mother could pass. . . ." She paused. "She never has, though. My parents tried to buy a house on the east side of town when they first moved here, and when my mother went by herself they showed her a place over at French Woods. Then when my father showed up, they said the house was already sold and brought them right away over here to the west side." There was a long pause, the implications settling over them both. Before Tish could say anything, because what was there to say to that, Angela remarked, "It be's that way sometimes," and refilled their glasses.

Tish conveyed the information as quickly as she could to her mother, who never seemed to believe that such things happened in Brazil. Mrs. Espy had raised her eyebrows, then said, "Oh, really, there must be some mistake. I'm sure a black family like the Thompsons could live anywhere they chose." But they don't, thought Tish, they don't. Don't you ever wonder why?

There were the long nights with Angela of confessions (crushes on white boys/black boys/mixed boys, intrigues, conjecture, lies, and speculation), ever since they were kids, of sitting on the old glider in the Espys' backyard, first sucking on popsicles and then slyly graduating to Kool Longs late into the humid darkness of cricket-filled summer nights. Over and over in that backyard they'd taken apart the crazy world piece by piece, their longings exposed, and then tried to reassemble the fragments, as the glider clicked back and forth. Bare feet stacked on top of the other's bare feet, legs entwined, heads flopped over on each other's shoulder. Beyond, the illuminated windows of the Espy house winked out one by one as everyone else went on to bed. But the girls sat and rocked, talking, while the moon rose overhead, and spread its cold blue light over the darkened tree limbs and yard. Then from an upstairs window Mrs. Espy's voice would float thinly outward—it was past midnight, did they have enough sense to get inside? Finally they would, unraveling themselves from the fabric of night, separating. Under the harsh explosion of the kitchen light overhead, their bodies shrank back startled, each having become too real, too fast. But there were still times just before they fell asleep in Tish's double bed that Tish wondered which one was breathing for whom.

When Tish drove with the Thompsons up to Cobo Arena in Detroit to see the Temptations perform in person, she began to believe earnestly the possibility of passing. If the hotel people mistook Tish for Mrs. Thompson's daughter, and assumed the Thompson children belonged to someone else (an incident that caused Mrs. Thompson to go scarily stern as she made it perfectly clear who was who), then why not let Angela tell the group of black boys who accosted them in the refreshment line that she and Tish were cousins? It made sense, it was easy to believe. "You're not white-white, Tish," Angela said.

Walking home from Angela's in the dusk, sated on Mr. Thompson's barbecued ribs and grilled corn on the cob, or slightly tipsy from snitched scotch, Tish felt comfortably suspended in time and place, the light of day gently siphoned off by evening. The slower she walked, the more she delayed returning home. At this distance she could imagine her own household changed, reconfigured, her parents and brothers no longer white, but slightly blurred into something less definite, filling the spaces in between. Her sandals scraping against the pavement, with toenails freshly painted, belonged to someone else, someone long and leggy and moody, someone with unexpected desires, who had begun to take over her body. She moved along with an easy swing to her narrow hips, each square of pavement reminding her of the board games she and Ford had played obsessively as children when they were both down with flu and the weather outside was miserable. A contained contentment, each of them having memorized all the cards with instructions, able to anticipate what would happen with each roll of the dice. She was prolonging the time on the west side of town, where older people rocking on porches called out hellos, and children scampered through the dusk relaying messages from one adult along the way to another down the street. Young brown girls double-dutched in the twilight, the eggbeater motions of their ropes matching the rhythm of their chants. Grown men and women flowed like water between fenceless yards. Children earned dimes or ice creams for running an errand to Slim's tumbledown corner market with its dark, musty interior so different from the lighted aisles of Fisher-Fazio. Each time a passing car slowed, Tish's pulse quickened. She hoped it was someone she knew, someone who would pull to the curb to chat for a moment from the car window. An acknowledgment. Inclusion. Maybe one of the older boys like Reggie Moore with their gentle flirtations as harmless and easy as breathing. "Big Legs," he'd called her once, much to Peachy's hilarity, and it was only later as she examined herself in the mirror that Tish realized his teasing had been a veiled kindness. Only a trick of fate sent her home to the wrong side of town, where things were so graveyard still she sometimes thought it was inhabited by the dead. Spooks. White people, not black people, were spooks. Soon it would be dark and she would move down her silent street past blank-faced houses where cicadas sizzled in the wide, manicured lawns. Later she would hole up in her room scribbling poems on one of her father's old drafts, while the Isley Brothers revolved on her turntable. *It's your thing.* Without music, she thought she would die in the emptiness of her parents' home, where the whirr of blades from the box fan in the window drowned out the hopeful hum of an occasional passing car.

* * *

Angela lived on the right side of Brazil to be friends with girls like Wanda and Tina, but she'd only been peripherally accepted all these years. Behind Angela's back the voices went, *The girl's sadiddy, boojee, a Tom, Miss Thang thinks she's too good, Girl gots bo-coos nerve.* Angela with the "good hair," Angela who had gone for a while in seventh grade with a motherless white boy named Flash whose own hippie professor father smoked weed and slept with female students. Angela had eventually tired of being "exotic," tired of being "my brown sugar," and turned briefly to a square black boy named James. Flash left town on a motorcycle and never returned. Angela still listened secretly to blue-eyed soul like the Righteous Brothers ("Girl, one of them has a black wife," she said by way of defense), and once chummed around with the popular white girls, even going so far as to cut her hair for a brief time in a pixie like Holly Penn's.

Angela and Tish had been stuck with each other as best friends since grade school, partly because their parents had urged the friendship as a step toward integration. It survived because when it came right down to it, they had no one else: Tish sliding through the cracks when it came to the popular white girls, and cautious, goody-two-shoes Angela never quite making it with the black kids. Angela fervently focused on such trivia as not wearing more than two colors at a time (unless you had on black or white—and shoes should always match your belt or handbag), and privately thought all the talk of revolution was nonsense. She also worried incessantly that her straightened hair would nap up in the rain—"make me look like Buckwheat," she said with an edge of shame.

It was hard to say exactly when it started, but things had been changing. Neither wanted to admit it, and so they kept up their same old routines, mostly out of habit. "Because we have no one else but each other," Angela said once, her arm over Tish's shoulder, but all Tish could feel was the weight of her desperation. Face it, they each trod a line, the edges of which dropped off sheer, like the sides of folding tables.

During the riots there'd been an edge to everything, as if something else besides airborne ash had gotten under people's skins. Tish felt so jittery she couldn't keep still. Even her parents remarked in their belea-

guered way how old black acquaintances seemed more standoffish.
Afros replaced straightened hair, only magnifying difference. "Separat-
ists," her mother murmured, lips pursed. Her father spoke gloomily of
"changing attitudes" and "growing hostility." He had long taught a
course called "The Negro in America" for the sociology department,
but now students were demonstrating for a black professor to teach the
course. Her parents expressed puzzlement and hurt, as if they'd been
betrayed. "Your father does such a good job. They couldn't find anyone
more dedicated," said Mrs. Espy. "And he's invested a lot of his own
time to bring Negro students to Brazil." Tish felt sorry for her parents.
How she hated to hear them say, "It's nice to see that Angela hasn't
changed. She's going to weather this storm." Tish cringed at her parents' counterfeit affection for Angela, mincing her words at the Espy
supper table, easing everyone's troubled liberal consciences by her very
presence. Angela, the Good Negro, polite, agreeable, and self-effacing.
Angela understands the importance of moderation, Mrs. Espy liked to say.
She's such an elegant girl. There was a whole litany of Angela's attributes, her manners, her beauty. What her mother really wanted to say,
thought Tish, was *She's almost white. Underneath that caramel skin, she's
just* like us.

Tish often considered the irony of how Angela's blackness was
wasted on her. As Wanda repeatedly quoted, *Black isn't just a color, it's
a state of mind.* Give your color to me, Tish wanted to say to Angela. It's
wasted on you, girl. I'd know what to do with it.

VIII

Martin Luther King, Jr., had been shot down in Memphis in broad daylight, as he was leaving his motel. That spring (an appropriately rainy night in Brazil) the news of his assassination hit like a thunderbolt. Footage of the shooting aftermath appeared on the nightly television news. But even with all the replays and eyewitness accounts, Linda Thompson still secretly suspected a trick of light and emulsion. King couldn't be dead. Impossible. It was a mistake, some terrible confusion. In her grief, she remained silent, cut off at the root. There were teachers at her children's schools and whites at work who thought he'd had it coming and couldn't look black people in the eye in case they could read the deceit. But it was the white folks' own sheepish expressions that gave them away. Black friends clucked their tongues and said the FBI finally got him, *just like the brother predicted they would.* Even after all these months, the images of his murder haunted, popping up from time to time like a hammer in her head and knocking her senseless with despair.

Now, exhausted from a day on campus and preparing her husband Harry's favorite stuffed pork chops, she was thinking how the murder still felt like yesterday, like a terrible, fresh tear in her heart. Everyone knew that white man Ray hadn't acted alone. It had been a setup, and long in the planning. In the living room Angela and her little girlfriend Tish harmonized over and over to Marvin and Tammy's "Precious Love" until Linda thought she'd lose her mind with the refrain: *Heaven must have sent you from above.* How uncomplicated the world still was for them, two young girls firmly grounded in the moment. Fragments of their conversation reached her ears, made her shake her head and smile: their adolescent worries and attempts to sound grown, when they still had no idea what lay ahead. What did they know about suffering? *Let's do it again. This time you get to be Marvin and I'll be Tammy.*

The night King was murdered Linda had returned from work, deadened by shock. There were no words for what she felt, no consolation, only the aftermath of impact with something of such force it had left her senseless. Nothing seemed quite familiar. Even her children sprawled on the living room floor, strangely quiet, their bodies illuminated by the flickering light of the television, struck her as foreign. She thought of all the missing children, sacrificed first to slavery and then to years of racial violence. Panic clutched at her. How could you not feel angry, full of hate? Harry was out of town on business. Usually in his absence the household loosened, and she and the kids happily let things go a little, but that evening Linda wanted him there, the missing bookend holding things in place. She recalled her own helplessness in front of her children, their faces garishly swimming before her in the cold blue light of the television. Tish Espy was spending the night. She and Angela had their arms around each other. What did they know? In her pink wool suit and matching pumps, Linda perched on the arm of her husband's easy chair, pretending she knew what to say. "Children, this is a very difficult and sad night." The measured words sounded so inadequate she wished she hadn't even bothered. And then even though she thought she'd cried away all her tears, she found she hadn't, and had to go in search of a cool wash rag to wipe her eyes. She remembered thinking as she tried to contain herself, but failed, just how unsettling it was for children to see an adult cry.

Her grief was infectious and even her youngest boy's agitation was in full evidence. "Mama, what's going to happen?" Soon she was taking turns gathering the children to her, including Tish and Angela. They couldn't possibly realize, she thought, how things would never, ever be the same again, and that the next morning they would wake to would be unlike any other morning they'd ever known.

They sat in darkness, no one bothering to turn on lights. Outside a light rain fell. The phone rang a number of times—friends calling to talk, then Martha Espy to inquire about Tish and say how she and Martin were so shocked, wasn't it awful, how could this have happened, Linda, I'm so sorry, as if she herself were the perpetrator and

Linda the victim, as if somehow this all boiled down to something that involved only the two of them. Eventually the younger kids went off to bed, but Angela and Tish clung to each other and cried some more, embarrassed and self-conscious in their grief, for which they could only repeat the same words: "Why?" and "How?" Then Harry phoned late from Philadelphia. He wanted to check on them all, make sure they were safe. His voice was strange, taut and distant. No one seemed immune to harm, he said tersely. "What kind of harm?" Linda wanted to know, and he had replied, "Baby, just tell me you're all right." He said it over and over until she wanted to scream. Back in the living room, she got herself under control, feeling a duty to the girls, who now sat quietly talking. She stayed up with them until almost midnight, nursing a martini and trying not to think the worst for the future. Look where dreams got you. She'd looked up at the picture of Martin, Bobby, and John hanging crookedly on the wall, the one that adorned the living rooms of so many hopeful black folk she knew, full of dreams. Of course all three men eventually wound up dead, Bobby two months later. Integration was never going to work, she mused, because deep down inside white people didn't really want it to. Oh, sure, they'd talk the good talk, and in such convincing ways you could almost believe they really meant it. But when push came to shove, they didn't want to have to sacrifice for it. They were for it as long as it was no skin off their teeth. She looked at her oldest daughter's rich butterscotch skin and the beauty and grace of her movements. She thought how she had brought into this world four beautiful brown children of increasing darkness who naturally deserved to have the things they wanted.

But life would not be easy for them. She had learned that early on, hadn't she? She still felt ashamed of how, on occasion through the course of her life, by omission and silence, she had occasionally, albeit briefly, allowed those around her, strangers, to presume she was white. Whiteness was always presumed until it was abruptly contradicted. Blackness, she thought now, is just that—a disagreement with whiteness. Those moments she had not "disagreed" had been a test, of herself and others, and she had been shocked by how much easier the world seemed for that moment. She learned a lot that way about human nature, including her own. She would never have openly claimed whiteness, had no desire to. But her brief silences were lie enough. The truth was she had experienced a guilty pleasure, the trickery of her own fair skin and light eyes, and because sometimes she just had things to get done without a whole lot of nonsense, she told herself she was doing it the easiest way. But it wasn't easy, knowing what she had done.

It only happened when she was alone, in private, like the time years ago she drove down from Michigan to house hunt in Brazil, and the realtor had sized her up and taken her to the West Side. They had chatted with such ease as they walked the rooms, and Linda Thompson had commented with pleasure on the mature trees in the backyard and the room for a swing set she would have installed for her children. "This is a nice neighborhood," the realtor kept saying, with emphasis on that eerie word "nice." And Linda had known, hadn't she, with a prickling of her skin, what the realtor had meant, but she had also hoped with equal vehemence that she was wrong. When she and Harry came back together for a look at the house, the realtor grew flustered, claimed she'd made a mistake and the house was no longer available, she was so sorry, but—oh, yes!—she did have a nice place on West Grant. And Linda knew with that sinking feeling that of course they were being redirected; why had she even thought otherwise? "I'm sure you'll find this neighborhood quite suitable to your tastes," the realtor had said, as more and more black faces began to appear on the street.

Linda Thompson never had been free of the gut-wrenching anguish of her own duplicity, the twistings of truth, as recent as a month before when she had returned a blouse to a store in a nearby town and the saleswoman had made a face behind the back of another black woman customer who came in and tried on a hat, drawing Linda, whom she presumed to be white, into complicity. *They have all that grease on their heads. It gets all over the hats,* she'd whispered, and shuddered.

Linda could almost imagine her brown-skinned grandmother asking her what did she expect, letting people assume she was something other than who she was. But it was never that clear. Should she always assume when white people were pleasant and helpful that they thought she was white too, based on the lack of pigment in her skin, the contrary color of her hair and eyes that whites didn't bother to look beyond? Her grandmother had all her life railed about colored folks who deny who they are and disappear to "pass." But she also made it clear you didn't want to be *too* black (everyone said "colored," anyway), as if blackness were an extreme you needed to take the edge off of. All those creams promising to bleach you a few shades lighter, and hair pressing to straighten out the kinks. No one ever said they would rather be white, because Lord knew they didn't want that either. No, what they said when they oohed over Linda Thompson's fair skin and praised her "good hair," without saying it, was "It's best not to be too black."

The night King was killed Linda took in the two pairs of eyes before her—the troubled dark brown ones of her firstborn, who suspected more than the haunted gray ones of the redhaired child she'd come to think of as almost her own, a picture of integration, ironic evidence of King's dream. "Mama," said her own child, as if beginning a question that she didn't know how to ask. And all Linda could think to say was "It's time you girls got some sleep now. We'll talk in the morning." Because she herself was so weary with it all. She had run out of steam, and wanted only to lie down in the quiet of her dark room and hope that morning wouldn't come too soon.

Pork chops eaten, dishes cleared, the boys asleep in their bunk beds, Harry was down in the family room drinking a scotch in front of the television, while Linda curled up on the living room sofa in her robe and smoked a cigarette before going to bed. She felt pensive, out of sorts. Why was it she couldn't get King out of her head? She and Harry had experience behind them, almost twenty years of marriage, so that silence and habit, no longer words and intimacy, now connected them. Gazing at the two almost-grown girls spread out before her on the floor, fallen asleep in each other's arms like babies, the turntable on the hi-fi still revolving, Linda recalled the night King died, felt the old twists and turns of doubt of her own being. She was grateful her own daughter was not beholden to those strict social conventions that had proscribed her own life growing up in Virginia: the blue-vein debutante balls, the social clubs, the parties, the right men of the right complexion. She wanted Angela to discover herself without the constraints of expectations that had limited her own self-definition for so many years: her mother's fussing about this boy and that boy—too dark, too poor, not the right status. It had been so important to her mother, who struggled on the edge of the middle class, for Linda and her sister to meet up with the "right kind," meaning fair-skinned with good hair and a pedigree. "Right kind. I've never heard a phrase so overworked," she joked now to her friends. Rightness had been stifling. Because when you are colored, her mother was letting her know, you need to be more than right. You need to be twice as good, twice as polite, twice as pretty, twice as smart. You never went out "without your face on," you never walked in bare feet out of your front door like a pickaninny, you never appeared on your porch in a bathrobe, you always made sure your clothes were ironed to a T, and you always spoke to everyone you knew, addressing your elders as "ma'am" and "sir." You never looked white folks right in the eye, but averted your gaze, a little to the right or left, but never down. And at college, despite all her mother's warn- ings about "dark men," she'd met and fallen in love with Harry Thompson, a walnut-colored track star with broad features and nappy hair. The memory of their first encounter still made her smile. But in her mother's book, success ultimately trumped blackness. "At least he's an educated professional," she had said of her new son-in-law, resigned but proud. Of course it all worked out. With the arrival of each of the four grandchildren, Mrs. Thompson's mother pored over their bodies with the fine-tooth comb of her experience, predicting just how dark each one would be, what texture of hair they would have, what relative they favored from the "lighter" side of the family. And as each child successively increased in darkness, drawing from Harry's side, Linda Thompson felt an odd relief, as her mother's consternation rose, de- lighting in the variations on mocha she and Harry had produced. "Thank goodness it's the boys who got the darkest," her mother said. "Life is so hard on dark girls."

Linda Thompson wanted to say, "Life is hard for light girls too," but she didn't, because her mother had always seemed blind to Linda's struggles, writing off her mistreatment at the all-black school she at- tended as "Oh, those little dark girls are just jealous of you." Jealous they might have been, but their cruelty knew no bounds. She had sought and found solace in a friendship with a little white girl several blocks away whose parents didn't realize for some time that Linda was black, and when they found out didn't seem to mind, and welcomed her into their home without question. With her own fond memories of the warmth of that household, Linda Thompson thought she understood Angela's attachment to the Espys. It wasn't anything to worry about. Her daughter seemed secure in herself. There were more choices now, weren't there? King had helped make that possible. She got up off the sofa, and bent down toward the girls, urging them to get themselves to bed. When they resisted with little moans, both smelling of sleep, she went to the closet and found a blanket large enough to cover them both. She stepped back, and clicked off the light. Their breathing synchronized, they inhaled and exhaled as one.

IX

The *Brazil Gazette* ("Queen of the Weeklies Since 1880") lay folded on the sofa next to Tish's mother where she rocked baby Francis in her lap. Every Thursday the paper appeared like clockwork on a metal rack inside the Lawson's on Main St. Rain, snow, or shine, Mrs. Espy stuck Francis in his car seat and chuffed down to retrieve it in the bronze Checker, a practical, no-nonsense car they'd traded in the old Pontiac Star Chief for. The Checker mortified Tish, its boxy bulk the only one of its kind in town. You could see the Checker coming a mile away; its broad grille as familiar to Tish as her mother's own face.

It was hard to live in Brazil and not, at some point, end up in the *Gazette*. Mostly the headlines featured issues of civic interest: tree plantings to offset the ravages of Dutch elm disease, parking problems, the beginnings of a Head Start program on the west side. The *Gazette* did report last year the hostilities by the all-white Pinkton High football team, who had greeted the Brazil Indians with catcalls and racial slurs. There had been a fight. Three black athletes from Brazil were suspended. A group of Pinkton athletes joined the Farmers to prowl the west side of town, "lookin' for niggers' heads to bash." But nothing much came of it. *Niggers die* was spray painted across the sidewalk in front of the A.M.E. Zion Church, but then quickly obliterated, though black kids at school lamented it and swore revenge for weeks afterward. The town's more unexceptional events were chronicled under captions like "Fire Runs," "Ambulance Runs," "Obituaries," "Hospital News," and "Legal Notes."

Separations, divorces (a lot of male faculty were ditching their tired old wives and hooking up with students), engagements, marriage licenses (to people you'd never heard of—"Dee Ann Martin Marries Willie Ray Lucas," and Dee Ann, a hairdresser from a neighboring town, would be photographed all smiles in her white dress). Tish's mother didn't miss a trick. In combing "Hospital News," she would remark pointedly on the occasional admission of a single girl who was then dismissed a couple days later with "baby boy or girl." Or if in turning to the "Police Blotter," just opposite "Good Neighbor News Bits," she discovered a match between the surname of a guilty party and someone Tish knew, she would inquire, "Now, don't you know a Tidwell? Don't you have a Burney in your grade? Wasn't there a Pickering girl you talked about in your science class last year?"

Getting into the *Gazette,* even under the best of circumstances, was always tinged with mortification. Caught in the odd locutions of the Brazil idiom, Tish herself had been reconstructed in appositives, embellished by journalistic curlicues, as in the following: "The part of Ann in *Cheaper by the Dozen* was played enthusiastically by Letitia Espy, a seventh grader at Brazil Junior High and daughter of Professor and Mrs. Martin Espy." Her mother had clipped them all and tucked them away in a scrapbook.

Martha Espy had also appeared in the *Gazette,* once for having won a gallon jug of M&M's at the grocery store for coming closest to guessing how many there were, and another time for being the victim of a mugging: "East side woman robbed by west side assailant in parking lot behind student union." Tish heard her parents' ongoing debate about whether Mrs. Espy had been right or wrong to try to conceal the "race of the suspect." Finally, under pressure from the one black officer, she admitted the boy had been Negro. "I didn't want to say," she told Angela and Tish sadly. "It shouldn't matter what color he was." The officer had said to her, "It does if you want us to catch him."

Like most of the kids of professors and other professionals, Tish and Ford had generally shown up on the *Gazette* honor roll, though when Tish hit junior high her *C*'s in PE for refusing to undress for gang showers consistently dropped her to the merit roll. In seventh grade she, along with Tina and another white girl, had accused the prejudiced Ohio history teacher of being a white racist (he let it slip one day that it was proven Negroes had inferior intelligence), and ended up receiving a *D* for the quarter.

Afterward, she got the Holly Penn stamp of approval for being brave enough to stake out such strong opinions—"I've always admired your forthrightness, Tish," Holly remarked, even though Tish knew she was lying through her perfect white teeth. As was always the case with interactions with Holly, Tish felt the knife edge of contempt barely concealed. It made her mad. Everything made her mad now, including having to go to school at all, which more and more felt pointless; it was a holding tank and little more. How she despised the hypocrite teachers and their lame excuse for education, including everything from subtracting slavery from the history lessons to the art teacher's insistence on calling the beige crayon "flesh colored" as he roamed the aisles among his brown-skinned students.

For the last couple of weeks the sight of the paper made Tish's nerves jump. She had been vaguely worried that the incident with the police would be recorded, her name brought to her mother's attention. How to explain what had happened in language her mother understood? Instead, she'd written a poem about it, worked out the words on the page in violent strokes.

As she passed through the living room, her mother unwrapped the *Gazette,* spreading it out across the sofa. She would go through it all, inch by inch, saving the "Police Blotter" for last. Tish couldn't stand it.

Most were a stretch: "Loose goat reported running amok on campus is nabbed outside Rush Hall" or "Red bicycle reported missing; chagrined brother of east side owner confesses to having borrowed it for joy ride to Curtis Pond."

For her children's benefit, she turned to juicier news that she served up as moral object lessons: divorce announcements, domestic quarrels, assaults, robberies, and the DWI's, usually a half-comatose soul weaving back from the bars one town over in the wee hours on Route 52. Lately, there'd been reports of drug dealing and marijuana smoking, particularly on campus, which was a place Tish was strictly forbidden from going. Ford was always sneaking off there, claiming to be at the library when Tish knew for a fact he had been smoking dope for a year now, and he was only thirteen and a half. But she'd thought it was advantageous not to bring any of this up since she didn't want Ford snooping in her business any more than he already did. Of course her parents didn't have a clue, and Tish felt nothing but disdain for their ignorance. Ford was too clever to be caught, and he clearly benefited from all the focus on Tish.

"Letitia, don't you know someone named Rogers?"

Her mother's assault carried all the way into the kitchen, where Tish foraged in the refrigerator for a snack for her and Peachy. They were supposed to be studying, but instead they'd gotten sidetracked memorizing the Panthers' ten-point program, copied onto a pamphlet from the Black Student Union meetings Wanda attended at the university. Now Tish pretended not to hear her mother, who was including Ford in her question. She circled back through the living room, quickening her step before her mother could call her back. The fragment from the *Gazette* caught up with her: " '. . . found walking down Route 52 at night in a dazed state. . . .' " And then her mother's commentary, "He was on acid. Like that boy from Parma who pulled his eyeballs out!"

Tish took the stairs two at a time. With the door of her room closed on the rest of the household, she sank down on the floor with sweet relief next to Peachy, sprawled on the bed under the Huey poster. "Okay, girl, I got it. Number one—We want freedom. We want power to determine the destiny of our school. Number two—We want full employment in our schools for our people. We want an end to the robbery by the white man. . . ." There was force in Peachy's voice, the same clipped, syncopated rhythms Tish recognized from TV footage of Panthers speaking.

"Don't forget decent housing," said Tish, tossing down a half-empty box of Oreos.

"And an end to police brutality and the murder of black people," said Peachy, reaching for a cookie.

"What about military service?" said Tish.

Peachy glanced back at the pamphlet. "Oh, yeah," she said. "That's next. 'All black men should be exempt from military service.'" She paused, scraping the white creamy filling along the edge of her front teeth. "You know, that's a damn shame, sending black men off to kill Chinese people just so the white man can profit. Ain't it?" She looked right into Tish's eyes. Tish wanted to say, "They're Vietnamese," but she didn't.

"Yeah," said Tish. All the wrongs of the world seemed to have clustered in that room. Once Tish and Peachy had calculated the probability that Tish's mother's southern ancestors might have held Peachy's father's ancestors as slaves in Tennessee. "Yeah, it's really messed up," she sighed. The whole thing made her feel ashamed, and for a moment she and Peachy faced each other in startled silence.

Now she plopped down cross-legged on the floor. There were things she couldn't say. Apologies to be made, but to who, and for what? There was the double lexicon of her friends, the idiom that circumvented white people, went right over their ignorant heads, spoke to historical truths no one wanted to hear. There were all the in references that Tish absorbed but ultimately had nothing to do with her. And there was the unspoken understanding they could call her *nigger,* but she couldn't say it back. And how when they talked about white people, she knew they didn't really mean her, but then, where did that put her? Sometimes she felt great relief; sometimes it just about broke her heart.

X

"What on earth did you do to your hair? You look like Medusa." That was all Mrs. Espy said when Tish walked in late, her tone rimmed with accusation.

As was her custom now, Tish didn't bother to answer. There had been an unexpected early snow and the walk home from Angela's was cold and wet. Her feet had grown numb. She'd run into two of her father's students, both white, on their way back from tutoring black elementary school children at the park and rec building on the west side. "Aren't you Professor Espy's daughter?" the one asked, knowing full well she was. Tish had hoped desperately that anyone passing would not link her with them, or assume her purpose on the west side was also to improve the minds of young black children. Enthusiasm for their own good intentions was written all over the students' faces. "What are *you* doing over here?" one of them had asked pleasantly.

Tish threw off her parka and began wordlessly setting the table, her fingers clumsy with numbness. Napkins, plates, silverware, glasses. Her hands felt alien. Mrs. Espy's voice seemed oddly weighted. "Your hair—you walked home like that?" Pause. "What do the boys want to drink? What does your father want? You better check." Tish had the routine memorized. The words buzzed in her head.

Dinner was always at the same time, no matter what.

Mrs. Espy stood at the counter in her apron fiercely chopping onions. She wasn't even disguising the irritation in her voice. "I asked you, what happened to your hair?"

"Dev cornrowed it."

"Dev? What was Dev doing at Angela's?" She wheeled around, paring knife in her hand. It sounded as if she hardly knew Dev or, worse yet, held something against him, when in fact she adored Dev—

old square, easygoing, bookworm Dev—and considered him a "very nice boy." "I thought you and Angela were studying *alone.*"

"We *were* studying alone. Dev and Peachy stopped by when we were *through.*" It was a slight exaggeration; they'd all been down in Angela's family room practicing the breakdown, but Tish had certainly thought about studying.

Mrs. Espy sighed.

"Watch the tone of your voice. I don't like the way you're speaking to me." She paused, laid down the knife, and went on. "I got a phone call this afternoon." She leaned back against the counter, wiping her hands on her apron. "It was Lynn Springer's mother."

Tish shrugged, but the quality of her mother's voice signaled trouble.

"I'm afraid I have some bad news." Was it kindness softening the tone? Or worry?

"Mrs. Springer . . ." Mrs. Espy cleared her throat. "Mrs. Springer doesn't want you and Lynn talking to each other any more. Not at school, not on the phone."

"I hardly ever see Lynn anymore," said Tish, hardening herself, "except in English."

"It seems Mrs. Springer found something . . . a note in one of Lynn's books . . . to you . . . Do you and Lynn still write notes?"

"Not really," said Tish, on guard now. "We're not really friends." With all the confessing that went on in notes passed at school, she could only imagine what Lynn Springer's mother had come across. Some old bit of mischief from one of those boring hours in English when Mr. Crawford droned on and on about Pip and Estella and Miss Havisham until Tish thought she couldn't stand another minute. Now she felt slightly queasy.

"Mrs. Springer said . . ." Mrs. Espy seemed to be in the grip of some overpowering emotion. "What she found was a note from Lynn addressed to you—a very explicit note—about her interest in a certain boy at school." Her tone dropped. "A *black* boy." She seemed to have difficulty going on, and the words "black boy" hung abstract in the air, tainted by the emphasis, and disembodied, as if they referred to an idea, not someone in particular. "The note talked about things that Mrs.

Springer said she couldn't repeat, about Lynn's fantasies—about this black boy. Apparently it was very explicit." Mrs. Espy turned away, embarrassed. For a moment Tish thought her mother wasn't talking just about Lynn, but was implicating Tish as well.

She felt a dull thud in her stomach. She remembered the note.

"It's very dangerous to pass such material around at school," said Mrs. Espy, implying that Tish was somehow to blame. "I hope you're not encouraging this sort of thing." She paused. "I hope this isn't what you've been writing as well. . . ." Worry lines appeared.

Mortification set in. Tish fought a sudden overwhelming urge to fall asleep right there, to curl up on one of the chairs and never wake up again. She didn't know whom she was most embarrassed for—poor little Lynn Springer with her feeble attempts to enlist Tish as conspirator in her crush on one of the black basketball players, or her own mother, now standing before her.

"I understand you want to defend Lynn—"

"I don't want to defend her. I don't know anything about her now. And her mother's a prejudiced witch. Everyone knows that."

Mrs. Espy looked crestfallen. "Tish, you need to know what Mrs. Springer said." There was a slight hesitation. Her voice edged into pity. "I'm sorry, but her exact words were that she didn't want her daughter to hang around with a nigger lover. She said she didn't want the influence."

Tish wasn't sure if she was more shocked by the words themselves or hearing them drop so effortlessly from her mother's mouth. There in the bright square of kitchen, indignation mounted inside her. "And you didn't say anything back? You let Mrs. Springer talk to you that way?"

"What was I to do? I was totally unprepared . . . It's a terrible thing to say . . . what would you have done?"

"I would have told her she had no right to talk about my daughter that way," Tish said, chest heaving. "I would have told her to go straight to hell."

She felt the heat in her face, as if summer had burst in unexpectedly and out of season. She started toward the door of the kitchen, still clutching napkins and silverware. She paused. Her mother remained uncertainly against the sink, the dusk gathering behind her head and muting her features. In that moment Tish didn't recognize her, felt as if she were staring at a stranger.

"I would have stuck up for me. You could have at least done that," she said.

Mrs. Espy was caught. "It just happened so fast. I didn't realize—"

"You didn't realize because you didn't want to realize," said Tish. She felt reckless with anger. Her voice took on the inflection Wanda used when she was telling white people off. "And now you have the nerve to wonder . . ." she said ". . . you wonder where all my white friends are going. That's where they're going. Do you get it now? They don't want to be with *nigger lovers.*"

She leaned over and threw the remaining silverware onto the table, where it scattered. A fork fell to the floor, bounced, then lay facedown. Her mother's stricken voice followed. "Please go tell Ford and Fisher it's time to wash their hands. And bring the baby down for dinner."

"Sure," muttered Tish. "Life just goes on as usual around this place. Let's not face the truth." *No one says what they really mean.*

Ford, sitting on the living room floor with his homework, glanced up. It was obvious from the expression on his face that he'd heard everything. He had a strange cowlick, which, now that his brown hair was longer, caused the left side of his head to look crooked and windswept. Peachy had long had a secret crush on Ford ("So cute for a white boy," she would gush). She was always asking Tish if Ford would go with a black girl, and Tish would sigh and say, "Don't be crazy. He's only thirteen." It embarrassed her thinking of Ford as anyone you could have a crush on. Poor Peachy, was she that desperate?

"What'd you do to your hair?" he smirked as Tish stepped over him. "I didn't know I had a black sister."

Tish kicked him, not hard, just hard enough. "Shut up, boy," she said. He clutched his leg and feigned pain.

The front door banged open, and in walked her father, dragging with him the smell of cold. He greeted them absently, and laid his briefcase full of student midterms on the sofa. He was growing a beard and there were flecks of gray in it. He gave Tish a passing look but said nothing and went on into the kitchen.

In the darkening front hall, Tish caught sight of her own reflection and paused in front of the mirror to look. She murmured to the image before her, *Mrs. Springer's an old white two-faced bitch.* The words gave her pleasure, separated her from the sting of the ugly words her mother had repeated. Now she felt angry with herself for the times she and Angela had sat politely at the Springer dinner table out on Christ-Cripple Road, helping themselves to homemade noodles and fried chicken and biscuits. And her own silence the time Mrs. Springer had asked Angela, "Are you Eye-talian?" and Angela had looked a little uncomfortable, and said, "No, I'm colored," and Mrs. Springer had drawn back and made an O of surprise with her mouth and said, "Well, my goodness, you don't *look* colored." And later she'd taken Lynn aside and said, "I don't mind, but please don't tell your father."

Tish crossed her arms, set her jaw, and stared defiantly back at her reflection in the hall mirror. She liked what she saw. Anger had burnished her cheeks. There was her oval face with its high cheekbones, the solid features and full mouth ("liver lips," Kim Mahelko had once taunted her), and the twinkle of glass stars in her pierced ears. Dev had plaited rows of red braids into the shape of a sun while Tish sat on the floor between his bony knees, like a boat in a safe harbor. That's what it was like being around Dev. And it felt good the way he'd made the careful parts and then pulled the hair so tight, causing her scalp to tingle, and her eyes to turn up at the corners. She had yielded to his fingers, to the sense that she was being remade. And there had been Angela and Peachy hovering: "Check out Tish. Girl, that looks so tough." Then a giggle: "She doesn't even look white." Now if she squinted in the low light, she could imagine herself blurring just a few shades darker, her features just a little broader, her full lips even fuller. It was that easy.

From the kitchen her father's voice droned on, detailing the ups and downs of his day, while her mother embraced him in the warmth she reserved just for him. Their voices blended and Tish no longer distinguished their words, just the loops and lines of years of repetitions.

Pots and pans clanged. Her father's voice continued. Tish went up and got the baby out of his crib and brought him down to the sofa. He struggled to get down so he could crawl on the floor in search of bits of dust to put in his mouth. Sometimes Tish liked to pretend he was her own baby, and when she'd take him out in the stroller, she'd make shocking remarks loudly enough to attract the curious attention of some stranger, like "Be a good boy for Mommy."

From the kitchen she heard her name. Only once, because then "Tish" became an impersonal, anonymous "she" with all the contempt her mother's tone could muster. She wondered if her mother was re-counting the phone call, or if she'd wait until later behind their closed bedroom door. Ford glanced over as if to say "See what you get?" Mr. Espy murmured something, and then her mother responded, with an edge. Tish leaned over and buried her face against the back of Francis's neck, closed her eyes, and breathed in his milky smell. He was small, and sweet, and it made her sad. If she pulled his little shirt up over her ears, she could drown out the voices, find the quiet in her own head, counting on the rhythm of his baby heartbeat by which to set her own.

The truth was, Tish thought as she pressed her face against the soft flesh of her brother, her mother had stopped loving her some time ago. She'd filled in the blank space between them with three other children, all boys she could love. Tish was already a head taller than her mother, and sometimes when they came across each other in the house at unex-pected moments, she lowered her head even farther and hurried around Tish as if she were an obstacle in her path.

Her father came into the living room and plunked himself down at the piano. "Come here, Tish, sing me a song." It was an old routine, something they'd done together ever since she was a child. He'd taught her corny old standards, and used to get a kick out of her singing things like "Smoke Gets in Your Eyes" when she was a little girl.

She got up, depositing Francis on the floor in a Buddha lump. She was dreading that her father would say something about her hair, but he was too busy concentrating on the opening bars of "Don't Fence Me In." She dropped onto the bench next to him and began to sing along. She craved the scent of his aftershave and the graceful motion of his slender fingers on the keys. She leaned against him, rocking in rhythm. There was a comfort to his solidity. It drew the sting from those shock-ing words like a poultice.

*   *   *

At the table, everyone took turns staring at Tish's hair, but the conversation carefully circumvented any mention of it. There was the opening discussion of politics, with Ford arguing with their father, and Martin accusing Ford of falling for conspiracy theories. "In case you don't know, the CIA," said Ford, "is behind *everything,* and you just don't see it."

Through the clatter and rattle and bang of dinner (Fisher fidgeting, the baby fussing), Ford turned and asked with faked innocence, "Tish, what did you do to your hair?"

Tish shot him daggers with her eyes, and mumbled the words "cornrowed" into her plate. This drew only a puzzled look from her father, who glanced at her mother for an explanation.

"It's a Negro hairstyle your daughter is wearing."

Inwardly Tish recoiled. Everything about her mother's tone, pursed lips, and the slight arching of one eyebrow were adversarial.

"Black," said Tish dully. "It's *black,* not *Negro."*

"Thank you, Le-*ti*-tia!" said Mr. Espy sharply. The room grew tense.

Tish couldn't stand it. "Well, the word *is black,"* she said, feeling a duty to explain. "You know, as in 'say it loud' . . . Nobody says *Negro. No-*body."

Mr. Espy's fork dropped onto his plate noisily. Whether it was deliberate or accidental, Tish couldn't tell.

"I know the word," he said angrily. "Don't patronize me, young lady."

"I'm not," said Tish. "I'm just saying the word is *black—"*

He didn't let her finish. "I'm not sure what you think you're trying to prove."

Tish rolled her eyes and slouched in her seat. "I'm not trying to prove anything." The table fell silent.

"She thinks she's black," snickered Ford, and he tried to make a joke. " 'Don't be talkin' 'bout my mama,' " he said in clumsy imitation, his voice straining and missing the inflections. "You should hear how she talks and acts at school—trying to sound like a soul sister." Tish could have killed him.

Mr. Espy sighed. "Tish, you need to accept who you are, or you're going to be a very confused young lady."

"I know who I am," Tish snapped back. As soon as she said it, she realized how foolish she sounded, and the familiar walls of her parents' kitchen struck her suddenly as strange and foreign. She couldn't look at her father. They were on uncertain ground, and they both knew it. She wanted to say to him, "It's you who don't know who I am. None of you do."

Ford grinned and stirred his mashed potatoes.

"What does a cornrow even mean, exactly?" asked Mrs. Espy, now trying to recover the situation. "Is it a symbol for something? I see black girls at the university wearing them. Tell us, Tish, we want to know."

Tish withdrew into angry silence, her appetite gone. The cultivated ignorance of her family infuriated her. Thank God none of her friends were here to witness her shame.

"Well, you might want to think about what it could signify," her father went on, chewing his roast beef. "What point you're trying to make."

"I'm not making any point," Tish said helplessly. "Dev was just messing around."

Fisher started crying because he didn't want gravy right on his potatoes. Mrs. Espy immediately threw herself into trying to separate them on his plate. She let her frustration escape. "Maybe you need to study at home if you're just going to fool around at Angela's."

Outraged at the presumption, Tish protested. "We *did* study. *Ma-a-a-n!*"

"I think she thinks this is what it means to be cool," her mother said tersely to Tish's father. There she was, talking about Tish in the third person again. In her precise diction the dimensions of the word "cool" flattened into two soulless syllables. Tish felt a duty, a quickening of reflexes.

"You don't know what 'cool' is," she challenged sharply.

Her father jumped in. "Isn't that what this is about—what you're trying to be? Cool like your black friends?"

Exasperated, Tish heaved a huge sigh and quoted from the don lee poem she had memorized: ". . . after detroit, newark, chicago & c., we had to hip cool-cool/super-cool/real cool that to be black is to be very— hot." She knew her parents wouldn't get it, and for the moment she found pleasure in their ignorance.

Mr. Espy threw his hands heavenward in disgust.

"You see," he said to the air. "This is what happens when our liberal chickens come home to roost."

Mrs. Espy was quieting Fisher. "We never heard this kind of talk from Angela or Peachy," she murmured. "It must be Wanda Beals's influence—"

Her father broke in. "I want to know what's going on with you. We've always encouraged you to have different kinds of friends, but you seem to have eliminated white from your vocabulary. What about the Mahelko or the Penn girl and some of the others you used to know? There hasn't been a white face in this house for over a year!"

Ford stifled a laugh and Mr. Espy glared.

The only response Tish could give now was one neither of her misguided parents wanted to hear, so she said nothing. Rejection by the "Penn girl" was her own parents' fault for being liberals and opposing the war and capitalism, and demonstrating for civil rights. In fact, Tish's father and Mel Penn had argued violently at a school board meeting, Martin expressing concern over the low number of black students in advanced classes. Mel Penn had scoffed and publicly accused Martin of being first a bleeding heart and second a communist. In turn Tish's father called Mr. Penn a fascist, just one step away from the Klan. That was the start. Then scandal erupted shortly after the retirement of one of the guidance counselors when it was discovered she had kept separate files on black students, directing them to vocational courses. During this volatile time Bunny Penn snubbed Mrs. Espy in the supermarket, as if the whole thing had been her fault. Eventually it all came to a head, and Mr. Penn pulled up to the Espys' rickety front porch in the family's Buick Electra, with his crew cut and bow tie and an invitation to Tish's father to join him for a game of golf at the country club, which, he seemed to have forgotten, excluded black members.

At the time Tish was proud of her father's stance. Now she felt differently. So much for their stupid ideals when that's all they were— ideals. What had Wanda called her parents once—armchair liberals? Perfect, thought Tish. Even her father had double-crossed her.

What none of them recognized was that somewhere, sometime, maybe when Tish was sleeping, an unseen hand had reached inside and rearranged her whole genetic makeup, creating a freak of nature. She wasn't who they thought she was. She had never been. Not white or black, she was something other and in between. Not even like Tina, and not like Angela, who had for a time with some small success straddled both worlds, but more like the people who fell between the cracks and lived in the spaces. Living with her parents required that she become two people, split, like the baby Solomon threatened to cut in half. At home she was expected to talk white, act white, think white, to pretend she was as white as the whitest girls at school. Girls whose voices rang with bland privilege, girls who had long ago decided in the unspoken language of caste that Tish would never be one of them.

"Maybe we should think about private school again," Mrs. Espy said softly. She reached for the mashed potatoes. "Her grades are terrible, you know." They went on like this, back and forth, while Tish stared hotly into her dinner plate, hating them all. She blocked out their rising voices, full of innuendo and speculation, until her eyes burned and the Currier and Ives pattern of sleigh and horse melted into a swirl of icy blue.

Finally they turned to other things, precise, modulated voices murmuring "please pass the salt" that blotted out her very existence. Tish watched the opening and closing of their mouths. She had the odd sensation she was staring through the wrong end of her father's telescope at strangers now receding, distant as planets in a far-off galaxy.

*   *   *

In her room Tish paced, unable to shake the sensation of being stranded inside her own head. Nothing matched up. Not herself with this family, not her mind with her body. Wait until she told Angela about Lynn's prejudiced mother! *A nigger lover.* How dare she? What did that make Angela? Or Peachy? Or Wanda? That's what it all came down to. If Wanda found out, she'd want to kick some ass. Tish could hear her now: *If you're a nigger lover and you love me, what does that make me?*

She flung herself down on her bed. Bit by bit she let herself be swallowed up by the encroaching darkness. A disappearing act, like erasing an Etch A Sketch figure. She craved a cigarette. Three Newports she'd bummed from Peachy and an old stale Benson & Hedges menthol were crammed into the old Kool Longs pack hidden in her notebook. But she knew better than to take the risk while her parents were still awake. She yearned for an intrusion, someone to phone and ask for her. As night came on, the house fell strangely silent, except for her mother's voice off in the distance reading *Winnie the Pooh* to Fisher and rocking the baby in her lap.

Downstairs her father began the first movement of a Beethoven sonata on the piano, something he did when he was either happy or sad. In any case, Tish felt he was making a point. She rolled over on her side and reached out to the rack of 45's. In the dark she grabbed several without knowing what they were and stacked them on the yellow plastic core in the center of the turntable.

The street outside her window was winter-still under an early coat of snow. A full moon showed through the mackerel clouds, but there were no stars. Rising, it cast a shaft of eerie blue light down over the snowy yard. Tish felt the moonlight enter her, like an arrow. With all the foliage gone, she could make out snow on the flat roof of the Hardlove house kitty-corner to the Espys'. Gina Hardlove was now a grown woman in her late twenties. How she had scandalized all the lily-white mothers in town who had cautioned their daughters in urgent tones about "what happens" when a young white girl from a good family "goes black." Tragic Gina Hardlove, they'd murmured to themselves. "Such a waste. Such a shame."

Gina was probably the most beautiful white woman Tish had ever seen—olive skin and Sophia Loren eyes that slanted, and a voice like velvet. Her short black hair was trimmed into a V on her neck. She seemed to defy race altogether, too dark to be white, and too light to be black, with features that suggested numerous possibilities in between. Angela remarked once she didn't think Gina was "all the way white." Someone said one of her grandparents had been full-blooded Apache. Someone else said she was part Greek. Which meant she wasn't white-white, the kind known as "Wonderbread," soft and bland and forgettable.

Her father, Bertrand Hardlove, was a famous art historian and well-known faculty radical. He'd marched with King in the south and helped register black voters. Rumor had it that he had at one time owned an orgone box, and he and his wife were devoted practitioners of free love (despite the fact, Tish's mother joked, that Brazil offered limited opportunities). Gina's mother was an invalid for a year before her death. Many people in town tried to say Gina was fast and unruly. She was a talented jazz dancer (she used to practice in her front yard in a leotard, looping her shapely arms and legs, throwing her hips to the side), what Mrs. Espy once wistfully referred to as "a true free spirit." Dr. Hardlove still lived in the old family house (Mrs. Hardlove had been dead for years), and was now notorious for his reclusiveness and glacial demeanor. Mrs. Espy once surprised Tish, revealing she had always found him profoundly charming, and had actually gotten him to thaw a little one evening at an anti–Vietnam War gathering held at his house.

When she was only sixteen, Gina married her high school sweetheart, a handsome black basketball star, Popeye Moody. (Because she had gotten pregnant, was the whispered subordinate clause. Because she "had" to. And she was just a young girl entering her junior year of high school!) Their marriage by all accounts was tempestuous. They argued constantly. Every few months Gina would run home and hole up in her father's house. Popeye would come around, heart in hand, and woo her back, and Gina, so the stories went, would relent because she couldn't resist. They would fight, reconcile, fight; it went on like this for some time. Mrs. Thompson once told Angela and Tish, "Gina couldn't keep away from him. He was such a really good-looking fellow back then, but there was always something about him . . ." Her voice trailed off, leaving Tish to wonder.

Jumping rope on the front walk with white neighbor girls *(I'm a little Dutch girl dressed in blue . . .)* Tish had watched Popeye Moody, then a handsome, sandalwood-colored man with a shining process, sauntering by in sharkskin trousers, on his way to the Hardloves to reclaim Gina. The other girls all stared and the rope buckled in the middle and limply fell on Tish's head. Once when she was alone, she stood just behind the dogwood tree in her yard and watched Popeye take the steps two at a time to the Hardlove front porch. He knocked loudly on the door, then paced, squinting into the street with impatience, humming to himself. When the door finally opened, Gina's faint outline was visible behind the dark screen. She and Popeye talked for a few minutes—Tish could see Popeye cajoling and pleading—and then the screen door swung open, and Popeye went in.

Mrs. Espy told Tish that once Popeye showed up drunk or stoned and was yelling in the street for Gina. Dr. Hardlove came out and tried to calm him down. Popeye cursed Dr. Hardlove up and down. It turned out Gina wasn't even there. "Popeye broke Dr. Hardlove's heart," Mrs. Espy liked to say. "After all Dr. Hardlove did for him. All the support he gave him . . . to turn around and treat a wonderful, noble man so dreadfully . . ." Ruefully, Mrs. Espy pointed out on more than one occasion, that for a white father in 1961 to approve the interracial marriage of his only daughter was courage at its most superlative. But Popeye was Popeye, and he chafed under his father-in-law's expectations. Dr. Hardlove was always riding him about going to college ("trying to give him an opportunity," from Mrs. Espy's point of view), taking him into his personal library and choosing books for him to take home and read. Pretty soon Popeye tired of old Hardlove's efforts, told Gina he wasn't going to sit through any more boring dinners with her father's colleagues and be grilled about Negro rights. He was a small-town boy longing for big cars, gold chains, and pretty women.

Two years after marrying Gina, Popeye turned around and joined the navy, against Dr. Hardlove's protestations—"part of the military-industrial complex," he groused. He wanted to work out a scholarship for Popeye to attend the university, but Popeye "never was into the books," as Mrs. Stubbs remarked once to Peachy and Tish. He was "street smart," but he didn't care about school. When he returned from Nam, she added, "That boy was ruined. Had him right up in the front lines where they put all the colored boys. Seems like he just lost his mind. He always was wild, but after that he just wasn't right in the head."

In Popeye's absence, people said Gina changed too. Loneliness got to her. She was young and unhappy. She scandalized folks by going out with an older black man briefly before Popeye returned. People talked when Gina was once again pregnant, tried to say the months didn't add up right. Nasty gossip circulated, how she was loose and irresponsible— what could you expect with bohemian, hippie parents? Tongues clucked, heads wagged. More black folks than white took her side. At one point Linda Thompson befriended Gina, hiring her to baby-sit Angela and the others. She was angry at how white folks in town vilified Gina. "She was the sweetest thing, young and pretty and all alone," Mrs. Thompson said. "She needed company, that was all. Nothing wrong with that. There was never any question that second child was Popeye's. He was just born premature, that's all. You look at that boy and you're looking at Popeye. He's got the Moody nose and the Moody eyes. I don't know why some narrow-minded people wanted to treat her that way."

When Mrs. Thompson was in a relaxed mood, after a couple cocktails, she would tell Angela and Tish stuff, stretched out in the living room with her stockinged feet propped up on a hassock. These were moments Tish craved, lapses in the normal, rigid boundaries between adults and children, when you could soak up the essential details of adult truths.

"You all didn't know Popeye Moody in the old days," Linda Thompson told the girls one night. "He was just as handsome as he wanted to be, like all those Moody men." And she shook her head. Tish savored the gesture and the sound of those words: *Moody men.* Something so powerful you couldn't even speak it. The words reminded her the way it feels just before a summer storm, when the sky turns first violet, then black, and the air thickens to the point of suffocation. *Moody men.*

In Vietnam Popeye had gotten hooked on junk, and even after he'd been back in the States, his habit worsened. He thieved from his poor mother. *Took her last fifteen dollars just to get himself some of that dope.* Gina gave birth to the second child and divorced Popeye. Shortly after, he went around bragging how he'd mail-ordered himself a Vietnamese bride named Mylinh and had her shipped over. She didn't last long. It was rumored she'd been a prostitute in her own country, cast out from society for sleeping with black American soldiers. Soon Popeye could be seen with some of the local winos like Pepe and Rudy, hanging out in the square near the track, downing Night Train and Richard's Wild Irish Rose and Boone's Farm or Ripple and not caring who saw. More than once, Tish and Angela came upon the empty bottles, evidence of a night's revelry, and they'd kicked them disdainfully, talking about just how low some people could go.

Popeye no longer had direct dealings with his own children, except by accident if they'd run into him downtown. For a while Popeye had a new old lady, "some skanky white broad from Elyria," Peachy called her. Tish had seen her too, a skinny woman with long gray hair and tattoos on her arms, getting out of a beat-up car. People were always making fun of Popeye. Someone said he was schizophrenic. Someone else said he was just a fool. Peachy and Tish, crossing the square after school to go to Nickles' Bakery for barbecued chips, would run into him sometimes. Peachy liked to mess with him. "Say, Popeye, what's happenin', brother?" and he'd eagerly summon them over. "Come here, pretty mamas. You lookin' good, baby." They would fall out laughing and take off running, repelled by his pathetic gestures. Deep inside, Tish was fearful of the deathlike cast to his face, the rakelike thinness of his arms and legs.

Still dauntingly beautiful and graceful, Gina and her two mixed children were a fixture in Brazil, their dark heads full of ringlets, their butterscotch skin the texture of silk. The girl, now in elementary school, had green eyes, the boy dark brown like his father's. Gina dated, mostly black men from out of town, Angela reported, and once Tish's mother remarked (in front of Angela) that she supposed with mixed children it was hard for a woman like Gina to find a white man. When Tish looked at her sharply, she hastened to add, "I only mean when you make choices, certain options get closed off." Angela didn't say a thing, just turned her head as if something beyond them had caught her attention.

Tish sat up on her bed. Through the cold glass windowpane, she could imagine Popeye Moody on the darkened sidewalk below calling out Gina's name. Had she ever really heard him call, or had she only imagined what she'd been told? In the frozen air, his voice would take on the sharpness and clarity of ice. It would cut through the chill, echo off the other snow-covered roofs, and ricochet from house to house, summoning all the sleeping daughters from their beds and into the winter night. Popeye, the Pied Piper. She closed her eyes. She tried to picture herself so drawn to a voice that she would, like Gina, be willing to leave the comfort of her home. Climb from an upstairs window and scale down the rough trunk of a fir tree to the ground below.

The voice Tish imagined though, was not the summons of a boy, but the pull of something much more insistent. One of these nights she too would start off, passing her father's office at Rawles Hall on the edge of campus, detouring around the high school, following her feet across the open field behind the stadium bleachers to the north side of town that would put her out on Christ-Cripple Road near the old mental hospital, and eventually the two-lane highway traveling east. If she kept on, she'd walk right along the edge of Lake Erie and out of Mohawk County forever. Cornfields would mutate into woods, and woods into housing developments, and then other towns would appear, strung together like beads on a necklace, until she reached the smoke-stacks of Cleveland and the clots of traffic thickening along Lake Shore Drive. And after she'd passed the most easterly edge of the lake, she'd find herself crossing the state line and heading into the green hills of Pennsylvania, where two years ago three white men tortured and murdered a black man from Cleveland, and left his mangled body in a hunting cabin in the mountains, skinned like a deer. If she kept on walking, the soles of her shoes surely worn thin by then, she'd eventually cross the New York state line, and soon after that she would be drawn to the dizzying thrum and beat of a real city, thankfully anonymous and lost to Brazil and her family forever. And this is where her thinking got fuzzy, because she could no longer picture herself or what she looked like; there was just an empty place in her mind where she had been, like the gravitational collapse her father once explained that happens when a star dies and there's nothing left but a black hole.

She was jarred by the sound of a 45 dropping onto the turntable next to her. Then came the rhythmic sloshing of waves and the soft croon of Otis Redding: "Sittin' in the mornin' sun, I'll be sittin' when the evenin' comes, watchin' the tide roll in, then I'll watch it roll away again . . ." She reached up, and one by one, undid each braid from her head.

XI

Brazil High sat on the north edge of town, a one-floor modern struc-ture built in the late fifties to replace the old stone, three-story edifice that had served generations before. Even though half the white in-crowd came from her side of town, Tish usually walked alone to school, unless in a generous mood she let Ford accompany her partway, or Angela had spent the night. Occasionally she fell into awkward step with Holly Penn and her main sidekick, Kim Mahelko, on one of their more tolerant days, but it was obvious from their carefully coded speech and eye rolling that they were "enduring" her. For a while they amused themselves by asking her questions and then feigning interest in her answers. Only later, when she'd heard her words repeated in Kim's screechy voice at the in-crowd lunch table, did she feel the weight of humiliation crash down on her. And after that, she began to fantasize how she and Peachy and Tina could catch Kim alone sometime and threaten to sic a bunch of tough, older black girls on her. Convince her they'd kick her ass. Give her a good scare. It was after teasing by Holly and Kim and Lisa that Tish gave up riding her bicycle altogether, suddenly ashamed of the balloon tires and clunky, rusted fenders. Her father had bought the adult-sized bike secondhand at a police auction, and presented it to her with much fanfare when she turned eleven. But now she saw it for what it was—ugly and childish, with its wide pink fenders and pedal brakes. After junior high, with the complications of stockings and garter belts and heeled shoes, many of the east side girls were being chauffeured by their parents, or escorted by boys who carried their books, not left to pedal their way to school, risking runs and grease streaks on their legs.

It gave Tish a pang thinking about how pleased her father had been to surprise her with the bike, and how she'd circled their block over and over thinking she would never need to ask for anything again as long as she lived.

Now the bike was propped in the garage, where each time her mother passed it she remarked she couldn't understand why Tish was letting it go to waste, it was a perfectly good bicycle, and if she rode to school she'd get there on time. But Tish had her mind on one thing. In the spring, an eternity away, she would take driver's ed and get her learner's permit. Her father had promised her driving lessons, and then in July, when she turned sixteen, she'd get her license. Her picture on a real Ohio driver's license, authorizing her to be in a car without an adult. There were even hints that she might get the two-toned white and turquoise Rambler Ambassador sitting out in the garage awaiting a few minor repairs. She'd use her babysitting savings and the money she earned waitressing at the Memorial Inn that summer to cover gas. If it really came to pass, she could always get Wanda and Peachy and Tina and the rest to chip in, and they could go all the way to the east side of Cleveland if they wanted, where Peachy's older sister lived and Wanda had some cute boy cousins she was always bragging about.

For now Tish walked everywhere—to Angela's and Peachy's, downtown on errands (often stopping by the appliance store to buy a new 45 for 89 cents of hard-earned baby-sitting money), to school. She must have walked the world that year before she learned to drive, choosing alternate routes through and around campus, in order to increase her chances of running into someone that mattered.

The trick to walking was making it seem you were walking because you wanted to. You had to adopt a casual air, as if you had somewhere to go, but you weren't in a hurry to get there because whatever was at the end of the line could wait. Even if the light was green and a car stopped to let you cross the street, you'd signal it to go on by, just so you could take your good, sweet time getting to the other side. Sometimes on more ornery days, if the light was red, you might still step out as if you were too busy with important thoughts to pay any attention to whether it was your turn to go or not, just to see how long it took for the driver to slam on the brakes, and for you to then motion the car to take the right of way. You could stand there like that for some time, acting as if it didn't matter if you got to where you were going or not, while people drove by noticing you.

"Fools' names and fools' faces," Mrs. Espy like to quote, "are always seen in public places." Tish cringed.

By the time her last-period class, general math, rolled around, Tish was antsy for the walk home, imagining whom she might run into. This year she'd gotten stuck in general math, after her poor showing in ninth-grade algebra (she had spent the year "reading for pleasure"). The only other smart person in the group was Camille Szonski, whose father taught in the Romance language department at the university. Camille was only a freshman, but looked almost twenty. She had long black Indian hair from her mother, who was Mexican and black. Her father was an Eastern European Jew whose family had been mostly wiped out in the Holocaust. Ever since her arrival in Brazil, people had badgered Camille to "make up her mind what she was." Camille's answer was silence and hanging mostly with the white professors' hippie kids. But on her own volition she staged a one-girl protest against the name of the school's football team, the Indians, saying that it insulted Native peoples, as she put it, a phrase which impressed Tish with its elegant ring. After that, Camille began wearing feathers in her hair and leather pouches of spicy-smelling granules around her neck. Rumor had it she stood up in the middle of her social studies class and argued the plight of Indians. "We were," she said solemnly, "the original people until the white Europeans raped our mothers." Even though Peachy and Wanda made fun of Camille because she wouldn't talk about her black side, Tish found her intriguing and her stance brave. Occasionally she stopped off at Camille's after school and listened to Laura Nyro albums in Camille's room, decorated with posters of the Beatles and various tribal artifacts. Camille's parents were counterculture types who allowed Camille to have boys in her room with the door closed.

The other members of general math included a triflin' Tidwell and the one low-class Burney released from special ed. And there were all the other mediocre kids, many of whom would either forget their books, if they ever had any books at all, or eternally request bathroom passes or dreamily carve their initials in the desktops. Tish knew she was smart, and it was her own indifference to mathematics that had landed her here. When the teacher, a nervous blond woman from Kentucky with an Appalachian accent, tried to make an ally out of her, Tish balked at the presumption of whiteness meeting up with whiteness, and turned tough and sullen. "I know your father is on the faculty at the university," the teacher made the mistake of pointing out as if this should make her more responsible. Tish slouched down in her chair until her back was almost parallel to the floor and rolled her eyes and sighed in that loud, disruptive way kids did to signal scorn and boredom. Everyone laughed. Ignoring her assigned seat, she moved to the back with soft-spoken twin black girls who were Seventh-Day Adventists and didn't believe in dancing, and a brassy white farm girl named Samantha Yoder who was inclined to interrupt class halfway through to announce that she was bored. Across the aisle sat Juice Washington, a dark-skinned black boy who reminded Tish of a giant cricket. He had been held back three years in a row, and spent most of his time sprawled in his seat, playing air guitar and singing the opening stanza of the Temptations' "I Know I'm Losin' You." In the middle of the teacher's explanation, Juice's singing of the opening guitar line was loud enough to drown her out. When she tried to go on, her hands trembling, her voice uncertain, he practically shouted out the lyrics. Tish reveled in his boldness, grinning back as he flashed her a wink that seemed to say, If these people had any sense, they'd just hand me my diploma and let me go work. The fact that the teacher, with her soft, Kentucky twang, blushed instead of reprimanded only made matters worse. "When you're trying to solve for x . . ." she would try, her voice lost in the hubbub, too scared to discipline, and the noisy class, abuzz with chatter, would shriek with laughter. It was cowardly, but Tish found secret pleasure in the woman's humiliation. She was scared of black kids, it was obvious. If one of them came to her desk to ask for help, she turned all shades of red, even down her neck, and began to stammer. After that, no one showed her any mercy, except the Seventh-Day Adventist twins, who almost never said a word.

There were only three black kids and one poor white kid in sophomore Advanced English and math. If your father worked at the university, however, you were generally a shoe-in, which was the only reason average white students like Mickey Carter, whose father was a college dean, showed up in Advanced English. Angela, Dev, and an uptight, hinkty girl named Mary Youngblood (whose father insisted she wear red lipstick and wouldn't let her date dark boys—*no dealin' in coal!* Peachy laughed) were the only black kids routinely placed in advanced classes. Dev was the only black boy, which meant he got teased a lot and called "Uncle Tom" and "schoolboy." Generally, Peachy and Tina made it into only the "average classes," even though they too planned to go to college. "That's because," remarked Wanda, whose Grandma Esther had made a big enough stink that Wanda was moved into advanced junior classes, "white folks are just naturally more gifted, right?"

So while Angela and Tish were reading *Great Expectations* and *Hamlet* in Advanced English, Peachy and the others were assigned short books like *The Pearl* and *Old Man and the Sea*.

Honors and average students were blended in history, science, and first-year foreign language, though of course black kids were traditionally steered away by the two white counselors from academics into vocational classes; everyone got lumped together in PE, typing, and music—black-white, rich-poor, smart-dumb alike. This was integration. *Racism was a southern problem.*

Though the school prided itself on its elite classes, the truly elite had long ago abandoned public education. The few blueblood kids in Brazil, like the Cranes and the Merrill-Brownes, went away, as family tradition dictated, to East Coast boarding schools. Their names almost never appeared in the *Gazette,* except in tasteful acknowledgment of some charitable donation or a merit scholarship award. When the Crane and Merrill-Browne kids returned to Brazil for holidays, they carried with them an air of the exotic, like foreigners dropped down in the middle of nowhere, biding their time for the next connecting flight.

The world of the Cranes and Merrill-Brownes was as far removed as anyone could imagine from the Tidwells'. As Wanda once remarked knowingly when she and Tish walked past the Cranes' brick mansion in French Woods, "It's a long way from this place to Roosevelt Court."

And she was right. Because while Wanda was fully aware of French Woods, where Holly lived, very few white kids ever had reason to go as far east as Roosevelt Court. "Black people make it their business to know what white people are up to," Wanda liked to say. "It's the way we've survived." When Roosevelt Court addresses showed up in the *Gazette,* it was always over trouble—drugs, knife fights, assaults, domestic quarrels.

The first night Tish spent at Wanda's, she recalled with great clarity the tone of her mother's voice remarking, "I didn't realize Wanda lived on Roosevelt," the word gone strange in her mouth. Her inflection, not unkind, more surprised than anything else, suggested something deeper than the word itself. But it remained unspoken, a question hanging there behind the question she had asked. And then Tish remembered. The "west side assailant" had lived on Roosevelt, a place that for her mother might as well have been on the other side of the moon.

Roosevelt. The word always made Tish think of fine velvet. Like the dark blue dress she once had when she was little, with a satin ribbon around the middle. *Roosevelt.* But the truth was that behind the thick, rich velvet curtain of a president's name lived some of the poorest black people in town.

The wooden houses on Roosevelt were mostly small and dilapidated. Some had sagging front porches, others dirt lawns. Laundry was hung out to dry on clotheslines or laid on whatever grass grew in the side yards. When you walked by, you could smell the leftover aroma of fatback frying in its own grease. In good weather, old people and kids sat outside on broken steps and chairs, and nodded to whoever passed by. In bad weather, residents taped plastic over the windows to keep out the cold. At Christmastime the Espys donated toys to the most indigent on the west side, and very likely something Tish had helped pick out at the five-and-dime made its eventual way to a less fortunate classmate on Roosevelt. Tish remembered the odd feeling of seeing the winter coat she'd outgrown in sixth grade show up on the back of one of the Tidwell girls at school, and Mrs. Espy had cautioned solemnly, "Don't ever tell her. Let her keep her pride."

It wasn't that Tish's mother deliberately avoided driving on streets like Roosevelt, she simply had no reason to go. The only white women who went to Roosevelt Court did so to pick up their cleaning ladies. But unlike a lot of the women on the east side, Mrs. Espy cleaned her own house, with Tish's help, of course. "With four children and a mortgage and a leaky roof, how could I even think of hiring a cleaning lady?" she said. Instead she donned an old shirt of her husband's and a pair of jeans and got right down on her hands and knees and scrubbed floors and waxed baseboards. She also did her own repairs, climbing up on the roof to clean the gutters one fall, and tearing apart old pipes to unclog drains. It set her off from other university and professional wives, many of whom employed "housekeepers," like Wanda's own Grandma Esther, and other "helpers."

Driving Tish to Wanda's, Mrs. Espy fell silent. It was obvious she was preoccupied, but wouldn't say why, and Tish, with growing dread, wasn't about to ask. In the Checker, neither spoke, so Tish flipped on the radio. Aretha was midwail in demanding respect. Tish started to sing along, imagining herself in a sea of bright lights before an audience. "Please turn that off," said Mrs. Espy sharply, making clear her distaste. Tish obliged, burying a sigh deep. The tension thickened. Mrs. Espy, tight-lipped, wended her way down Division Street, away from the university, across the tracks, and through the park on Spring Street. Her reluctance was palpable. Someone had spray painted *Honky pigs must die* in giant lettering on the backboard of a basketball hoop.

It was obvious from her mother's stiffening expression that she saw it too. Under other circumstances she might have sighed and made her predictable comment about not understanding "the growing anger," but she didn't.

Instead she cleared her throat. "Isn't that Peachy's house over there?" grasping for something familiar. Peachy's house was several blocks over. Tish burned in the silence. "No," she uttered coldly. "Peachy lives on Washington."

Mrs. Espy prattled on. "You know how fond I am of Angela. Both your father and I are. I'm glad you two have been able to maintain your friendship under difficult circumstances. I'm very proud of you girls."

Tish winced at her mother's carefully clipped phrasing. With rising impatience, she felt herself retreating from her mother's well-intentioned slips.

The Checker turned onto Roosevelt. Mrs. Espy slowed way down, taking in the unfamiliar houses one at a time. In the silence she radiated discomfort. A fragment of loud music burst from one of the houses as a front door opened, and then closed again. When Tish got out of the car, she noticed her mother was still wearing her homey apron, the blue one with the white ruffle on the front. That detail moved her to momentary pity.

But Mrs. Espy didn't drive off right away. While Tish crossed the yard to Wanda's, her mother lingered, exhaust steaming from the tailpipe. She didn't turn around, and when Wanda's tiny grandmother opened the front door, she slipped inside fast, with a sense of relief. What capacity did her mother have for taking in Wanda's poverty, the peeling linoleum in the kitchen, the tattered curtain on a rod instead of a door separating Wanda's closet-sized room from her grandmother's? (Wanda's grandfather, a retired janitor, had died the year before.) How awkward her mother would have looked when Wanda's Grandma Esther invited her to have a seat in front of the television, on a sagging sofa with the springs poking through. She imagined her mother's gingerly attempts at politeness, the clumsy effort to appear comfortable with battered furniture and plastic-covered windows. Wanda didn't care about being poor (she loved her grandmother fiercely and all the sacrifices her grandmother had made for her after her mother died).

She recited all the jokes ("I'm so poor couldn't even buy a mosquito a wrestling jacket" or "I was so hungry I got up and ate the bait right out of the mousetraps"), and teased Tish about "livin' in the Big House."

Peachy and Tina were already in Wanda's room, harmonizing along with Martha Reeves and the Vandellas, while Wanda's grandmother, with a passion for Westerns, had *Gunsmoke* blasting on the TV screen. "You eaten yet?" she asked Tish. "You awful skinny. Set your little bag down and go on in the kitchen and get you some dinner." She paused solicitously. "You eat chitlins, child?" A smile played on her lips. Tish knew why she asked, and that she wouldn't have asked Tina or Peachy that question. Yes, she was quick to assure her, yes, she loved chitlins. Grandma Esther shook her head. Tish got a plate and filled it, even though she was still stuffed from dinner, and then went on into the cramped bedroom where Peachy was already flung across the mattress on the floor. Tina sat on the edge, French-braiding Wanda's hair, separating even sections with the teeth of a comb, and rubbing Afrosheen into the exposed scalp. Familiar posters of Huey, Malcolm, Bobby, and Eldridge stared down from the walls. Wanda's tumbledown bookshelf to the right of the mattress was full of books by black writers, some of whom Tish had already read, like James Baldwin and Ann Petry, and some she was only beginning to hear about. The girls' harmony braided together so perfectly that when the song finished, there was a swell of good cheer. "Give me some dap, girl. That was tight. Hey, Tish . . . check us out. . . ." And they began again, Wanda, her hair freshly braided and oiled, motioning for Tish to join in.

She sank cross-legged to the floor, with the plate of food in her lap. Hot sauce burned the edge of her mouth. She took a deep breath, brought her face in close to the circle of the others, and following Wanda's command, came in on the chorus. "Mighty, mighty spade and whitey . . ." Every time Wanda hit the word "whitey," she bugged her eyes at Tish and when she said "spade," she elbowed Peachy in the ribs.

XII

Outside, Martha Espy, taking in the foreignness of the street, debated with herself whether to go up and officially introduce herself to Wanda's Grandma Esther. They had never met, though Tish had pointed her out on occasion downtown—a small, nondescript, brown-skinned woman with graying hair who held herself upright. A woman with dignity, Martha thought to herself, like so many black women in this town, holding themselves slightly apart, so there would be no mistake. But on her own, Martha worried that once she'd confused Esther Beals with another woman about the same age who always smiled graciously at her in the store. And she didn't want to make a mistake of the "all of you look alike" sort so she just smiled back and went on about her business, afraid to ask.

Now that same uncertainty took over, and she imagined how startled the black woman might be to confront a nervous white woman on her doorstep trying to make conversation where there really was none to make. There would be awkwardness about whether to invite her in or not, and she might be seen as an intruder. She recalled the woman's voice from the phone, a heavy, distinctly southern-black accent that seemed homey but impenetrable, calling once to ask for Wanda, who had dropped by after school with Tish and Angela. Something both alluring and unfamiliar about that voice. It had startled her, reminded her of the inscrutable woman who used to help her own mother out occasionally when she was a child.

Now, what would there be to say after the first polite words? She tried fashioning an excuse to go to the door, a reminder for Tish, a double check on the ride home in the morning, but she feared it might be construed as mistrust. Things were so different with Angela's mother, Linda Thompson, who was very much like other women

Martha knew, even down to the mannered way she spoke and the familiarity of her physicality—creamy skin, freckles, auburn hair, not so unlike Martha herself, from whose side of the family Tish had inherited that wilderness of kinky red hair. All through the early years of civil rights, she had found herself increasingly encouraged by Linda Thompson's polite agreement on everything, from busing to the acceptability of interracial marriage, the whole time conscious of their respective roles as pioneers—a black woman and a white woman forging connections, earnest in their mutual convictions. Linda had made it so easy, and Martha had often felt pleased with herself. Their friendship had been invigorating and reassuring. It was through their same-age daughters that they formed the strongest bridges. Enhancing race relations was a joyful process, and the brown and white bodies of Angela and Tish leaping in and out of a sudsy bubblebath or curled together in sleep had touched both women as they witnessed the unknotting of their own differences, smoothed out in the innocent bodies of their children.

Now, sitting in her car on Roosevelt, Martha began to grow faintly uneasy as a group of young black men emerged from one of the houses. They stood drinking around a parked car, talking and laughing in high falsettos in the chilled air. To her ears the sound was "decidedly Negro," curious and foreign. Martha tried to assure herself that all was well, that her daughter was safe inside. And she watched for a moment the dark men jostling and elbowing one another in what she felt must be camaraderie. She glanced back at Wanda's house. The blinds were drawn over the lit squares of windows. The house was modest, yes, but it looked cozy enough from the outside. She could understand Tish's attraction to Wanda—her feistiness was impressive, even if she did seem a little fast and brash at times. But perhaps it was that warm Negro laughter that Martha had often felt herself drawn to, the zest-for-life-despite-hardship so many Negro entertainers had demonstrated over the years, that her daughter was attracted to. She was thinking this as the young men began to spread themselves out into the street. As they came closer to the car, two of them now looking directly at her, she felt a rising uneasiness. After all, what business did she have here in their neighborhood? She shifted into drive and moved cautiously past them, looking straight ahead. Her breath clutched in her chest. Once she was past them (one of them turned to look), she peered into neighboring windows, searching for a clue as to where exactly her daughter had gone.

XIII

Tish awakened each school morning with a knot in her stomach. It was what happened when you no longer belonged to your own body, your insides twisting themselves into odd shapes and angles. Eventually she imagined herself wasting away to nothing. That had happened to a girl at school who, they said, started out with an ulcer and ended up losing an intestine.

From downstairs came the sounds of her mother's morning preparations, the clatter of breakfast dishes in the kitchen, her unvocalized "up and at 'em" permeating the air, the slamming of doors, the quick tromps of her father bolting purposefully down the front stairs to the university to get to his eight o'clock, her younger brothers' voices, the sound of the baby fussing. The din seemed to belong to someone else's family, as if a cosmic prank were responsible for her awakening to pink-rose wallpaper and her grandmother's vanity set.

She'd hide as long as she could in her room with the door shut, delaying her descent. Her stack of 45's had been played so much they were worn thin as dimes: Lorraine Ellison wailing out "Stay With Me, Baby," or Aretha joining the "Chain of Fools." Let Angela pretend she was whitewashed Marilyn McCoo singing about "up, up, and away"; Tish would take earthbound Aretha any day, the raw, throaty siren overripe with pain. Aretha knew about love and life. Rumor had it her husband beat her, but she couldn't bring herself to leave. Love was that binding, and that sorrowful. Tish imagined herself singing backup in sister Caroline's high soprano, soaring into the heavens on "Ain't No Way." Mrs. Espy's irritated voice traveled up through the stairwell, on cue, as Aretha faded out, "Letitia, are you dressed yet?"

Tish stood mute and morning-stunned among silhouettes of clothes she knew to be hers but clearly seemed to belong to someone else. Either they were all wrong or else she was. Nothing fit anymore, and even the new skirt and pullover sweater she'd wheedled out of her mother to start off the school year had cheapened into dowdiness when she wasn't looking. It was the wrong combination of blue and green plaid, with too much white in it, and the sweater was already beginning to unravel along the hem.

It wasn't long before her mother's footsteps mounted the stairs with firm purpose. Mechanically, Tish yanked off her nightie, pulled a skirt from the hanger, and added a blouse. Piece by piece in the dark closet, with Etta James's "Tell Mama" crescendoing in the background she created a reasonable facsimile of herself. By the time her mother lurched through the door to threaten her with God knows what, she presented her with a halfway dressed, uncombed version of progress. They would stare at each other, wordlessly, and then Mrs. Espy would turn on her heel and leave.

Overnight, it seemed, Tish had become a stranger, a clumsy, looming reminder to her mother of some vague disappointment. The accusations were that she'd become taciturn and sullen (her mother's exact words), a mediocre student (true) with a negative attitude (sometimes— she just had moods), she lacked interest in her family (untrue—she still liked looking at stars with her father), she was mean to her younger brothers (half true: she just didn't want them poking through her stuff), she was reckless and self-involved (translated: her room was always a mess), and she tied up the phone line for hours (more like a few minutes) talking to Peachy or Dev, or that old silly bucktoothed boy named

Melvin Goins she'd once French-kissed at the show when they'd all gone to see *Lilies of the Field* starring fine Sidney Poitier, about the only black man you'd ever get to see on the big screen. She went off to parties on the east side of town on streets named for presidents at houses where her mother didn't personally know the parents *(Will the lights be on? Will there be adults in the house? Will you be the only white kid there?).* Truth be told, she mostly hugged the wall at the few parties to which she was invited. There weren't too many guys with the nerve to ask the only white girl at a black party to dance in front of everyone. There was always Dev to fall back on, Dev who was just as awkward as she, always a little too formal and a little too stiff when he'd see her in public. But together they danced well enough that she avoided any of the stiff, jerky, white-girl movements she and her friends ridiculed. *Come on, Tish, show us how those white girls do it,* and she'd convulse and spasm her way across the room *(Don't forget to fling your hair back,* but her springy hair didn't fling and she'd have to pretend), and they'd all fall out laughing about how honkies didn't have any rhythm, and Tish would feel relief when one of them picked up the imitation, and then it was her turn to laugh.

A couple times when slow dragging she found herself pressed against a skinny boy named Ricky Jenkins who seemed to be able to slide his arm around her and get his tongue in her mouth before she could figure out what he was up to, mostly because he was so funny and could make her laugh. Once he'd put his mouth on her neck and she'd had to jerk away at the sting of his lips sucking so hard at her flesh. It wasn't until later when a small bruise appeared that Angela explained to her what a monkey bite was and how they were to be avoided, since boys used them to mark fast girls they'd "done it" with. She painstakingly applied mint toothpaste to Tish's neck, and they'd sat around in the family room listening to Dionne Warwick find her way to San Jose, waiting for the red mark to fade.

This morning the last thing Tish wanted to do was face the mash and chaos of the school hallways, the rituals of snubbing and being snubbed, only to discover that for some unknown reason today she was out, not in. No, that wasn't exactly right; she was never in, which was why she took refuge where she could. But sometimes she was less out. And those temporary moments of blending at the edges allowed her to see the possibility of belonging.

On her way out of the house, Tish passed Ford and two of his friends, one black, one white, on the front walk. She'd decided on her favorite navy and green wool skirt and a matching navy sweater. For once, her red hair actually was staying in place, parted on one side and held down with a clip. Just as she got to the street, she heard one of the boys say, "Your sister is pretty." She didn't dare turn around, and she didn't want it to matter what a thirteen-year-old thought about her. Silly boys. She kept on going, but the words kept returning, curling inside her like a comfortable cat.

It almost didn't matter that she hadn't studied for her French test. What was the point? She swept in through the back door of school and cut down what was called the chemistry hallway. She caught her reflection in one of the exhibit cases featuring photos of the cheerleading squad. Not bad today, she thought, though her one knee sock had lost its elastic and kept sliding down her calf. Damn it all, now someone would call her Pippi Longstocking. She went in search of a rubber band.

The white in-crowd, with Holly Penn and Jeff Anderson at the nucleus, had draped themselves and their coats over chairs in the multi-purpose room, laughing and talking in that knowing way they had. Years of affinity, social standing, and advanced classes held them together like glue. Semester after semester Tish had watched them like a foreign movie without subtitles. Most of the time they didn't even glance her way, except by accident. She thought of how pathetic she must have looked trying desperately for years to reinvent herself as someone who deserved their interest. She remembered with a certain wryness her feeble efforts to be what she thought they wanted her to be, which only made them more derisive. It took her years to understand they spoke a different language, and that even their silences and gestures were marked by a secret code. How was it that they were able to determine who was in and who was out with barely as much as the blink of an eye? Let them have their cliques, their funky little attitudes. Let Kim Mahelko and Lisa Mains giggle and make faces behind people's backs. Let Jeff Anderson roam the halls with masculine confidence, deliberately dropping his voice to fake sexiness as he murmured, "Hello, Letitia," just to make the others double over. Why did she care about his pasty white face stretched into mockery?

He had gone with every girl in the white in-crowd and had now turned his attentions to Mimi Dunlap, newly arrived from Los Angeles, California, a week into the school year. Her father was a religion professor, and Mimi was immediately placed in the advanced classes, where the in-crowd claimed her. Her big draw was that she'd been an extra in *The Endless Summer*. She was a short, chubby brunette who otherwise might have been negligible. But because she used to "hang ten" with surfers, and knew terms like "when the waves are two to three and glassy," Holly Penn conferred on her instant status. Mimi's best friend had been a girl she casually referred to as "one of Paul Newman's nieces." These were clearly credentials no other girl in Brazil wielded, and to the landlocked in-crowd, Mimi's experience offered a vicarious glimpse into a world they'd seen only on the movie screen. Holly, ever astute, immediately made Mimi her friend to ensure they would never be competitors, and now the foursome of Holly, Mimi, Kim, and Lisa made up the social center of the in-crowd's lunch table, with Jeff and boys like Mike Pratt and Peter Schiff hanging along the edges, their primary function to amuse and await instructions. This year Holly had begun going with a very senior boy named Taylor Weems, who had already been threatened with expulsion for growing his hair below his shirt collar. As a result, it was rumored Mr. Penn was not happy with the relationship.

Tish dreaded walking by them all, suffering the group's quick surveillance, and the collective inhale by which they assessed her passing. "Hello, Tish." That was Holly. Then a chorus of "Hi, Tish," all dutiful. She rounded the corner, half expecting an echo of laughter. To her relief there was none. She checked her reflection again in the mirror hanging just inside the choir room door, pleasantly surprised by what she saw. How she craved a cigarette, but hated to smoke alone. She'd go find Angela. This meant backtracking and walking by the in-crowd again, since she knew Angela would most likely be over by the vending machines, where the black kids all congregated. Holly Penn gave Tish

another glance-over. Was it Tish's imagination, or had Holly murmured something to Kim, Lisa, and Mimi, who now turned to look?

All the Penns (descendants of William) seemed genetically pro-
grammed for good fortune. A staple of the *Gazette,* their photos were
poised above captions like "winner" and "high scorer" and "best" fill in
the blank. There were seven Penn children, all perfect in their own
ways. It was clear Holly had inherited her mother's imperial generosity:
Bunny Penn ran about half a dozen charities and was always being
honored for some act of kindness. Her life was a series of ribbons and
plaques and speeches, and when she wasn't busy, she lay outside on a
deck chair by their kidney-shaped pool (it had the bluest water Tish
had ever seen) and sunbathed until she looked like a blackened redfish.
Mr. Penn owned a huge medical supply company on the outskirts of
town, which employed a number of Brazil residents.

More than once in one of his dinner table rants Mr. Espy had used
the Penns as an example of capitalist greed (much to Tish's delight), but
there was no animosity, just a matter-of-fact reference to a specific
example of what he called "the culture of accumulation."

"Tish," Holly once asked after she'd seen Mr. Espy demonstrating
on the square against the army recruiter sent to campus, "are your
parents communists?" Another time she remarked with aristocratic curiosity, "Your parents are so unusual. I saw your mom out mowing the
lawn, and she was wearing *jeans* and sandals. She's not really a hippie,
is she, just a little eccentric?"

Tish joined the tide of students moving down the main hall. There
was a restless air in the hallways, or was it her own inner agitation?
Beyond a clot of black students she spotted Angela on the arm of
Michael Brown. What a relief. She yanked up her knee sock and
flagged Angela down. Angela waved back and reluctantly pulled herself from Michael's proprietary grasp. A moment later, shoulders
pressed together, they banged through the swinging doors of the girls'
rest room, laughing to themselves about their "nic fit."

"Hurry up, Negro, you got the squares," said Angela, as Tish fumbled down in her bra for the crunched-up pack of Kools. "You are so
slow, girl." They slipped into adjacent stalls. Tish struck a match and
felt the welcome pull of smoke into her lungs.

"Don't bogard it," Angela demanded from the other side. Her index and middle fingers scissored the air under the stall. Tish slipped the cigarette back. Angela was beside herself about a fight out by the flagpole. Had Tish seen it? No, she hadn't. She'd come in the other way.

Angela loved dispensing news. Her voice reverberated. "Well, this little redneck white girl smart-mouthed Wanda Beals, called her Brillo Head, and Wanda jumped her." (A deep inhale, a deep exhale of smoke.)

"Who?"

"One of the Farmer girls who digs brothers. Anyway, Wanda was all over her—snatched half the hair out of her head before old Tommin' Mr. Foster came out and broke it up."

"Is Wanda getting suspended?"

"No," said Angela. "They tried to, but her grandma has been down here for the last hour arguing with the principal."

The toilet paper dispenser in Angela's stall creaked. Tish could hear the paper unwinding. Angela went on. "I'm tellin' you, some of these white broads get on my nerves. Like the ones that mess with brothers on the sly and then don't speak to them in public. Now, you know I don't have anything against black and white together, but . . ." Her voice trailed off in exasperation.

Tish stuck her fingers under Angela's stall and retrieved the cigarette. She knew how some of the white girls talked and giggled about their flirtations with "soul brothers," imagining black boys to be more knowledgeable sexually than white. White boys didn't rap. Black boys did. It drove the white girls giddy, gave them status. And why was it some of the ugliest white girls could get the finest black guys? She'd heard Wanda's theory, and Peachy's too. They were right. Forbidden fruit.

From the other side of the stall wall, Angela said, "I'm still trying to get that french inhale down. Tell me how again."

"Like this." Tish climbed up on the toilet seat and peeked her head over the edge of the partition. Down below, a foreshortened Angela crouched on the toilet, stockings crumpled comically around her ankles. She glanced up. "Are you crazy, girl?"

Tish laughed. "Yeah," she said. "I'm crazy." It felt good saying that.

She liked the sensation of being dizzingly at the top of the world. As little girls they used to cram themselves on the toilet at the same time, and race to see who finished peeing first until Mrs. Thompson caught them and said they were too old for such games. Tish had been puzzled, unsure of what she meant.

"First you let a little smoke out your mouth like this." She pulled the smoke in a perfect loop up through her nostrils. She poked her lips forward.

"Damn, that looks so nasty," said Angela approvingly. Tish handed Angela the glowing butt so she could try herself.

Angela clenched it between her teeth and shifted on the toilet. She held a wad of toilet paper in her hand. The smoke curled into her eye and caused her to squint.

"I'm thinking of getting another perm," she said, wiping herself. "Get my hair cut again . . ."

Tish steadied herself against the partition. She was imagining what it would be like to be this tall, to be able to see behind walls and over the tops of things. "Tish, are you even listening to me?"

"I think you'd look better with a fro," said Tish. "You've got the face, the features for it." What she wanted to say was, Why do you want a white girl's hairdo?

Angela sighed. "Girl, you sound as trippy as Michael. My hairdresser says my hair's too fine for a fro—" Her voice was drowned out by the flush of the toilet. Excuses, excuses, thought Tish. Angela just doesn't want to be black. It was that simple.

The first bell rang. Tish jumped down. Angela could be such a Tom sometimes, still stuck on chemicals and straightening her hair, and grinning at Holly Penn. It irritated Tish, the way Angela could talk so black on one hand and act so white on the other. She went out to the sink to wash her hands and slosh water in her mouth.

Behind her, Angela clicked open the stall door and emerged.

The outside rest room door swung open, letting in the hall hubbub. Three white juniors came in, blond hair rolled under, and one of them waved her hand in front of her nose and said, "Pee-yoo. Who's been smoking in here?" She glanced accusingly over at Angela and then Tish. Angela said, "Don't look at me, we just came in." Tish was terrified the girls would figure it out and report them. They were the kinds of girls who would do just that. She pretended to concentrate in the mirror on getting her hair to lie flat.

Nothing worked. She'd tried everything: smashing it down hard with her palms, pressing it into place with a barrette on either side of the part. Rollers only made it worse. She had tried sleeping on orange juice cans (Angela's suggestion) but they left dents and ripples, and it was only a matter of time before her hair resumed its own snaky shape. Peachy tried to hot-comb it once and burned her scalp, leaving a tiny bald patch on the side of her head. She'd even tried a little bergamot, but it only matted up her hair and turned it greasy.

The other girls adjusted skirts and stockings, checked makeup. Tossing knowing glances, they left. Angela and Tish were alone again. Tish was still in desperate need of a rubber band for her sock. She'd stop by the secretary's office and ask. Angela bent over to dust off the tips of her loafers and Tish wondered if the roundness in her hips was really caused by sex. Peachy claimed it was one test to tell if a girl was lying or not. Tish couldn't help but wonder if Angela really was still a virgin. Peachy was a virgin, for sure, swearing up and down no boy had touched her below the waist. From the way Wanda talked so tough about how no man was ever getting more than a whiff until she was good and ready, she was too. Jasmine Robinson probably wasn't, not with a boyfriend like Lamar.

She stared at her own hopeless reflection in the mirror. "Sometimes I just can't stand myself," she sighed, and then realized she'd spoken the words aloud.

"You and James Brown," said Angela. "You just need to do something with your hair, because you're really cute, Tish." As if that's all it took to remedy a problem! Angela reached over and gathered the unruly red mess in her hands. "Like this, why don't you just tie it back?"

She held the hair away from Tish's face and ordered her to look at herself. "That's a pretty girl," she said.

Tish pulled away and shook her hair back out. "I hate pulling my hair back," she said, sliding the barrette back along the side.

"How else can people see your eyes?" Angela asked. "I think you try to hide under all that hair."

"I can't do anything with it."

Angela got a gleam in her eye. "Girl, could you imagine if you showed up at school with a fro? You'd have people tripping big time."

Tish shrugged, momentarily startled by the version of herself Angela had just offered.

Angela began to dig in her streaked makeup bag for eyeliner. "Come here," she said impulsively, waving the little black wand like a magician. Tish moved closer and hunched down, her face eye level with Angela's. She felt the soft pressure of Angela's hand against her cheek, and then the faint tickle of the brush moving across her bottom eyelid. She held very still. "You're so much prettier than you realize," Angela said almost tenderly, licking the tip of the little brush. "Just be happy for who you are." And she flicked another dark line under Tish's eye. Tish lowered her lids and imagined herself transformed under Angela's patient hand.

XIV

With her three oldest off at school, Martha Espy cleared the breakfast dishes. Then while Francis napped, ritual dictated her pilgrimage through the children's rooms, checking to see who made the bed and who didn't, and collecting dirty clothes, and otherwise assuring herself the house was in order (on occasion scanning her children's dresser drawers for evidence of unnamed transgressions). She paused in Tish's room—the framed pictures of Beatrix Potter characters now replaced by the silk screen of Che over the bookcase, Huey Newton above the vanity, and Malcolm X glaring down, finger raised toward the ceiling. A ceramic burner held upright three long sticks of incense that reminded her of miniature cattails. She bent over and sniffed. One smelled like vanilla. She had heard from Lilly Anderson, whose son Jeff was in Tish's class, that kids were using incense to cover up the smell of marijuana smoke. Could it be possible? Just to be sure, Martha opened the top drawer of Tish's dresser and peeked inside. She felt only a small pang of guilt when her fingertips connected with the cotton fabric of her daughter's crumpled underpants and a fading sachet smelling faintly of violets that Tish's grandmother had made one long-ago Christmas.

She withdrew her hand and closed the drawer. She suspected Tish smoked cigarettes, she so often smelled of smoke. She turned and observed the bed, made in haste, the blanket lumpy, the pillow smashed flat, with a renegade red hair coiled like a spring on its surface. Bending over, she held up the edge of the mattress with one hand and felt around underneath with the other. What did she expect? Something other than empty space? She dropped the mattress back into place. Relief caught in her throat. She pulled herself up, smoothing down her skirt with her hands. Tish no longer left her notebook around. It was there that Martha suspected lay the clue to her daughter's secrets. She had seen some of what Tish had written in the past, words she had been shocked to see her daughter knew. *You should be careful what you write down for people to see,* she'd said cryptically to Tish, and received only a scowl in answer. Well, you couldn't be too careful these days.

She left the room, hoping Ford had remembered his book report and trying to remember whether or not Tish had lunch money. In that empty house, with its leaky roof and creaky stairs, she rarely took a moment for herself just to think. Think of the choices she'd made in life, think of what she might have done differently. She had yearnings sometimes, but they were eclipsed by her family responsibilities. She had trained to be a high school English teacher, and had taught for two years before marrying Martin, but now she had five people to tend, to keep watch over, four of whom would be returning in a few hours expecting dinner. She ran the house like clockwork—up at five, asleep by ten, and even then it seemed as if she couldn't keep the laundry from piling up or the dust out of the corners. And then there were all of

Martin's books and telescopes to stumble over. Impossible to manage it all! It was difficult, in the face of all the changes, to maintain standards for her own children. She worried about Ford and Tish growing up in such a chaotic era, especially with all the permissiveness (teenagers necking on the streets in plain view, and neighbor children being caught with marijuana and hallucinogenics!), but mostly she worried about Tish.

Francis woke, fussing. Martha stuffed him into his snowsuit, preparing for morning errands. As she chugged downtown in the Checker, with Francis in his car seat next to her, she was pleased to make out the trim figure of Linda Thompson in a powder-blue overcoat carefully picking her way through the slush before turning in to the post office. The timing was such, thought Martha, that by the time she'd parked and lugged out Francis, heavy in the winter snowsuit that made him look like a spaceman, Linda would be finished with her errand and on her way back out, and they'd bump into each other naturally and maybe have a moment to talk. She could casually ask Linda, whom she hadn't seen in a long time, if she had a minute to have a cup of coffee at the Woolworth's counter and catch up.

By inquiring about the Thompson children, she might get around to gleaning some insight into Tish, who was becoming increasingly unfathomable. She also hoped to renew old ties to Linda herself. Too much time had passed.

She opened the car door slowly in the brisk, pleasant air, thinking any moment Linda Thompson would be exiting, but when she didn't, Martha felt foolish, like a kid in junior high waiting to be noticed. As she withdrew Francis's stroller from the trunk and set it up on the pavement, she heard a voice behind her. She turned. Behind her stood a small, light-brown woman, vaguely familiar, wearing a rumpled car coat and an odd little felt hat pressed down on her head.

"Hello, there, Mrs. Espy," the woman said with that formality of an older generation, and for a moment Martha thought she recognized the pleasant black woman who cleaned house for her neighbors the MacGregors, the people Tish baby-sat for.

"Why, hello," she said back, hoping that in the next few moments it would become clear who exactly this was.

The woman extended her hand. "I'm Peachy's mom. Connie Stubbs."

"Oh, Mrs. Stubbs, of course! I was just distracted here. . . . I apologize for not recognizing you right away."

She tried to stop before she appeared flustered.

"Please call me Connie," said Mrs. Stubbs. Before Martha could say "please call me Martha," the woman began cooing at Francis through the car window.

"Ooh, what a little sweetheart. He your youngest?"

Martha nodded, pleased that the other woman approved. She wondered if they were both feeling the self-consciousness of their intersection. She felt a jolt of excitement, a glimpse into the potential for normalcy if only color could be ignored, because after all, they were both mothers, and their daughters were friends, and shouldn't they naturally come across each other in the course of their daily doings? Wasn't that the promise of integration?

"I always wanted a boy," said Connie Stubbs, "but the Lord chose instead to bless me with three girls."

Mrs. Espy was startled by the fact that she hadn't realized there were two older Stubbs sisters.

"Well, girls are nice too," she said placatingly, trying to adopt a tone that would match Mrs. Stubbs'.

"Girls are a gift," Mrs. Stubbs went on earnestly. "I never had a moment's worth of trouble out of the first two. And then Peachy was a surprise in my old age"—she paused and laughed—"yes, a surprise, but she's proved to be a real blessing to me. Your little Tish is a sweet child."

For a moment Martha felt a pang, because she herself would never have thought to describe her daughter in those terms. Then she wondered if the brown woman peering out from under the awful hat had a special knowledge that she herself didn't, and she felt a momentary twinge of envy, wondering if this was what drew Tish to spend time at the Stubbses'. Some kind of maternal warmth from this woman that

Martha wasn't able to give her own daughter. She herself had always thought of black women as warm and maternal.

"Peachy's such a dear too," she replied dutifully.

"Oh, you won't find a sweeter child than Peaches," said Mrs. Stubbs proudly. "She's my heart, she really is. You know you can have so much trouble with children these days. . . ." She paused and let the words sink in.

For Tish's mother, the remark was a heaven-sent opening, a cracked door through which she proceeded to place her foot.

"Yes, it can be a real test," she said. "I'm never sure what to think."

"A *real* test," repeated Mrs. Stubbs, gripping the front of her car coat as if to ensure it didn't unwrap itself from her body. "But I thank the Lord every day that He watches over my Peachy. When I think of all that could happen . . ."

"Perhaps," said Martha, trying to hang onto the thread of the conversation, "it's best not to think of those things. . . ." She herself was iffy on the subject of the Lord, and wasn't sure whom to credit or blame for the ups and downs in life.

"Yes, well, you're right about that," said Connie Stubbs agreeably. There was a pause. "Well, I shouldn't keep you standing out here in the cold," she added awkwardly. "It was so nice seeing you."

"Yes, so nice to see you too," said Martha, desperately trying to think of a way to keep the woman from walking away. But Mrs. Stubbs was already waving to Francis through the car window. "Good-bye, precious," she said sweetly. To Martha she said, "You take good care now." And then she turned and started across the street.

"You too," called Mrs. Espy into the gray air, hoping the phrase nicely echoed Mrs. Stubbs's.

She pulled Francis in all his familiar winter bulk from the passenger seat and settled him into his stroller. Agitation quickened in her chest. They had made a connection, the two of them, and in that moment she imagined the boundaries of race and class disappearing. Here she, a white professor's wife living on one side of town, had met up with an uneducated black laundry worker from the other side. They had exchanged kind words about each other's children. Mothers under the skin. Isn't that what it was all about? She pointed the stroller with determination toward the front door of Woolworth's with a rising sense of optimism. Perhaps the solution to all the world's troubles was really this simple. If only people could get off this race kick and treat one another as human beings, the fragments would all reknit themselves and the world would be color-blind. She glanced behind her several times, but Linda Thompson was nowhere to be seen.

XV

Their arguments always seemed to rise up out of the blue, with the blinding force of a blizzard, catching both by surprise. This one had something to do with her mother's frustration over unwashed dishes, a mess of the boys' toys littering the living room, unfinished household business. It escalated to include a lecture on Tish's music, the sad state of her grades, and the threat that Tish wasn't going anywhere all weekend. "All weekend! I'm going out tonight," Tish called out in panic. Mrs. Espy wasn't even listening, Tish was sure of that, and she felt herself sink in the quicksand of hopelessness. And just moments before Angela was to arrive to walk with Tish to a dance at the parish house of the Congregationalist church, where they would meet Michael Brown and, if Tish was lucky, someone for her! Her mother had misunderstood, hearing only the words "Congregationalist church" and imagining something related to the youth group there. When she realized that the parish house was being rented out for a private dance and that it was not a church event at all, but a party put on by a group of black athletes to celebrate their latest win, she began to reverse her decision. Tish strode off into the living room, furious, and close to tears. Frustration threatened to fill her right up to the eyeballs. Her mother trailed behind. Gone was her sternness. She was now pleading.

"When I said yes, I thought you were going to a church event. I didn't realize it was a boy-girl party."

Boy-girl party. As if there were any other kind at her age! Tish cringed. Why such a big deal over this one and not the others?

"It's just a dance," she said wearily. "I told you exactly what it was a week ago when you said I could go. And Angela's already on her way over."

Before Mrs. Espy could respond, Angela was letting herself in the front door, with a cheerful "Hel-lo!" She had on her maxi coat and a matching skirt and knit vest. Her hair was wound in a twist, held high in place with a gold barrette. She'd added a red rinse to it for "highlights."

"Hello, Angela," said Mrs. Espy, smoothing out her voice and withdrawing to the edge of the living room.

Tish suddenly feared her mother would say something stupid and offensive in front of Angela. Her breath caught in her chest and tightened. Was it boys her mother was worried about, or black boys in particular? If so, why didn't she just say it, and get it over with? If Tish were going off to dance in stiff, jerky movements to the Mamas and the Papas with Jeff Anderson and Mike Pratt, would her mother raise these objections? She was sick of the interrogations.

"Are you going like that?" Angela wanted to know, observing Tish still in jeans and T-shirt.

"Course not. Come on upstairs," Tish said glumly, and her mother retreated back to the kitchen, where her voice mingled with the voices of Tish's brothers.

In the safe haven of her room, Tish put Aretha on the turntable and flung herself backward onto her bed. "Ain't no way," Aretha sang. Tish was too dispirited to cry. "My mother's tripping—really hard," she moaned. "She's trying to find some reason not to let me go tonight."

Angela narrowed her eyes. She was a quick study.

"Like how?"

Tish shook her head. "It-shay," she said. "Ull-bay it-shay." The bed underneath her yielded to the motion of her tosses and turns. Aretha's voice climbed higher, inching up the scale of agony.

Angela sat down at the vanity table and spun around on the stool to face Tish. At this angle, she looked grown up, like a young woman, and for the first time Tish thought how Angela seemed like someone much older than herself.

Tish sighed. "Martha's so strict."

Angela chewed her bottom lip. "It's not just strictness. *My* mother's strict." She paused. "Your mother's—well, scared. Scared for you, Tish." She paused. "She's really changed. She acts different now. It's obvious she's worried about you going to black parties—even with me."

Tish felt the sting of truth. Even if her mother had never come out and said these things, how long did Tish think Angela could turn a blind eye? In her mother's mind there was an unleapable abyss between black and white, and a reason why the black kids went home to one side of town and the white kids to another. She rose half-heartedly to her mother's defense, resorting to words like "old-fashioned" and phrases like "I'm not sixteen yet."

Angela's mood change was almost palpable, her tone increasingly somber. "I don't think your mother trusts *me* anymore," she said. There was no disguising the hurt in her voice.

"It's not you, Angela," Tish was quick to say. "My mother loves you."

"Maybe in her own way," said Angela, "but now that we're growing up she doesn't want you going *out* with me." She gave Tish a long, meaningful look. "Going out with me means meeting black boys, Tish, boys like Michael."

Tish tried to correct her. "It's not that—"

"Your mother's hypocritical. It's so obvious, Tish. Let's face it, she's going to take you away from me." The words hung there in the air between them. Tish felt her insides twisting into familiar knots. She got up and silently took the brush to her red curls.

Angela let out a deep exhale and began fingering things on the vanity table, examining each item as if she'd never seen nail polish and emery boards before. "Did you tell her the party's for the athletes and that Michael's one of them?"

Tish nodded. That should have been enough. For Angela's mother it was. Tish felt a gulf open between them. She concentrated on trying on white lipstick while Angela took an orange stick to her cuticles. The white lipstick made her look like a ghost. She wiped it off and tried to stave off the rising anguish of being caught in her mother's predictions and what it would mean shortly to stand along the edges of the dance floor while dark bodies pumped like pistons to the beat. Someone would occasionally reach through the dark and yank at her hair and murmur loud enough to embarrass, "What's she doing here?" She didn't blame them one bit for not wanting white girls at their dances, white girls who, in Wanda's words, "had gone coo-coo for cocoa puffs." She wanted them to intuit just how wrong they were about her, that she did what she wanted and went where she belonged.

"How does this look?" she finally asked Angela, as she stood in her navy-blue pleated skirt and a red poorboy.

"Fine," said Angela without much heart.

"No, I mean it," said Tish. She wanted Angela to look at her, to see her as she really was.

Angela cocked her head slightly and gave Tish the once-over. "Come here," she said, "your hem is dragging on the left side. Do you have a safety pin?"

Tish dug one out of the drawer and handed it over.

"Here," said Angela, almost maternally, and turned the bit of loose hem under and fastened it. "Turn around. Okay, you can't see it."

"Thanks," said Tish. She got down on hands and knees searching through her closet for the sensible patent leather pumps her mother had bought her for ensemble. She'd give anything to have pointy-toe shoes like Angela's, but she didn't, so the patent leathers were the next best thing. The little heel made her long legs look even longer and gave them some shape.

"You look cute," said Angela. "Come on, let's go."

"Are we walking?" Tish asked.

Angela nodded. "I couldn't get the car tonight. My mother dropped me off. She's got to take Monica to a slumber party. I'm riding home with Michael."

On their way out, Tish tried an offhand good-bye, then felt herself stiffen as her mother advanced toward them. She was assessing Tish—her hair, her clothes. She was taking in both girls, making a comparison of some sort in her mind. Why couldn't it be Mrs. Thompson giving casual approval with a wave and a "Have a good time, you two"?

"Your mother's picking both of you up?" Mrs. Espy asked Angela right to her face.

Tish winced. She was caught now. Angela was a terrible liar. But if she didn't say yes, Tish knew she wouldn't be going anywhere tonight or for a long time to come.

Angela turned, the upturned collar of her maxi coat throwing half her face in shadow. "Yes," she said, simply and cleanly. Tish could have kissed her. She knew Angela would be furious at having to lie, but Tish could deal with that later on the walk over. Right now, she just wanted to get out of the house before her mother changed her mind.

"Eleven-thirty, Tish," Mrs. Espy said, knowing full well that the dance ended at one. Tish felt the old anger wedge itself into the center of her gut. There was the pull of loathing as she looked back into her mother's strained face, with its mask of courtesy.

"I know," she said coldly. "Come on, Angela."

"Good-bye, Mrs. Espy," Angela said in her politest voice. Tish could see how Angela's pleasant tone smoothed out the wrinkles of her mother's worry. Maybe now her mother would imagine the party in whatever way she wanted: a well-lit room with plenty of adults crowding the sidelines, observing to make sure no one danced too close. How out of touch she was, Tish thought sadly with a yank of pity.

Outside she and Angela hurried shoulder to shoulder down the walk through the cold air. Once they'd gotten to the street, Angela said, "I don't appreciate your using my mother like that. I don't like being put on the spot."

"What was I supposed to say?" said Tish. "That you'd be meeting Michael and going off with him to make out, and leaving me stranded at the party? That I didn't have any way home and give her a great excuse to say I couldn't go?"

"Why didn't you just say you were riding with someone else? If your mother checks with my mother—"

"She won't," said Tish uncertainly. "They never see each other anymore."

The streetlights cast a dim glow every half block. Angela looked at her watch. "It's still too early to show up. Michael doesn't get off work until nine. I don't want to be the first ones there. It would seem really square. Let's go to the campus snack bar and get a Coke."

Tish agreed, envious of the casual freedom Angela enjoyed. She knew that if her mother caught her on campus she'd be in trouble. So many restrictions she lived under. Now the guilt of her small deceptions joined the chill of winter in her bones. More important, she was worrying how she would get home. Certainly there would be someone willing to leave early and drop her off. If they let her out at the curb, instead of pulling into the drive, they would most likely be gone before her mother could raise the blind in her bedroom window and discover it wasn't Linda Thompson at all, but some tall, lanky afroed youth her mother would assume the worst about. Tish arriving home with a carload of black boys. That's how Gina Hardlove started out. She'd heard the story told many times. The voice went on in her head, drowning out Angela saying, "Tish, are you even listening to me?" She nudged her. "Hey, isn't that Wanda's man Grover over there?" Tish looked up. A tall afroed man was exiting the university library and now striding their way. He was alone, a half dozen books clutched under one arm. Tish imagined the weighty thoughts he, as one of the Black Student Union leaders, must be thinking. As he passed, Angela called out, "Power to the people, brother," and Grover, wire rims framing his almond-shaped eyes, glanced over and replied, "Right on, sister, right on." Tish felt the brief connection they made, one in which she was not included. How she envied Angela. It was that unspoken language of fraternity, of black acknowledging black regardless, a subtle nod, gesture, or tip of the head that meant so much more. Grover had looked right past her. In that split second she did not exist.

XVI

For the English class assignment the following Monday, Tish recited Langston Hughes's, "The Negro Speaks of Rivers." She practiced it on her family at dinnertime, and repeated it every morning before school while she was dressing until the words felt like her own. She loved the rhythm of the repetitions. After her recitation, Mr. Petit asked the class earnestly, "Who is the 'I' in this poem?" and then stupid old Mike Pratt, who was now going with Lisa, brayed out in his high voice for everyone's amusement, "A guy who travels a lot?" This made everyone, except Dev and Angela and Tish, laugh. It was that laughter and the yawning mouths and wicked sparkle of all those white faces that gave Dev the idea to organize the recitations of other black poets, poets not chosen from the assigned list. After careful thought, Angela chose "The Blackstone Rangers" by Gwendolyn Brooks. Dev did Claude McKay's "If We Must Die" and "The White City" in an emotional voice Tish hadn't thought him capable of. They were making a point—the Hughes poem had been the only work by a black poet included in what Mr. Petit called "the poetry unit." Naturally, they couldn't count on Mary Youngblood to do a black poet; instead, when asked, she hesitated, pursing her pink-lipsticked mouth, back-pedaled with a lot of "oooh-ahhhh's," and finally said "maybe," and then turned around and chose Emily Dickinson, much to Angela and Tish's disgust. One of the four half–Puerto Rican sisters at school, Alicia Gonzalez, agreed to memorize a Leroi Jones poem as a "show of solidarity," she said, even though she mostly hung with white kids. And a hippie white girl named Susan Wax, who called herself "very political" and wore anti-war buttons all over her sweaters (*Girls say yes to boys who say no*), agreed to memorize a poem by don lee. But it was Holly Penn who received a standing ovation and an A-plus for her rendition of Frost's

"Mending Wall," which she gave with just the right dramatic flair and confidence to cause the class to erupt into applause.

In the gym locker room later, Holly sidled up to Tish as she struggled to snap up the regulation navy-blue one-piece before anyone could see exactly how flat her chest still was. "Those were interesting choices of poems you and the others made."

Tish nodded.

"I guess you were making some sort of a statement," Holly probed.

"Maybe," Tish mumbled. She felt edgy under Holly's scrutiny, particularly in such a public place, with Kim and Lisa just on the other side of the lockers listening and measuring every word to be served up later for ridicule. She was desperate to get herself covered again.

Just then Wanda strolled in, slamming through the swinging doors, and laughing loudly. She was lugging her trombone from band practice, and blowing a big bubble of gum from her puckered mouth, knowing she could be given demerits for chewing gum on school property and not caring one whit. She dropped her trombone case next to Tish and said, "Hey." When Tish bent over Wanda observed for the amusement of anyone who cared to hear that Tish had an "ironing board behind." "Look," she crowed, then pointed out how Tish's thighs "gapped" at her crotch so you could see the light coming through. Tish pretended to be too busy searching for her crew socks to notice. Why didn't she ever have a comeback for Wanda? Disrobing beside her, Wanda demonstrated how her own heavy dark thighs touched when she stood motionless. Then she turned to illustrate with Peachy and Tina, yanking on them so they'd hold still. "White girls have gaps," she announced to the rest, now half in and half out of clothes. There in the crush of bodies, and the ripe locker scent of sweat, musk, lotion, and perfume, Tish inhaled the odor of her own body rising up from the neck of the slightly sour suit. It made her feel strangely ashamed. Brown, yellow, white, and black bodies crowded together, elbows and breasts only inches apart, flesh gone garish in the fluorescent overhead, stretch marks, scars, birthmarks, and baby fat all revealed. Tish had come to think of white girls as ghosts, the way they could almost vanish under harsh light, the way they went deaf when black girls loud-talked them. "Puerto Rican girls have half a gap," Wanda went on, taking on the next-to-oldest Gonzalez girl, Louise. She was enjoying herself thoroughly. "Puerto Ricans are kind of like in between black and white." She pointed to Louise's chunky thighs. "You're part soul sister, aren't you, girl?" she said, laughing. "You got a black girl's legs." She looked over at Tish and muttered for everyone's benefit. "You know what I'm sayin', don't you, girl? You know I'm telling the truth!"

Tish tried to laugh it off as a sign of inclusion that Wanda could be so personal with her in such a public way, but it became unclear as she sealed herself up with the last snap of the tight gym suit who was laughing with her and who was laughing at her.

"Notice," said Wanda, strutting across the locker room floor in just lace bra and panties, breasts bobbing, "how black girls' booties go all the way up in back like this [she pointed to her own] and ride high in the air, but white girls' just go flat." (And she pointed back at Tish.)

There came cries of "Wanda, you're crazy," and "Wanda, you are too much," but most of the black girls were laughing, and the ones who weren't pushed past and headed out to the gym for lineup and roll call, shaking their heads. There was one, though, named Annetta, who was desperately squeezing herself into invisibility against the row of lockers. She wore gigantic spectacles like insect eyes, and Tish saw the anxious look on her face. Annetta had seized a towel to cover herself, but not before Tish noticed. "What about Annetta?" she said. "She's flat all over." The moment the words came out she regretted them, but it was the only weapon she had.

All heads turned on Annetta, and everyone stared. Wanda strutted back across the floor to her locker and began to squeeze herself into the uniform. Her developed body stood in stark contrast to Annetta's little stick figure. There was an awkward silence, some mutterings, and a few icy looks. "Annetta?" said Wanda, glancing over. "Turn around, Annetta." Annetta did, her shoulders hunched. Wanda paused and pondered. "No, see she doesn't gap," she said earnestly, and then burst into laughter. "But she sho 'nuff has on some raggedy-ass drawers." The gym teacher's whistle blew and everyone began streaming out to the gym floor. Tish waited until the

locker room was almost empty before turning to apologize to Annetta. In that pasty-walled, windowless room, she could almost imagine they were serving time in prison.

"Hey," she said softly. "I didn't mean it like that."

Annetta seemed to retreat even farther into her body.

"It's okay." She even forced a funny, puckered smile.

Such forgiveness was undeserved. Tish would have preferred that
Annetta had flown into a rage and threatened to kick her ass. Instead
she continued calmly buttoning up her blue uniform with the methodi-
cal precision of someone accustomed to doing things right. Tish turned
and walked out onto the gym floor, where the teacher's voice echoed off
the walls. She took her place in line.

There was no way to undo what she had done, but over the next
week, Tish went out of her way to greet Annetta in the hallways,
something she had never done before. Guilt drove her to walk partway
home with Annetta one day when they both happened to exit out the
back door of school together. Annetta lived with an aunt, it turned out,
because her parents were dead. She had only one kidney, and as a child
she'd had rheumatic fever. "I'm undeveloped," she explained solemnly,
"because of all my illnesses," which only made Tish feel worse. She
feigned deep interest in the specifics of Annetta's conditions, all the
special medications she was on, and the fact that she wasn't allowed to
do hard sports. This information made Tish feel even sadder, more
ashamed, because she had nothing in common with Annetta. But she
went so far as to invite Annetta home to study one night, knowing
Annetta got poor grades and had a hard time concentrating. To her
surprise, Annetta declined. "My aunt doesn't allow me to go to—
well—*other* people's houses," she said softly. "She's afraid something
will happen to me." Tish pressed. Annetta grew quieter. Tish offered to
have her mother call Annetta's aunt. Annetta seemed to shrink even
more. "I can't," she said, terrified. "I'm not allowed. I can't come to
your house."

It wasn't until Tish and Annetta parted ways at Division Street and
cut across campus that it dawned on her what Annetta meant. She
wasn't allowed to go to white people's houses. When she mentioned this
to Angela, Angela cut her eyes. "What are you doing inviting her over

for, anyway? Tish, she is the *weirdest* person. And her aunt's stone crazy, you know, keeps Annetta locked up in the house all the time, won't let her out to do anything, and Annetta doesn't stand up to her."

Annetta was a coward. It showed in the way she walked, her body bent from the fatigue of the effort. At school she hung around with a mildly retarded white girl who lived out at the orphanage and who, it was rumored, had been dropped and then burned with boiling water when she was a baby, which accounted for the bald patches on her head. After that, Tish detoured around Annetta when she saw her, and it was as if they'd never spoken.

XVII

For the Christmas ensemble concert, Tish was selected to solo on "O, Holy Night." A corny song, but she didn't care. Singing it made her feel angelic. Nervous about performing in front of half the town, she was thrilled when Wanda remarked without an ounce of guile after the final rehearsal, "Girl, you sure can sing the hell outa that song." And then because she couldn't resist, she added, "For a white girl," and punched Tish in the arm.

The part rightly should have gone to Wanda, who, as everyone pointed out, "had the most soul" and "the most mature voice" of anyone in ensemble. Wanda was so musical—could play any instrument she got her hands on, and could sing for days. But she'd already been selected to solo on a gospel piece. The fact that only Tish and Wanda had been chosen for solos increased Tish's pride. The choice equated her with Wanda. They both got to step away from the rest of the chorus and distinguish themselves. They were fore-ground, the others background. It became a connecting point. *Did you practice your song? Are you ready, girl? I'm so nervous. Girl, you'll be just fine.*

The night of the performance Tish could see how pleased her par-ents were, sitting there with Ford and Fisher, baby Francis on her mother's lap, smack-dab in the middle row of the auditorium. In her navy-blue skirt and white blouse, Tish stepped down off the riser next to the piano and tried to forget there were several hundred people staring at her. She began to sing. A few times her voice faltered, like tripping over a stone, but she yanked it back on track. She got through, and when she was done, the auditorium erupted in applause. It swelled like waves. Numb and hot all over, she squeezed back onto the riser between Peachy and Tina. The piano started up and she joined in the melody of *"Stille Nacht,"* still flushed under the harsh stage lights.

Afterward, everyone congratulated her (even Wanda came up and said she'd sounded "goo-ooo-oood"), and she got permission from her parents to hang out for a while at the Campus Restaurant downtown with the others for an ice cream sundae. She'd catch a ride home with the Stubbses's. She could see the brief hesitation in her mother's eyes, some unspoken suspicion, before she relented.

Full of dessert, Tish, Angela, a junior named Sharon, Peachy, Wanda, and Tina clowned around under a streetlight across from the square waiting for Mr. and Mrs. Stubbs to show up. There had been a brief warm spell, and the night was rainy in a series of rainy nights. The drizzle had stopped long enough for the humidity to build. Tish could feel her hair, which she'd spent hours trying to straighten on giant juice cans, now spiraling out of control. Not now, she prayed. Not now. She reached up and desperately tried patting it down flat, but it wouldn't obey. Red corkscrews formed around her face. Wanda reached over and snatched up a swatch in her fist. For everyone's ben-efit, she laughed and said, "Damn, Negro, what you got there?" The others, including Angela, started laughing. Wanda was up to her old tricks. "You got you some righteous-ass nappy nigga hair. Look at this."

Tish yanked herself away. "Stop, Wanda," she pleaded. Damn the rain! She tried pressing her hair down.

"Well, it's true," Wanda said. She had everyone's attention. "Check it out. Look at Tish's hair. Girl, what you been hidin'?"

Peachy said, "You know, Tish looks like she could pass . . . look at her hair and mouth," and Sharon agreed, "She does look like she could have some blood," and then they all started speculating and messing around, pulling on her hair kinking in the dampness, and laughing and teasing about how "you could have a little nigga in you, you know." Peachy pointed out how Mr. Espy tanned awfully dark in the summer for a white man ("You got a fly in the buttermilk, girl?"— more laughter), and Tina insisted earnestly how Tish's hair was just about the same texture and color as her cousin Niecie's in New Orleans, and then stuck her own arm alongside Tish's to prove there wasn't much difference. Peachy suggested, "We might as well just go on and make her an honorary Negro, she thinks she's one anyway." Tina said, "For real." Angela kind of glanced away, as if she hadn't heard, cautious to the last, and Tina challenged, "What you lookin' away for, Angela, like you all embarrassed or something?" Wanda immediately jumped on Peachy for taking things that far.

"What you all talkin' about, honorary Negro and it-shay like that? Y'all crazy sayin' you can make a white girl black. What's wrong witch'all?" She launched into a tirade about slave masters and slaves, persecution mentality, centuries of oppression. "It ain't funny," she said. "Y'all really messed up."

Sharon said, "Right on, sistah," and Tish felt the discomfort of too much attention.

Behind them on the square, she concentrated on two winos emerging from behind the upended track, one of them carrying a bottle of screw-top wine in a sack. She thought she recognized the thin, bent frame of Popeye Moody. His voice carried through the night air. She started to make a joke, to take the pressure off herself, but Peachy and Tina were on a roll.

"Come here, Tish," said Peachy, pulling Tish over against her, and glaring at Wanda and Sharon. "Girl, you gonna hang with us, you gonna be one of us."

Tina said, "Right on."

"Damn!" Wanda blurted out. "It's bad enough we got your little yellow ass, Tina."

Everyone said, "Oooooooh," and Tina said, "Wanda, why don't you shut up sometimes?" And Sharon said, "Make her."

Peachy started in earnest. "Tish, repeat after me. 'When the Revolution comes . . .' "

Tish hesitated.

"Go on, girl, say it." There was an edge to her tone.

"When the Revolution comes . . ." Tish said slowly.

Wanda's eyes got fierce. "All right, all right. You need to get some soul, girl. When the Revolution comes, you gonna be right there with us blowing honkies away, right?"

Tish nodded.

"Then *say* it. Say it like you mean it."

Peachy interrupted. "But we will spare your family. Okay? Martha and Martin—and your brothers—we'll let them slide. Just like Tina's mama."

There were some groans from Wanda. "Damn, y'all really some serious fools. . . ."

With a few nonsense words and a flourish of her hands over Tish's head, Peachy announced honorary Negrodom had been conferred. There was an awkward pause. Tina giggled, then clapped her hand over her mouth. They were all looking at Tish. The mood changed, everyone got quiet. "This is some serious-ass shit," said Wanda and kicked at the curb. "Y'all shouldn't play like that."

Peachy and Sharon started linking arms. "Beep, beep, umgowa . . . black power's gonna get yo mama." It felt natural and right that Tish should be here like this. She never wanted to go back to dead old Woodland Street, and the careful, insular world of her parents, who believed in the egalitarian dream, that all people are created equal and therefore, underneath it all, are really alike. What a lie. *We'll save you when the revolution comes. We'll save your family too.*

When the Stubbses finally pulled up (Mr. Stubbs in hat and tie, and Mrs. Stubbs in her nightdress with a coat thrown over it), the girls were all so high on their own silliness as they piled into Mr. Stubbs's Mark

III that Mrs. Stubbs asked suspiciously, "What you all been up to? I just know you ain't been smokin' any of those funny cigarettes," which only made them fall out more with laughter. Mrs. Stubbs murmured to her husband, "Nnnnnh-nnnnh, they some silly girls tonight." And he grunted his sympathy. Peachy said, "Oh, Mommy, we just made Tish an honorary Negro." Mrs. Stubbs's eyebrows shot up and she just shook her head and muttered, "Y'all somethin' else." The air thickened with her disapproval.

Packed in the Mark III, bodies flush and compressed, Tish felt fused to the others. The flesh of Wanda's arm against her own was now connected through her to the bone of Angela's knee. She felt pleasantly sleepy, body flowing to body. In the shadows they might have been sisters, jammed together on a family outing. For once she didn't fear getting lost or slipping away.

It seemed like a mistake when the car made its turn onto Woodland. The houses along her street appeared severe and empty, the pristine lawns antiseptic. The Mark III sailed up to the corner.

"I used to go to that house there when I was a little boy," Mr. Stubbs pointed out. It was an old stone house set back from the street. "My daddy had a little junk business way back when, and we'd go around there to pick up all kinds of things that man threw away. That was back in the days when folks didn't have nothin'. . . ." He paused and let them all fill in the blanks.

Peachy was embarrassed. "Da-ddy," she said.

"Well, it's true and there's no shame in hard work. Hard work's what bought this new automobile you're riding around in, young lady." Then for Tish's benefit, he added, "The white fellow owned it was a nice gentleman. Always treated us with respect."

"Da-ddy," Peachy said again, and punched Tish in the arm. Tish wanted to tell Mr. Stubbs not to take her home. After all, she was an honorary Negro. She didn't belong on Woodland Street.

Tish didn't care if her mother thought she'd gone mad. Blackness for Mrs. Espy, well meaning as she was, remained a mystery. So much easier to believe it shouldn't matter. *White and black are the same. Why all this emphasis on blackness? Peachy Stubbs isn't black, she's light brown.* Tish started to explain. "I can understand," Mrs. Espy interrupted, "how exciting people like the Black Panthers must seem to you, but they would reject you for being white." And as if responding to her own unnamed worries, she drew on more non sequiturs as feeble proof: "That poor Mrs. Grotz from Elyria—her granddaughter was going with a Negro man who shot her in a fit of rage. She fell in with the wrong crowd—she didn't understand his world and he probably deep down inside resented her for being white and that led to her death . . . remember *Native Son?*"

For every tale of injustice and humiliation Tish brought home from school (like the time Mickey Smith was suspended for refusing to sing solo on Negro spirituals as punishment for talking in music class, or the way the football coach called the black team members "Schwartz" when he was mad), her mother seemed determined to create an alternate possibility. *Racism is a southern problem.* Tish turned away again and again, angry. *Privilege is always gained at the expense of someone else.* She didn't have the words to explain how little daily things made up the convenience of being white, how Mrs. Espy had never suffered rude stares on the street, how she didn't have to think twice about stopping in small towns outside of Brazil, how she took for granted her pleasant exchanges with the old German ladies in the outdoor market, who on other occasions had been overtly cold to Mrs. Stubbs and Peachy, telling them they weren't allowed to touch anything.

Little by little the gap between Tish and her mother widened.

XVIII

Overnight, a bad winter storm arrived with wind, and snow so thick and fast that the world in the morning looked shapeless and white. Mrs. Espy stuck her head through Tish's bedroom doorway with a curt, "I don't want you late today." Dutifully, Tish crawled out of bed, skin hardening against the cold. She wrenched tights from her dresser drawer, then a turtleneck. In the harsh winter light she seemed to disappear. In the bathroom she scrubbed her sleep-stiff face until color flushed the pastiness from her cheeks. She brushed her teeth. Her hair, consigned to lifeless waves by the dry air, stuck to her scalp. She yanked it back hard and jammed it into a barrette, where it stuck out on both sides of her head. What she would give to see Angela's broad, light-brown face with its perfect symmetry staring back at her, and her own head framed by an afro. Instead, there was her pale, moon face lit up in that awful light like somebody's jack-o'-lantern, surrounded by a tangle of unruly red hair. *A pale white girl.* How she'd come to despise those words. Like the day Wanda was joking around about how pale senior class president Bonnie Nixon was: "She needs to go sit in the sun."

Tish swiped a little of her mother's Cherries on Ice lipstick, dabbing some red into her cheeks with her fingertips.

She went on down to breakfast, with the heaviness of failure on her shoulders. She was facing an algebra test in general math she hadn't studied for, and why should she have? She'd written three poems instead, one of which she imagined as a song to be sung some day by the Temptations. Numbers bored her. It was a stupid class filled with stupid people, the Seventh-Day Adventist twins in their matching pleated jumpers twisting their pencil erasers in their mouths, hopelessly searching for square roots, and the little blond teacher pacing and nervously eying everyone to see who was cheating, but too scared to confront two black kids who were openly slipping each other the answers.

"My, you look pretty today," Mrs. Espy said brightly.

Tish winced. She wasn't fooled one bit by her mother's lame effort.

Outside, the yard lay shrouded in white, and more snow fell. The trees and bushes looked as if they'd been cast from molds. Already, Ford and Fisher were pulling on their jackets for school, and Francis sat propped in his high chair. Tish leaned over and planted a soft kiss on his cheek. He grinned up at her. *You're the only one,* she thought, with a sigh.

She had no appetite this morning, but feigned eating, and got outside as fast as she could, stepping carefully into the deep footprints left behind by the paper boy to avoid covering her loafers with snow. By the time she'd made it to Division Street, she had worked up a sweat. If she ditched the wool pullover under her parka, everyone would see where she'd rolled her skirt at the waist. She'd just have to suffer.

From Division, she made a hard right and cut across campus past Afro House and then Duvall Union. Last summer she and Peachy had gotten into ripping off books at the campus bookstore there. It happened almost by accident the first time, when each was too embarrassed to go in and ask for a copy of *Candy* because they knew the store manager, a humorless older white man, would accuse them of being too young for dirty books. In an impulsive moment of terrifying bravery, Tish grabbed the book and stuck it in the waistband of her shorts. Then she ran from the store, sandals clacking, Peachy following behind in hysterics. They were laughing so hard they had to throw themselves on the ground. Even before Peachy ever swiped anything, the manager always eyed her suspiciously, asking her to leave her book bag at the desk while he let Tish go on in without a word. "I'll give him something to look at me about," Peachy said, and made her first rip-off.

Even now sometimes they'd go there after school just to prove they could outfox that prejudiced old man. Tish liked the bold feeling as they smiled their way past him. While he trailed after Peachy, trying to be surreptitious as he straightened books on shelves, Tish took whatever they wanted, slipping the books into the big inside pockets of what she'd come to call her ripping coat. Then they'd walk right back out, saying exaggeratedly polite thank you's. The last was a nice touch and put them into stitches. Outside they split up the loot. Tish had gotten a bunch of books that way: W.E.B. DuBois, Booker T., *Soul on Ice* and Malcolm X's autobiography, for starters. *Autobiography of an Ex-Colored Man* and *Souls of Black Folk*. Louis Lomax's *The Negro Revolt*. Marcus Garvey. Peachy called the thefts a revolutionary act against the Man, and Tish, high on the words themselves, agreed this all served a higher purpose.

She stopped at Nickles' and bought a cream-filled doughnut, lingering for a few minutes to see if anyone interesting came along. The woman behind the counter was the one who had given her and Wanda and Peachy the hard eye on several occasions when they'd stopped in for snacks after ensemble practice. She followed Wanda and Peachy the length of the counter, scrutinizing every move. Wanda, never missing a beat, would pretend to touch things, causing the woman to jump protectively and say in that exaggerated voice of contempt, "May I *help* you?" over and over when she had no intentions of helping at all. This was the same woman who greeted Tish's mother warmly, and when Tish tried to explain to her mother about the woman's duplicity, Mrs. Espy accused her of having an overactive imagination. She simply could not conceive of the parallel lives people lived in Brazil, clinging fiercely to the notion that everyone in town, black or white, was treated with the same courtesy.

Tish stood out on the street for a moment, gathering the loose ends of hatred for the woman inside now calmly wiping down the glass counter. Angela's boyfriend, Michael Brown, zoomed by in his car, eyes straight ahead. Tish gave a feeble wave, then stuck her cold hand back in her parka pocket.

As she walked past the square, Reggie Moore sauntered around the corner, wearing an eggplant-colored walking suit. He was older, at least twenty or so, and still wore a do-rag over his processed hair. But, as everyone concluded, he was triple fine and quadruple sweet. And even Angela, who didn't have much patience with "jive men," had to admit Reggie was sexy. His face lit up when he saw Tish.

"Hey, sweetness," he said. Tish warmed to the attention.

"Hey," she said, cool as she could, trying not to let on how flattered she felt.

"How ya doin'?"

"Fine," she said. "Just fine."

"Where's your little girlfriend?" he asked.

"You mean Angela? She's already at school."

"No, the other one I see you with sometimes."

She ran through them all.

"Yeah, Peachy," he said. "Little short brown-skinned girl?"

"That's Peachy," she said, smiling.

"Tell her I said hello. You take care," said Reggie, lightly touching her arm. "And stay sweet."

By the time the icy pea gravel in the school parking lot crunched under the thin soles of her loafers, the first bell was ringing. She didn't even care.

The halls were ominously quiet, and each step on the freshly waxed floor announced her tardiness with a loud squeak.

She paused to adjust her book bag over her shoulder when a voice from behind startled her. She wheeled around. Lamar Holiday just exiting the boys' rest room. He was wearing tinted granny glasses, even though the school had banned them.

"Hey, Tish, wus happenin'?"

She hadn't realized he actually knew her by name, but then it shouldn't have surprised her. Girls and their names were Lamar's business. "Nothin'," she said amiably, setting the clumsy book bag on the floor. "What's up?"

"You," he said in that corny, flirtatious way he had. "You're what's up."

He moved so close then that she could smell his sweet breath. The gold Africa medallion flashed at eye level.

"Go on, Lamar," she said, pushing the air close to him with her hand.

" 'Go on, Lamar,' " he mimicked. He stepped back and stroked his chin slowly, eyes searching her face. "You look good, girl, you know that? You're starting to fill out in all the right places."

This was a lie and she told him so. He laughed and backed off. "Naw, you're gettin' a little booty, girl. No shame in that. You can't blame a man for noticing." He spread his arms in a gesture of helplessness.

"I bet your old lady Jasmine doesn't appreciate that," Tish said boldly.

He laughed. "Aw, now how come you gone bust my chops. Jasmine ain't here. What she don't know won't hurt her." He winked, as if they shared a secret. He knew she knew he was a dog, and he liked her for knowing it. He sauntered on down the hall snapping his fingers and singing, "Who's makin' love to your old lady, while you were out makin' love?"

In the principal's outer office, Tish stood nervously against the counter chewing the edge of her thumbnail while the dyed-blond attendance secretary wrote up her pass. She tried out an excuse in the most affectless tone she could adopt. "My mother's sick. I had to get my brothers ready for school."

The secretary's plucked eyebrows rose. "Are you saying that's why you're late?"

"That's what I'm saying." She shifted her weight to the opposite foot, her hip jutting out, the way Wanda did.

The secretary stared at her a moment, then wrote "excused," and her initials below, and handed her the slip. "I hope your sick mother feels better."

In the hallway Tish double-checked the slip. She'd been given both a pardon from detention and a release from homeroom by the check next to the box saying "Admit to first period." Call it caprice or carelessness, the secretary had done her a favor. Past the closed door of her homeroom she went. Through the frosted-glass window she caught the blur of faces—Angela and Peachy and the others would be shuffling their papers and arranging their books and gossiping and praying for the bell to ring.

She had ten precious minutes to do as she pleased. There in the silence of the army-green walls, she was, for the moment, unaccountable. When presented with these occasional glimpses of freedom, she could never come up with much more of a plan than to sneak in the rest room for a smoke. But today she walked instead past the hall monitor, a blond senior boy who never looked up from his studying, over to the vending machines at the back of the multipurpose room and bought herself a Snickers bar, and perched herself on the back of a chair. She ate the Snickers in quarter-inch bites. To her right just above the pencil sharpener there was a leftover dent in the wall from last year's school riot in the spring after King's assassination. The white football coach had put a black kid's head into the wall with a sickening thud. There'd been an uproar. Black parents showed up at school. The Farmers squared off against the more militant black kids, threatening to start a race war. Word traveled fast. Black kids were throwing their books down in the middle of the hallway and running toward the multipurpose room, fists ready.

Angela and Tish had been in the girls' rest room when the doors flew open, saloon-style, and three black juniors burst in and said, "There's a riot, and the white boys are getting their asses *kicked."* In her rage, one of them turned to Tish and said, "What are you doing in here, bitch?"

She and Angela got out of there fast. Tish had never felt so aroused, so full of anger. The halls were deafening. The only other time she'd ever seen so many black kids crowded around one place was right after Otis Redding died. Police arrived, and the halls swarmed with angry and terrified kids, black and white. It was hard to tell who was fleeing and who was participating. She and Angela pushed their way right up to the front of the crowd gathered around the multipurpose room. At that point it was mostly black, and she got bumped and jostled.

"I'm gone," said Angela. She was scared. They left together, uncertain, and hid by one of the deserted exits. They clutched at each other and cried, too afraid to take a stand, but not ready to ignore. A group of black students stormed past in protest. One of them turned to Angela and said acidly, "You comin' with us, *sister?"*

She didn't answer, just kind of ducked her head. And Tish felt ashamed for her. Shortly after, they both went on to class. There was no learning that day or the next.

When things cooled down, ten black students were suspended. Only two white kids were. The injustice was so blatant it split the school in half like a coconut, with fights breaking out every few hours for the next several days. A lot of the white kids were either indignant or scared, and some stayed home, claiming to be sick. There were rallies and boycotts. It seemed as if everyone was threatening everyone else, and the principal called in the state troopers. For a week, the school was under guard until "things settled down." Nothing had really changed, Tish thought. There was only the veneer of resolution.

The hall clock jumped ahead with several little clicks, and the bell rang, catching her by surprise. In a moment the hallway was flooded with swarming bodies, and she felt cheated of almost two minutes. She joined the flood of students, a minnow following the sharks upstream: Tish Fish, the mean kids had called her in elementary, and now she swam along, just trying to keep her head above water. *Hello, hello, hey, how ya doin'? (smile, nod) hello, hey, hi, hi, hi.*

Halfway down the hall, she spotted the note poking out from one of the ventilation slats on the metal door of her locker. Probably some outpouring from Angela, pleated meticulously like origami. They still wrote in a blend of pig Latin and Franglish to disguise their true meanings. *Chère Ish-tay, Let's allez à la bibliothèque après l'école for udying-stay.* She tugged the note out, unfolding several layers of binder paper. The lines were thinner than the college-ruled Angela and she used.

In blue ink someone had scrawled at a deep slant, *Don't look now, Miss Fine Thing, but you have a secret admirer.*

That was all. Her first thought was that the note had gotten into her locker by mistake. She ran the tip of her finger over the unfamiliar writing as if touch might reveal something sight didn't. She could feel the slight indentations where the pen point had pressed too hard. Then because she didn't know what else to do, she refolded it, and slid it inside her French book.

Last winter in ninth grade an anonymous enemy had scribbled *Nig-*

ger Lover on a piece of paper and dropped it inside her locker. *Be careful, or you're going to get hurt.* The note had fallen to the floor under the bottom shelf, where the toes of her muddied snow boots kicked it around for a couple of days before she noticed it. By the time she pulled it out, it was spotted and smeared, and before her eyes focused properly, she misread the mud-streaked salutation as, *zipper loser.*

At the end of the week another note showed up on her locker. Same paper, same writing. She half wondered if someone was mocking her, then desperately hoped not. *I'm watching you, you fine thing. Your secret admirer.* She looked around. Students pushed down the halls on their way to classes. Dev stopped to ask if she'd read the English assignment. He ended up walking her to class while she surreptitiously folded the note into a tiny square and slid it into her jumper pocket. She wasn't paying attention to a word he said. And when he took his seat next to Holly's flunky Jeff Anderson, and Jeff flashed him one of his phony Jeff grins, Tish turned her head in disgust. Dev was too Tommish sometimes, she thought. If only he knew how Jeff ridiculed him behind his back.

More damp snow fell, coating the streets in a thick wet layer of white. A third secret admirer note lay folded in her pocket. *Sweet Thing, You make my heart sing.* Corny, but maybe he was joking around, whoever he was. Soon she would consult with Angela to see what she thought, decipher all the clues. The day was dreary. Ensemble practice had been canceled again. On her way home alone (Peachy and Wanda were driving with Jasmine Robinson over to the mall in Elyria to buy ID bracelets because the jewelry store in town was run by a white man who wouldn't let more than one black teenager in his shop at a time) she paused in the square and idly sketched out her initials on a section of the snowy track. T.E. for Tish Espy. Then she wrote a plus sign after it. She followed that up with a question mark.

$T.E. + ? = ?$

The only algebra she cared about. Who was her equivalent? Certainly not the silly boys, white or black, in her class. Certainly not square Dev, though as Angela put it, "You could change him, girl." She had smiled and added, "Give him some back, and blow his mind," which made Tish think for a split second that maybe it would be a relief if she just pursued Dev and asked him to be her man for the rest of the year. There had been talk that Dev "didn't like girls *that way*" (Angela had gone so far as to say he acted like a "punk," though Peachy was protective of him and insisted he was "just shy"). Tish thought how much easier it would be for them both.

Before her lay the unsolvable equation. Her frozen fingers, reddened from the contact with icy steel, seemed no longer to belong to her. She looked up at the oppressive dome of gray sky and then across the square at the faded brick facades of dull downtown, where silhouettes of passersby in winter clothes pressed themselves forward into the cold.

A little over a century before, slaves fleeing on the Underground Railroad traveled these streets in lanternless carriages, pulled by horses whipped into urgency, arriving at the shore of Lake Erie to board boats to Canada.

The passing of slaves and their pursuers made this a haunted place, full of ghosts. Some of the freed slaves returned to settle, like Peachy's great-great-grandfather, their descendants populating the west side of Brazil and select areas of nearby towns, unable to speak to one another about what had happened many years before. Such a history does not end with a written proclamation, but continues to accumulate in echoes and reflections and memories over the years, wafting into the present.

Whites saw the world one way, blacks another. A piece of track upended in the square was simply not enough. Covered now by snow it disappeared into the white landscape like the slaves themselves scrambling across the ice of Lake Erie to Canada to freedom. No one ever talked about slavery in American history. Their teacher last year had carefully skipped over that chapter.

She trudged on, wrapped in her old J. C. Penney's parka, deeply regretting not having bought a maxi coat. Life would improve greatly with a maxi coat. And then she'd get some shoe boots, like the ones some of the senior girls were wearing, and her life would take another turn for the better.

"Tish!"

She didn't think she'd heard right, but there it was again, her name, flat and one-dimensional against the cold dry air.

"Tish!"

Footsteps crunched behind her in the snowfall, and when she turned around, Holly Penn and Kim Mahelko were striding purposefully toward her. Their eyes were bright, their cheeks flushed. Holly with her pale skin that never reddened in the cold and dark hair perfectly aligned under her navy-blue tam. She was wearing knee-high white vinyl boots and a white wool minidress under her unbuttoned maxi coat. Tish thought enviously how she could have been a model from one of those mod catalogs from London.

"Hi, Tish," both girls said in their shared voice.

They came up on either side of her, and Holly put one gloved hand gently on Tish's shoulder by way of greeting.

"I hardly ever see you," said Holly. This was a stretch, since they saw each other daily. "How are things going?"

"Fine," said Tish. "Just fine."

They were walking almost exactly in rhythm, three abreast on the sidewalk. Self-conscious, Tish broke her stride, tried to look nonchalant, even a little tough in case someone who mattered passed by and saw them together. She didn't want the fact that she was walking with Holly and Kim to be misinterpreted.

"Oooops, you dropped something," said Holly and stooped to pick up one of Fisher's mittens that had fallen from Tish's parka pocket. In her elegant gloved hand the mitten looked childish.

"Oh, that's not mine," Tish said quickly. Holly looked puzzled. She held the mitten in her hand a moment, then dropped it back down. Tish kept her hands stuffed in her pockets.

"Are you still writing poetry?" Holly asked amiably. "I'm the assistant editor of the school newspaper, and I was wondering if you might want to submit one of your poems for the next issue."

Tish shrugged. She couldn't ignore the flutter in her stomach at the flattery, the old yearnings to be accepted, but her guard was up. Why, all of a sudden, after months of aloofness, was Holly showering her with attention?

"I don't really have anything for the paper," Tish said matter-of-factly.

Kim changed the subject. "I heard your solo in girls' ensemble this year."

Tish nodded. The girls' breath collected in a smoky blur in front of her face.

"It seems like they picked more Negro girls than white this year," Kim went on. "Not that it matters or anything, but I figure they just feel pressure to make up for the past or something."

Tish felt the burn of anger. Her frozen fingers had gone numb in her pockets. "They choose the best singers," Tish said tersely. "They have auditions."

"Oh, I know, I know," said Kim lightly. She glanced over at Holly. "You know what I mean."

Tish had never liked Kim, especially after hearing her pronounce that blacks and whites mixing made mongoloids.

She let her shoes scuff over the snowy pavement, feeling carefully for ice underneath. The last thing she wanted to do was slip and make a fool of herself going down.

"We don't talk much anymore," Holly was saying, with a sweet, easy regret. If Tish hadn't known better, she might have thought she herself was to blame.

"Frankly," Holly went on with only the slightest hesitation in her tone, "we worry about you sometimes, Tish." She paused as if preparing her words exactly. "We worry about—well—the direction your friendships have been taking and what that could mean for you in the long run."

"What she means," Kim chimed in earnestly, "is lately we noticed you've been spreading yourself a little thin."

Tish felt a knot developing in her stomach.

Kim cleared her throat. "You know, like where you sit at lunchtime. Some of those girls you hang around with—"

Holly interrupted. "We don't mean Angela. We all think highly of her. I mean, she's one of the smartest girls in our class." She shot Kim a purposeful look.

"It's some of the others—like Peachy Stubbs," said Kim, and in her mouth Peachy's name twisted into something sour and unpleasant. "I mean, Peachy's kind of—well, you know. . . ."

If Tish had been Wanda she would have put them immediately in their place. But of course if she'd been Wanda, they wouldn't talk to her like this to begin with. Cowards and bullies, so sure of themselves.

"You come from a good family," said Holly. "I guess we can't figure out why you'd be attracted to some of the people you are. It's like lowering yourself."

Kim added, "Don't take it wrong, Tish. I know we haven't always been fair to you. I mean, we did some thoughtless things in the past. You're a unique person. You're not afraid to say things like how you're against the war in class and stuff like that. It's"—Kim paused again— "it's noble."

"Exactly," Holly agreed. "You know, people like you, even if they don't always show it. We think—well—maybe we didn't give you enough credit in the past."

Tish's body began to overheat in the parka. She had a sudden urge to begin running as fast as she could. Where was Wanda when she needed her?

"In fact," Holly continued, "I'm having a party this weekend, and I'd like you to come. There'll be some boys from private school there— boys of your caliber."

Kim was saying, "I don't want you to think we're prejudiced in any way, because we're not. I'm all for civil rights, you know that. But there are things to consider, Tish. You know, about your future."

"I don't know what you're talking about," Tish said weakly.

Holly leaped to reassure. "I think it's great the way you reach out to others. But all we're trying to say is that choices you make now could affect the rest of your life. You know, you don't want—you don't want to end up . . . well, like Gina Hardlove."

Her voice, clear as a bell, chimed out across the snow, so reasonable, so matter-of-fact, that it was hard not to believe she had Tish's best interests at heart. In fact, her tone implied, it was Tish who had gotten it all wrong, and now here was a chance to start over. The layers of meaning began to peel away like skin, Holly Penn was trying to save Tish from herself. This chance meeting was a little mission. It was duty and obligation, pure and simple. Holly and Kim were offering salvation.

A red Dodge Charger pulled up. Holly's current boyfriend, Taylor Weems, leaned out. Tish declined his offer of a ride ("Come on, Tish, we'll drop you"), and turned on her heel. Under her breath she was cursing to herself.

"See you Saturday maybe?" Holly went smile first into the car, followed by her white vinyl boots. From the backseat Kim's dark hair swung in its perfect arrow cut, just clearing the collar of her maxi coat. Tish imagined their smug laughter.

After they'd pulled off, she crossed the street and began picking her way through mounds of unshoveled snow toward home. Shame made her sick to her stomach. A moment later, Lamar Holiday appeared alongside her, winding down the window of his Chevy. He was alone, wearing a bulky sweater under his red leather coat. A cap was pulled down, squashing his afro.

"Hey, Tish." His breath smoked in the cold air. "You need a ride?"

She could almost believe that he cared and that they might be friends.

"Come on, baby," he said, "it's cold out. You look like you're about to freeze to death."

"I'm almost home," she said, "thanks anyway." She managed a strained smile.

"Okay, keep warm then." He winked and pulled off, wheels crunching over ice. It was only a minute later after he'd turned onto Elm that she wondered what business had brought him to the east side of town.

The one party Tish attended at the Penn house was back in eighth grade. In school Holly handed Tish an engraved invitation to her thirteenth birthday party. "It's sort of formal," she'd explained. "Girls are going to wear dresses and stockings. Angela's coming too."

The evening before the party, Tish was in a panic sorting through her clothes. She practiced hooking and unhooking her garter belt and carefully pulling the sheer stockings taut so they wouldn't sag. First thing in the morning she was down at Woolworth's with her latest stash of babysitting money in search of a worthy gift, something Holly would be impressed with. Angela had informed Tish she was taking Holly a bath and shower set her mother had picked out at the shopping center in Elyria. Tish didn't dare ask what a "bath and shower set" was, but it sounded sort of sexy and grown-up. Without help or advice, Tish finally settled on a red cotton dickey and matching headband, enclosed in a clear plastic box, which cost a dollar more than she'd planned, but would be worth the splurge.

But at the party, in Holly's pearl-colored hands, the dickey suddenly transformed into what it really was—something cheap and useless. And Tish hadn't noticed the headband was stitched unevenly, but it was the first thing Holly made note of in her gentle, objective way. From her sea of gifts, she flashed Tish a benevolent smile and murmured a polite thanks, and that was the last Tish ever saw of either the dickey or the headband, which she suspected eventually got "donated." Gradually she came to understand how her choice paled next to the bath and shower set, not to mention the travel manicure kit in a little red leather case from Kim, and the white windbreaker (with "Holly" stitched in green leaves and red berries on the sleeve) Lisa had brought. Stricken with the realization she'd gotten it all wrong again, she threw herself into playing "pin the mustache on Ringo Starr," and when, blinded and dizzy after being spun, she pinned it to his crotch, the other girls erupted into laughter. When the blindfold came off, she saw what she'd done. Everyone was giggling. "Did you see where Tish put it? Right on his *thing*." There were nasty jokes, and everyone kept laughing, even Angela, while the strains of "California Dreamin'" emanated from the record player. This was followed by more giggling and suggestive references to "Twister later." The significance of "later" didn't register until around eight when it became clear to Tish that Holly's invitation to her did not include the coed party at which Twister would be played, to be followed by an all-girl sleep-over. That was reserved for her circle. Tish and old Homely Hannah (a piano professor's daughter) were the only two of the ten girls to be not so discreetly dismissed before the boys arrived and other festivities began. Tish imagined the look Angela gave her was rueful, even sympathetic, but she couldn't be sure. Angela said nothing, just sat with prim discomfort over in a corner, pretending to talk to the other girls. Tish remembered well the sound of Lisa screeching with laughter. It was only sometime later when Tish and Angela talked about that night that Angela confessed she'd been ashamed of herself for not sticking up for Tish. She'd been afraid, she admitted, because of her own tentative position. She said, without guile, "Tish, sometimes I just get so scared."

Tish had never gotten up the nerve to tell her mother what really happened the night that Mrs. Espy drove her the three blocks down from Woodland to French Woods. Maybe it was because her mother had seemed so thrilled Tish was being included that she couldn't bear to disappoint her. Even though Mr. Espy had winked and made cracks about how he hoped Tish could survive a night with Republicans, it was obvious her parents were pleased their daughter was expanding her social life to include white friends. Tish had given one backward glance at the festooned veranda of the Penn porch, where Hannah still waited glumly under a bouquet of balloons for her mother, and climbed into the cavernous old Checker. She was drowning in humiliation, for herself and for her oblivious mother, who inquired eagerly about the party. For some time after, Mrs. Espy spoke of Holly as if she and Tish were friends. "I ran into Bunny and Holly Penn today at the Sparkle Super. Holly said to tell you hello. Why don't you give her a call? See if she'd like to go ice skating with you and Angela. Aren't she and Angela good friends too?"

Tish could hear the urgency in her mother's voice.

"Not anymore," said Tish angrily. "They never really were. Holly's prejudiced. She won't be friends with black people."

"Oh, come on!" said Mrs. Espy, clearly running thin on patience. "You say that about everyone. Maybe Angela was the one who stopped hanging around Holly. Maybe Angela doesn't want to be seen with white people. Prejudice goes both ways."

It doesn't, thought Tish, it's not the same, but she didn't know how to explain. It was a test without exact answers. She turned for a moment and snapped, "If that were the case then Angela wouldn't hang around me." And she stormed out of the room. Why the refusal to see? What was everyone so afraid of?

XIX

Mostly Linda Thompson kept an even temper. But she'd had a long day in the provost's office trying to negotiate with leather-jacketed, afroed representatives from the Black Student Union who wanted more black faculty, and a group of stuffy, bow-tied white regents who thought the whole place was going to hell in a handbasket. She had been selected to sit in, she knew, because she would be seen as an ameliorating force, a safe black presence, a concession to the stiff-jawed, angry students whose faces closed down to the damn-near-white-woman mouthpiece for the Man, talking to them about procedures. One of them, Grover Pace, had turned to her at one point and challenged her silence. "I'd like to hear what the *sistah* has to say." From the tone of his voice she knew he was baiting her, asking, in less than subtle terms, *Whose side are you on, ours or the white man's?* More deeply, she was being asked, as she had been asked so many times throughout her life, *Who are you?* Returning home after days like this to a houseful of noisy children, she occasionally let her nerves do the talking. Hadn't she made it clear she wanted things in good order when she arrived? That she didn't have time to come home and clean up behind them all, now that they were old enough to show some responsibility? But there were the boys' bicycles thrown down across the walkway—again. She slammed the door of the Catalina and almost stepped on a saucer sled. "Damn it!" she muttered, and kicked it out of the way. Silhouettes flashed in the picture window, then came the pounding of running feet from inside. Tish Espy would be there—she practically lived at the Thompsons', eating them out of house and home. You'd think her own family didn't feed her.

Mostly Linda didn't mind the girls having company when she was gone, so long as they kept the boys from destroying the house, and everyone was getting along.

But on this particular afternoon, as she swung through the front door lugging a bag of groceries from Sparkle Super, she was in no mood for foolishness. So why was Monica, tears streaming down her irate face, wailing, "Mo-m-my," in the voice of the broken-hearted. Behind her, arms crossed in indignation, was her little sidekick, a fast-talking black neighbor girl named Diana who didn't seem to know she had a home either. Her eyes were big as saucers.

From the back of the house came Angela's muffled voice, "And don't you even try to come back in here, you little black tar baby," and then the slamming of the bedroom door.

Linda Thompson set down the bag and her purse, the weight of the day descending on her. She drew in a deep breath to steady herself and kicked off her pumps. In stockinged feet she strode to the back of the house, and yanked open Angela's bedroom door. Her anger was exacerbated by the sight of Tish Espy on the bed, looking startled and nervous. There was the faint scent of a recently extinguished cigarette. Linda ignored it.

"I want to see you, Miss Angela, right now," she ordered. "Out here." Her voice was shaking.

She grabbed Angela by the arm and pulled her into the hallway. She wanted to knock some sense into her pretty head. "Don't you evah," she instructed in a thick voice, "evah, evah, evah let me hear you say something like that again to your sister. You don't need to show off to your little white friend." And when Angela opened her mouth to protest, Linda did something she'd never done before—she slapped Angela across the mouth, and instructed her to take her little triflin' self to the kitchen. The contact with her daughter's flesh surprised Linda. It had happened so fast. Her hand stung from the effort. She poked her head back through the doorway and told Tish she'd have to go on home. She could barely control the trembling inside, or the shrill timbre of her voice. To make a point, she apologized for Angela's behavior as Tish slid down the hall past an anguished Angela, now mutely stumbling toward the kitchen. In the living room, Monica sat rocking furiously in the big moving armchair braids loose in her head, a look of pure revenge on her face. Linda had no way of knowing that Tish felt as humiliated as Angela, having been reduced in Mrs. Thompson's perception to Angela's "little white friend," complicit in her whiteness. Nor did she know that for days after Tish was furious with Angela for implicating her, and furious with Mrs. Thompson for diminishing her.

Linda Thompson knew only one thing—Angela was not going to get away with that kind of talk in her house, favoring fairer skin in a conspiracy of superiority with her white girlfriend. "What a terrible thing to say to your sister," she said later, when things had settled down, and Angela's father had said his piece. They were all sitting around the kitchen table, the two parents and the two girls (the boys were not included), and Mrs. Thompson admitted she might have overreacted, but that didn't mean Angela was any less wrong. She reached out one pale milky hand and laid it conciliatorily on Angela's caramel one. With her other hand she touched Monica's café au lait wrist. She launched into a speech about respect and family, the importance of loving yourself for who you are, the beauty of being black. Her words felt insufficient. Her husband nodded, put in his two cents, cleared his throat, and went down in the family room to watch wrestling with the two boys.

There was the strained apology from Angela, and Monica's strained acceptance. Linda oversaw Angela's wooden efforts to make up (an offer to take Monica shopping downtown on Saturday), and prayed her words would make sense. When she got up from the table, she kissed each daughter good night. What she feared most was that she was somehow responsible for her oldest daughter's breach, that deep down inside, her firstborn, who flipped through beauty magazines where white women lounged, sprawled, posed splay-footed, and pranced, yearned for good hair and lightness, for the privileges lightness could bring. That she saw modeled even by her own parents the preference of black men for light-skinned women, women who looked almost white. She sat for a long time, well after the bedroom lights had gone out, and her children were sleeping, trying to gather in her mind all the loose ends of uncertainty, only to find them unraveling again. Later that week, she made a point of calling her old friend Nancy Sims and suggesting a shopping trip and lunch for herself, Nancy, Nancy's daughter Edna, and Angela, in Cleveland. Edna was a solid dark-skinned girl, and a year ahead of Angela in school. Edna would help restore a balance, give Angela a touchstone and maybe an "in" with her black peers.

XX

"Tish, Tish, I gotta talk to you." Angela was frantic. She'd rolled her brown hair into a flip, and pulled it back from her face with a cloth headband. Tish thought it looked terrible. Why did Angela want to wear white girls' hairstyles? She needed to get those relaxers out of her head and grow herself a fro. Get real. Get down. Be a righteous sister. Angela had hold of Tish's sleeve and was glancing up and down the hallway. "Listen," she said dramatically, her beautiful features contorted, "I don't want to scare you, but I just overheard Jasmine talking to Maxine and Benita, and Jasmine is on the *warpath,* girl." She lowered her voice as several students paused in a clump at the end of the hall.

Still half asleep, Tish didn't register the words. Angela's theatrics were old hat. Her slightly smoky breath grazed Tish's nose. "Listen to me, girl, Jasmine Robinson wants to ick-kay your little utt-bay."

"What?" That got her attention. But the words still weren't quite making sense. "What are you talking about?"

"It's Lamar," said Angela. "Jasmine was pitching a fit down at the end of the hall, about how Lamar's been messing around with a white girl, and she was talkin' about kickin' some booty, and then I heard your name. Tish, be careful."

The ringing bell jarred them both and Angela let out a deep sigh. "It-shay, I can't be late for class. Are you coming?"

Tish felt sick to her stomach. "In a minute," she said. Her mind was racing. She didn't want Angela to see how jumpy she was. Maybe she could talk to Peachy, get Peachy to act as intermediary and find out what this was all about. She could tell Mr. Cox she had a personal emergency (implying something of the feminine variety, guaranteed to make male teachers wince and send you off readily without a pass) and summon Peachy into the hallway. How on earth was it even possible that Jasmine would single her out? What had she ever done to Jasmine? Nothing, except to tell her jive-ass, Uncle-Tomming boyfriend to stay away.

Tish slammed her locker shut. The clang echoed in the empty hallway. She considered going to the nurse's office and claiming cramps so she could hide out in the dark room, safely shut away. Let things blow over. Let Jasmine figure out she'd made a mistake. There were quick, staccato footsteps behind her. Startled, she looked up. To her disbelief, Jasmine was just rounding the corner. Out of nervousness Tish grabbed her locker padlock and began fumbling with it, muttering the numbers to herself—22–2–26—as if they were amulets against disaster.

Maxine and Benita were right behind Jasmine, tall, imposing girls, both seniors. One of them used the heel of her hand to pound out a quick rhythm on a locker just before Tish's. Tish closed her eyes, expecting to feel a blow or a push. She concentrated on the padlock, dreading that she might lose her balance and fall over.

Then just as quickly as they'd come up on Tish, they passed by. Tish didn't move. Jasmine hadn't even noticed her. Or had she? Tish observed from the corner of her eye. Jasmine had paused outside senior math and was still talking in an angry voice to her girlfriends. Fragments of words exploded: *I saw . . . she said . . . unh-unh, girl . . . little white ho . . . sick of these little damn bitches be givin' it up to every brother they can . . . calm down, Jasmine . . .*

Tish took a chance. She gently shut her locker door, juggled her books into the crook of one arm, and started down the hall with what she hoped was a confident and purposeful stride. She was going to pass them, but it wouldn't matter, since she knew she hadn't done anything wrong. The girlfriends were already drifting away, one of them calling back down the hallway, *We gonna get her. Don't worry.* Jasmine, a wad of gum jammed in her jaw, blew a perfect, elegant bubble. Mesmerized, Tish caught the motion of her popping it with her teeth and drawing it back, in one smooth motion, into her mouth. At the same time Jasmine turned toward her in slow motion.

"Hey, 'scuse me, you're Tish, right?" The tone was aloof, matter-of-fact, almost careless. Hardly the tone of someone intent on kicking ass.

Tish slowed and turned. Her body suddenly felt heavy. "Yes."

"You're the one hangs around with my little play sister Peachy Stubbs." She sucked the gum back onto her molars and gave a loud crack. Up close, Jasmine was so beautiful it was frightening. Perfectly smooth milk-chocolate skin and a high forehead. She was taller than Tish and broad-shouldered, with shapely legs and thighs and the carriage of a grown woman. Her fro was even bigger and fuller than Wanda's. "You know Lamar Holiday?"

Was this a trick?

Tish imagined him materializing between them—tall and dark with his Ban-Lon shirts and the gold Africa medallion hanging on a slim chain from his neck. Hesitantly, she nodded.

"I need a favor." Jasmine's voice lowered. "Peachy says you have study hall with Lamar." She paused. "I want you to keep an eye on him. Tell me what he does. Who he talks to." She paused. "Anything. You knowwhatI'msayin'?"

Tish nodded. In study hall Lamar sat one aisle over and took copious notes from his senior civics book in small, curved handwriting. He seemed innocent enough then, the model of studiousness.

"I heard he's been messing with that little half-and-half broad . . ." She clicked her fingers. For a moment, Tish thought she meant Tina, and her stomach knotted. "You know the one . . . young bitch . . . Jeannie Lyons. She's in your study hall too. Peachy said she lives over by you, so maybe you can pay attention. Tell me if you see his car over there, or catch him doing anything."

There was a brief flicker of fire in her eyes. Tish couldn't catch her breath.

"I know you'll be cool," said Jasmine. Make no mistake, she was saying, don't take my business into the street. Tish nodded a final time. "Right on," said Jasmine and then turned, still cracking her gum, and strolled on into class on her pointed-toe sling backs as if she had all the time in the world to get to where she was going.

Now Tish was late again. Stranded in the hallway by herself, she tried manufacturing an excuse. There was the threat of detention, the lectures from her mother, the restrictions. But what did it all matter? She wanted a cigarette so badly to calm her nerves she thought she'd die. Sometimes she felt like just taking off and doing whatever she wanted for twenty-four hours. She'd pay the consequences later. There had been girls from Brazil known as "incorrigibles" who were so bad they'd been sent off to "juvey" in Cleveland, where they lived in detention with other troublemakers. That might be better, Tish thought, than going home every night to a mother who nitpicked her to death.

She hiked her books up against her chest and started on down the hall to class. In the split second of an ordinary moment, Jasmine Robinson had taken account of her, a ghost of a girl, a girl who could be absent for days on end without anybody but Peachy and Angela noticing. Tish—she was that invisible girl passing down the halls like vapor. And Angela, Miss Thinks-She-Knows-It-All Angela, was dead wrong!

When she slipped in the door, Mr. Cox was too busy chalking key dates for the American Revolution on the board to notice. She took the side aisle past Angela, who had artfully slung Michael Brown's letter jacket over the back of her chair. (Once she even made Tish sniff the collar to inhale the scent of his Old Spice cologne as she detailed their most recent close encounter.) Angela's eyes widened. *"Qu'est-ce qui ce passe?"* she mouthed.

Tish flashed a mysterious smile and shrugged. Let her wonder. Let her guess. She swished on by, wishing she had gum to crack, and dragged her loafers across the linoleum in that carefree, reckless way cool girls did.

At the back of the room, Peachy hunched over her open book, bulky plaid coat flung over her shoulders. Her hair was jammed and pinned haphazardly on top of her head. Tish recognized her look of desperation. She hadn't done her homework. Procrastination was Peachy's downfall. Behind again, she was trying to finish up her formal chapter outline, which she'd gotten stuck with as a punishment for never having the right answers in class. It wasn't that Peachy was stupid, she just had distractions.

Behind Peachy's back, Angela was always saying how Peachy could be really cute if she just did something to fix herself up: quit frying her hair, put on some makeup, took time to match her outfits, stopped playing the fool so much.

"That sort of behavior might have gotten her over in grade school, but now we're in high school, and almost women," Angela would sigh.

When Tish plunked down her books with a thud, Peachy's head shot up, her face ancient and drawn with effort. A fresh row of pinkish-brown pimples marked her forehead. "I've got something to tell you," Tish whispered, and Peachy said, "Not now, I'm trying to book, girl."

On the first day of class, they had requested seats next to each other, for the express purpose of cheating on tests together. It was Peachy's idea: she could get the multiple choice answers from a girl who had Mr. Cox first period, if Tish would memorize the answers and then discreetly hand-spell the letters to her using the deaf alphabet from under her desktop. Angela and Peachy and she had all three learned to finger-spell when they volunteered at a summer camp for deaf kids where Mrs. Stubbs had been one of the cooks. Occasionally they still used the alphabet as a secret code if they didn't want others knowing something.

Because she had a good short-term memory, Tish could memorize test answers in no time. And Peachy and she figured if Mr. Cox was lazy enough to give the same test to every period, why should they bother going to the trouble of actually studying?

It was obvious, given all the tensions at their school, that Mr. Cox saw their request to sit together as a chance to "enhance integration," which is how Peachy and she joked about it later when they were both pulling *A*'s they didn't deserve. She was too ashamed ever to confess to Angela that Peachy and she cheated. Angela would have had a fit. She could be really uptight about stuff like that.

"How do you write Roman numeral fifteen?" Peachy whispered.

Tish drew an inconspicuous *X* and then a *V* in the air with her index finger. Mr. Cox turned to face the class. "About next Monday's test . . ." he began.

"Damn," Peachy murmured, "but this white man is breakin' my back." Her pencil point pressed so hard against the paper it snapped. "Dang! This isn't history, this is slavery. Ain't this man ever heard of the Thirteenth Amendment?" The white girl in front of her shifted uncomfortably in her seat, signaling she'd heard but was too embarrassed to say anything. "Yeah, you heard me," Peachy mumbled to the back of the girl's head and made a face.

Tish dug out a pencil and tossed it over. Peachy grabbed it up, too irritated to be grateful.

Up front, Angela, whispering animatedly to Holly Penn, had spiraled around in her seat. Tish felt a pang of annoyance. How long was Angela willing to play the token Negro, the black girl who could be forgiven her blackness? Uncle Tom, Oreo, house nigger. No wonder Peachy and Tina were always joking about Angela behind her back. Deep inside, Angela still cared what those two-faced white girls thought. You couldn't have it both ways—black and white, that is. One way or another you had to make up your mind—even the mixed kids—and then stick with that. Whiteness was a sickness. Desiring it was even worse. *We want education for our people that exposes the true nature of this decadent American society.*

Now Mr. Cox clapped his hands and asked for everyone's attention. He began to talk, but his voice was a distant drone. The brightly colored, psychedelic tie he wore was knotted too tightly around his neck. His words faded in, faded out. Tish tried to concentrate on the test review, but her mind was drifting far away from the Declaration of Independence and the truths it held to be self-evident, to the snow coming down again, the violence of her own thoughts, and the sweet memory of Jasmine Robinson enlisting her for a favor.

Without warning, Angela started getting tight with Edna Sims, a dark-skinned black junior whose mother played bridge with Angela's mother at their social club. It seemed to happen overnight, catching Tish off guard. Edna was mildly popular with both white and black kids, neither out nor in, and no one ever called her a Tom for talking to white kids, she was just Edna, passing the halls with her books cradled against her narrow chest. She was preengaged to one of the quietest, smartest junior boys, Charlie (Skip) Nelson, whose father ran a mortuary. Angela had recently remarked, "You can't be my only friend, Tish." She was right. What she really meant was, I need more than a white friend.

So Tish spent more time on the fringes with Peachy and Wanda and Tina at the big table jammed against the south wall of the cafeteria where a lot of the black kids sat. Or sometimes she just sat by herself and pretended to study, when instead she was pouring out her heart in her notebook. People never said what they really meant. White people had been lying to black people for years, and black people knew it. There were double and triple messages, things implied, messages inferred, so that what was being said was not the same as what was meant. She wrote a poem about this called "White Lies," and turned it in to the student teacher in English. It was returned with a long note of praise that ended with "You have a lot of wisdom, Tish, for someone your age. But you should try not to be so pessimistic. The world is changing for the better. As good as this is, it doesn't fulfill the assignment."

*   *   *

In study hall she was filled with a secret purpose. Lamar Holiday didn't know it, but they were now connected. She pretended to play with her pencil, tapping it against the top of her French book, allowing it to balance itself between her index and middle finger.

Generally, she used study hall for what her last year's algebra teacher, Mr. Phipps, disparagingly referred to as "reading for pleasure during class time," for which she was repeatedly punished. "You can read for pleasure later," he admonished, yanking the book out from where she'd hidden it inside her algebra text and stashing it away in his desk drawer. He'd confiscated everything from *Manchild in the Promised Land* to *Lady Chatterley's Lover* to an Iceberg Slim novel, and when Peachy was circulating what she referred to as "a nasty book" called *The Nigger Bible,* he found that on her as well, and refused to return it. "For the content," he said, his white face reddening, "I'm surprised a girl like you, from your kind of family . . ." He didn't finish, just leaned on the implication. What he meant was "a white girl from a white family," but he didn't dare say it. Tish clucked her tongue and stared at that man so hard he gave up calling on her and left her alone. After that, and well into this year, she gave him the evil eye all the time, because she could get away with it. It was a victory of sorts and when she'd see him slinking down the hallway, she'd tap Peachy on the arm and loud-talk him in an exaggerated voice, "That man bugs me to death with his old prejudiced self," just to watch his face redden.

Jeannie Lyons, the girl in question, sat by the window of the multipurpose room that doubled as cafeteria and study hall. She was only a freshman, but she was almost six feet tall and well-developed for her age. Her sandy hair was naturally nappy, but she'd straightened, lightened, and greased it into submission in imitation of her white girlfriends'. Angela and Peachy had independently written her off as "a Tom," "doofus," "too white acting," and therefore not worthy of their attention. Black girls threatened to beat her up from time to time for just being. She had allergies that made her slightly red and watery around the eyes, and her mouth was always swollen as if she'd just finished crying. She wasn't exactly pretty, she was too yellow for that. She had sea-blue eyes and a flat, broad nose. She hung around with two countrified white girls (she *thinks* she's white, Peachy liked to say, and that makes her the most dangerous of all) who had reputations for doing *it* with any black boy at school, or so Peachy claimed. Up until now Jeannie had always gone with white boys. Lately, someone had seen her around with pink-skinned Bill Penderson, who, as the saying went, "wouldn't know he was black if black jumped up and hit him in the head."

The Lyonses lived one block over from Woodland on Beech, in a white, triple-story house with a mansard roof. Jeannie's dad, a soft-spoken man, was the east side postman, black as the ace of spades, the kind of dark that a lot of black kids joked about ("your clothes got out at night without you" and so on). Mrs. Lyons was a tiny blonde who worked as a nurse at the Brazil Memorial Hospital. Once she'd given Tish a tetanus shot after she stepped on a rusty nail in the sand at Curtis Pond.

The Lyonses had once belonged to the Espys' integrationist group before everything fell apart. Tish remembered her mother saying once how "brave" she thought Mary Lyons was to have married a Negro man in the 1950s, in the face of such tremendous prejudice and social pressure, and for the two of them to raise "mixed children." "It must be so confusing," said Mrs. Espy, "not to be sure what you are."

To which Tish had responded, "What would you say if I fell in love with a Negro?" and her mother had turned to her in that thoughtful way she had and said, "If you love him, Tish, that's all that matters. Love is color-blind."

The group had included two other white university families, and six black families, two of whom had since moved away. By the time it all dissolved, the Espys were the only white members left. Some of the black couples turned militant and separatist (like her mother's acquaintance from church, Gertrude Price, who had taken a Muslim name, and now wore dashikis and a big natural and on principle no longer spoke to anyone white, including God). Whatever the myriad reasons (moves, births, deaths, illnesses, politics), gone were the sunshine days of integrated barbecues in folks' backyards and the careful efforts to prove "We're all the same" (*Your baby walked at ten months? Oh, mine too. Yes, yes, I agree, I've always preferred iris to gladiolus. You'll have to come over and I'll cut some for you.*), and those who had once been connected by the strain of polite optimism now spotted one another around Brazil with embarrassment and tight smiles. The Lyonses withdrew into their own tight-knit circle of friends, mostly white.

Jeannie's younger, egghead brother Roger Lyons was one of Ford's best friends, and the two often played chess in the summer on the Espys' screened porch, or in winter up in Ford's room, which Tish referred to as "The Pit." Angela called Roger "white boy" behind his back and when she'd run into him at their house, hunched over the chess board with Ford, she'd always shake her head in that way she did when she thought someone was hopelessly pitiful. Together, their contempt for the Lyonses snowballed: the nerdishness of Roger, Jeannie's desperation to be white *(She even listens to the Beach Boys!!!)*, Mr. Lyons's Uncle Tommish grins of greeting to his white customers ("Booker Lyons has such *dignity*," Tish's mother had said ecstatically once as Tish cringed), Jeannie's predilection for a white-girl hairdo and pink lipstick. "It's truly sick," Angela said.

All study hall Tish kept her eye on Lamar, sly as a hawk. There was power in knowledge. And it was payback for his presumptions with her. He'd underestimated her, was counting on her white-girl silence. Guys like Lamar played black girls off against white, trusting in mutual dislike. But he was slick. In study hall he mostly yawned a lot and stretched his arms up over his head, or picked out his afro, or stared out the window, waiting for time to pass. But he never so much as glanced at Jeannie. And Jeannie, sallow and freckled, sat engrossed in *Valley of the Dolls,* sniffling and licking her long slender index finger carefully before each turn of the page.

Tish pretended to study French, the one class she still liked, but all the while her mind was riveted to Jeannie and Lamar, *les deux ensembles—les amants.* There was the thrill of deceit, theirs and hers, and the delicious possibility of having something to report to Jasmine.

While she waited, she conjugated Lamar's name in French on her tablet, as a joke for Jasmine. *Je lam, tu lams, il/elle lam, nous lamons, vous lamez, ils lament.* Much to her disappointment, nothing happened, not so much as a look or a signal. At one point Jeannie's chair tipped back with a loud squeak that broke the silence. Tish's chest tightened. Jeannie put one thin, stockinged leg on the rung of the chair in front of her.

Her pleated skirt swung wide with the grace of an accordion, and exposed a pale upper thigh. The skin on her leg was as white as Tish's own. She glanced over at Lamar. But he was napping, head down on his folded arms. His gold ID bracelet, with Jasmine's initials and a heart etched inside, hung from his dark wrist. The metal reflected a weak ray of winter sunlight from the window.

Far as Tish could see, Jeannie's eyes never left the pages of her wrinkled, dog-eared book. There was only the slightest movement of her chest when she breathed, and the barely perceptible flicker of her lashes. Under the layer of makeup, her yellow skin thickened like wax. Then, without warning, Jeannie looked over and caught Tish staring. Tish averted her eyes fast, but maybe not fast enough, because a shadow passed over Jeannie's face. Tish pretended to be focusing on the window beyond to the snow piling up, threatening to bury them all in whiteness. The breath swelled in her chest.

Then the bell rang, and amid scraping chairs and books thumping into bags, she gathered up her stuff and filed out along with everyone else. Lamar brushed past to catch up with two other basketball players. "Hey, sweetheart," he said with a faint wink of recognition. It didn't mean anything, he did the same to all the girls, but she couldn't undo right away the little knot of excitement in her stomach.

In the meantime, Jeannie walked off down the hall in the opposite direction, her shoulders slightly hunched over the load of books she held against her chest. For a moment Tish felt almost sorry for her. She was just a big old gangly girl, as awkward as Tish, and every bit as much a misfit. But there were hierarchies to be observed, and Tish knew the importance of her role. Any sympathy she might have dredged up quickly metamorphosed to scorn. Just like any white girl, old Oreo Jeannie was stupid enough to fall for Lamar's jive-ass lines.

Tish couldn't really blame her, but Angela began going to parties with Michael and Edna Sims that she didn't mention until afterward, as if sparing Tish embarrassment. Or was it that with her new status, she was able to push Tish from her mind so easily? Was this another admission that Tish really was a liability? Was it her whiteness, or just the fact that she was a clumsy girl with red hair who still couldn't rap to boys? Was this the way Angela had felt that time in seventh grade when Tish went swimming with a white classmate at a private club just outside of town where black people were not allowed to be members?

Her father's question echoed in her head: *You think your Negro friends will like you better if you pretend to be like them?* So much for honorary Negrohood. Tish spent more and more time sequestered in her room, playing records and harmonizing along with Jerry Butler singing "Never Gonna Give You Up." Even though she had never loved anyone, she lay flat on her bed with the ache of the lovelorn.

Things got worse. Angela began going with Michael to the Boot Center on Saturday nights, which was what all the black kids called the town rec center on the west side of town because no white kids showed up anymore. They were scared of the fights, and as some of them said, "We just don't feel welcome." The Boot Center was known for being kind of rough, and Mrs. Thompson deep inside really preferred Angela didn't go, but she didn't want to deprive her daughter of social acceptance by her peers. And Edna Sims was allowed to go, and Mrs. Thompson figured Michael would take good care of Angela. Michael was Angela's "in" to parties she wasn't personally invited to. Angela acknowledged she owed it all to Michael, but she kind of rubbed it in too. It made Tish crazy. Angela was quick to repeat over and over details of what people wore and said, and who slow dragged and who was grinding with who. Vicariously Tish absorbed these experiences. Desperate to be included she suggested, "Maybe I can spend the night and go with you and Michael next Saturday." Angela's expression hardened. She looked Tish dead in the eye. "Your mother wouldn't approve. Please don't try to use me as an excuse." She paused. "I can't get you in with the black kids, Tish, if that's what you're asking. I have problems of my own."

Tish had underestimated Angela. Now she felt ashamed of herself for being so transparent. Angela had given her legitimacy. Without her, Tish was nothing.

She couldn't count on Peachy, especially since it turned out Peachy had gone to the show with Wanda and Tina without asking her along, and afterward they'd ended up on campus at a university party where Wanda knew everyone, and danced with college boys like Grover. Where would Tish fit in? She knew without asking. Her role was to listen as Peachy bragged how Reggie Moore had showed up, and they'd all gotten high on Boone's Farm apple wine out behind Afro House. Tish tried not to care. With a sinking feeling she thought how little she had to offer them. Soon her girlfriends would tire of spending the night at her carefully ordered house, squeezed into the double bed, stuffing themselves on chips and dip, and listening to records when they could be out dancing with university boys. Why should they live by her limits, cut themselves off from real pleasure? Subject themselves to her parents' polite cross-examinations that only showed how out of touch they were? It was hard to know whom to pity—her friends, her parents, or herself, caught somewhere in between.

On weekends when Tish was feeling morose and left out, she stayed home and made caramel popcorn, and by default sometimes ended up playing duplicate bridge with her parents and Ford, which seemed to reassure her family that she wasn't completely lost to them. They had no way of knowing that in the stillness of that living room, with her grandmother's clock ticking away the seconds, she was suffocating. That the air in that house might as well have been from Mars. Her breath would lodge in her chest, and whole minutes seemed to pass before she was able to exhale. The cards blurred before her eyes. *Tish, pay attention. Trump is hearts.*

The phone would ring, and she would leap for it with hope (maybe she was being remembered at the last minute). But if it was for her, it would only be some oddball like Dev calling to ask about a homework assignment. She came to be grateful for at least that much comfort, a disembodied voice in her ear, a lifeline to the outside world. Someone else who was stuck at home on a Saturday night with no particular place to be. Dev was a patient listener, and sometimes Tish would confide in him, counting on his sympathy at the other end. Her words were a repetition, like a refrain in a poem: *I'm so sick of not fitting in anywhere. I don't belong.* This in muffled tones while the household went on obliviously in the background.

If the call wasn't for her, she thought she would choke on the silence. The caller would be a distressed student for her father, or a neighbor calling for her mother, or one of her brother Ford's mysterious older university friends. Ford never talked long, but shortly after they finished playing their hand, he'd go slinking off into the night with Jeannie Lyons's brother Roger on some cryptic undertaking, free to roam as he pleased, even though he was younger, because he was a boy. And her—she'd sit in that stifling house with all the junk piled up around—shelves and shelves of books, and old chairs and sofas and telescopes, listening to the musicality of her parents' voices, calling and responding, and the clicking keys of her father's typewriter.

Eventually they headed off to bed, and her mother would remind sweetly (or was it pityingly?), "Don't forget to turn off the lights when you come up." One night she paused by the stairs, but not so Tish could actually see her from the living room. It was the shadow she cast backward through the doorway that caught Tish's eye. She hesitated there for several moments. Then Tish heard the creak of the first stair, and the whisper of her mother's slippers on the bare wood. Whatever she might have said she didn't.

It was her mother's idea to drive into Cleveland for Handel's *Messiah*. "Can Angela come too?" Tish begged, and when Mrs. Espy said of course she could, Tish was elated. But Angela had already made plans with Edna Sims to go to Edna's cousin's cotillion in Elyria *(Girl, I'm wearing this bad-ass dress, wait 'til you see it)*, and Tish felt again the sinking sensation of being replaced. Angela hadn't seemed all that sorry she couldn't make the *Messiah*, a fact Tish silently noted. "Is there someone else you'd like to ask along?" Mrs. Espy asked. "How about Holly or Kim?" The omission of Peachy and Wanda angered Tish, even though she knew they were sneaking off to another party on campus at Afro House. And she couldn't realistically picture Wanda, even as much as she loved music, suffering through the forty-minute drive to Cleveland in the backseat of her parents' car, with the Espys making polite conversation.

"No," she said dully. "I'd rather go alone." She dressed in her favorite white lace dress with the Nehru collar and yanked her red hair up on her head so that it sprayed out from the top, but her heart wasn't in the event. She and her parents left, with Ford in charge at home, and drove the hour to Severance Hall. Tish sat scrunched in the backseat, absorbed in the dark, observing the lights of boats winking out over the water of Lake Erie. Up front her parents chattered about the soloists, the problems at the university, the world at large. Tish felt the old tear of separateness, the world of her parents, and the world that was hers. She could barely recognize these two silhouettes in the front seat, taking their lives for granted so easily. As they passed through the predominantly black neighborhoods, Tish felt the tension rise in the car. She could sense her parents' discomfort, and she cringed at the quick image on one street corner of a rough-looking black man in handcuffs being led to a police car by two burly white policemen. They passed rows of dilapidated brick houses. Here and there people huddled in the cold, drinking and smoking. There would be the sharp spark of a match and the clatter of breaking glass as a bottle was thrown to the pavement. Tish's mother, muffled in her good coat, murmured exclamations, and Tish wasn't sure if she was responding to the poverty, or the prevalence of blackness, or both.

Inside Severance, Tish was caught in a tangle of emotions. Without Angela, she blended in with this pasty crowd of colorless people. She was struck by the sameness of whiteness, the flat blond faces and transparent eyes. If she'd been with black people, someone assuredly would have pointed out the dearth of black faces. But her parents chattered on obliviously, their ticket stubs torn and pocketed, their faces radiant from the pleasure of a night out. Her father bought Tish licorice caramels from a black-jacketed concessionaire at one end of the hall, and winked as he suggested she slide them inside her purse so no one would see her take them into the concert hall. Tish kept straining her eyes for a black face. Instead she saw rows upon rows of faces that all seemed to have been painted with the same white brush. No nuances, no distinctions. She could hear Wanda's chuckle in her head—*All white people look alike*—and she had to admit that in a crowded room it was true, everyone roughly the same hue.

At intermission, her parents ran into two other Brazil professors and their wives, and Tish shifted from one leg to the other, a forced smile on her face, pretending to care about the conversation ("So, let's see, Letitia, you must be—what—a sophomore in high school now?"). The little coos of approval, the men's chuckles, stiff as the bow ties at their necks. She nodded, answered their questions, and tried not to shift around too much, though her legs were starting to ache from standing. Across the room one lone black man was making his way through the crowded foyer. Tish turned abruptly, feeling a sense of relief, as if someone had just opened a door. If she'd been with Angela or Peachy, they would have said with heartfelt sighs, "Dag, check out the brother," and nodded in acknowledgment. The man was probably her father's age. He had a little gray in his hair and in his beard. He was on the pudgy side, plain-featured and dark-skinned. He carried himself with the self-conscious wide-shoulder stroll some men adopt in public places. He must have caught her staring because he turned his head, and for a split second their eyes met. Tish shot him a smile of recognition, the way her friends did when encountering other blacks. The man smiled reflexively, almost out of surprise, then went on, heading toward the rest room. When Tish turned back, she ran smack-dab into her father's furious expression. His eyes were lit up as if on fire. For a moment she thought she'd missed something, and then the full weight of his misunderstanding descended on her shoulders. She felt as if the floor underneath her had begun spinning. He took her by the arm and pulled her away from the conversation, gently, as if he were going to show her something on the other side of the foyer.

"I'm shocked," he said in a forced whisper. "What on earth was that look you just gave that black man?" His voice was taut, on the verge of breaking.

"What do you mean?"

She had never heard this tone before. "It was a come-on, Letitia, if I ever saw one."

"A come-on?" At first she didn't understand.

"You know exactly what I mean, young lady. You single out the only black man here—don't think I didn't know what that look meant."

Tish thought she was going to be sick. She had meant only to repeat the gesture of her friends she had seen time after time. "I didn't do anything," she said weakly, rolling her program into a tiny tube between her agitated hands and bringing up the open end of it to cover the trembling of her mouth.

"I want you to know something, Letitia. . . ." her father said. "I will not have a daughter who makes a public display of her *thing* for black men."

"But I don't . . ." she said. "It's not like that. You don't understand."

Her mother, still at the center of the foyer, turned to look at them, a sweet smile of puzzlement on her face.

"I just hope," said her father in the same strained, hoarse whisper, "that Mr. and Mrs. Donaldson didn't see what I saw. What do you think that poor man thought? You embarrassed him, a young white girl giving him the come-on?" There was that awful word again— "come-on." It made her think of women movie stars in the old black-and-white forties pictures lowering their eyelids seductively and uttering double entendres before exiting with a swish of their dressing gowns. "You're going to give yourself a reputation, young lady, if you're not careful. And one that I don't think you're ready for."

Then he turned and stalked off, leaving her standing there, open-mouthed in shock, breathing into her rolled program. Shame washed over her like waves, embarrassment for herself, and embarrassment for her father's misinterpretation. What did he think, that she really would make a play for some man old enough to be her father because she was a white girl with a jones for black men? Is that the way he saw her? Was that the truth? Surely, she prayed, the man hadn't misunderstood also, or had he?

She stood there, empty of words, empty of feeling. Moments later, the man made his way back across the foyer. This time there was no acknowledgment.

XXI

It was Peachy's idea on a cold night in late January to double date with two boys from Elyria. It also, Tish knew, was the only way Mrs. Stubbs was going to let Peachy out of the house with a boy.

"I didn't tell them you were white," Peachy informed Tish casually as they dressed in her bedroom. Good, thought Tish. Let them assume whatever they damn well want to. "Here, you can borrow my mini-skirt, it'll look tough on you. I'm going to wear this midi so I don't freeze my delicate, thin African blood." It was all arranged. Tish had told her mother she was spending the night at Peachy's, and nothing more. She made some vague reference to the fact that they might stop by Angela's too. But the truth was that Eddy and Vic Wooten would pick the girls up at the Stubbses' and drive them downtown to see *Rosemary's Baby* at the Orpheum Theater, where they would have an official, normal boy-girl kind of date.

"Eddy's cute, and built too, girl," Peachy kept reassuring. She added a third layer of deodorant ("to cover up any funk," she laughed) and was now spraying the crotch of her panties with Femguard. "And he's sweet, but kinda shy. And Vic—first time I saw him, I knew he was for me."

Tish felt anticipation building, the nervousness of meeting a boy. She swabbed on purple eye shadow, then decided it made her look slutty, and wiped it off. She pulled her hair up on top of her head and fastened it with a rubber band. It reminded her of a red pineapple turned upside down. She licked her lips to moisten them and then took the jar of Vaseline Peachy used to eliminate ashiness, and vigorously moisturized the skin on her arms and legs.

"Honey, I don't mean to interfere," said Mrs. Stubbs dubiously as Tish emerged from Peachy's room in the borrowed miniskirt, which barely covered her thighs, "but are you sure you have your mother's permission to go out tonight?"

The question was doubly loaded. There were those unspoken questions, the ones Mrs. Stubbs really wanted to ask, but was trying to avoid. Tish saw the glance over the length of her exposed legs. It wasn't her fault Peachy was so much shorter. And Peachy was too busy fussing over her new fake suede jacket with the fake fur cuffs to pay much attention.

"Sure," Tish said, trying to manage her voice. "She knows we're going out."

"I think you know what I mean," said Mrs. Stubbs, rising up from the dining room table, where she'd been watching television. She cleared her throat. "Does your mother allow you to date colored boys?"

"Ma-ma!" Peachy heaved a huge sigh. "It's *black*—B-L-A-C-K. Mommy, no one says *colored* anymore."

"No one?" Mrs. Stubbs's eyebrows rose high on her forehead. "I beg your pardon, but I don't believe I'm a no one."

A car door slammed outside. The boys had arrived.

"I just want to be sure you girls aren't doing wrong," said Mrs. Stubbs in a voice that suggested she had her suspicions.

Peachy's groan was her answer. Lies to adults, even by implication, always made Tish nervous. If she had answered honestly, she wouldn't have known what to say. That her mother would go into a tailspin seeing Tish, dressed in a skirt up to her ears, going off to a dark theater with a black boy she'd never met?

Heavy footsteps clomped up the front porch. "It never hurts to have a reminder," said Mrs. Stubbs. "Nowadays you can't be sure. In my day young girls knew how to act around young men." She pressed forward. "What I'm tryin' to say to you both and, Tish, I'm talkin' to you, honey, just like you were one of my own, you hear me? is remember to keep your panties up and your dresses down." The doorbell rang.

With Mrs. Stubbs hovering, and the proximity of two nervous young men crowding into the tiny living room, Tish wanted to faint. They entered reeking of cologne and hair pomade, removing their leather caps, and trying to look upright. Their presence seemed to fill the room. Tish, uncertain which boy was which, found herself tongue-tied. Her eyes kept dodging theirs. Mr. Stubbs, napping after work, emerged from the back bedroom, tying his plaid bathrobe around his waist. "I just wanted to introduce myself to the young men here," he said, squinting against the bright light and extending his hand. The boys were uncomfortable, but they shook hands and "yessired." Tish tried to imagine this scene taking place in her own living room. This double life she led. Why was it she couldn't imagine her father greeting Eddy and Vic Wooten with the same humor and firmness Mr. Stubbs did?

Mr. Stubbs said, "Now, I'm sure I don't need to remind you that these here are young ladies. You gentlemen know exactly what I'm talkin' about."

There was another earnest chorus of "yessirs."

Peachy was noticeably irritable.

"Good night, Mommy. Good night, Daddy."

Mrs. Stubbs followed them right out onto the porch, and stayed there in the cold while the boys with exaggerated chivalry helped the girls into the car and cast reassuring smiles back up at her.

"Y'all be home by eleven," she called out. "Drive carefully. The road could be slick."

In the backseat, next to Eddy Wooten, the shorter of the boys, Tish hugged the door. The car smelled of stale cigarette smoke and old french fries. From the opposite corner Eddy sized her up, his eyes darting nervously from under his leather cap. "So you're Peachy's cousin," he drawled.

Tish nodded, not caring if he had his doubts. He wouldn't dare press; it would be considered rude. "You got a square?" she asked. Eddy dug down in the pocket of his leather jacket. "Help yourself," he said and gallantly lit her cigarette for her. The smoke soothed her. She french inhaled, but Eddy wasn't paying attention. He was cutting his eyes down at her legs. She started worrying how much of her thigh was exposed in Peachy's skirt, and she didn't want Eddy getting the wrong idea. Up front Peachy chatted away with Vic, who was the taller and handsomer of the two, though his eyes were too close together and he reminded Tish of a moth.

All the way down Division Street, she kept expecting to see her mother's Checker approaching, the headlights illuminating the inside of the car. How in that awful moment of recognition her mother would screech to a halt and demand to know what she was doing. She smoked furiously.

At the movies, when Tish started to go into her pocket for money, Peachy yanked her to the side. Vic and Eddy were busily combining change to get the tickets. "Let yo' nigga pay," Peachy whispered. "You never go dutch or they don't respect you."

Tish felt uncomfortable letting a boy she hardly knew pay her way. She didn't want him to expect anything from her.

"Isn't Vic fine?" Peachy gloated. "And Eddy is so built. He wrestles, you know. Come on, Tish, what's wrong with you, girl?"

Tish couldn't say why, but she felt stricken. Eddy was dull and uninteresting. She wasn't attracted to him in the slightest. She tried to force a smile, but it didn't work. Was it this awkward for other girls on dates? Just then Holly Penn and Taylor passed by, and she caught the ease of Holly's smile and the slow arc of Taylor's arm as he brought it down gently on Holly's shoulder.

Inside the lobby, Peachy announced she was hungry and then waited for the boys to dig in their pockets for more money to buy popcorn and Red Vines and Red Hots. All the while, as kids from school passed by, Tish grew more and more anxious. She shifted from one leg to the other. Peachy had such rotten taste in boys. A couple of black juniors she'd seen around with Wanda passed and said hello. Tish resisted a sudden urge to bolt.

"Come on, girl, let's go find seats." Peachy dragged her down the aisle while the boys negotiated the concessions. "You're actin' all weird, Tish." There was irritation in her voice. "What you got rocks in your jaw for?"

Tish couldn't explain even if she herself knew what was wrong. She was ashamed of the whole situation. And she hated herself for the extra care Mrs. Stubbs had taken on her behalf, as if white girls wouldn't know better than to put out to a black boy, especially one as pitiful as Eddy. The theater was darkening. As Eddy settled in beside her, she could feel his hand edging up on the armrest next to hers. She moved her own hand, keeping her eyes focused straight ahead. She was panicked by the thought she'd be seen by someone who would report her to her mother. A moment later Eddy offered quietly, "Here, you care for some Red Hots?" and passed her the whole box. "Thank you," she said softly, feeling miserable. She popped a handful into her mouth, where they burst into fire and brought tears to her eyes. Just punishment, she thought.

The huge red velvet curtain covering the screen drew back. Now the manager, a notoriously prejudiced white man named Pat Walker, stalked up and down the aisles with his flashlight, on the side of the theater where the black kids sat, ordering legs off the backs of seats and telling kids to sit up. When he shone the light on Tish and Peachy and the two boys, he made a stern point of saying to Eddy, "Keep your hands to yourselves during the show." Further humiliation.

Tish glanced apologetically at Eddy. The ghoulish light from the screen bleached his face for a moment. He caught her staring, mistaking her embarrassed glance for interest. He passed her a Red Vine, slow to let it go so his fingers would brush hers. He leaned over and murmured, "You sure are lookin' good." His breath was rancid. She ignored him.

The opening scenes of *Rosemary's Baby* began, and Tish concentrated on the screen, trying to block Eddy from her mind. Each time he shifted next to her, she dreaded the thought that he was working up to putting his arm around her. Already Peachy and Vic were holding hands, and Peachy was placing popcorn in Vic's mouth with her own fingers. Tish felt envious of Peachy's knowledge. She couldn't imagine herself having the nerve. She was sorry now she'd come, sorry for the deceits all the way around.

Up in the front row a group of black girls from school were talking back to the movie.

"You better watch out, girl," one of them cautioned Mia Farrow. "The Devil's after yo' baby."

Gentle laughter rippled through the audience.

"She's so *stupid*," said another girl. There were murmured "mmmmmms" and "uh-huh's," followed by "Are you *blind*, woman?"

As the suspense mounted, the commentary continued. Mia Farrow had all the clues, Tish thought, but she wasn't acting on her instincts. Couldn't she see what was coming?

"Don't trust him," one of the front-row girls warned, as Mia's husband tried to reassure her everything was just fine.

"Why don't y'all shut up?" said one of her friends. But Tish was grateful for their chatter. Each time they cracked a comment she found herself laughing and able to breathe again. Then Pat Walker scurried down the aisle, running the beam of his flashlight over the rows of black kids, in search of the talkers.

"Damn! Shut the light off!" someone said, and then the words "prejudiced honky, stupid-ass white man" floated out over the theater just as the Devil baby was unveiled.

After the show, Eddy and Vic took the girls to Dogs-N-Suds. Eddy kept looking at Tish. It occurred to her he was determined to figure out if she really was a light-skinned black girl, maybe mixed. But he was too polite to ask. It was to her advantage to let him think so for now. She wouldn't have to explain why she wasn't interested, and he wouldn't think she was either prejudiced or easy. Peachy gave Tish conspiratorial winks as they devoured burgers and fries. It was obvious she was happy to have a boy's attention, and wanted Tish to feel the same.

In the harshly lit booth at Dogs-N-Suds, Eddy grew more talkative. He had popped a mint in his mouth and, now with confidence, draped one arm over Tish's shoulders. He told a funny-bitter story about being the only poppyseed in a wrestling match in Parma, and how when he won, the white opponent's side booed and shouted "nigger." Tish brightened to the unexpected revelation of a political side, imagining Eddy transformed into the revolutionary perfection of Wanda's friend Grover, speaking the gritty, informed language of black resistance and pride. No such luck. Eddy shrugged, said he tried not to let things get to him, and leaned over to plug the tabletop jukebox slot with a couple of quarters. Now he was singing along with the Originals' "Baby, I'm for Real" and staring meaningfully at Tish. Bits of dandruff dotted his jacket collar like snow. The ear closest to her was buckled like a cauliflower. She felt herself sinking in the quicksand of her own disappointment. She imagined Angela laughing at Eddy, and she made a firm resolve right then never to see him again.

Outside, she turned up her coat collar, lit a cigarette, and stared up at the night sky. The Tish star was nowhere in sight. She wondered sometimes if it even existed or if it had been a well-intentioned invention of her father's, a game to get them both through childhood. Eddy's voice, just inches from her ear, startled her. In the cold air his breath flickered like fire against her cheek. "I really like you," he whispered. She flinched. "I'd like to see you again, Trish."

That did it! She shot back, "It's *Tish,* not Trish."

"Okay, then, Tish. Can I call you? Can I see you again?"

"I don't know," she said coldly and turned her head, not sure what words should follow next. Angela would have known what to say, how to discourage him. No, Angela would never have ended up on a blind date with someone as square and simple as Eddy. But here she was, stuck with old Eddy Wooten, helpless and annoyed, while Peachy playtussled with Vic in the parking lot.

"You're sweet," Eddy tried again, shifting his awkward bulk in front of her.

"I'm not sweet." Stiffly, she drew her coat around her. "I'm not sweet at all."

He didn't seem to notice the change in her mood. In fact, he didn't seem to notice much at all. All the way home he badgered her. "You got a ole man?" he wanted to know. His hot breath caressed her ear.

"Yeah," said Tish, pulling away and lighting one cigarette after another to keep him at bay. He pressed for details. She would go no further. At the Stubbses', she was the first one out of the car. Her insincere thank you trailed behind through the frosty air to where Eddy sat awkwardly, half in and half out of the car. She glanced back once and caught him shifting himself to the front seat. There was no moonlight and his face was eclipsed by shadow, but she suspected he was watching her go. She hadn't meant to hurt his feelings. But what did he expect?

Thrust back into the bright light of Peachy's living room, she felt hung-over, the way she did mornings after she and Angela had been filching scotch. Mrs. Stubbs in her housecoat drowsily interrogated them for signs of misbehavior. "Did your little boyfriends smoke?" she wanted to know. "Did they pay for your tickets? Were they gentlemen?"

Later, feeling ashamed and depressed, Tish crawled into bed next to Peachy wearing a borrowed nightgown that was too tight in the shoulders and musty in the armpits. This wasn't the way things were supposed to be. She had nothing in common with Eddy Wooten. She didn't care about wrestling. He had briefly fallen asleep in the movie. He was as slow and dull as a lizard. Was this the best she could do? Maybe love was reserved for girls like Angela and Jasmine. Tish felt it was sure to elude her all her life. Stretching ahead were years of awkward dates with awkward boys like Eddy, cast-off friends of boyfriends of cast-off friends. She fell asleep thinking, oddly, of her mother. There was a pang about deceiving her. Tish's punishment was the lousy time she'd had, and would go on having for the rest of her life if things didn't change. In the dark of Peachy's curtained room, breathing in the ripe odors of cooking grease and house, she couldn't even make out the hand she brought up to her face to rub her eye. For a moment she panicked, imagining she was disappearing, but then in the dark she began to touch herself, taking inventory of her body, and fell asleep only after she was assured she was all there.

On Monday she crowded in to the lunch table with Peachy and Wanda and Tina, and several other black girls who eyed her dubiously. "Hey, Tish," Tina said, scooting over. "Tough earrings," she added, and reached out to touch the little peace symbols twinkling in Tish's ears. They were new, bought with saved-up baby-sitting money. The conversation was already in progress, centered on Jasmine and Lamar. Wanda had learned through her university girlfriend Simone at a Black Student Union meeting that Lamar had spent the night in a white girl's dorm room. The same white girl ("this old hippie chick") accompanied him to the Five Stairsteps concert in Cleveland because Tina's older sister Cheri had spotted them there.

Damn, but that brother is messed up. How can he do that shit? I always knew he was into white girls, like half these so-called brothers around here. Tongues clucked, necks snaked, heads shook, sighs circled the table. Murmur: *How does that go—you got an afro head and a processed mind?* Bitter laughter, building from loud to louder.

Tish seized the moment to contribute something. "He was messing with Jeannie Lyons not too long ago." No sooner were the words out of her mouth than she realized her error. Peachy looked down at her bologna sandwich and cleared her throat. One of the other black girls gave Tish an indignant look as if to say, Why don't you mind your own business and shut your mouth?

"Conversation was going *this* way," said Wanda. And she made a little joke about how "some people" had brought their "dipping spoons." More laughter. Tish felt herself flush. Wanda was fronting on her.

"Jeannie Lyons is a breed, she ain't white," someone else said.

Peachy jumped in. "She might as well be white, way she act. And everybody knows she digs Lamar."

Someone else broke in. "Jeannie Lyons is old news, girl. I heard Jasmine put a foot in her ass a long time ago."

"You a lie," said someone else. "Jasmine doesn't fight."

Murmurs. Feet scuffled under the table. The multipurpose room was hot. Tish began to sweat. She had cramps. She tried wishing herself away.

"I just don't get it," Peachy said. "I mean, it seems like a lot of these brothers around here would go with even an ugly white girl over a black girl. I wanna know what a white girl has that I don't."

Several afroed heads nodded sympathetically. Wanda, sitting on the edge of the table, turned and replied without hesitation, "A white pussy." Heads shot around from the neighboring table. There was astonished silence, and then Peachy and Tina and the others just about lost it. A tidal wave of shocked noise rose up from the table. Tish saw some of the popular white boys glance her way, and their collective look was one of curiosity.

"Look," Wanda went on, and her sharp eye fell right on Tish, half-taunting and half-apologetic. "You know I ain't talkin' about you, girl." But Wanda couldn't be trusted, not when she had everyone's attention like this. The world was her stage. "I'm not talkin' about you, 'cause I don't know *what* you've got under your dress, dick or pussy, or whatever."

The words rose up crude and horrid, attaching themselves to Tish's own flesh. Laughter washed over her, punctuated by murmurs of "Wanda, you are so wrong" and "Wanda, stop." She'd gone too far, even for her ardent admirers. Tish's body stiffened, and suddenly the place between her legs, no matter how tightly she pressed her knees together, was no longer private. As mortification set in, she had the sensation she was drowning in her own flesh. She wished herself into oblivion, to a point in time when she hadn't yet arrived. Wanda laid her head on the table and laughed so hard Tish thought she was going to be sick.

"Tish, girl, I'm just messing witchyou," Wanda said, eyeballing her through her fingers. "Okay, sister girl? You cool with me, you know you are." She was almost tender. She turned around to the others, some of whom had their heads in their arms they were laughing so hard. "I didn't mean nothin'. I just talk alotta it-shay, y'all know that." When the laughter didn't subside, her tone grew harsher. "It ain't that funny. Tish is my girl. My ace boon coon. Why don't y'all shut up? I was just messing with her."

But Tish knew she'd been set up. Wanda had used her, made her look foolish. There was no taking back the ugly words. They reverberated in her head, the lunchroom was shot through with them. She crumpled her paper lunch bag with the cheese sandwich and carrot sticks into a ball. The assistant principal was walking through the room, feigning friendliness in his greetings to students clustered at different tables, reminding everyone the bell was about to ring. Tish started to get up. Peachy put a hand on her arm and cast her a sheepish glance. "Don't pay her any attention. Wanda's a mess."

"It's okay," Tish said softly, "it was kinda funny." Her voice was barely audible in the din of scraping chairs and pounding feet.

Tish lost herself in the hall traffic and headed down to the back exit to the parking lot, the one mostly white kids used. She pushed open the door. Outside thick snow fell. Coatless, she stood in the doorway, surveying the student cars lined up like little metal toys. In warm weather there were fights in the lot, and couples made out furtively against car hoods. Now the lot was empty. She felt like one of those little figures trapped inside a paperweight. The world began and ended right here at Brazil High. It was like living in a tight, airless cave. There was nothing beyond, nothing to move toward. She imagined herself stepping out into the white falling snow, and vanishing.

XXII

After the business with Wanda, Tish toughened herself and feigned aloofness. Embarrassment drove a wedge into her pride. But she was determined not to let it show. She blamed herself, for not having a comeback, for being so thin-skinned, for putting herself in the situation in the first place. She should have known better, given the way Wanda liked to mess with people. Tish decided to play it cool. Like the way she'd avoided Holly Penn's crowd for days after overhearing Kim and loud Lisa joke (to Holly's amusement) about how "that freaky Tish Espy" (eye rolls and giggles) probably ordered all her clothes out of the JCPenney's catalog (giggle, giggle). "Did you see those clodhoppers she wears?" Through that lens her own wardrobe was suddenly distorted into shabbiness. Shamefully, she started coveting the warm, rich plaids and solids of the skirt and sweater sets the in-crowd wore, the endless procession of mix and match outfits that meant girls like Holly could go a whole month without wearing the same thing twice. Tish never let on that not only were her new clothes from Penney's, but most came secondhand from the older daughter of her mother's old college roommate, a girl she'd never met, whose slightly outdated cast-offs Tish gratefully sorted through and donned. At lunch, she hid herself in a corner of the cafeteria, her clunky Hush Puppies tucked up out of sight under the chair rungs, the total weight of her deficiencies descending on her. Her body felt all wrong, her clothes didn't fit right. She'd give anything to be someone else. She chewed off her fingernails and devoured Faulkner. Preoccupied with the long, sensuous sentences, she purposely ignored the mindless parrot chatter from the surrounding tables. How long she could fake lofty grandeur she wasn't sure, but she wanted to give the impression she was too cool to care. Occasionally, she glanced backward to see if anyone had noticed her absence. Finally, when the bell rang, she watched them all get up to leave, listened to the shuffle of feet and bump of chairs. Shouts of recognition, but nothing for her. She waited, picturing herself sucked into the din of voices, and disappearing without a trace.

Over the next week Eddy Wooten phoned three times. "Tish, telephone!" Her mother's voice rang out with cheerful expectation. She clamped her palm over the mouthpiece and whispered, "It's a *boy*," before handing over the phone. Tish managed to cut the conversation short by resorting to monosyllables and finally begging off with the excuse that she had to study. It was a lie, she almost never studied, and when she did, her mind was always deserting the work sheets and textbooks to roam in daydreams while she listened to records. When she'd hung up, Mrs. Espy wanted to know (with carefully crafted casualness) who this boy was. It was as if Tish could read her mind: her mother making a lame effort to be involved in her daughter's life. As if they could ever be confidantes and talk about anything real. Tish accepted the dish towel her mother handed her to help dry silverware. She was on guard. "He's no one," she said coolly.

"Well, he sounded nice," said her mother with exaggerated cheer.

"He pronounced your name *Tre-ish*. That's how I could tell it was a black voice."

It was a black voice. The alien words went off like so many wrong notes in Tish's head. Eddy wasn't an "it" and he wasn't "a voice." There was that impenetrable wall, her mother's inability to go around and really look at what was on the other side.

Tish drew in a sharp breath, felt the air clutch in her chest. She clanked several plates together yanking them from the drainer.

"Tre-ish," her mother repeated, thrusting her hands into the soapy dishwater. She was amused, charmed. "I think that's kind of cute. Remember the little Negro girl in your first grade who called you Artisha?"

Tish felt herself withdrawing even farther from her mother.

"No," said Tish hotly. "I don't. I think you made that up."

There was a strained silence. Her mother's face tensed.

"I don't know why you're so defensive, Letitia. You take all this so personally."

Tish stuffed the dish towel inside a glass to absorb the drops of water.

"The boy who called—he *is* Negro, isn't he?" Mrs. Espy asked tentatively. There was an edge of hesitation in her tone. She was trying to get something right.

"Why should it matter?" said Tish, smacking one of the plates hard against the shelf.

"Oh, just curious," said her mother. "I mean, not that it matters. I just wondered. You should be careful about hurting his feelings—you don't want him to think—"

Tish threw down the dish towel. "Think what? That I know he's an Uncle Tom and I can't stand him and I don't care what he thinks?" She couldn't look at her mother. But she knew for the moment she had the upper hand. Her mother would be too confused to stop her. And for once she didn't follow with questions either. Tish fled. Upstairs, she took satisfaction in slamming her bedroom door as a final shutting off. Let her mother come after her and put her on punishment. What did she have to lose? Nothing. Out her window everything, including the sky, was a white wilderness. She felt like a caged creature in the zoo.

She looked up at Huey on the wall and imagined herself standing next to him in solidarity. He would need her. There was a war on out there, and her mother didn't even know it. Outside her window the snow seemed never to stop, but kept coming, flake piling on flake, muting the world of all color. She turned the record player up full blast and danced to Stevie Wonder's "Uptight."

Angela still called every night as she always had to talk about Michael and school and who was digging on who, and who messed around, and how close people slow dragged at the most recent party. Now that she and Edna Sims exchanged confidences, Tish knew things about Edna too. *Edna says, Edna told me, Edna can't stand* became a thread in the fabric of their talks. Edna's authority loomed large. "Edna thinks I should get a fro." Tish couldn't believe her ears. "I've been telling you that all year," she said. Angela didn't seem to hear, but went on with her litany of what Edna said. Edna had this hairdresser, Edna knew where to buy formal gowns for the prom, Edna said you should never wear white before Memorial Day, or after Labor Day. Edna, Edna, Edna.

But Tish was not so easily impressed. She would hold the phone away from her ear for a full minute at a time, while Angela's voice buzzed incomprehensibly like a fly through the receiver. When she did respond, Tish maintained a dull, flat tone, answering mostly in mono-syllables. Eventually Angela would say, "What's wrong, Tish?" and Tish, pleased by the interest, the sudden turning of Angela's attention from the larger world she inhabited back to Tish, would utter in her gloomiest voice, "I'm depressed. I'm going through some changes." It sounded grown-up and important, an antidote to Angela's schoolgirl cheer.

"You need a man," Angela said one evening. "I've been thinking . . . Michael's cousin is visiting from New Jersey. They're coming by later. Why don't you come over?"

In a split second Tish felt a rush of hope. Angela hadn't abandoned her after all. And certainly Michael's cousin would have to be a big step up from Eddy Wooten. By Angela's own account, Peachy had terrible taste in boys—"She likes those illiterate, jungle niggas," Angela said, with her nose-in-the-air tone. "Half the brothers she knows can't even talk right. They sound like they got mush in their mouths, talkin' 'bout 'Baby, I lub you' and it-shay like that."

Tish had to laugh. She imagined the cousin—a nice-looking, smart boy like Michael Brown or an older, solemn, intellectual sort like Wanda's friend Grover. They would discuss politics, debate why Du Bois was hipper than Booker T., and she would explain how she had lately been considering a career in law so she could defend Black Panthers, who were being tracked down and murdered by the FBI. On her way to Angela's, silenced by discomfort as her father drove in the cold air, she predicted the failure the meeting with Michael Brown's cousin inevitably would be. It would go like this: The boys would show up casuallike, almost accidentally, while the Thompsons were off at their social club. It would seem unplanned, except for the fact that the cousin was wearing cologne and a new shirt, and Tish had on her best hip huggers and eye makeup. And he'd be not so good looking, almost guaranteed, on the doofus side and either shy or not too smart, and neither of them would know what to say, so he'd stare a lot and Tish would look away and he'd ask stupid questions like why she wouldn't look at him, and Tish would try hard not to laugh. While Angela and Michael whispered and touched and kissed, the cousin and Tish would end up slow dragging in Angela's family room to the Intruders' "Cowboys to Girls." The cousin would start nervously sweating until he had soaked through his Ban-Lon shirt all the way down his slacks to his thick and thins, and the very ripe boy smell of him would stir in her both horror and fascination. He'd want to kiss and make out, and she'd have to get it straight right off the bat that she wasn't easy like other white girls. And he would draw back, shocked that she would think he'd think such a thing, and he'd reassure her that she was cool, down, the kind of smart, sassy girl who commanded respect. And finally, she would yield half-heartedly to his kisses and gropings just because it was so much easier. Maybe love could happen after the fact. But, no, it would turn out he wore braces he'd been trying his best to conceal, and the hard metal would collide with her teeth, and then his tongue, thick and furry, would slide without warning between her lips. And she wouldn't stop him, even though her stomach would be roiling. Instead she would detach herself and hover above, observing with a kind of scientific curiosity herself in the awkward clutches of a nervous boy who kept catching his fingers in the ringlets of her frizzy hair. How to tilt her head? How to follow the shape of his arm? Her neck would stiffen. In her mind she would calculate just how much was too much. And then his hands would be fluttering at the hem of her blouse, his fingers suddenly moving downward. Such a shock! She would push him away. Enough was enough. She wanted him to be so much more. Instead there would be confusion and the scent of a strange boy's sour mouth, a boy whose clammy touches left her cold, whose apologies for rushing only made her deeply sad. It was nothing like love—just a clumsy fumble between the furnace and Angela's father's woodworking table where the sawdust on the floor would cause her to sneeze. And later when she'd find bits of wood chips stuck to her bellbottoms, she'd pause and wonder with some chagrin why she even bothered. And when this boy with the braces later phoned long distance in his high-pitched, nervous voice with the thick Jersey accent, she would lie straight out and say she already had a boyfriend—his name was Grover Pace. Was he a brother? the boy wanted to know. Yes, she'd say, and slam the phone down, while her mother, all ears and not two feet from her stirring spaghetti into boiling water, pretended not to pay attention. And Tish, appalled by the memory of the labored sound of the boy's disappointed breathing on the other end, and ashamed of her own cruelty, would take herself upstairs to listen to 45's. When Angela called, she'd want to know exactly what Tish thought of Michael's cousin.

How could Tish explain? She was sick of the details of Angela's romance with Michael, the endless repetitions of "we almost did it" and "his thing got so hard" hissed in sepulchral tones through the phone into her ear. How long had she continued patiently to tolerate the particulars, musing over explicit expressions such as "fingering" and "going down," the meanings of which she could only guess at, but which made her feel jumpy and queasy with such knowledge. Unattached to someone she could love, sex struck her as an awful, desperate thing.

It was after an overnight at Angela's that Tish, crossing Division Street, spotted Lamar's white '63 Chevy convertible whistling south toward Route 52.

He wasn't alone. No question it was Jeannie Lyons pressed against him shamelessly, her sandy bangs pasted by the wind to his dark chin. It was as if a big Lake Erie wave had risen up and smacked her in the head.

She ran herself into a sweat getting home to dig in her schoolbag for Jasmine's phone number. Phone privacy at her house was almost impossible, what with her younger brothers swarming (her brother Ford spying), and her parents materializing as unexpectedly as apparitions. She took a chance, shutting the door to her parents' room and crowding in close to the black phone next to their four-poster bed. Her heart was a rock in her chest when she dialed, her fingertips feeling out the unfamiliar numbers.

On the other end, Jasmine's mother answered sharply.

"Who's calling, please?" she asked.

"Tish . . . Tish from French class."

"Tish?" Pause. "Just a moment."

The phone receiver clanked against something Formica-hard. Time inched along. Nervously, she chewed her thumbnail. Downstairs, her mother was yelling at one of the boys, and then she heard the slam and bang of cupboard doors in the kitchen. In the background at Jasmine's she caught the faint sounds of Gladys Knight wailing how she heard it through the grapevine that her man was planning to make her blue.

Finally Jasmine picked up on the other end. She was crunching potato chips into the receiver.

"Uh-huh?" Her voice sprawled long and lanky on the other side of town. Tish imagined her in perfect silhouette with her big natural blooming, edges carefully pruned, around her beautiful face.

"It's me, Tish." Conspiratorial. Hard as nails.

"Mmmmmmmmmm."

Tish threw out the bait. "I saw Lamar today."

"Ummmm-huh? Where?"

A woman's voice snapped in the background, and Jasmine said, "All right, all right." Into the phone she said, "My mother has to make a call."

This forced Tish to the point. Did Jasmine remember what she asked? Mmmmmmmm-hmmmmm. Well, she'd seen Lamar's car. Oh, yeah? Yeah, and Jeannie Lyons was in it. What did Tish mean in it? *In* it. You know, close to Lamar. How close? Close. Just close or very close? Very close. It got so quiet on the other end you could have heard a rat pee on cotton.

At last Jasmine said fiercely, "I knew his black ass was up to no good," and hung up.

That was it? She turned around and dialed Angela. She prayed her mother downstairs wouldn't hear from the kitchen phone the residual clicks of her upstairs dialing.

Angela said, "You saw what?"

Tish acted casual, introducing Jasmine's name with the smoothest inflection. She repeated their whole conversation, word for word, without one interruption from Angela. A long silence followed on the other end.

"I didn't realize," Angela said coolly, "that you were currently *friends* with Jasmine Robinson." She paused. When she didn't say anything, Angela added, "I know for a fact that she's two-faced and uses people."

"Maybe *some* people," Tish shot back.

"Sounds to me," said Angela sullenly, "like Jasmine isn't interested in you at all, she just wants information on Lamar. Besides, she doesn't even like white girls. You better be careful."

"What do you mean, 'careful'?" Tish's nerves hovered right on the edge of excitement.

"You'll find out," Angela retorted in that knowing way she had when she didn't know anything at all. "You don't seem to realize you and Jasmine can never be *real* friends."

When they hung up, Tish felt hollow inside.

She sat for a moment on the edge of her parents' unmade bed, looking around the room and taking in the casual evidence of their years of intimacy—her mother's white nightgown slung over the back of a chair, her father's socks tossed in a corner on the floor, their nighttime reading laid out, pages marked, on the nightstands on either side of the bed. There was a framed galaxy chart on the wall, just like the one her father had given her when she was little so she could memorize the planets and the constellations. But she never had. The galaxy chart had eventually seemed all wrong, an artifact of naive childhood. She claimed she preferred not knowing the names of constellations and planets, believing that ignorance was the magic that kept them suspended up there in a place so vast it was beyond imagining. She felt the familiar texture of her parents' chenille bedspread under her fingers, and recalled the way they both used to smell dewy and sleep-drenched in the predawn mornings when she was still a kid and came to crawl in with them. It had made them all three laugh, the way she burrowed down between them, separating them, and claiming each one for herself.

Now she ignored her mother's voice calling for her to come set the table, to rock the baby, to fold the laundry, or whatever else she was being summoned for.

Contrary to Angela's prediction (and much to her annoyance), the next day in French class Jasmine passed Tish a note, folded into a fat triangle. Tish hadn't seen it start down the row, and when it dropped onto her desk, she felt a quick twinge of elation. She didn't want to appear overeager, so took her time getting around to unfolding it and peering at it from the corner of her eye.

Just wanted to say HIGH to Tish, the note said. *That was a bad sweater you had on yesterday. Peace and love, Soul Sister Jazz.* There was a heart with Lamar's initials, L.H., and *Black love is forever* scrawled across it. At the bottom in her own invented calligraphy she wrote, *Free your ass and your mind will follow.*

Uncertain about whether or not Jasmine's note required an answer, she played it cool and waited a day, flushed from the sweater compliment. Then she passed along a poem she'd written (no capital letters anywhere) about why the war was wrong and how many more black men than white men were being sent to the front lines (she'd heard her father talking about this). *Brothers dying in the rice fields in Vietnam, beaten on the streets of Birmingham.* Jasmine stopped her in the hall. "You're on the ball, girl," she said. "I dig that. You ever read Nikki G.?"

Now in class, even if she was talking to one of her "girls," Jasmine would make a point of turning to her as she came down the aisle. " 's happenin', Tish?" And Tish would mumble, "Not much," or "Nothin'," because the point was that if you were really cool, nothing much was going on—not in this rinky-dink school, and not in this little backwater town.

It wasn't much, but what attention Jasmine did pay her gave Tish a sudden charge of confidence. She loaned Jasmine *Facing Mt. Kenya* and Faulkner's *Sound and the Fury.* Jasmine loaned her *Valley of the Dolls* and a Frank Yerby romance *(Girl, did you know that man was black?).* Tish sauntered by girls like Holly Penn without caring one whit if they noticed her. If they spoke, she'd just sort of nod and smile. And occasionally when she did stop to talk, she acted as if she just had a minute because she had some place else to be, and she saw that her new nonchalance left them open-mouthed.

The next secret-admirer note read like this: *You are too, too fine, won't you please be mine, can you dig it?* The words crashed in her ears. It was worse than a corny Valentine. She felt let down, even embarrassed, but with a bit of imagination she was able to elevate the clichés to something much more estimable. After all, it had been scrawled in haste, and there was a certain rhythm to it, a kind of cadence of urgency she could appreciate. She pressed the note inside her binder. So what, not everyone could be a poet. And maybe poetry was really whatever came from the heart, raw and unpolished. Passing down the hall, she imagined herself into the heads of various boys strolling by. Fine Tony Purify, half-black, half-Hawaiian, smiled as he passed, but gave nothing away. Jeff Anderson paused at his locker and turned to say hello in that way he had of feigning niceness on the sly when the rest of the in-crowd wasn't around to witness. On down the hall she went. There were no knowing looks, no rings of connection, just an occasional "Hey, Tish," a nod, a wave. She even sidled up to Dev at one point just to see if something in his expression would give him away, but he said nothing revealing, just mentioned he was nervous about his test in advanced math, and asked if she had an extra eraser he could borrow. Then he put on his reading glasses, which always made his eyes look even bigger than they already were. For a moment a softness entered them that almost broke her heart. She gave him her last pencil by way of apology, and trudged on down to class. It was a cold, snowless day in February. She paused for a moment to look through the plate-glass front doors of the school out across the bare, frozen ground. A wind stirred the American flag out front, causing it to flap around the metal pole, the sound a sad, pointless one. It was the only movement for as far as her eye could see.

The following day Jasmine accosted her. She was wearing a blue denim shift with a partially unzipped zipper that ran from the bottom hem to the base of her neck. Her hair stood out in a perfect globe around her head. Huge silver hoops dangled from her ears. She was clearly in no mood for small talk. "Was Lamar in study hall yesterday?" Her tone was severe, face stony.

Tish assured her he was, but didn't mention Jeannie wasn't. There seemed to be no point. Angela had informed Tish that Jeannie had left school early with cramps, and Wanda remarked in her knowing way that cramps could be caused by an illegal abortion. Tish pondered this. She'd heard stories of other girls, girls who had been whisked off suddenly claiming mononucleosis, when in reality they were being sent out of the country to rid themselves of an unwanted pregnancy. Somehow the idea of pregnancy and Jeannie became entwined in her mind, and the next time she saw her she glared at her fiercely, as if in warning.

The next day in French Jasmine passed Tish a note asking if Lamar had talked with *anyone* in study hall. Her jaw was hard, she looked determined. Something was up, and with her usual tenacity she was bound to get to the bottom of it. She had signed off with *Power to the people, Jazz* and drawn a clenched fist next to that. Politics and love hand in hand. *Hey, Jazz,* Tish wrote back, leaping to the intimacy of the diminutive. She began, *Lamar didn't talk to a soul.* She went on to say how boring school was and how she wished she could get the hell out of Brazil, and how with all the terrible things going on in the world— poverty, war, racism, and so on—why were they sitting up in this stupid school being made to learn about the exports of Ecuador? At the end of the note she took a chance and added a quote she'd read on a poster hanging in the student union. *The voice of the people is the voice of heaven—Mencius. Later, Tish.* She refolded the note, scribbled Jasmine's name on top, and handed it to the girl in front of her. Like connecting dots from one point to the next, the note made its way up the row. She felt the heat rush to her face when it arrived in Jasmine's hands. Jasmine turned ever so slightly in her seat, then tucked the note inside her red leather purse. Tish pretended to focus her attention on the oral quizzes now starting in the class: question-and-answer dialogues. But all the while she kept an eye on Jasmine's expression, which remained impassive, waiting for her to open the note. Spectacled Madame Zietlow wandering the room in her long skirt started with easy stuff as warm-ups: *"Qu'est-ce que c'est?"* pointing one by one to the items she pulled from her net bag. Down the aisle each student took a turn. *"C'est un livre," "C'est un mouchoir," "C'est une pomme de terre."* There were giggles, corrections. Madame Zietlow was a stickler for pronunciation. Tish could name objects in French all day long: pens, paper, notebooks, combs, rings, keychains, tables, chairs. The world was full of nameable objects in whatever language you chose. What about love? *"C'est l'amour."* But love wasn't about to appear from the net bag. Tish wondered what would happen next time Madame Zietlow stopped in front of her and asked, *"Qu'est-ce que c'est?"* and she responded, *"C'est moi, c'est une Tish,"* as if she herself had been drawn from the net bag, a separate, invented category, like any other common noun. As if there were such a thing as "a Tish."

"Jasmine's false," Angela kept warning, now that Tish was growing less patient with details of how far Angela and Michael Brown had gone in the backseat of his Cutlass. *(One itty-bitty millimeter more and it would have been in me,* and *Dag, it hurt, girl, you wouldn't believe how big it gets.)* Tish could no longer look Michael straight in the eye without imagining him in the throes of passion. His good-boy, polite grin now struck her as amusing, since he had no way of knowing the alternative images of him Angela had conjured up in her late-night recaps. Tish had run out of curiosity about Angela's adventures, was tired of her pronouncements that she was "still a virgin" (emphatic shake of her head), but "came this close" (eyes closed as she exhaled loudly). She kept wondering why Angela was even bothering to hold out. She might as well just go ahead and give it up all the way; she'd had all her clothes off and had done everything else under the sun.

"I'm telling you," Angela said coolly, "Edna says watch your back with Jasmine. She's using you for her little spy."

"Jasmine's cool," said Tish. "It's not what you think."

"I know this much," Angela insisted. "She calls herself being tight with Peachy Stubbs, but Edna says she puts Peachy's business right out on the street."

"What business?" said Tish, unable to conceive of any "business" Peachy might have.

"Just business," Angela said, tight-lipped and knowing. "Some things you don't know about Miss Peachy and her fast self."

Tish was dying to know, but didn't want to give Angela the satisfaction of thinking she didn't know something.

"Oh, I know about that," she said, not to be outdone. "Ain't nothin' but a thing."

Angela arched her eyebrows. "Well, if that's what you want to think," she said, "but Peachy's heading for serious trouble."

Tish was dying of curiosity to know what "business" and "serious trouble" Peachy could have, but she was more fed up with Angela's knowingness. Whatever it was, Angela had to be making it up.

"Well, Jasmine says . . ." Tish liked to say, only Angela wasn't buying it.

Whenever Jasmine swept by, either locked in Lamar's proprietary grip or flanked by her girlfriends, Angela would roll her eyes meaningfully in Tish's direction. *See what I mean? She can't even speak. She thinks she's too good. Too cute. She's playin' you off.*

"She didn't see me," Tish would say, unsure.

"Sure," said Angela in a voice that implied Tish was just too deaf, dumb, and blind to understand.

XXIII

"Why didn't you tell me you were invited to Holly Penn's party?" It was one of the coldest days of the year, and Mrs. Espy had just come in the door. "I ran into Bunny this afternoon at Fisher's school book fair, and she seemed surprised you weren't there."

Tish concentrated on pulling on her skating tights. "I forgot." How slippery truth could be, wriggling away from itself and escaping like that. She imagined it slithering behind the radiator with serpentine quickness and disappearing through the floor.

"Well, that strikes me as odd since you never seem to forget when Peachy or Angela invites you to a party." Mrs. Espy hung up her coat. Her patrician syllables clattered in Tish's ears. Recriminations weren't far away. The radiator hissed. There was no way to explain the truth.

"I forgot . . . I said I forgot. . . ." In her head, she heard the
words "bitch, bitch, bitch" and worse. Hypocrite! It's what her mother
was and of course Holly too, underneath the glossy hair, smelling sweet
from daily shampoos, and rosy skin enhanced by foundation, pretending generosity just to set her up for this very moment.

Mrs. Espy's tone clouded over. "You mean, Holly didn't invite any
black kids, is that it?" She said it almost tenderly, as if Tish were to be
pitied. As if Tish had fallen away from her careful control, and gone
beyond what Mr. and Mrs. Espy had ever intended in the name of
integration.

More sighs. "Tish [sigh], your father and I raised you to believe that
people are equal, but that doesn't mean forgetting who you are. Sometimes I think we don't know you anymore. I know you're at that
awkward age . . . and these are strange times." (Her voice was picking up speed in the home stretch.) "Your loyalty to Peachy and Angela
is admirable, but they go to their parties without you. You can't just
have only black friends, you know. It's not natural. You're white.
You're not black. You're cutting yourself off. You're limiting yourself."

You're white. That's what her mother was saying, as if tossing her a
lifejacket. As if she were drowning, like the time out at Curtis Pond
when a girl fell on her and towed her under, and Wanda and Peachy
went into stitches on the beach. *You see that? Big fat white girl almost
drowned Tish!* Tish couldn't bear to look at her mother, the enemy, lips
moving, uttering nonsense.

"For starters," Tish said, grabbing up ice skates, scarf, mittens, and
blue knit hat, the one just like Angela's that Mrs. Thompson had given
her two Christmases before, "Holly's a big prejudiced phony." Her tone
lacked the conviction she felt and the words fell dull and lackluster on
her ears. She jammed her red hair up into the blue hat and went on.
"Her mother doesn't want black people in their house." Even that came
out childish. As soon as she spoke, she knew she sounded foolish. "You
don't understand. She doesn't really want to be friends with me, she
only pretends. And she stopped inviting Angela to her house last year."
She accidentally got caught in Mrs. Espy's sorrowful expression, the one

that accused her of exaggerating, even inventing. Her mother could be so naive.

And then, because it was the trump card she'd been holding, Tish blurted out the truth about the birthday party two years before at Holly's.

Mrs. Espy's face got strange. "I can't believe that," she said hesitantly. "There must have been some misunderstanding."

"No misunderstanding," said Tish triumphantly. She pointed to herself. "Me—I—Letitia Espy—your daughter—not wanted. And why? Well, for starters, the Penns think my parents are communists . . . freaks, weirdos. Don't you get it?"

The spark of anger ignited, and lit the wick of rudeness. What did she have to lose? The words fell from her lips, as if she were writing them on a page, instead of speaking them. "You're too blind to see it. Holly Penn invited me to her party because she and her little phony white friends are trying to save me from being a nigger lover. Ask her. Ask Mrs. Penn next time you see her in the Sparkle Super, or wherever it is you're always running into her."

Mrs. Espy looked as if she might cry.

Tish stared back at her, felt the brief burst of power as her mother grew weaker. "Don't you get it? I'm a *freak*, Mom. A *freak*. Like a two-headed calf or Siamese twins! You think so, don't you?"

She could no longer feel her own body, and the house had all but vanished. Outside, beyond the half-opened front door, the white snow fell silently.

"You've alienated all your white friends . . ." Mrs. Espy began.

"Like who? Like Lynn?" Tish snapped angrily and then faked a sarcastic laugh. "Right." Her mother didn't answer, just grew smaller and smaller in the dim light. Tish went out then, slamming the door behind her. She half expected her mother to storm after her, tell her she was grounded for life. But there was only silence, and the house sat like a dark, square box, uninhabited.

It was her legs that started moving on their own over the snowy walk, and the rest of Tish just followed, numb even though she wasn't cold. Every time a car came down the street, she turned, half expecting it to be her mother in the old Checker. Tight-lipped, she would order Tish to get in, and at that moment Tish's life as she knew it would end. They would ride in that confined space, the unbearable silence broken only by the engine humming, and together they would enter the darkened garage, where the dying of the engine would mirror the last happy breath Tish would draw. As they were getting out, her mother would inform Tish she was not going anywhere, not that night, and not for many nights. Tish knew a girl whose parents had chained her to her bed when she wasn't in school, and finally shipped her off to some detention camp for kids who were acid freaks.

But none of that happened. Each car that passed was not the Checker. By the time Tish turned the corner, passing the gate to French Woods, she had the odd sensation that her mother had no intentions of following her, and that she was free to do as she pleased. She daydreamed of being adopted by the Thompsons and living out the last two years of high school in normalcy, sharing the bedroom with Angela, and eventually going off to college with her. She and Angela would make things like they were before, when they were two halves of the same person. They'd both get afros, and hip boyfriends who were friends, and sign up for all the same classes, and major in Black studies. Together. But she needed Angela. She couldn't do it all herself.

She walked the six blocks to the skating rink in the dark gray light, with her skates clanging around her neck. In her head she was reciting her favorite poem, Hardy's "Darkling Thrush," mostly because the gloomy words cheered her, like singing the blues: "I leaned upon a coppice gate when frost was specter gray, and winter's dregs made desolate the weakening eye of day."

From the open sides of the skating rink, the chorus of "Everlasting Love" crescendoed. First session was almost over. Second session would begin shortly. Generally on Saturday nights there were more black kids than white at second session, which was why her friends jokingly called it "Boot Nite." In the parking lot she spotted Lamar's white Chevy with the red, black, and green flag displayed on the dashboard.

At the entrance, she paid her 50 cents and went in under the canopy. The rink was already full of skaters, a lot of them young kids. It took Tish a minute to search out Peachy and Tina and Wanda, who were huddled in the low bleachers drinking cups of the watery cocoa from the vending machine. To her surprise, Angela and Michael were just walking in too. Angela was wearing her identical blue knit hat, and for a moment this fact brought them closer together.

"We came by to pick you up, but your mother said you'd already left," Angela said. She had on a whole skating outfit, with matching mittens and scarf.

The three walked past Holly Penn and Taylor Weems, who stood hand in hand along the edge of the rink. Kim and Lisa were with them as well, Lisa with her thin lipsticked mouth talking in a loud, unbearable voice.

"Hey, Tish. Hey, Angela." The hellos were extra hearty, as if they were trying too hard. Tish turned and gave a gentle wave of her hand that could be read as greeting or dismissal.

She could feel the wind sharply blowing off Lake Erie, occasionally stirring up a cloud of snow and causing it to drift in through the open sides of the rink.

Dev was sitting with Peachy, Tina, and Wanda on the bleachers, looking skinny as a string bean in his skating tights. He was the only boy Tish knew who wore tights to skate in. He was also wearing a red knit cap and a scarf wrapped up around his face. She squeezed in next to him and blew on her fingers to stay warm. "Hey, Tish."

"Here, have some," said Peachy, thrusting her cocoa at Tish. "This shit's nasty."

Tish pushed the cup away. "Get it out of my face."

Wanda and Tina were laughing.

"Don't nobody want Peachy's old leftover cocoa," remarked Wanda. "She's tried to make us all take it."

"Y'all messed up," muttered Peachy, still sipping her cocoa and looking evil.

Wanda and Tina took turns talking about the skaters: *There goes Jasmine; look at her tough skates, girl. Ooooh, I can't stand that boy there— look at him with his lips all poked out. Terry Miller's going with that Gonzalez sister now—what's her name—Miriam. She's all right—they make a cute couple.* The words took on their own rhythm. Wanda complained about the cold, and Tish offered her the blue knit hat, which she was sick of anyway. Wanda accepted, grateful, and in her appreciative hands the hat suddenly took on a surprising grace and flourish. Tish felt a pang of jealousy as Wanda clamped the hat down over her ballooning fro, tucked the edges of her hair up inside, and pronounced herself much warmer, thanks, girl, right on.

Dev asked Tish if she wanted to skate, and she said in a minute, trying to find her equilibrium, and distressed about the hole she had just discovered in her tights. Her nose turned red and damp in the cold. It was depressing. She withdrew like a turtle into her oversized jacket and watched through blurred eyes as skaters soared past: the oldest Gonzalez girl with her dark brown hair in two braids, Holly Penn in a plaid skirt, Tony Purify with Jasmine's friend Maxine. Odd little Dana Savage who was still in elementary went by with her three white adoptive siblings, and someone murmured what a shame it was she'd been adopted by white people who didn't even know how to do her hair right. The Savages were in the art department, and Mrs. Savage had gone to a lot of trouble to do her part for civil rights.

At one point, Jasmine and Lamar came around the corner in one smooth movement, arms intertwined, skate blades flashing. Jasmine pulled herself free and scraped to a stop on the ice in front of them. Lamar skated backward to the center, and stood there doing little loops, showing off his new black skates.

"Hey, y'all."

"Hey, Jasmine."

She leaned against the railing, keeping herself sideways so she could talk and keep an eye on Lamar at the same time. Her breath smoked in the cold. "I'm going to California in two more weeks for spring break, thank God. Visit my Aunt Yolanda." She was smiling and her eyes were bright. Small flakes of snow that had blown in under the rink dome had lodged in her hair. "She's having a fortieth-birthday party. About time I get out of this dead town and party on the Coast."

She clicked her fingers for emphasis and slid her skates back and forth while she talked. Tish felt envy rise. California!

Lamar moved off toward the entrance of the rink. Jasmine followed him with her eyes. He was so good-looking and so wrong. At the far railing he came to a screeching stop, cutting up a mist of powdered snow with his blades. He exchanged a soul handshake across the railing with a tall older boy in a full-length leather coat who stood in street shoes. Fingers curled, fists clenched, fingers interlaced, knuckles tapped. Big smiles, a flash of communion. Even as far away as she was, Tish could see that underneath the leather coat, the boy was wearing a copper-colored turtleneck and a large peace medallion around his neck. He had long, soft hair in a well-groomed natural, and smooth brown skin. Tina had spotted him too. She leaned over to Tish. "Who's that, girl? Check him out. Mmmmmmmmm."

Tish shrugged.

Jasmine used her front teeth to pull one mitten off her hand so she could adjust the hoop earring in her lobe. "That's just Marcus Goodman," she said casually.

"You mean *Goody?*" Peachy squinted. "Joe Faison's cousin? That's not the Goody I remember. When'd he get so fine?"

"Marcus was always fine, just square," said Jasmine dismissively. She drew a square in the icy air and wiped her mittened hand across her nose. "He's sweet, just can't dance, can't rap, and from what I heard, can't kiss." She laughed.

"How come you call him Goody?" Tina teased. " 'Cause he looks so *good?*" She elbowed Tish and grinned.

Jasmine sighed. "Negro, please. Y'all can be so pitiful."

"What school does he go to?"

"He graduated already—from Catholic school in Elyria."

"Who he go with?" Wanda asked, interest piqued.

Jasmine shrugged. "Y'all should see yourselves with your eyes bugging. Why don't you ask him yourself?" She called out, "Hey, Goody, come here!" Everyone started protesting then and Wanda ducked down and hid her head in Peachy's lap, and Peachy pushed her off, and they were all falling out and practically fainting on themselves. Dev said, "Y'all can be so silly," and stretched his arms over his head with a sigh.

Goody looked over. "Yeah, you!" said Jasmine. Baffled, he pointed clumsily to himself. With that gesture, something rose up inside Tish— pity for his awkwardness?

"Come on, good-lookin', good thing Goody!" Jasmine laughed. She motioned him over.

Shyly, he started toward them, Lamar following on the edge of the ice and making slow loops.

Lamar announced, "This is my ace boon coon, Marcus Goodman." Then, he laughed. "He's free, black, and single . . . but the nigga ain't got a rap and he can't skate."

Jasmine said, "Stop, Lamar."

Lamar reached out and slapped Goody on the shoulder. He was performing for them all. "Can you believe that? When we were little kids—remember, man?—I tried to get you skating on Curtis Pond, and you freaked out and started cryin', talkin' about the ice was gonna break."

"Yeah," Goody grinned genially.

"Nigga's scared of water," Lamar went on. "I pushed him off the dock once at Curtis Pond and he was screaming and crying, talkin' 'bout 'Mama, help me!' "

"Man, you're lyin' now." Goody chuckled. He had a nice, easy manner, and he wasn't at all rattled.

"You really can't skate?" Peachy asked. "It's easy. Go rent you some skates, baby, and *I'll* teach you how."

"Oooooh, girl!" said Wanda and fell out laughing again. "You are so fast."

Peachy tightened her jaw and moved her shoulders up and down to an imaginary beat. She could get away with that sassy, bold stuff, because she was so little and funny.

Now that Goody was in front of them, fully tangible, no one really knew what to say. The boldness wore off. Awkwardness took over. Tish bent to peel off her boots and wedge her feet into the skates. They'd gotten too small, but Mrs. Espy said they were good for one more season. She laced them up loosely. Wanda and Tina simultaneously got off the bleachers and tiptoed in their skates over to the edge of the ice. Peachy announced she was off to the snack bar again.

Goody sort of squatted down on the bottom bench and studied his hands. "How you doin', man?" he nodded to Dev, and Dev said, "I'm fine," and looked away.

Tish elbowed Dev gently and mouthed, "Let's skate." She was feeling self-conscious, nervous about being left alone with Goody.

When she glanced back, Goody had turned, and his eye rested briefly on her. It was so unexpected that she was caught off guard. She tried to smile, but her face was so cold she couldn't make sense of her own features. Dev extended his gloved hand and she took it gratefully.

They skated past Jasmine and Lamar, who had now moved center ring and seemed to be arguing. Jasmine was sulking, her face turned away from Lamar, who'd grabbed her hands and was pleading with her. She could tell Jasmine was upset again, and she wondered what it was Lamar had done now. A moment later as they came back around, she caught sight of Jeannie Lyons in a red quilted jacket over by the skate rental sign. It looked as if she'd done something weird to her hair; she now had bangs, and her hair had been straightened and greased and pulled up in little ringlets on her head. She had on red earmuffs and was standing there casually with a couple of younger white boys from junior high. It was hard to tell if she'd come alone or with them. She kept glancing around as if she were expecting someone. "Uh-oh," Tish said. Dev drew her closer as they rounded the corner, hands crossed.

"I'd stay out of that one if I were you," Dev murmured.

They came around past Peachy and the others, now all on the ice, and Peachy yelled out, "My turn next!" and she grinned and waved. The skates felt good cutting into the ice. It was almost like flying. Dev gave Tish a half turn, and she skated backward, catching a glimpse of Goody still sitting by himself on the edge of the bleacher. He seemed to be waiting, but for what? Her scarf whipped back around and caught her on the chin. Dev said, "Concentrate, Tish," and she realized she was out of step and throwing him off balance.

Jasmine was now sitting on a bench on the other side of the rink, knotting her skate lace, while Lamar hovered with a sheepish grin on his face. It was hard to tell what her expression was because her head was bent, but it was clear from Lamar's body language that he was trying to make up. Tish waved, but Jasmine didn't look up. Jeannie has her nerve, she thought, showing up like this. She and Dev circled around again and again, and when she looked over, she saw Lamar exiting to the parking lot. He passed right by Jeannie, and didn't even give her a look. Tish elbowed Dev. His only response was "Y'all need to leave that girl alone. She never did anything to any of you."

They went around several more times. Tish closed her eyes. For a moment she felt like a little kid who assumes if she can't see that she can't be seen. "Everlasting Love" began again. She felt a sudden chill, and then realized Jasmine had skated up alongside. " 'scuse me, Dev, I need to talk to Tish a minute." And as Dev released Tish and skated a polite distance away, Tish slowed to a stop and faced Jasmine.

"Goody's asking about you, girl. Just thought you'd want to know." And she winked and turned a quick circle on the ice.

When Dev came back around for her, Tish did some figure eights in time to the music, just in case Goody was watching. She came off the ice with an awkward stop and took a seat on the far side of the bleacher, away from Goody, who was now talking to one of the Gonzalez girls and a little bright-skinned black girl named Patsy who had gone to French-speaking school in Canada. Peachy and Wanda were still on the ice clowning around, and Tina was at the pay phone.

Self-conscious, Tish pretended to concentrate on unlacing her too-tight skates, to let her feet breathe.

"Hello, there."

She pretended not to hear. "Hey, there," he said again. This time she looked up. Goody was leaning across the bench toward her.

"Excuse me. Jasmine says your name is Tish, is that right?" His open coat brushed against her arm, startling her. She nodded.

"You're a friend of Jasmine's?"

She nodded again.

"I've never seen you before."

She couldn't think of a response, so concentrated on unlacing her skates.

"You getting ready to leave?" he asked.

"No, my skates are too small and they cramp my feet." She paused, embarrassed. He didn't want to know all that. Why wasn't it she had ever developed the ease around boys that other girls had?

"Maybe you could teach me to skate," he said.

The very thought made her breathless. Just then she caught Wanda, who didn't miss a trick, looking over. She could read Wanda's mind as if it were her own: *Check him out, goin' for the white girl.*

"Mind if I sit next to you?" he asked, even though there was plenty of room on the bench.

"Suit yourself," she said, then regretted the coldness in her voice.

Wanda, grinning widely, called out, "Hey, Tish, what's *happenin'?*" and Tish knew she was being messed with. It was mortifying. She turned around and made a face at Wanda.

"You want a cigarette?" Goody asked, close to her ear. He was already thumping a brand new pack of Kools with his fingers.

"Sure," she said, relieved.

"I don't think we can smoke in here," he said, looking around. "What do you think?" She knew then he was waiting for her to suggest they go outside together. Like her, he probably felt exposed and uncomfortable under the bright lights of the rink.

"They make you smoke outside," she said feebly.

"Come on," he said.

She knew only that she set her skates aside and got up to start toward the entrance. Her movements were stiff and mechanical. She had no idea if Goody was following or not, but she couldn't risk looking back. Her legs felt tight as if she weren't used to walking. On her way out, she paused briefly to let the woman at the ticket booth stamp the palm of her hand. She was certain the woman's expression signaled suspicion. Out in the dark parking lot, away from the lights, she stopped and looked up at the sky. She shivered in the night air, but the cold sharpened the edge of her daring. From the corner of her eye she caught a movement, followed by the rhythmic crunch of footsteps on the icy gravel, and even though she knew it was Goody, she still didn't turn.

"Hey," he said at her side. He had turned up his coat collar, throwing half his face in shadow.

"Hey," she said back, and caught his smile. Understanding passed between them like a flash of heat. No one had ever looked at her like that before. She glanced away, trying to maintain her cool. She imagined what Angela might do and say. He shook out two cigarettes from his pack, placed both in his mouth with a gloved hand, and lit them. In the brief flare of match, she caught his profile, the elegant slope of nose, the intense gleam of his eye. He handed her one of the cigarettes straight from where it had just rested on his full bottom lip. She imagined his velvet mouth on hers as she took the first drag. She french inhaled, letting the smoke loop back in through her nostrils. Words stuck in her throat. She inhaled again, grateful for the nicotine rush. A sweet ginger smell floated through the night air. Startled, she recognized the suggestive scent of men's cologne. It made her weak in the knees. Panicking, she realized she didn't know where to start. But he did. Gently, he began to speak.

It was small talk at first. Did she come here often? Did she know this and that person? Did she ever go to the roller rink in Elyria? Underlying the questions was the unspoken substance of deeper meanings. Their conversation seemed so natural—effortless.

"You live near here?"

"Woodland Street." But she didn't want him to get the wrong idea, put her in the category of rich white girl. "Our house is kind of run-down. It's not one of the fancy ones."

"I know someone over there," he said. She felt an odd pang of jealousy. Some other girl. Some *white* girl. After all, why was he out here with Tish when he could have started talking to Peachy or Wanda or Tina? "You know a girl named Mona Penn?"

"I know her sister Holly."

"Mona's cool. She and I went to Catholic school for a year together. She went off to college already. Me, I wasn't sure what I wanted to do, so I'm still stuck here in Brazil trying to figure things out."

What was he trying to tell Tish? That he dug Holly Penn's older sister? That they'd had a thing? That he dug white girls?

"You ever go to the rec center?" he asked.

"You mean the Boot Center?"

He tipped his weight back on his heels and laughed. "You're all right, Tish."

He made it easy to be with him, telling her about having gone to Catholic school, how his mother wanted to make sure he had a disciplined environment. "I'm not a troublemaker," he said. "I don't want you to get the wrong idea. But you know how it is. There's a lot of temptation in the streets . . . she didn't want me messing up. Now she's worried I'm gonna get drafted, and she wants me to start college."

"You might get drafted?"

He shrugged. "My number's really high, but you never know. I try not to think about it. I'm thinking about going down to Ohio State next year."

In the cold, dark parking lot, she leaned against someone's car hood, and confided in Goody about the Tish star. He made a point of showing keen interest, searching the cloud cover with his eyes. "I think I see it there, right behind the moon," he said, and she was embarrassed to think he might be humoring her. They had been standing about a foot apart, but now he squeezed in to lean against the car too, and their shoulders touched.

"Lamar and I are talking about getting an apartment together until he leaves for college in August. We both want to get out of the house." He paused. "Tell you the truth, I'm not much for conversation. People say I'm on the shy side."

Tish was touched by this admission. "Me too," she said. "I never know what to say, and I hate small talk."

"I think you're pretty cute," Goody said. "I mean, if you don't mind my saying so. I don't mean any offense."

She felt just the edge of suspicion. "What about Peachy and Wanda and Tina? You don't think they're cute?" She was testing him.

He shrugged. "Wanda's cute, but she's too loud, and I don't like girls that big. Peachy's sweet . . . is Tina the little light-skinned one? She's nice-looking, I guess."

"You don't like black girls?" Tish asked.

He seemed taken aback. "Whoa!" he said. "Why you wanna ask me something like that?"

Her voice hardened. "You're out here with me. . . ."

"Naw, naw." He smiled awkwardly. "You're kinda tripping." He added softly, "Just like a sister."

"I'm not tripping, I'm just trying to figure out where you're coming from," she told him.

"Whew! You're tough," he said and laughed again. "Anyone tell you you sound like a black girl?"

"Not tough," she said. "Just observant. I pay attention."

"Ohhhhh," he said, with a smile. "You think maybe I have a thing for white chicks. Naw, it's not like that. Not at all."

"Because if you do," she said boldly, "you're talking to the wrong girl."

He laughed. "You're tough, little one, I like that."

This was so different from the clumsy make-out sessions at parties, or the fraternal walks home from school with Dev, or the clumsy attempts at dates with boys like Eddy Wooten. She felt important and grown-up talking to Goody.

"I like you, Tish," he said earnestly. "You're different, you know that?"

She didn't ask different from what, but basked in the compliment. For once, difference sounded good.

"I told you," she said, gaining confidence. "I pay *attention.*"

"I'd like to see you again," he said softly. "Would that be possible?"

His question came so unexpectedly that she felt herself choke.

"I don't mean to embarrass you," he said, and then very tenderly tucked his index finger under her chin and gently pulled her face upward so that she had to look him straight back in the eyes. "Something about you just got under my skin, that's all." He paused, maneuvering his body close to hers. "You don't have an old man, do you?"

"No," she whispered. Slowly he removed his finger, but she could still feel the gentle pressure of his touch.

"So what else should I know about Miss Tish?" he asked.

"What do you want to know?"

"Tell me anything you want me to. I want to know you."

She felt herself come open all at once. How easily the words came. As she talked, she forgot the cold, so it took her by surprise when she began to shiver.

"Here, let me warm you up," said Goody. It was as natural as breathing when he put his arms around her.

She felt herself melting against him, grateful for his warmth. He was so much bigger than any of the boys she'd ever hugged before. Held against him that way, it was so much easier saying what needed to be said. And when in the moonlight he bent down and put his mouth on hers, she never flinched, but yielded right up, because it seemed so natural. He led, she followed. They stayed that way for a long time, swaying against each other in time to the music coming from the rink, pausing just long enough to catch their breath. It seemed they'd only begun kissing before the skaters began to flood into the parking lot from the rink, and they had to pull apart. In the confusion of bright headlights snapping on, Tish panicked a little and pulled herself free. "I've got to go home," she said abruptly, suddenly chilled and exposed.

She caught sight of Dev's red cap, and she excused herself, hurrying through the slush, past Peachy and Wanda, whose heads both turned. She ignored Wanda's teasing, "Where've *you* been, girl?" and sorted her way through all the exiting skaters until she'd found Dev. "Can you walk me home?" she asked, panic tinging her voice.

"I thought you already left," he said a little coldly.

"No, I was just out having a cigarette."

Dev slung his skates over his shoulder. "I hope," he said quietly, glancing back as Goody emerged from the shadows, "you're not getting yourself in over your head." She hated him for his self-righteousness. Was he just a bit jealous? Or did he know something she didn't? Well, she wasn't about to ask old square Dev anything about Goody, and give herself away.

The moon had all but disappeared, and the air was cold and dark. She turned around, but Goody was no longer in sight. She tromped along beside Dev as if in a trance, unable to think of anything except the memory of Goody's mouth on hers. Peachy passed in Lamar's car with Jasmine and Wanda and Tina. They slowed and Peachy rolled

down the window. "I want to know what you and Goody were doin'
all that time out in the parking lot." And there was a hoot of laughter
from the car—probably Wanda—and she wondered if they were all
making fun of her.

"There's nothing to tell!" she called back, but they had already
passed.

Next to Tish, Dev was just a silhouette—another pair of footsteps
crunching on the icy walk. He might have been anyone, or no one. Tish
didn't say a word, and at one point she glanced over and saw just how
rigid his jaw was. The rhythmic clanking of his skates was driving her
crazy. And then suddenly she realized with horror that she'd left her
own skates back at the rink, on the bleachers. Now the rink was closed,
and the skates were locked inside. Her mother would find this an odd
oversight, and want to ask for details about the evening to determine
how on earth Tish could have left her skates behind. Mentally she
began to concoct an excuse, but her heart wasn't in it. She was so tired
of the little lies. As they reached her block, she confessed, "Dev, I forgot
my skates." Her mittened fingertips burned from the cold. He wasn't
answering, but was concentrating on something ahead.

"There are people out in front of your house."

"What do you mean?"

He pointed. "Down there. Isn't that your yard?"

She couldn't tell. They began to walk faster, past the MacDonalds,
the Prices, the Marshes, and the Hobarts. All fast asleep in their beds.
Ahead, on the edge of the snowy yard, blinked the red light of a police
car. She made out the silhouette of her mother out in her coat and boots
talking earnestly to a small group of neighbors, and as Dev and she
drew closer, everyone turned to look.

"Is that her?" the cop asked, and she had the oddest feeling she was
being accused of something. Already she was preparing her defense: *I
stayed until the end of second session and then I left my skates and had to
walk back to try to find them, and no one was around, and so I waited and
waited . . .*

Mr. Espy called from the porch steps. "Tish!" His tone echoed a
mixture of relief and impatience. He came down through the snowy
yard, leaving a trail of dark footprints in his wake.

Several neighbors from across the street, including the young faculty couple renting out the Hardlove house for the semester, her parents, and the cop were standing around the charred remains of a wooden cross, still smoldering in the snow.

Mr. Espy's voice was a strange rattle in his throat. "Thank goodness you're all right," he said. Tish heard the deep inhale of his relief, the emotion he was trying not to give into in front of the others. He turned to the cop, who, for a moment, Tish thought she recognized as the one who had stopped Mrs. Stubbs's Fleetwood that afternoon last fall. But he wasn't. Mr. Espy was saying, "Thank you for coming out. Everything's okay now."

She caught the double take the cop gave her and Dev. It was *that look*. He asked Dev who he was, and Mr. Espy stepped in and said, "One of her school chums." The words sounded old-fashioned and false. She felt a roar in her ears, sensed the cop's disapproval watched him turn and head back to his squad car, probably thinking how his time had been wasted coming out for some white girl off with a black boy. What did her parents expect?

Now that she'd arrived, neighbors began quietly to disperse with soft murmurs of "good night." One of them said, "Glad everything's okay." How long had they been out there? Tish wondered.

Mrs. Espy gently snuffed out one of the embers with the toe of her boot. Worry lines spread over her face. "You're late," she said sharply. "We've been worried sick." It was obvious she was trying to keep her temper under control.

Mr. Espy looked at Dev. "I'm sorry you have to see this. You two kids sure you're okay?"

"We've been worried sick," Mrs. Espy repeated. Her tone was tight, edged with hysteria. "Where have you been? I called the rink over half an hour ago and tried to have you paged. They said no one fitting your description was there."

"There were a lot of people," Tish said quickly. "And you can't hear anything over the loudspeaker." She prayed Dev would stick by her, not give her away.

"But you *were* at the rink, were you not?" said Mrs. Espy. "The whole time? I was all set to drive over to try to find you."

Tish felt Dev tense beside her. She imagined the unimaginable—herself in the arms of Goody, caught in the headlights of her mother's Checker as it pulled into the snowy parking lot. Just imagining the close call was heart-stopping.

"Come on inside," said Mr. Espy, his brown hair tousled. "Let's have a little hot chocolate and get warmed up. Dev, I'll drive you home whenever you want. I don't want you walking alone."

Dev fell even more deeply into silence.

"I'll have the boys get rid of that thing in the morning," said Mrs. Espy. "What a contemptible thing to do!"

Inside the house, all the downstairs lights were on. Ford was still up and waiting for them in the living room.

"Well, this was quite an evening," said Mr. Espy, once they were all seated in the bright light of the kitchen. In that one word he seemed to annul the evidence in the yard, which now took on almost a dreamlike quality.

"I think probably the less we make of this, the better," he went on with forced heartiness. "Pranksters. Some crazy kids playing a thoughtless joke."

Tish interrupted. "Dad, they were *racists,* not pranksters." She turned to Dev in disbelief. "Tell him, Dev," she urged. "Tell him how it really is." But beside her Dev shrank as though trying to disappear. He didn't answer. Disappointed, Tish fell into sullen silence.

She half-suspected Lynn Springer's redneck brothers who hung with the Farmers. But, sadly, it could have been any number of white boys from school.

"I can fill in that burned place tomorrow," Mr. Espy was saying. "It will look as if nothing ever happened."

Tish felt two distinct kinds of anger: her fury toward the most likely culprits, the Farmers, for daring to trespass on their lives in this way, and a more diffused fury toward her parents for calmly writing off the incident as little more than a mean-spirited prank. She was struck by the fact that while a cross as tall as a man burned on her front lawn, she was kissing Goody in the parking lot.

The conversation turned to small talk as a way of easing tensions. Everyone was trying too hard. Dev, looking frail and mouselike beside

Tish, was politely holding up his end of the conversation with her parents. Tish knew full well if Dev hadn't been there they would be having a very different conversation.

Mrs. Espy plunked down mugs of steaming cocoa. There was an almost celebratory spirit, as if something unpleasant had been avoided and now life could return to normal. The conversation turned to the debate club Dev was involved in, and then Mrs. Espy asked after Dev's mother, who was exactly the sort of salt-of-the-earth brown woman whose rights Mrs. Espy would have imagined marching for in Birmingham.

While her father drove Dev home to Park Street, just a few blocks south, Tish slouched in the backseat. She watched for signs of life on the street, but it was too cold for anyone to be walking. When Dev got out, he thanked her father in his polite, soft-spoken way, his breath forming clouds in the night air. He gave one wave of good-bye to Tish. She wondered what he really thought. Mr. Espy waited for him to get his key in the door before pulling away from the curb. "Nice boy," he said in a thick voice. "Very nice boy." It was always this way with her parents, never saying what they really meant. And as if in response Angela and Dev flattened themselves into whiteness, like the way Dev shut down in silence in her parents' presence and quietly sipped his cocoa as if all was well. Her parents had missed the cop's look and the pointed question about Dev. Now her father's voice went on about how these were complicated times. Did Tish know the Websters down the street were divorcing? Mrs. Webster was going off to the Himalayas in search of spiritual rejuvenation, and Mr. Webster, now sporting a beard and sandals, had found nirvana right here in Brazil, with a college junior. Tish half smiled at her father's dry humor, but didn't answer, just nodded now and again and yielded to the rhythm of the moving car. "You were at the skating rink tonight, weren't you?" he asked as they pulled into their own driveway. He shut off the engine. They just sat there, the yard so dark Tish couldn't make out a thing.

"Yes," said Tish. Her father took the keys from the ignition and jingled them in the palm of his hand.

"I hope," he said, "that there isn't something you're not telling us."

* * *

The *Gazette* would report the cross in the "Police Blotter" as an act of juvenile vandalism by "unknown suspects." The Espys' was not the only cross that night, and the fact that crosses appeared on the lawns of two other white families, both known to be anti-war and vocal, seemed to take the sting out of things for Tish's parents.

The *Gazette* did not name the other two families, but Mr. Espy quickly discovered that one of the crosses wound up in the front yard of the Steinbergs, another university family—Jews—and the other fizzled on the lawn of the *Gazette* editor, whose editorial the week before had supported the students demonstrating against the ROTC recruiters outside the administration building.

Proudly Tish mentioned the cross-burning incident to a few of her friends, thinking it proved something. But no one seemed particularly interested. Angela sighed and said meaningfully, "I'm sure glad I wasn't there." Peachy said, "Dag, Tish, for real? That's a trip," and went back to clipping her fingernails. Wanda crossed her eyes. "Girl, why would someone burn a cross on *your* lawn?" *We need the revolution,* thought Tish. *We need it bad.*

XXIV

"Marcus asked about you. He wants to see you again."
The ensemble room seemed to shrink as Tish's chest constricted. She might as well have just swallowed a hot brick for all she

could speak. The sheet music slipped from her hand to the floor. She bent over and picked up loose sheets of black notes, trying to stack them as she went.

Peachy grinned ear to ear. "He wants to know if he can call you."

Wanda was laughing. "He probably thinks your daddy'll shoot his black ass through the phone."

Tish stiffened. "My parents aren't that way, Wanda, and you know it."

Wanda sighed and rolled her eyes. "Whi-ite pe-ople," she sing-songed.

Peachy said, "So it's cool if he calls?"

"You know it is, girl. Why do you even ask?"

Peachy shrugged.

Tish couldn't help herself. "Where'd you see him?"

"Jasmine's—"

"Jasmine's!" Tish said, and immediately she heard how overeager she sounded. She hadn't meant to give herself away like that, especially not in front of Wanda.

"Yeah, he hangs with Lamar sometimes. Anyway, me and Wanda were walkin' by and he was coming out the front and he called me over and started asking about you. He digs you, Tish." Peachy put her hand on Tish's arm and gave a squeeze. "Girl, I mean *really* digs you."

"Go ahead," said Wanda with a wave of her hand. "I ain't trippin'. You're my nigga, Tish. My little honorary nigga." And she threw back her head and laughed.

Peachy cut her off. "Goody'll be at Jasmine's eighteenth birthday party. And you're invited. She's rented out the Boot Center. You can go with me and Dev if you want."

Tish's mind clicked through the permutations of her parents' protests, and her own pleas. *The Boot Center.*

"He's so fine, girl," said Peachy dreamily. She poked Tish in the side. "You landed you one fine-ass brother."

"I didn't land him yet," said Tish, balking at the terminology, her face growing hot.

On the riser, Tina scooted over to make room. They were running through "Steal Away." Tish picked up her sheet music and joined in, but she was too distracted to focus. When she sang, her voice faltered, and she couldn't find her place on the page.

It was her father who gave her permission to go to Jasmine's party, even extending her curfew to midnight. He still managed on occasion to take Tish's side in things. Tish had overheard him trying to wheedle her mother into agreeing. "Martha, what's the harm? She's almost sixteen. Let her go." For the moment he was her ally in those uncertain swings between friend and foe. Then she remembered he was gearing up for a conference in London, and mostly didn't want the house in upheaval for the two weeks before he left.

She could have predicted her mother's counterargument, the old refrain carbon copied from the last discussion of its kind: *I don't even know this Jasmine. Is Angela going? Well, why not? Won't her mother allow her to go to the rec center downtown? You know what that place is like. It's always being mentioned in the paper for one trouble or another. . . . I don't think any white kids even go there.* In the days preceding the party, Mrs. Espy observed Tish with stony silence, pointing out extra things for her to do, a kind of penance: closets in need of cleaning, basement cupboards that required sweeping out. At one point she came right out and asked, "Will you be the only white person at this party?"

"I don't know, probably," said Tish, with as much rock-hardness as she could muster. "Why do you always ask me that? You wouldn't ask Angela if she was going to be the only black person in a place."

"It's not the same," said her mother. "I just think it must be hard putting yourself in situations where you're the odd one out." In the silence that followed, Tish looked up into her mother's face. She read a kind of pity that she wanted no part of. Then her face shut down altogether, and Tish realized how pointless it was anymore to try reaching across the divide.

*　　*　　*

The night of the party a freezing rain began, hovering on the edge of sleet. Mrs. Espy insisting on driving Tish to the party, but Tish knew this would be a bad idea. She pictured the Boot Center through her mother's eyes and knew that would never work. The parking lot would be full of black teenagers, kids that would appear to her mother in their blackness as rough and even frightening. Inside there would be wall-to-wall partygoers, the lights dimmed so low you could barely make out your hand in front of you, people slow dancing so close they appeared to be fused. She was desperate to get over to Peachy's to try on makeup and maybe even hike up her skirt a little without her mother's hawk eyes assessing her every move.

"Then how will you get home?" Mrs. Espy pressed.

"Peachy," Tish said, without thinking.

"Are you sure? I don't want you driving with strangers." Tish knew Peachy wouldn't appreciate the lie, but she let it go.

"I don't understand why these parties start and end so late. When I was a girl . . ."

Tish resisted saying, "When were you ever a girl?" Imagining her mother, showing the first signs of gray in her hair, as a girl was an impossibility. Adrenaline coursed through her body. She was having a nic fit and if she didn't get outside with her cigarettes soon, she thought her head would explode.

By the time her mother dropped her off at Peachy's she was almost mute under the strain of reproach: *Your skirt's too short. Please go change. I don't want you wearing eyeliner. It makes you look cheap. Cheap.* Tish winced at the quaintness of the word. *You mean like a ho,* she countered recklessly under breath.

Rain had begun to fall heavily as she came up the Stubbses' front stairs. Inside, Mr. and Mrs. Stubbs sat together on the sofa watching television. Tish slipped past with a quick hello. There was no indication Peachy was even close to being ready ("Slow down, you're on CP Time now, girl"). Anxiety gnawing at her, Tish plunked down on the un-made bed and chewed her fingernails and read about the most eligible bachelor in *Jet,* while the minutes ticked away. Miles Davis's *Sketches of Spain* revolved on the turntable. Something about the sadness in the horn and the percussion of rain on the roof brought Tish close to tears.

"I've got something for you," Peachy said. She pulled three dashikis from the closet. "You can wear this. Wanda gets the red, black, and green one. We'll be matching." Tish's dashiki was a loose pattern in blue, white, and black, with a little red splashed in. "This is boss," she said, touched.

"It's easy to make," said Peachy breezily. "If you can sew a neck hole, you can make a dashiki."

Tish removed her blouse and slipped the dashiki over her head. *Tough, bad, outa sight. Go 'head on, girl, witch yo' bad self.* Encouraged, she tried on a pair of navy fishnets Peachy offered and let Peachy have her red ones. Excitement brewed in her pores. In the mirror she couldn't help imagining how Goody would perceive her, red hair spiraling over her head, her high cheekbones lightly rouged with Peachy's mocha rose blush-on. Next to Peachy, she almost believed they could be related—two girls, sisters in spirit, in matching outfits, off to a party together, fed on the final strains of Miles Davis.

They drove house to house to pick up the others. The delays only made Tish more frantic. "Relax, girl," said Peachy. "What you all uptight about?"

Next to squeeze into the car was Tina in a white pantsuit and big red earrings, then Wanda in her dashiki, and as if that weren't enough stops, Jasmine's running partner Chick, an evil-looking girl about whom Mrs. Stubbs had once remarked "a whole lotta yellow wasted," and finally, at last, Dev, shirt pressed, loafers polished, looking square as ever, but fine, too, and as Wanda pronounced, "good enough to eat."

It was now ten o'clock. No time to mourn the two precious, wasted hours waiting for everyone to get ready. Jammed in the Fleetwood, she thought she'd grow faint from the mix of perfumes, the swell of body heat, and the anticipation of seeing Goody again. Wanda cracked on Tish's dashiki, and then reached back and thumped Tish good-naturedly on the arm. She was clearly in a good mood. "I hope Grover's fine black college ass is there. Don't any of you fast heifers get any ideas either, 'specially you, Miss Chick."

From the front seat she proceeded to light up a joint and get high right there in Peachy's mother's car. Tish expected Peachy to object, but she didn't, just rolled down the window to let in a little fresh air, and concentrated on driving. The sharp, acrid smell filled the car. Wanda passed the joint back to Tina, who with a quick toke, passed it on to Chick. By the time it got to Tish, she thought her nerves were about to snap, but she grasped the joint as if she knew what she was doing and put it to her lips. She wasn't prepared for the bitter, tarry taste. She caught herself before she choked, suppressing a cough deep in her throat. "Take it all the way in," Wanda directed from the front seat, her eyes rimmed in kohl. "Don't waste my stash." Tish took another tentative drag, and passed the joint back up to Peachy. To her relief, she felt nothing more than a brief sensation of light-headedness, as if she'd breathed too quickly. Passing headlights washed over them, causing them to light up briefly in flashes, then settle back into darkness. On the radio Stevie Wonder sang "Ma Cherie Amour," and everyone joined in. Next to Tish, Chick patted her fro into shape. Tish felt her own hair, thickening into ringlets in the swamp of body heat and cologne and Afrosheen. When they pulled up to the Boot Center, she felt as if they had all melted into one body, unfolding from the car to join scores of afroed silhouettes dashing through the rain to get inside.

Beyond the heart-bending wail of Junior Walker's sax blaring from the window speakers, red, black, and green crepe-paper streamers hung from the ceiling. Vanilla incense thickened the air. Coming up the steps behind Peachy and Dev, Tish had a bad case of the jitters, but she tried to keep her cool, setting her jaw into the square shape of confidence. A dark-skinned girl with straightened hair yanked back in a bun and keen features sat smoking on one of the steps. She was a senior, someone Tish vaguely recognized. "Wasshappenin', sisters?" she said to everyone, pointedly omitting Tish, her eye skipping over the vacancy and back to Peachy. In that moment Tish felt herself shrink away from her own skin.

At the top of the stairs, they were greeted by Cintrilla Moore's older brother, Reggie. Two other young men in their early twenties, acted as door guards, checking invitations and asking people to put out their cigarettes. A sign on the wall announced PRIVATE PARTY. There had been rumors of a fight, a bit of leftover trouble with some dudes from Lorain who had a bone to pick with somebody's cousin who had disrespected somebody else's old lady and started a whole lotta shit. "And how are you foxy mamas doin' tonight?" Reggie smiled, the gold cap on his front tooth gleaming. His flirtations were smooth and seamless, his stance charmingly self-mocking. For a short time Tish and Peachy had both had wild crushes on Reggie Moore. Angela called him a "street nigger," made fun of his gold tooth, and his processed hair, but Tish knew better. Reggie had more sex appeal than ten Michael Browns put together.

"Hello there, beautiful," he said, taking them in, marking their individuality with a smile that insinuated each was special. "Jasmine and Lamar ain't here yet, but there's plenty of food and drinks inside. Help yourselves. Good to see all of you."

Inside, strobe lights pulsed. Anyone wearing white, like Tina, was lit up and freeze-framed for an instant right on the beat.

Out on the dance floor Tommy Tidwell and his nasty white trash girlfriend Roberta Micks did the hustle. It was rumored around school she had actually kissed Melvin Goins's penis. The very thought baffled Tish, trying hard to imagine what would possess someone. As the story circulated, girls clucked their tongues and shook their heads. How was such a thing possible, and why would any girl want to touch her lips to that part of a boy? *She is sick,* Wanda had said. *These brothers will go with a skanky white girl over a black one just 'cause of what a white girl'll do. Ain't no sister in her right mind gonna put her lips on somebody's old nasty jones.* But then to Roberta's face she smiled and acted all chummy, so it was hard for Tish to know what Wanda really thought about anything. Now Roberta was centerfloor, filling out a short pleather miniskirt and see-through blouse, and dancing confidently with Tommy. Everyone agreed she could dance "black," from years of growing up on Roosevelt Court and hanging around the Tidwells. Her brown greasy hair was yanked up tight on top of her head in a bun. Two oily curls of hair spiraled down on either side of her acne-red face, pinned at the top with a metal clip. It was a bad imitation of a black girl's pressed-hair style. Tish turned her head and tried to pretend she hadn't seen Roberta. The girl embarrassed her, made her feel she would be automatically compared with her, and a connection made, as if there weren't an infinite chasm stretching out to separate them.

Squeezed among all those bodies, the humidity rising, Tish began to panic that she'd gone to all this trouble for Goody and maybe he wouldn't show. All she had to go on, after all, was Peachy's word.

The room was so crowded it was impossible to move without touching someone else. Along one wall, a table was spread with paper cups and punch, bowls of chips and pretzels, paper plates, and several Crock-Pots full of gumbo, neat yellow squares of corn bread stacked on the side. On the wall, black-light posters hung: stylized silhouettes of men and women with exaggerated afros, their naked torsos embracing over captions like "Afro Love" and "Black Ecstasy" that throbbed in rhythm to the music.

Right away, Peachy was asked to dance, and then Tina, and then Wanda, leaving Tish hugging the wall. She staked out a place with Dev over in a corner. He was trying to look indifferent, his eyes focused just above the bobbing heads on the dance floor, as if he had better things to think of. Poor Dev, Tish thought, he was so square. Maybe it was true what everyone said about him, but she couldn't imagine that he could actually like boys instead of girls. What did that even mean? How could a boy really like a boy? She couldn't imagine. She edged closer, letting her shoulder nudge his, trying to take comfort in his familiarity. He looked over and smiled and asked if she wanted to dance. With relief she let him lead her out on the floor. It was a slow dance, Nancy Wilson's "You Better Face It, Girl," which made Tish want to weep every time she heard it. She was grateful to Dev for saving them both. He was very careful, almost wooden, when he took her in his arms, and she didn't mind at all his light, careful touch. He deliberately kept the lower half of his body at a respectful distance. She sang along, uninhibited. Someone thumped against her. An accident? She turned her head slowly and saw a girl. It was the smoking girl from the porch, such a pretty dark girl with features now pressed into meanness. She was furious. She mouthed something, but Tish turned away, pretending not to have noticed. Instead, she and Dev dutifully rocked back and forth in the sea of dancers. When she looked again, the girl had turned her back and was elbowing her way across the room. Maybe it hadn't been intentional after all. She closed her eyes, getting lost in the music. The song ended and they separated with mutual relief.

There was a flurry on the stairs, and a commotion in the doorway. Someone screamed. Someone else yelled something. For a moment Tish thought a fight was starting. There were always fights at the Boot Center, mostly when out-of-town people showed up. But it was only Jasmine and Lamar arriving. Everyone started cheering and clapping as they pushed through the crepe paper streamers in the doorway. Jasmine was wearing a red velvet minidress and white stockings and black heels, her beautiful face framed by the globe of hair. Lamar was extra fine in a crisply ironed shirt, tie, and gold leather jacket. They squeezed through the crowd, Lamar grasping hands and soul shaking his way along. When Jasmine spotted Tish, she grinned and pantomimed the peace sign, and Tish mouthed "Happy Birthday." Girlfriends like Cintrilla and Maxine and Benita had crowded around, and Tish could see Jasmine was showing them something in her hand, but she couldn't see what. The Delfonics' "Ready or Not" began to play. What if Goody wasn't coming? She didn't dare ask about him, didn't want to appear overly eager, but she was running out of time.

Over by the refreshments Lamar grabbed Jasmine proprietarily and began kissing her neck, murmuring in her ear. She pushed him away, rolling her eyes and protesting, "Stop!" in that mock playful way she did when she didn't mean stop at all. The record ended, and then the Isley Brothers started up: "It's your thang . . ." Tish stood woodenly. Jasmine was popping her fingers and laughing. Belonging was effortless, acceptance natural. Without a word, she pulled on Lamar and they disappeared into the crowd.

Peachy appeared briefly at Tish's side, beads of sweat on her face. "Goody's here. He just walked in." Tish felt herself go strange in her own body. Desire and panic collided. She was all wrong, she knew it. She should never have worn the dashiki. What would he think? "He's right there. Here he comes, girl," and Peachy was back out on the dance floor. No escape. Stranded, Tish panicked. Where was Dev?

Before she knew it Goody had sidled up to her in his leather coat. So much taller than she'd remembered, so grown. In his presence she was so stricken she pretended not to see him.

"Hey," he said gently, face softening. He touched her arm. "How you doin'?" but Tish didn't think she'd heard, and asked "What?" and then he looked a little embarrassed and leaned forward and repeated his question right into her ear. There was his warm breath entering her as if he had just blown life into her. But she was also embarrassed, now understanding what he'd said hadn't been anything worth repeating, and she said aloofly, "I'm fine," and the conversation stalled again. How did other girls do it? How did they know what to say after hello? He asked how long she'd been there, she said not long (not wanting him to think she'd been waiting), and he asked if she'd gotten his message, and she folded her arms across her chest and copped a little attitude, and said what message, and he said he'd left a message with her father. When? Just a little bit ago. Tish thought she would die. Did Goody mention the party? No, he just asked if she was home, and her father had been very nice (Goody emphasized this).

"Would you like something to drink?" he asked.

Tish nodded anxiously.

"I'll be right back." Cologne fell off him in waves as he eased away through the crowd. It was a scent that made her dizzy and stirred her longing.

Along the way, people were greeting him. A girl's voice screamed out, "Hey, Goody!" and Tish felt herself shrink. She focused on trying to find the feeling in her legs. The dashiki felt voluminous and awkward, and she wished she'd worn something else. Where *was* Dev when she needed him? She'd forgotten how close to being a man Goody was, how fine he looked, how deep his voice was, how terrified the whole thing made her.

Why had she even bothered to come? Someone jostled her. Two girls were forcing their way to the other side of the room. Someone was yelling. She turned around to see two older boys pushing each other. One was cursing. She didn't recognize either one. A brown-skinned girl with her hair in a twist smiled at Tish and shrugged, as if to suggest she too thought the floor too crowded.

And then like magic there was Dev! Tish immediately latched on to him. Goody was returning with drinks, and Dev looked over at Tish and said, "So, he came, huh?" And Tish nodded and said yes. Why did she get the impression from his frown that Dev didn't approve?

The boy in an apple hat acting as deejay stood up on a chair next to the record player and yelled out something to the crowd about gettin' down in a romantic mood. A moment later came the hesitant opening of the seven-minute Dells' "Stay in My Corner." Goody handed Tish a cup of punch. Mortified by Dev's scrutiny and the suggestive start of the Dells' song, she drank the whole cup in one long swallow. What she hadn't realized was that it was spiked. Hard alcohol stung her throat. Then came almost the instant relief of smoothing out. She wished Goody had brought her another.

Goody seemed amused. He leaned around and tapped Dev on the shoulder. "What's happenin', brother?" Dev nodded back and moved over an inch or so to give Goody room. In that gesture he'd signaled Tish wasn't really with him. It's what Goody had been asking, and now there was nothing else for him to do but take the empty paper cup from Tish's hand and draw her close to him onto the dance floor. She could smell the animal leather of his coat, the sweet scent of soap, and the unbearable heartache of Old Spice cologne. She wanted the floor to open up and swallow them both, to find herself held in Goody's arms for the long descent to the final drop below. She shut her eyes tightly, and yielded to the solidity of his body. Goody pulled her closer, in a determined move, and she stumbled against his feet, almost losing her balance. How clumsy. If only she could take back the moment and start all over! In agony, she struggled to get herself right, but not before she caught Dev laughing silently into the palm of his hand.

Then came the pressure of Goody's firm arms around her, and his mouth against her ear. In one smooth gesture, he'd gotten her back into place, was guiding her against him. "He your old man?" he asked softly. His breath was warm and sweet.

Tish shook her head furiously. Too furiously. Goody pulled her tighter and said, "I've been wanting to see you again," which only made her grow stiffer. She'd never really learned to slow dance, had always faked it with boys like Dev, and now her feet betrayed her. "Follow me," he urged softly. "Follow me. Stay with the beat." Then she felt oh-so-white, like a white girl out of place, who couldn't even keep the beat, who was making a fool of herself. In spite of her clumsiness, Goody began to sing earnestly into her ear in a precise, sweet falsetto. "If you stay . . . stay, baby . . . stay in my corner . . . ooooh . . ." It wasn't exactly unpleasant, just uncomfortable to feel so held. He slowed their movement way down, so that Tish felt her breath stopping altogether. And then he came to a halt, and pressed her close against a hard place on his thigh. Tish felt herself yielding, her whole body coming apart from the inside out. He pulled her even closer. Instinctively she resisted his attempt to grind, yanking herself away. "Quit," she said. He knew exactly what she meant, and immediately let his face soften into an apology. "Sorry, I got carried away. How's this? Let's try again," and he pulled her ever so gently toward him again, so that now her face barely rested against the leather coat, and there was space between their bodies. She had wanted it, hadn't she, wanted to be pulled close like that, but she also had a point to make. "I'm sorry," he said. "It's just that I really dig you, Tish. I've been thinking about you since the night we met. I can't get you out of my head."

The crowd swelled as more people arrived, hurrying inside to get away from the gusts of cold rain. Tish caught sight of the back side of Peachy in her miniskirt and dashiki being towed across the floor in the arms of Vic Wooten, who was dabbing his glistening forehead with a handkerchief. Wanda floated by in a slow drag with Grover. Tish closed her eyes and laid her head against Goody's chest. She suddenly felt very heavy and sleepy.

He murmured encouragingly, "Mmmm, you can keep a beat." What he meant was *for a white girl*. She let the comment pass. When the record ended, Goody held her a few moments beyond the last sigh of the record, as if unable to let her go. "The Look of Love" began. He took her against him again. After, they untangled themselves as if discovering again they were two separate people. She allowed Goody one last lingering caress on the small of her back, so sweet she thought she could never want anything so much again. Even after his hand was gone, the memory of the gentle pressure remained, guiding her and keeping her upright. The spiked punch had gone to her head.

It was impossible to try to carry on a conversation over the din of the next song. Tish mouthed that she needed a cigarette and excused herself. On the way to the back door, she grabbed a napkin and mopped her face. Someone thrust another cup of punch at her. Over in the corner by the record player, she caught a glimpse of Jasmine and Lamar making out shamelessly. From time to time their two silhouettes, topped by cottony halos of hair, seemed to merge into one. Someone on the dance floor shouted, "Y'all need to take that stuff on home!" and everyone laughed.

The back exit led to the fire escape. The rain had turned to heavy mist. Tish was still carrying the second paper cup of spiked punch. The cold air revived her. Dampness settled on her skin and her hair expanded in the wet. The rain had slowed to a drizzle, and the steps and walkway below steamed and glistened. Several senior girls from school stood talking at the edge of the fire escape. Reggie was leaning against the rail and smoking a joint. Cautiously, Tish joined them all under a couple tattered paper lanterns. "Hey, Tish," said Chick, accepting the joint from Reggie. Her maxi coat was unbuttoned and her eyelids had the same unbuttoned look. The air was full of promise. Spring would be along soon.

Chick passed the joint on. When it got to Tish, she declined, too nervous to smoke in front of the others. She was vaguely aware that Goody had followed her out, though he was trying to make it look as if their running into each other again was an accident. First he kissed Chick on the cheek, then bent over another girl named Ruby Mason. "Hey, Goody," they cooed, and in the dim lantern light the softness of his face almost broke Tish's heart. "Where you been keepin' yourself, brotha? You are lookin' good, Goody," teased Chick. She sniffed the air around him. "And you smell good too." She put her arm around his waist. "Ain't this one fine-smelling man?" She laughed. "Damn, baby."

The others began to laugh. Goody shoved his hands into the pockets of his coat. It occurred to Tish he was shy, that the attention embarrassed him. His awkwardness with women suggested he didn't have much experience. So they had that in common. He looked up at the sky as if he were searching for something, but he didn't say anything. Ruby started teasing him too, and he flushed and toed the ground like a young kid. Everyone laughed. Tish had missed the joke, but smiled anyway to show she was a good sport. She downed the second cup of punch.

"Who do you know here?" Ruby Mason asked her in a friendly, curious way. Jasmine and Lamar, Tish told her. It made an impression.

"I seen you around a lot with that little light-skinned girl, what's her name, Angela, the one go with Michael. She here?" Tish shook her head. She started to say where Angela was, but Ruby got distracted, and Tish found her words drifting pointlessly off into thin air. She never had it quite right; she knew she came across as too eager, too nervous, and it made people want to flee from her. But then she felt Goody coming up close behind her and she heard him say, "I thought maybe you had run off." And she smiled and said, "No, I just needed a square. You got one?"

He did, and he shook one out of his pack and then lit it for her from his own mouth in the slow, seductive gesture that almost made her lose her mind. He put it directly from his mouth into hers, and she imagined the sweetness of his lips.

Below, a car screeched to the curb. An older man Tish faintly recognized jumped out, the engine still running. He had on a black leather jacket and beret. He looked up at them all standing on the porch. "Power to the people," he said, raising his fist by way of greeting. He nodded knowingly at Reggie and Goody.

"Ooops, that's me," said Chick. "Later, everyone." She blew a kiss to the group and took one more hit off Reggie's joint before hurrying down the stairs. The man came around to the door for her. Chick twitched her behind and lifted the hem of her maxi coat as she folded herself into the passenger seat. The man raised his fist to the group on the fire escape. "Peace," he said and got in.

As they drove off, there were comments about "Chick's married man," and "It's a damn shame," and then speculation. Disapproval and envy intertwined.

She's so fast. Why don't y'all let her alone—she's cool. It ain't right to go with another woman's man.

Their words washed over Tish. She tried to absorb their experience through her pores. She was dying to ask who the man was, but she didn't want to look foolish. ". . . can't stand these brothers with white women. . . ." Tish snapped back to attention. It was Cintrilla talking. "I'm for real. Every time you turn around there's some brother with a white woman on his arm, and they don't even need to be pretty, you know what I'm sayin'?"

Ruby Mason and the others hmmm-mmmmm'ed their approval.

Reggie shook his head. "Y'all sisters are too damn cold. Y'all need to lighten up on the brothers. Sure, some of them have messed-up minds, but you got to cut them some slack. They know which side they bread is buttered on. I for one love black women. Every single one of them. Period." There was a murmur of laughter.

Tish was glad to see Goody had started joking with Ruby, and when he put his arm around Cintrilla she knew he was demonstrating where he stood. She warmed herself in the camaraderie.

Reggie leaned over, coughing, and offered Tish some of his joint. This time Tish accepted. "Check out Miss L'il Bit here," said Reggie with one of his irresistible grins, but nobody did. "How old are you anyway, girl?" It was a question Tish didn't want to answer, but she pushed forward through the months and said, "Sixteen." She passed the joint on to Goody.

He hesitated, then took a quick hit, and handed the roach back to Reggie, who was already digging a clip from his pocket. It was then that Goody moved over beside Tish, took off his coat and laid it carefully across the railing. "You can lean back," he said. "It will be more comfortable." No one seemed to object. They stood there silently among the others as if words weren't necessary. They were there together without really being together, laughing and talking. Goody eased his arm up against Tish's, and planted it firmly there. Tish thought how there was no language for this, that all the scribblings she'd made in her notebook about love paled against the violent longings erupting in her now, the unexpected charge of flesh against flesh.

Below, cars sloshed by in the rain-slick street, voices echoed, and each time the exit door opened, there was the reassuring beat of James Brown's "Mother Popcorn." Above, the moon appeared now and again.

Somewhere in the rainy night Angela was going just that much further with Michael, and Peachy was sweating off her eye shadow in the middle of the Boot Center with Tony Purify, and Tish's mother was pinning up her hair in the silence of her bedroom and wondering how she'd failed her daughter, and Tish's father was preparing his speech for the London conference, absorbed in his work, his daughter momentarily forgotten.

As for Tish, she heard Goody asking if she wanted to take a ride over to the lake with him and Reggie and Ruby.

"We like to go and watch the lights on the water," he said. Tish glanced down at her wristwatch. It was quarter to eleven.

"I can't. I have to be home in an hour," she said softly.

"You sure you can't stay out a little later? I'd really like for you to come." Here was urgency and opportunity together. She felt as if she'd been torn in two.

"I can't," she said. "My parents are—*strict.*"

The word tumbled out with all its possible implications. "Strict" from a white girl could mean many things. She didn't want him to misunderstand.

"You comin', bro?" Reggie interrupted. "We gonna stop by my crib for a minute and then make this little run." The whites of his eyes were red from weed. He seemed tougher, wiser, leaner than Goody. To Tish he said, "You're invited too, sugar." He added, pointing to Goody, "This here's a good man, a righteous brother. You ain't got to worry about him. I've known him since he was this high," and he held out the flat of his palm.

"Naw," said Goody. "I'm staying here. Y'all go on."

"You should go if you want," Tish urged. "I have to leave soon."

He shook his head. "I'll stay. I don't want to go without you," he said in a voice that turned her insides to butter.

A half dozen others were now congregating on the fire escape, mopping their foreheads and complaining about all the "body heat" being generated. *You get a bunch of niggas together* . . . Laughter.

Someone poured something from a flask into a paper cup. Then the flask was making its rounds. "Goody, you ain't drinking tonight?" asked a boy in a Lorain High School letter jacket.

He waved his hand to indicate he wasn't.

"Suit yourself," and the flask went by.

Goody drew Tish gently to the side.

"So your father's a professor, huh?" He paused. "Must mean you're pretty smart."

"I'm not a good student," Tish admitted. "I don't really care about grades."

"You don't want to go to college?"

"I don't know, sometimes I just think, what's the point? If you want to change the world, you don't do it by reading a book."

It was easy talking like this in the dim light, the voices of the others providing a reassuring backdrop. "You think you'll go off to college?" Tish asked, unable to imagine that he wouldn't.

He stirred his pockets with his fists. "Pops wanted me to go real bad. He died a couple years ago. Maybe next year I'll apply. I need to keep working for a while. You know, figure out what I want to do."

Tish's imagination took flight, her own uncertain future merging with his.

"You're sweet," he said, "and you're a thinker. I like that."

Encouraged, she started to tell him more, but a few sentences in and his attention was suddenly diverted. The keen-featured black girl who'd poked Tish in the back earlier waltzed up on the other side, and was stringing her arm playfully through his. She was prettier than Tish had realized, dark brown with slanted eyes. Jealousy only sharpened her beauty. She pulled him against her and said something Tish didn't hear.

"Go on, get off me, girl," he joked, trying to act casual.

"Go on, yourself." She peered over at Tish, and then back up at him. "What you doin' out here, Goody, talkin' to yourself?"

"Don't act crazy, Sonya." He was laughing nervously in a forced way that made Tish wonder if she should go back inside and leave him.

"Don't try to embarrass me, Goody," Sonya loud-talked to attract everyone's attention. "I asked you a question." She had turned her back deliberately to Tish.

Goody said, "Sonya, this is Tish."

Sonya ignored him. "I want you to come dance with me. You ain't paid me a bit of attention all night."

Goody seemed uncomfortable.

Sonya was insistent. "I'm serious. I ain't playin' with you, Goody."

He let out a sigh, and took his hands from his pockets. "Okay, but quit pulling on me, girl." He turned to Tish. "Excuse me, but I promised Sonya one dance. Do you mind?"

"You didn't promise me shit," snapped Sonya. "Don't make it like you *have* to dance with me. And you don't need her permission either." She was mad, teasing, and wicked, all at once. Tish swallowed and turned her head, trying to look as if she didn't care one whit. Didn't she have other things to do? Where was Dev when she needed him.

"I'll be right back," said Goody, and patted the leather coat where he'd laid it over the railing. It was a promise that he would return. She stood there uncertainly, stomach constricting. Goody's coat without Goody suddenly felt alien. Above, the clouds began sliding across the moon. Soon all she could see was a sliver, the shape of a Christmas ornament her father put on the tree every year with great pride. "We bought this the year we were in France when you were a year old," he liked to say. The drizzle began again.

One of the girls standing under the porch awning turned to Tish and remarked, "You're gonna get wet."

It was true. She didn't even know when to come in out of the rain. Their boisterous, high-spirited talk closed off into a tight circle that had nothing to do with her, and she wondered if she should join them or just stand there looking like a fool waiting for Goody to return. The rain picked up. The others began moving inside.

What she would have done next she didn't know if Jasmine hadn't popped her head out the door. She was pleasantly high and there was a rosy flush to her skin.

"Hey, y'all," she said to the group passing through the door. "Lamar out here?"

She looked at Tish. "What are you doing out here in the rain by yourself, girl?"

"Just getting some air," said Tish.

"Goody's here. You see him yet?"

Tish nodded. "He's inside dancing. With Sonya."

Jasmine rolled her eyes. "Oh, that," she said. She stepped out closer to Tish, but stayed under the awning. "That's old business."

She lit a cigarette. "Here, want some?" Tish joined her. They shared. "Goody digs you," Jasmine said, looking up at the sky. "He's cool. A little mixed up sometimes, but cool. He needs to get his ass in college and get with the program."

Tish checked. "He doesn't go with anyone now?"

"Naw," said Jasmine. "He messed with Sonya last year, but she's crazy—too possessive, and Goody ain't into all that. Over the summer I saw him around with Susie Purify, you know, Tony's cousin, but Susie's with Reggie's brother now." She handed Tish the cigarette. "You can have the rest."

Tish was dying to ask for more information, but didn't. The past was the past. She couldn't expect a boy like Goody not to have had girlfriends.

She reached out and touched Jasmine's arm. "Happy Birthday."

Jasmine grinned. "It is a happy birthday. Lamar and I are back together—for good this time. All that nonsense he had going on a few weeks back is over and done with. Check out the opal ring he gave me." She thrust her left hand out to reveal a flash of milky white on her finger. "Isn't it beautiful?"

Tish nodded.

"He's changed," she said. "I think he's finally straightened himself out. All it takes is a good woman. I mean, if you tend to business, it pays off."

Tonight, Jasmine could afford to be generous.

"By the way," she said. "Would you write a poem for Lamar and me?"

Tish was surprised. "A poem? What kind of poem?"

"You know, a love poem."

"I don't know," said Tish. "You can't really write a love poem for someone else."

"Okay," said Jasmine, leaning closer. "I'll tell you what. You write a poem for Goody, then let me have it, and I'll give it to Lamar and say it's about us."

Tish smiled. "That's plagiarism," she said.

Jasmine laughed. "Girl, just do it. You can write so good."

"I'm not that good," said Tish.

"Yes, you are," Jasmine insisted. "If I could write like you . . ."

Tish felt embarrassed. "Maybe you can," she said. "If you write a poem, I'll look at it for you."

Jasmine seemed to have lost interest. "Oooh, this rain is about to freeze me to death. I'll catch you later, gotta find Lamar. You want me to tell Goody to get his ass back out here?"

"No," Tish said, terrified. She glanced down at her watch. It was after eleven-thirty. "I really gotta go. You know—my parents . . ."

"Later for you, Cinderella," Jasmine teased. "I want that poem, you hear?" She breezed off, full of happiness.

Several more songs played, and Goody still hadn't returned. Tish spotted Angela's friend Edna Sims and they waved to each other through the open door, but Edna was talking to someone and Tish didn't want to interfere. The rain grew steadier. Tish felt slightly sick. She wasn't sure what to do, but she knew if she waited any longer she would not only be a fool, but a wet one. She tried not to imagine what was keeping Goody, but she knew she didn't dare go back inside. She moved away from the coat on the railing and stood uncertainly at the top of the fire escape looking down into the empty street below. She was debating whether to leave the coat, thinking if she went inside to hand it to him, he'd misunderstand and think she'd used it as an excuse to come looking for him. And then she'd have to suffer the indignity of Sonya's glares. She turned to leave, but paused, held hostage by the coat which seemed to be all that was keeping Goody's place, beside her, like a bookmark.

Two figures below in the misty street stepped out of the shadows from the side of a neighboring building. For a moment Tish thought she was seeing Goody and Sonya, but it was just her mind playing tricks. She stepped back from sight and watched. Two strangers arguing, maybe. She heard a woman's voice. Then the two figures came together in a kind of embrace, but no—not exactly—the woman had pulled herself back and was now gesticulating with her hands. Tish strained to see. No mistake—it was Lamar. And the woman with him—it wasn't Jasmine. Tish made out the dyed-blond hair and thick legs of a senior named Cindy Pavelka, a popular cheerleader who ran the cash register at Money's Drugstore on weekends. Lamar was cajoling. The girl distinctly said, "Then when?" At Jasmine's party! What nerve! The girl's voice drifted up, fragments of indistinguishable words. Were there tears? She wasn't sure. Lamar was backing away and the girl kept coming toward him. Now they had stepped under the streetlight. Cindy was clinging to Lamar's arm, but Lamar wasn't trying to pull away anymore. For a moment they clung there together, then Lamar said something that sounded like "good night," and Cindy moved off slowly down the street to a car parked at the curb. Someone inside the car snapped on headlights, the engine started, and Cindy got in without glancing backward. Tish strained to see who was driving, but all she could make out was another woman, probably one of Cindy's girlfriends. Lamar stood there a moment in the street as if undecided, then glanced up at the darkened windows of the Boot Center. From his posture, Tish could read his uncertainty. What a dog, she thought. The Bar-Kay's "Soul Finger" blasted from the open door.

She took a deep breath and launched herself down the fire escape into the rainy night. She turned right to avoid Lamar. But he had changed directions and rounded the corner of the building just as she did.

"Say, baby," he said. They were both surprised. "How you doin'?"

"I'm fine." She pushed past.

"You leaving already?" He was grinning at her with his sharp self, and she could smell the delicate lace of wine on his breath.

He looked her up and down in that slow, exaggerated way he had, as if his eyes were caressing her flesh. "Where're you going in such a hurry, sweetheart?"

"Home," she said. "I'm late."

He ran a knuckle under his nose. "I could give you a ride," he said. "My car's just over there."

"No thanks," she said.

"What, you too good to ride with me? I don't bite, you know that. Jasmine would want me to watch out for her little friend, right?"

"No," Tish said. "I just don't want to put you out."

"Baby, that's not puttin' me out."

He had hold of her arm again, and this time his grip was firm. She could feel his breath on her cheek, smell his cologne. His eyes went soft in their sockets.

She wanted no mix-ups or misunderstandings. "You need to stay here," she said. "It's Jasmine's birthday."

"You haven't danced with me yet. We need to do something about that."

"Lamar," she said firmly. "You need to take your ass upstairs to your girlfriend."

He smiled and let go. "You know, Tish, every time I see you I think to myself what a fine little thing you are. . . ."

He trained his eyes directly into hers. For a moment she saw what Jasmine must see, the look that corkscrewed down inside and pulled up need from the most private place in yourself. Tish broke the gaze.

"I've gotta go."

He glanced behind him. "Come on," he wheedled almost tenderly. "My car's just over there. . . ."

"Good-bye, Lamar."

"You know." He grinned. *"You're so fine. Please be mine."* The familiar words echoed in her head. A flash of anger tore through her.

"What? What did you just say?" she demanded.

"Don't think I didn't notice you staring at me all the time in study hall." He gestured with his thumb toward the upstairs. "But you know things ain't been right between her and me for a long time, but *you* . . ."

"Is that why you gave her a ring tonight?" snapped Tish.

He was only momentarily taken aback. "Hey, you don't think I'm gonna make her feel bad on her birthday."

"That's cold," said Tish, "really cold. I gotta go." She paused. "By the way, Goody left his leather coat up on the railing. Would you give it to him, please?" She turned with as much attitude as she could muster and took off into the night. She didn't dare look back because she had the feeling Lamar would still be standing there, waiting. He was used to getting what he wanted. Once she had gotten to the end of the street, she realized she was going the wrong way. Now she was really in danger of being late. In spite of her heeled shoes, she ran the two miles over slick, wet sidewalks, from the west side of Brazil to the east.

She didn't slow down until she was a block from home. She'd run out of steam. The temperature was plummeting. Her breath smoked in the night air.

Now came the tricky part. How would she explain why there were no headlights in the driveway? No sound of tires on gravel? What would her mother think if she saw Tish walking up?

She crept to the edge of the drive. The house sat drenched in rain and darkness. Was she late? She checked her watch under the street-lamp. Two minutes to midnight. No, miraculously she was on time. But it looked as if her parents had already gone to bed. She swallowed hard several times to clear away any scent of alcohol. To be safe, she chewed on a handful of pine needles she grabbed from a tree her father had planted the year before. Coming up the walk to the unlit house, she had an uneasy feeling. Something was wrong. She stood for a moment on the porch, then tried the door. It was locked. What to do? She knocked softly. Nothing. She knocked again, nervous as the rain began again in earnest. She invented a dozen lies in her head. How Peachy and Dev had walked her to the corner, then left. She knocked again. The street was silent as a grave. Finally from inside came the sound of footsteps and then the fumbling at the doorknob on the other side. The porch light exploded over her head. The door swung open. There stood her father in his robe and pajamas, hair mussed. She had gotten him out of bed. "Hi, sweetheart." He yawned sleepily. "Come on in. You have a good time? Your mother and Ford are in the back playing Scrabble. They must not have heard you knock."

Tish went on in, welcoming the warmth of the house. She kept her jacket on, covering the dashiki, and threaded her way through the darkened house to the kitchen. Mrs. Espy looked up from the table as

Tish entered the circle of light. Scrabble tiles were spread all over the table. She and Ford were playing earnestly. She didn't even glance at the clock.

"Did you have a good time?" she asked absently.

"Yeah."

"Peachy and Dev have a nice time?"

Tish nodded.

She scooted a chair up next to Ford and sat down for a minute. The quiet in the house after the din of the party was deafening. She could hear the blood pumping through the veins in her head, the faint groan of the refrigerator and the ticking of the clock on the windowsill.

Ford was high again. She could tell by his stretched lids and slow-motion gestures, and her mother didn't have a clue.

He spelled out "plague."

"Mmmm, nice," said Mrs. Espy. She leaned forward, eyes combing the board. "Let's see, I ought to be able to do something here with the *z*."

She never asked how Tish got home. She said nothing more about the party. Playing Scrabble with Ford had put her in a contented mood. A few minutes later Tish said good night, and went on up to bed.

The terrible truth hit her all at once. She loved Goody with every breath in her body. He had crept over her like an illness, and now she ached for him as if in a fever. Let him dance with Sonya! What did she care? It meant nothing. Jasmine had said so. "Old business." It wasn't possible for him to have held Tish the way he did without there being something more between them.

She removed her clothes slowly, studying herself in the mirror. She tried to imagine what Goody would think if he ever saw her like this. What about the gap between her legs and her flat butt? She turned sideways and considered herself. In the soft light, her skin looked golden. Her red hair stood out from her head in kinky ringlets. What was the stupid joke Jeff Anderson made one day in front of the whole English class about how you could tell a "true redhead," and then everyone had stared at her, and Holly and Kim and Lisa had doubled over in stitches? She hadn't gotten it right away. It was only later his meaning dawned on her. Now she looked down at the patch of wiry red hair between her legs, and imagined a hand touching her there. She got into bed and closed her eyes.

It took a while to fall asleep and when she finally did she dreamt of falling through the ice at Curtis Pond, and swimming through the murky water alongside spotted sunfish with frozen gills in the glazed underworld where nothing else moved. She was holding her missing ice skates, heavy as rocks, by their laces. A moment later, a shadow that dream logic dictated was Marcus Goodman appeared next to her, except that he was having trouble breathing, and his arms were flailing. In her dream, she put her arms around his waist and swam upward toward the surface, towing him. The skates came loose and sank to the bottom. Together they broke the surface and gulped in air. His hair held drops of water like tiny silver fish in a net.

XXV

Connie Stubbs had a sixth sense when it came to her daughters, and this morning was no exception. Peachy was all out of sorts, moody, acting funny. Connie pressed, Peachy retreated.

"It's nothing, Mama, I just have a headache."

"Well, maybe you're not eating right," said Mrs. Stubbs. It occurred to her that her daughter might have been drinking, but she didn't want to get into that right then. She had her suspicions about Wanda, but knew better than to accuse falsely. She'd seen parents drive their children to wrong by mistrusting them every step of the way. "Too many parties?"

Peachy groaned.

Connie Stubbs gave her daughter a good once-over with her eyes. "You want me to cook you some breakfast, baby?"

"You'll be late," said Peachy. "I'll fix my own."

Mrs. Stubbs already had on her white uniform and rubber-soled shoes. She was doing her hair. Sometimes when she looked at herself in the mirror she imagined herself as a nurse, which was what she'd really wanted to be, helping people get well, instead of bleaching out bed-sheets, but fate had other things in store for her. Her family had no money to send her to nursing school, and she'd begun working the second she graduated high school. When she married Jimmy, he'd promised to send her to nursing school, but then time passed, and bills mounted, and her first two daughters arrived, three years apart, and nursing school became a luxury she couldn't afford.

"You sure you're okay, honey?" Mrs. Stubbs asked, giving her hair one last smooth-over.

"Yes, Mommy." There was a slight edge to Peachy's voice, the kind of edge Mrs. Stubbs had heard other girls use with their mothers, but one she was not accustomed to from her own daughter.

"Well, you fix you some cream of wheat, child, and come straight home from school so you can rest, okay?"

Peachy shook her head. "I have ensemble practice."

"Well, I can't let you use the car because I have a doctor's appoint-ment at three," said Mrs. Stubbs. "But I can drop you off. You'd be a little early—"

"That's okay, Mommy, I don't want to go to school yet," said Peachy, and for a moment Mrs. Stubbs saw before her a child of five, with her hair plaited tightly, crying and stubbornly refusing to go back to school, because some white children at kindergarten had called her "nigger." She had known, hadn't she, that this was inevitable, the mo-ment when every black child becomes aware of what the world really thinks of her. Mrs. Stubbs had been so mad and so sad at the same time she hadn't found the exact words, so instead drew her child to her. She knew with a deep sense of dread that no amount of explanation would ever take the sting away from that. She could complain to the school until she was blue in the face, but an apology was all she would ever get, and that wasn't even a starting point, in her book. It was that same helpless feeling she had now, except she saw in front of her a young woman, almost a stranger, whom she could protect only so long from whatever burdens the world felt like dropping on her shoulders.

"Peachy, is there something on your mind? Did something happen?" she asked, picking her car keys off the table.

"Nuh-uh," said Peachy. The phone rang. "I ain't talkin'," said Peachy. Mrs. Stubbs answered. For a moment she thought whoever was on the other end would give her a clue as to why Peachy was so moody. But it was only Wanda.

"How you doin', baby?" Mrs. Stubbs asked.

"I'm okay. Peaches there?" said Wanda, and Mrs. Stubbs thought, by extension, that meant Peachy was okay too. Nothing troubled in Wanda's voice. She relaxed a little.

"Peachy can't come to the phone right now. But I'm making a cobbler this weekend," said Mrs. Stubbs, knowing how Wanda loved cobbler. "I hope you'll pass by to get some."

She said this also for Peachy's benefit, to see if she could get her daughter's spirits to rise. But Peachy was at the refrigerator pulling out the carton of orange juice.

"Well, you have a good day," said Mrs. Stubbs. "And give my best to your grandmother."

She hung up. "Is Dev eating over here tonight, baby?"

Peachy looked up. "Huh?" she said, and it occurred to Mrs. Stubbs that her daughter, who was now at the sink, hadn't heard her with the water running.

"I said, is Dev eating over here tonight?"

"He's got debate club," said Peachy.

"Well, I won't be cooking until around seven anyway, and I *know* debate club don't go that late. Tell him to come on over and we'll play some whist."

Peachy shrugged and poured herself a glass of juice.

"Are you listening to me, Peaches?"

"Yes, Mommy, but you keep talking and now I'm getting a worse headache."

"Lord," said Mrs. Stubbs. "You sure are trying my patience this morning. What's gotten into you?"

Peachy turned and looked her mother straight in the eye. It was the look of one woman to another, and Mrs. Stubbs saw before her a daughter who wasn't a child anymore.

"Nothing, Mama, I told you. I just don't feel good."

"Your stomach botherin' you too? There's some of your daddy's Pepto-Bismol in the bathroom cabinet."

"Good-bye, Mommy," Peachy said, with a wry smile.

The glimmer of smile relieved Mrs. Stubbs.

"You be good at school and study hard," she said, the way she used to when Peachy was in elementary. She opened the door leading to the carport. Jimmy had forgotten to set the garbage can out before he took off for the airport in his new Mark III, and it now blocked her way. But it was too heavy to move. She paused for a moment, thinking she could ask Peachy, but changed her mind. It wouldn't hurt anyone to let that can sit there for another day. She went on around it, closing the door behind her. Teenagers, she thought. Well, she had been one once too, almost forty years before. Things had been different in her day, but not so different that she couldn't look at her daughter and know something was wrong.

She sighed. She wasn't about to dwell on it too much, because most likely when she returned home in the evening, Peachy would be in better spirits. She was wiping off her windshield when she felt something like a tap on her shoulder. She wheeled around.

"Peachy?" she said reflexively. There was an odd, disconcerting silence. She was alone. She turned and opened the back door and poked her head inside. "Peachy?" she called into the house.

There was no answer, just the scent of burned hair.

"Peachy?"

Her heart jumped in her chest.

"What, Mama?" Peachy came to the kitchen door, hot comb in hand.

"Girl, don't you try to do your own hair," said Mrs. Stubbs. "It's already so brittle."

"I'm just touching up the ends," said Peachy.

"Let me do it tonight, sugar. Okay?" Suddenly she wanted desperately for Peachy to be the little girl again who needed her mother. She wasn't ready to let her daughter go, not just yet. Overnight, it seemed, little Peachy had suddenly turned sixteen, skipping all the years in between.

"Mmmm-hmmm," Peachy agreed, laying the hot comb back on the stove burner.

"What you want for dinner tonight, baby? Anything special?" She felt impulsive. Her paycheck had had a little overtime added to it. She could splurge. "Just tell me, sweetheart."

Peachy thought a moment.

"You know what I want, Mommy," she said and smiled. There passed between them the familiarity of two people who know each other's habits and desires inside out. Mrs. Stubbs felt relief wash over her like a wave. That's all it was, Peachy just needed a little attention.

"Yes, I do know what you want. And if you want Wanda or any of your little friends to spend the night, that's fine too." She left then, feeling better, glad things could be so easily resolved.

XXVI

Sunday Tish, pleading a stomachache, had spent most of the day in bed. Monday morning she awoke changed and amazed. When she went to sit up she realized she didn't want to do anything but burrow back into bed, pull the sheets and blanket around her like a cocoon, and plunge her face into the pillow, which for a moment she could imagine was Goody's chest. She heard her mother calling from the kitchen. Somewhere in the house the baby was crying. *Clatter, clatter.* Dishes were rattling. Her father had left for London on an early flight. Household sounds had nothing to do with her. She now belonged to a world that spoke a different language. This is love, she thought, as a tremor ran through her. She opened her eyes long enough to decipher the foreignness of her room, the flowered wallpaper, the shiver of the silver maple branch against the open window. The air held a hint of springtime, the raw, earthy scent underlying the cold. She imagined that somewhere over on Washington Street, Marcus Goodman was also coming to in his room, stretching his long self in bed, in the early fog of awakening and wondering when he would get to fold Tish Espy in his arms again.

Tish wondered if everyone could see the transformation written on her face. She smiled at her mother on her way out the door, and her mother said, "That's a happy face."

At her locker near Tish's, Holly Penn remarked, "You seem cheerful today," and Tish considered what that said about other days. Taylor Weems was standing there as well, and Tish noticed he was letting his hair grow out long, like a hippie's, and he wore a leather wristband with a peace symbol. He called out to Tish, remarked in his slightly sexy, smug way that he'd heard she wrote poetry, and would she want to let him read some. He grinned when he said it, as if the whole idea of her pleased him. And Tish grinned back, thinking momentarily how much more interesting Taylor Weems would find her than Holly if he overlooked superficial things like looks and just gave her a chance.

"What'd you do this weekend, Tish?" Holly asked conversationally. In the past, the question would have been accompanied by a knowing glance from Holly to one of her cohorts, and then their lips would purse to keep from smiling when she'd shrug and answer, "Nothing."

"I went to a party Saturday," Tish said as casually as she could. She couldn't resist. Now it was her turn to exclude. "You know Jasmine Robinson? It was her eighteenth birthday. Really tough party. Everyone was there."

She liked that last touch—"everyone was there"—because of course in Holly's world "everyone" had an entirely different meaning. And she counted on Taylor, with his gentle blue eyes sweeping over her, to catch the implication. She smiled and started on down the hall, tasting the sweet elixir of satisfaction. No longer did she have to care what lame white girls like Holly Penn thought. She had one thing on her mind. Marcus Goodman. Goody. What had he thought when she disappeared into that misty night?

She found out before French. According to Peachy, he had cornered her twice at the party to ask if she'd seen Tish. "When did you leave, girl? You didn't even say good-bye." Also, according to Jasmine, a concerned Goody had pressed her for details. Could he call Tish at home, or were her parents "that way"? When could he see her again? Could Jasmine arrange something?

Never before had Tish imagined such ecstasy. "Tell him he can call," she said recklessly to Jasmine. "Cool," said Jasmine. Tish's breathing thickened with anticipation, and she prayed the phone would ring when her mother was upstairs busy with the baby.

Passing Lamar in the halls, Tish laughed at him openly. She held the trump card. He'd wink at her and she'd roll her eyes. This made him laugh, and then she'd laugh and shake her head. Sometimes he'd stop dead in his tracks and tip himself way back, tugging his sunglasses down onto the end of his nose, until Tish would say, "Go on, fool." He was so stuck on himself he didn't even know to be sheepish. When Tish finally confided the truth about the notes, Angela shook her head in disgust. "I always knew he was full of it-shay," and then she listed all of Michael's attributes in counterpoint as if to reassure herself. Tish was astounded how Angela had transformed an ordinary boy like Michael Brown into the extraordinary human being she believed him to be. Perhaps that's what love did. *Made lemonade out of a lemon,* as her mother used to say.

It was all she could do to keep her mind on school. Minutes passed like hours, and she found herself changing classes and opening her textbooks in a daze.

She caught Lamar outside the gymnasium talking earnestly to Jeannie Lyons, her back against the wall. She was making pouty faces at him, and then Lamar reached out and touched Jeannie right on her breast. Jeannie brushed his hand off in awkward flirtation and twisted away. Then Lamar sauntered off whistling. When Jeannie passed by her, she was smiling, and Tish noticed the purple bruises of sucker bites edging out from the collar of her turtleneck. Disgusted, Tish deliberately bumped into her, and gave her a hard, meaningful look as a warning. Jeannie shrank back. Tish felt tough like Wanda, invincible. She wasn't going to take any mess from anyone. Later, she saw Lamar flirting with the white cheerleader Cindy he had been arguing with in the shadows. Her pink-lipsticked mouth was flung open in pleasure. "Oooh, Lamar!" she was saying, and Tish hated her for the squeal in her voice and the way she flipped her stringy hair back over her shoulder. How, thought Tish, with contempt, could he even waste his time on a girl like that when he had the most beautiful black girl in school in love with him?

It was pathetic. And all the while Jasmine sat confidently in the front row in French class, cracking her gum, and picking out her fro, and smiling at her girlfriends whenever she gave the right answer as if nothing else mattered in life. Tish felt sorry for her, not knowing. But she wasn't going to be the one to put her wise. Even Angela told her she'd be a fool to do so. "She'll take it out on you," she said, and it might have been the best piece of advice Angela ever gave. "Jasmine's blind where Lamar is concerned. You try to tell her anything now and she'll think you're lying."

Well, so much for Jasmine and Lamar. She had her own love business to tend to. For the next week she went about her mother's house with a brisk sense of purpose, poised for whatever would happen. There was a brief, awkward phone call from Goody, right at dinner, when everyone was seated there at the table listening, and her mother was giving her the hard eye. Tish breathed softly into the receiver, "I can't talk right now," and he understood: "I'll call you later." She didn't ask when, just trusted that they were now so synchronized he would intuit when the time was right.

She let slip to Angela that she was in love. Angela's eyes widened appreciatively.

"So, girl, give me the scoop."

Eagerly Tish launched into details that added up to larger implications. Just speaking the words brought Goody to life before them. It felt good, Tish with information and Angela attentive, offering commentary, but Tish was careful not to embellish too much. *Where exactly were his hands? There. Where? Okay, right there, or farther down? How did he touch you? Was there pressure or hesitation? What did he say? Did he soul kiss you?* That love could be dissected into such stark mechanics struck Tish as discomfiting. But she desperately needed Angela's help. They split the next cigarette, passing it back and forth. *And then what did he do?* What Tish left out, because there were no words for it, was the tenderness, the slight sigh that emanated from him when he put his mouth on hers and the rising excitement that caused him to pull her close against him, as if to make her a permanent part of himself.

"He wears Old Spice," Tish said, falling back on Angela's bed in a swoon. And Angela said, "All the brothers do," and she pulled from her dresser drawer a bottle of it and yanked off the cap, holding it out for Tish to smell. Immediately she was enveloped in the mystery of Goody. It was as if he'd appeared in flesh and bone before her, and she looked incredulously at Angela the magician. "Pour some on your pillowcase," Angela advised. And they drove together to the drugstore, where Tish purchased a bottle for herself.

It didn't matter what anyone thought, even Wanda, who made the expected crack about blackies, whities, and zebra babies. Tish laughed her off. Goody's name was a word etched into her brain, a clamor in her ear. Shut away in her room listening to Wilson Pickett sing about the midnight hour, she imagined their next meeting, what she would wear and say, how she would move, how he would look at her with those soft brown eyes, and the unspoken urgency that passed between them.

She burned from the memory of his body next to hers. The very shape and texture of it had surprised her. It was so different from the chaste touches of Dev or even the cartoonish smooching she'd done with no-count boys. Goody was a man. Longing took hold and went to war with her head. She would never get it right. Downright clownish on the outside and on fire on the inside, she slouched her way to math class, where the frightened little blond teacher dutifully chalked the homework assignment on the board. She took her seat, middle row by the window, agitation clouding any sense she might ever make out of algebra. She felt annoyed by the twin Seventh-Day Adventists and Samantha Yoder, whose loud remarks now struck her as rude and silly. "I *still* can't read what you've written!" Samantha was braying at the teacher, just to see how many times she could get her to erase and rewrite the same material.

Who cared about the teacher's equations and their X, Y, and Z's, Tish thought, idly scribbling Goody's initials all over her notebook. Those weren't the kinds of problems she wanted to solve. When the teacher asked for solutions, Tish was busy devising her own equations.

Marcus Goodman + Tish Espy = x Solve for x.

Then *Tish Espy + Goody = y.* She assigned numbers to the letters in his name, then to her own, added them, subtracted them, divided them, and multiplied them. She came up with a phrase, and finally a distillation. *Marcus Goodman and Letitia Espy. Letitia Goodman. Letitia Goodman. Letitia Goodman.*

Over and over, her pencil moved in the shape of those words. His name. The sound of his name. The shape of his name on the page. The blue ink against the white page. She tried just *Goody plus Tish.* With a little flourish. *GOODY* in all caps, filling in the O's. *goody* all lowercase, like e. e. cummings or sonya sanchez. As she concentrated, a faint memory of aftershave drifted over her. She bent down and sniffed her own hand. It wasn't there. But an acute sensation of touch washed over her like a wave tumbling her backward. It was all so preposterous and dangerous and she knew it.

"A boy called again last night while you were at the McGregors' baby-sitting," said Tish's mother, as Tish scrubbed potatoes in the sink for dinner. She paused. "He sounded older. He wanted the number where you were, but I didn't think that was a good idea. He didn't leave his name." She added, "He was very polite."

Tish played dumb and shrugged. The less her mother knew, the better.

"I don't think you should have boys call you when you baby-sit," she said. "The McGregors aren't paying you to talk on their phone."

Tish looked up, trying to suppress her irritation. "I don't have boys call me when I baby-sit," she said. "If I did, he'd have called me there and not here."

She waited for her mother to say, "Watch your tone," but she didn't.

There was only silence. At the McGregors' Tish had looked up Goody's number in the phone book, and memorized it until it took on a life of its own and repeated itself in her head. She had wanted desperately to call him, but she didn't want to seem fast. The phone was listed under Coretta Goodman, his mother, 578 Washington Street. Sandwiched in between Alta Goodheart and Marvin Goodyear. She'd started dialing, but chickened out.

While setting the table, she ran the number over and over in her head, adding up the digits, dividing by seven. Her father, just returned from London (he'd brought her miniature bottles of colorful nail polish and a vest), came in and kissed her on the cheek. "How was your trip, Daddy?" she forced herself to ask, though she could barely think of anything that didn't have to do with Goody. She pretended to listen patiently as he rattled off details, but her mind was a million miles away.

Later, in her room, she feverishly copied down the numerical equivalent of the letters in each of their names, then tried matching and scrambling to see what might be decoded. Tish Espy. Marcus Goodman. She was desperate to know his middle name, to know in what other ways they might find connection. The details of his face had begun to fade, but she had the most overwhelming sensation of his body, his breath, the face bending down close. Of the way they naturally fit together, mixed their limbs and mouths and breath. The scent of the cold air, the spice of his cologne. The smell of his leather coat rising up warm and ripe. *Tish Goodman. Tish Goodman.* It ran like a current through her head.

*   *   *

One evening on the way home, Tish and Peachy drove by Goody's house five times in Mrs. Stubbs's Fleetwood, when they were supposed to be stopping only long enough to get gas at Leon's Shell.

Tish slouched way down in the front seat so she wouldn't be seen. She peered out just over the window ledge, memorizing his house: the porch, the steps, the way the roof slanted down the front. The house became his body, the shape of his torso, as much as Tish could remember.

"You want to go see if he's home?" Peachy said.

"No," said Tish, almost fainting. "No, not yet."

It had been two weeks since Jasmine's party. She didn't want to rush things, seem too eager. Let him come to her.

"Some of us are going by Reggie Moore's crib later; you want to come?" Peachy asked. She tossed out the bait. "Goody might be there."

Tish felt a thrill of excitement. Imagine, herself at Reggie Moore's, hanging out with everyone that mattered. Being seen. Goody entering and being surprised that she was there.

"I can't," she said dully, glancing at her watch. "I'm babysitting at seven." She considered sneaking off after the McGregor children fell asleep. What harm would it do?

Peachy shrugged. "Too bad. What you want me to tell Goody for you if I see him?"

Tish felt anxiety rise up in her throat. "Nothing," she said. "Just tell him I'm baby-sitting."

"You want him to call you?"

"You really think he digs me?" she asked.

"Go on, girl, you can be so square. I told you he did."

Tish asked. "How late will y'all be at Reggie's?"

Peachy shrugged. "I have to be home at midnight or Mama will kill me. You know how she is."

Midnight, Tish thought. Midnight with Goody.

"Reggie stays over on Eden Street now, on the north side of campus. He just moved out of his parents' house. You could come by after baby-sitting."

Tish tried to imagine how she would orchestrate that. The McGregors would be suspicious if she didn't want them dropping her off at home. "What do y'all do over there?" Tish wanted to know.

"Listen to jazz . . . some people smoke weed."

"Damn, Peachy," said Tish, sliding back down in her front seat and covering her face with her hands. The enormity of her passion overwhelmed her. "I really dig this man. What if you told him that?"

"Girl, please . . ." said Peachy with a half smile.

"I mean it," said Tish. "I think I'm in love."

Peachy rolled her eyes. Tish thought to herself how simple Peachy was, how uncomplicated, how impossible it would be for her to grasp the significant connection between herself and Goody. After all, Peachy had never known love and was satisfied by dull dates with boring boys like Vic Wooten, proclaiming her virginity with a vengeance. What did she know of passion? What did any of them know?

A big rain came and melted the remaining patches of snow to slush. Temperatures jumped unexpectedly into the fifties, and a warm wind sprang up. Tish took Francis over to the reservoir and helped him fly a kite in a sudden burst of generosity. She half hoped Goody would come upon them unexpectedly, touched by the maternal way she guided Francis's little hand as she controlled the kite.

Later, temperatures dropped again. A light, wet snow began to fall. With Mr. Espy in the passenger seat of the recently repaired Rambler, Tish practiced driving. She had her temporary license now. *It's good to be cautious. Better safe than sorry.* She was desperate to be seen driving, and detoured past Spring Street Park, extending the trip and thinking with any luck, she might spot Goody walking down Washington. She'd rehearsed this possibility over and over in her mind. Goody would be loping along in his leather coat, and she'd casually honk and wave. He'd look over, and his face would light up. He would be impressed to see her behind the wheel.

"Always be thinking where you could go to get out of someone's way," Mr. Espy was saying. "Drive defensively. For example, take that car turning right there. Let's see, if he suddenly came straight at you, what could you do?"

"I could go up on that curb lawn," Tish said, but her mind wasn't on curb lawns, it was calculating the chances of running into Goody— slim to none.

She ran a poem through her head. He lived exactly:

One and a half blocks west of Angela
Three blocks east of Peachy
Three and a half blocks from Jasmine
A mile and one/tenth from Woodland Street

"Good thinking," said Mr. Espy. "You always want to be very alert. Like having eyes in the back of your head."

They hadn't talked much since the night the cross burned. Tish suspected he felt really bad about a lot of things, but didn't know what to say. He had his own troubles down at the university. There had been a recent sit-in by black students demanding more black faculty and when he'd gone in to try to negotiate, they sent him back out. His one black master's student, his pride and joy, had become sullen and uncommunicative. Lately Mr. Espy was talking about leaving teaching altogether. "I'm on their side," he said helplessly. Tish felt both the pull of her love for him and the push away from his wounded ego.

Tish turned the car toward Angela's. A group of boys were coming out of a house. One had on a long leather coat. For a moment, her pulse jumped. But it wasn't Goody.

Tish drove past and pulled into Angela's steep drive. The back bumper of the Rambler scraped against the pavement. She and her father sat there, the two of them, with the nose of the Rambler pointing upward toward the sky, like a spacecraft about to take off. The windshield wipers clicked, the heater creaked.

"I've been talking to your mother," said Mr. Espy. "She said you're planning to work again this summer. And I think I've almost convinced her that you can have the Rambler when you turn sixteen."

"Really?" said Tish, immediately imagining how easy meeting Goody would be if she had a car.

"You're getting to an age where you're going to want to go out with friends and maybe stay out later than your mother or I want to stay up, and you should have a safe way back home. But you're going to have to get your grades up and try to get along better with your mother."

She didn't answer right away.

"I want peace in our household," he said.

She nodded. She fought a sudden urge to embrace her father, to feel they were friends again. She remembered how they used to go off together when she was little, and how he'd taken her to the planetarium in Cleveland, and like magic, there in the middle of the day, they had had night. She had asked him then, "Is my Tish star up there?" and he had put his arm around her and assured her that it was, even when she couldn't see it. "You mean stars hide?" she asked. And he nodded.

Tish got out and her father slid over into the driver's seat. He sat with the motor running, waiting to see her safely inside. Angela had spotted them from the living room picture window. She came to the door in plaid slacks and a green sweater. She opened the screen and leaned out to wave. The gears of the car shifted into reverse, and the tailpipe scraped as Mr. Espy backed out.

Tish felt a pang watching her father leave. She knew they could never be close again, not the way they once had. Sadness overwhelmed her, drew her almost into grief.

Inside, Angela was grinning like a Cheshire cat. "My parents have company. We have the downstairs to ourselves. . . . What's wrong with you?"

Tish snapped out of her mood, and handed Angela her parka. They passed around the edge of the living room, where Mr. and Mrs. Thompson and two more couples, all spread out on matching sectional furniture, sat drinking cocktails and listening to Ramsey Lewis on the hi-fi. One of the women was clicking her fingers to the beat of "In-crowd."

"Hi, Tish, sweetheart," Mrs. Thompson called out, her stockinged feet propped on the ottoman. She was wearing her pink suit, the one Tish adored.

There was the tinkle of ice in glasses, and the low, knowing adult laughter. Tish heard Mrs. Thompson say to her friends, "Angela's little boyfriend is Michael Brown. You all know him, don't you? His mother is Vernetta Brown. Michael's such a doll. We just love him, and they are so cute together."

Angela rolled her eyes and moaned, but Tish secretly envied the warm way Mrs. Thompson described Michael, and her own connection to his mother. Angela's world made sense. It had cohesion. In comparison, her own seemed so jumbled, pieced together like a mosaic. There were times she felt as if she were living triple lives. She followed in Angela's wake, loading up a plate of food ("Mama cooked some soul food"), before heading downstairs to the basement rec room ("Michael's coming over soon"). Within seconds they had gotten into Mr. Thompson's liquor cabinet and were pouring caramel-colored shots of Johnnie Walker Red. Tish retrieved a pack of Kool Longs from her brassiere and tapped the bottom. She handed one cigarette to Angela and kept one for herself. They each lit up (both were carrying Come Back Inn lighters now, courtesy of Wanda) and kicked back, eyeing each other with confident ease, and licking the barbecue sauce from their fingers. It would be hours before Mrs. Thompson came down to check on them, and in that time they would have gotten rid of the evidence, rinsed out the glasses, and added water to the scotch.

Angela successfully french-inhaled and then blew out a steady stream of smoke. She looked poised, mature, worldly sitting there, her hair slightly rumpled.

"Let's call up Goody," she suggested as the scotch went to her head. She started to reach for the phone, but Tish grabbed her arm.

Angela shook her off. Being high gave her courage. "Come on, girl, trust me. I'll just act like I'm calling him for myself—you know, he and Michael kind of know each other." She was leafing through the phone book. How did she learn to do all these things? In a moment she'd found the number (Tish didn't dare let on she knew it by heart), and Angela dialed.

She edged over closer to Tish and held the receiver up to her ear so she could listen too.

Ring. Ring. The ring stopped. Someone had answered. A woman. His mother, most likely.

"Hi, is Marcus there? . . . Mmmmm-hmmmm. No, this is Angela. . . . Angela. Angela Thompson . . ." There was a pause, and Angela's eyes lit up. She covered the mouthpiece with her palm and hissed, "He's there, he's there. I'm gonna tell him to come on down, girl."

Tish really did think her heart and lungs would burst straight out of her chest. Her head began to swim. She jumped off the sofa. "Don't tell him I'm here," she said. Angela waved her off with her hand and spoke into the phone.

"Hi, Marcus, it's Angela Thompson. . . . Hey, how you doin', brother? . . . Nothing. . . . No, unh-unh. . . . No, Tish and I were just sitting down here. . . . Uh-huh, she's right here" (Angela's eyebrows went up and down. She shot Tish a grin), ". . . we thought you might want to come hang and have a drink with us. . . . Michael's on his way. . . . My parents have guests. . . . Just come on up the driveway and around back to the basement door by the patio. Uh-huh. Uh-huh." Tish couldn't bear it any longer. She jumped up and began to pace, inhaling so deeply on the Kool Long that she hot-boxed it and almost burned her mouth.

The warm scotch snaked through her. She felt deliciously dizzy, even a little crazy. The thought of Goody showing up with so little warning made her weak all over.

Angela hung up. Tish sank back on the sofa and moaned. "Angela . . ."

The old light was back in her eye. "Dag, girl, he couldn't wait to get over here. Just like that—no hesitation whatsoever." She squeezed Tish's arm. "You got yourself a man."

Tish took another swallow of scotch.

"Don't get too high," said Angela, alarmed. "Do you know what my father would do to me if he knew we'd been ripping off his Johnny Walker Red?" She resorted to her prim voice. "Girl, he would kill me. That's *k-i-l-l* kill." She got up and began to rearrange things while Tish put "La La Means I Love You" on the turntable and pretended to dance with herself across the floor.

There was a gentle knock at the basement door, so gentle in fact that for a moment Tish confused it with the percussion in the record. The sound of Goody's knuckles on the door made her almost insane with expectation. The knuckles would be attached to the longer, slender fingers of a hand, and the hand to an arm, and the arm to a man she had conjured up over and over in her mind. A memory that had replaced him in reality and filled her with unbearable longing. For the split second before Angela opened the door came the short delay in which desire overwhelmed. The door swung open, followed by a swift draft of cold air. Odd how anticlimactic it was catching Goody briefly framed in the doorway of Angela's rec room, suddenly too large, and too old. His face was different, it belonged to a stranger. The details had blurred in her memory. His cheeks were higher and narrower than she'd remembered, his shoulders broader. His hair wasn't quite as long, or maybe it had gotten pressed down under the cap he was removing from his head. Snow had settled along the exposed edges of his hair, whitening his temples and adding several more years to him. Tish was so nervous she instantly launched herself into the La-Z-Boy recliner, grateful for the wide seat. Trembling, she grabbed another cigarette and lit it. She was grateful to Angela for taking his coat and making small talk while she collected her thoughts. She tried to adopt a casual pose, knees drawn to chest, as if she'd been relaxing for hours. When he turned to her, his brown eyes smoldered. She felt exposed. "Hey," she said, pulling the smoke from the Kool Long deep into her lungs for reassurance.

"Hey, baby," he said. Angela smiled conspiratorially. It made things easier with Angela acting as a foil. *Remember this? Remember that?* They were putting on a show. She laughed too loudly, pulled back, grimaced when Angela grimaced, mimicking the ease of Angela's "hmmm-mmmm's" and "dag's." It was like acting in a play. There was polite conversation, Angela asking Goody with great poise about his job, his mother, the old high school he'd attended (they knew people in common). Then came the chime of the upstairs doorbell, signaling Michael's arrival. From above Mrs. Thompson was heard urging him to "go on down, the girls are listening to music." A moment later Michael descended the stairs. Tish almost choked as she handed her glass to Angela for a refill. "You sure your mother won't come down here?" she whispered.

"Positive," said Angela, going back to the cabinet for another shot. Michael kissed Angela, and then he and Goody exchanged black-power handshakes. Tish and Angela occupied themselves sorting through Angela's 45's, Tish's nerves on edge. Michael poured himself a small shot of scotch and offered Goody some, and they took seats on opposite sides of the room and laughed about an incident only they seemed familiar with. Tish listened for innuendo, anything she should know.

"I didn't know you drank," Goody turned to her. She couldn't tell if he was glad to see her getting loose or not, but she took the chance that it was a compliment.

"Lots of things you don't know about me," she said, and downed the shot. Everyone said, "Ooooooh." She smiled, wondering if she'd gone too far, and feeling the gentle numbing sensation of the alcohol in her head. Michael had his eyes on her too, as if seeing her for the first time. What impression was she giving? She prayed it was sophistication, the ease of someone at home in the world. She hoped they weren't thinking she was just a square white girl, someone easy to get over on.

Angela scooted in next to Michael with the intimacy of old habits and routines. Now she was gently rubbing her thigh against his knee in a teasing way and crooning to him in a soft voice, "What'd you do today, honey? You seem tired. Did you work overtime?" They sounded like somebody's parents, Michael grinning and murmuring in response, and Angela continuing in that honey-smooth voice she reserved just for him.

Each time Tish caught Goody's eye she felt her insides thicken to pudding. Now Angela was pleading, teasing, taunting, and pulling gently on Michael's arm. Michael wore a sheepish expression, but soon he was lulled by the sound of her voice into leaning back on the sofa, his letter jacket unbuttoned, grinning up at her. Goody inched over to Tish, drawing up his chair next to her. Now she was on her own. No Angela to help out. It was up to her to entertain Goody, and she didn't have a clue how.

"Let's put something different on, something slow and sweet," Goody suggested, and motioned for her to join him in selecting a record from the stack of 45's she and Angela had compiled. She was grateful for the scotch softening the edges of panic. It seemed natural squatting there on the floor with him, sorting through records. He put his face against her hair and murmured, "Mmmmmm, you smell good," and the compliment embarrassed her because it wasn't as if she'd put on anything special; it was either the Dial soap she'd used in the shower before coming over or Goody was making the whole thing up. She didn't know what to say, couldn't force herself to move up against him the way Angela had done with Michael. After all, Angela and Michael were going together. Angela had the right to behave that way. She and Goody were just getting started. She wanted so desperately to feel his arms around her, but there were steps in between to be taken. What were they? He chose an old Miracles song, "Ooh, Baby, Baby," that always left her weak in the knees. He extended his hand and drew her up off the floor. A moment later Michael had reached over and flipped off the main light switch on the wall. The room was now faintly illuminated by the dim lamp above Mr. Thompson's bar. In that dusky light, Goody pulled Tish close. As he sang softly in her ear, she imagined the words were his. He was letting the song speak for him. "Mmmmmmm," he murmured, towing her against him, and she thought how well she fit against his chest, as if a place had been carved out just for her. When she got the nerve to glance over, she saw Angela straddling Michael's lap and French-kissing him deeply. It was like a scene from a movie, and she imagined herself looking like Angela as she pressed herself back against Goody, and he said, "Oh, yeah!" into her ear with such force that she knew they understood each other without words. He gripped her tightly, yanking her closer and closer until she could go no farther. There was a hard place on his leg and she grew breathless with what it signaled. His mouth on hers, his tongue against hers, his breath moving in rhythm with her breath. Someone put on the Temptations' "In a Mellow Mood." She lost track of time there in Angela's basement, and it wasn't until the door at the top of the steps opened some time later and Mrs. Thompson called down, "Okay, girls! Time for company to leave!" that Tish remembered where she was. Slowly she and Goody disentangled themselves. In the corner a sleepy-eyed Angela, drugged on love, half-dozed against Michael where they had hidden themselves on the floor behind the La-Z-Boy.

An album revolved soundlessly on the turntable while the needle continued its rhythmic grind. Someone flipped on the light switch, shattering the mood. Tish flinched. The furniture, the objects in the room all took on the startling shape of normalcy. Before Goody left he touched Tish under her chin with his finger again. "Stay sweet," he said. The words wrapped her in the hint of promise. She got dizzy thinking of herself as sweet. *Sweetness. Honey. Sugar.* Then came the blast of cold air from the opening and closing of the basement door, the shutting out. Left was just the sweet memory of leather and cologne, and the pressure of a soft mouth on hers. Tish flung herself giddily back down in the La-Z-Boy, unable to think straight.

Angela, hair askew and blouse buttoned wrong, turned to her. "Girl, you're blowing that brother's mind."

Tish grinned, thinking how it was so much easier than she'd thought. All she had to do was sit back and let him love her. All she had to do was present to him the self she wanted to be.

XXVII

At school, the hours creaked by. Tish filled pages of her notebook with Goody's name and stared out the window. In those lazy moments while the teacher's voice droned on and other students napped or passed notes, she lost herself between the lines of binder paper, the letters of Goody's name repeating themselves into the deepest intimacy. In between daydreams, she jotted poems, fragments and images, each one returning magically to his name. How could she even think about her term paper for English or her math test? How pointless school was! The clock ticked. Peachy had been out sick for a week, and when Tish called to check on her, Mrs. Stubbs said she'd come down with a bug of some sort and was sleeping. "I'll give her your message, baby, and thank you for calling to check on her." At lunch, Tish sat with Wanda and Tina and their friends, but for once she felt superior to them in her new knowledge.

At home, she cranked up the Parliaments full blast until her mother yelled for her to turn down the damn noise. She practiced different selves in the full-length mirror, dancing and posing, then trying on wise, sexy, surprised. She piled her red hair up on her head. She took it down and pulled it back. She braided it on either side—no, too childish. She parted it on the left and then on the right. She left it swept up one side, imagining herself to be Flo of the Supremes. She sang along, playing the record over and over: *I just wanna testify . . . what your love has done for me . . . I just wanna testify . . .* She parted her hair down the middle and drew it down on either side to see if she could look like Cher. What she would give to be dark, with long black hair, or even an afro. But her hair sprang back, coiling into red spirals.

Then came a knock on her bedroom door.

"Telephone, Tish dear. It's that boy again." By the time Tish opened the door, her mother had vanished, words lingering, matter-of-factly, without question. Her mother was in her own way implying approval. Perhaps if Tish just let this unfold naturally, didn't push, didn't confide too much, her mother would eventually accept Goody as a fact of their lives.

Tish went right through the open door of her parents' bedroom, where Mrs. Espy had left the receiver on her nightstand. It lay there like an invitation her old black telephone transformed like magic just by the sound of Goody's voice. "Tish? Hey, it's me." It took her a moment to find the voice to answer. "Hey," she said back, nerves ajitter. His words bled into her ear, soft with expectation. It was so much harder this way, perched on the edge of her parents' extra-firm mattress, with the sounds of Fisher's electric train just one room away, to open herself up. So much easier just to drop her head against his chest and close her eyes. Let the broken bits of her, the odd fragments that made up Tish, come together for just a moment in the sweet swirl of words now pouring into her ear.

Goody was a slow, hopeless fact of love. She knew this from the songs, the overwhelming way in which he simply took hold and left her no choice. The way they could say so little, but so much passed between them unspoken, as if they understood each other from long ago.

"Stay sweet," he'd say at the end, as if to seal their trust. His hushed and gentle "Can you meet me later?" was the connection between one encounter and the next, but later never came soon enough.

Being with him never lasted long enough. The minutes they snatched here and there added up to only a few hours a week. The square and the arboretum were no longer the square and the arboretum, but meeting places full of memories of Goody. It was always Tish who had to leave first, conscious of time and panicked she would be caught coming out of the woods with him.

There was the slushy, chilly night he walked over to her baby-sitting job at the McGregors', just two blocks from her parents', and when he knocked at the door she thought she would faint. She'd been on the phone with Peachy, who seemed to have recovered from the flu. Tish asked her to hold on a minute while she checked to make sure it was Goody and not the Boston Strangler. Seeing him so tall and lanky in the doorway before her, so three-dimensional and fully himself, gave her a jolt, and she could hardly speak. How different he was in person from her imaginings, when she could speak for them both and will him to do what she wanted. She was grateful for the excuse that she had to go say good-bye to Peachy, a chance to collect herself, while he eased himself onto the McGregors' sofa and patiently flipped through a magazine, waiting for her to wrap up the call. She was glad it hadn't appeared she'd just been waiting there, with nothing better to do, but the fact that she was about to enter the room where he sat, with no one else around as a buffer, left her speechless. If only Angela were there! He called her "shy," teased her about being so withdrawn, sang a few bars of "I'm A Soul Man" to make her smile. How could she explain she was burning up inside, and all that was left of her was ash? "Can you braid hair?" he asked, and when she said she could, he slipped between her knees into a seat on the floor and handed her a comb from his pocket. She felt herself trembling with the weight of his body against her thighs, and when she plunged her fingertips into his hair, parting it gently with the teeth of the comb, it was like sinking into cotton. He was lulled into a gentle stupor by the rhythm of her fingers in his hair, and she felt as if it were the most natural thing in the world, a gesture of her love. Afterward, he took her gently into his arms, stroked her hair, chuckled at the clamminess of her hands, kissed each fingertip, called her his girl. Each passing car was certainly the premature return of the McGregors, and the unexpected footsteps on the porch more than certainly meant she'd been discovered. But it was only a neighbor returning a tricycle, dumped unceremoniously on the doorstep. There she was sprawled on the McGregors' sofa, with Goody gently kissing her along the neck and fumbling under her blouse. She let his hands touch her bare flesh, felt her breasts harden under his gentle pressure, then pulled back when he tugged at the waistband of her pettipants. *"No, Goody."* But a moment later it was no longer just his hands, but his mouth. She thought she would die. Then the baby let out a wail upstairs, giving her a good excuse to stop, though it was really Goody who stopped, and when she sat up looking at him from under her tousled hair she knew he understood. "I don't want to rush you" is what he always said, making each step they took together her choice and more precious than the last. She understood how different her explorations with Goody were from the insistent grapplings Angela had described with Michael ("He was beggin' me, girl, said I was causing him so much pain"). Tish knew better than to give herself up too easily. It was different for Angela and Jasmine; they were black girls with black boys. She had to be tougher, tighter, more certain.

In the couple of months before school ended, Tish was driven to distraction. Mrs. Espy was losing patience. "I ask you to do so little around here, and you can't even remember to do the minimum. . . ."

Tish felt reckless and uncaring. It was for Goody that she dressed and fixed her hair, just on the off chance she'd run into him. He'd quit his job at the Sparkle Super, where he bagged groceries, and started working at his uncle's barber shop, Skin's, just on the edge of the west side. It was an old storefront in a mostly residential area, left over from the early days when there had been a black "downtown," consisting of a corner market and a cleaner's. The shop was always full of black men having their hair cut and "telling lies," as Goody put it. There was even a striped barber pole outside and an awning. Goody could make her laugh by imitating some of the old men who came inside, and it was the laughter he could summon up in her that made her love him more. She was enchanted by the funny stories he told, the toasts he recited, his imitations of Rudy Ray Moore, and his keen observations on life on the west side in general. Tish had taken to detouring past Skin's on her way over to Peachy's or Angela's, in the hopes she would accidentally on purpose happen on Goody. She could never get up the nerve to actually stop, but counted on the chance he would be emerging just as she sauntered by. Serendipity would bring them together.

He began calling her "Red," something she wouldn't allow anyone else to do. She didn't like it, exactly, it embarrassed her, but he said it so endearingly she couldn't let on she minded.

At home, observing herself in the dimly lit mirror, she imagined his desire for her, in the poses she memorized and assumed in reflection, right, left, front, back. Once she brought her own two lips right up to the mirror and pressed them against the glass, imagining herself alternately as Goody and then as herself.

*   *   *

Spring came early. One morning green sprouts appeared on the trees, and warm breezes wafted off the lake. Tepid rains began, and afterward the streets steamed. "April showers bring May flowers," Mrs. Espy remarked, looking out the kitchen window at the budding yard. Spring also brought news that Peachy was in trouble—pregnant by four months—a fact she had up until now managed to keep secret not only from her parents but almost everyone else. Tish could have cursed herself for not realizing. She really was blind. The revelation that Peachy was not only carrying a child, but had been having sex while pretending otherwise, left Tish dumbfounded.

It was Angela who passed on the news with relish ("I've known ever since Edna told me," she said smugly). And astute Wanda, who further confirmed the truth in the girls' rest room at school.

"Whose is it?" Tish wanted to know, but Wanda just shook her head.

"Why should I know? I ain't askin'," she said. "Some nigga." Tish felt strangely aggrieved.

"Don't act like she died," said Wanda, pulling a rake through her hair. She leaned over and gave Tish's hair a quick comb-through, then returned to her own. "She's not the first girl to get pregnant. But don't tell her I told you. She's scared what her daddy will do."

The information weighed heavily on Tish, and she felt foolish that she hadn't been the one to figure it out, especially after several nights of lying next to Peachy in her bed when they talked their way into the darkness. And how she'd gone on and on about Goody with Peachy patiently listening and not saying a word about her stretching womb and the growing pressure on her bladder, and the knowledge that a new life was taking shape inside her. How was it everyone else knew things she didn't? Didn't Peachy trust her? Maybe it was because Tish had been all tangled up in herself, with no thought for anyone else.

"What's she going to do?" she asked.

Wanda shot her a look. "What do you mean?"

"You know . . ." said Tish.

Wanda sucked her teeth hard. "Black girls *keep* their babies."

Tish mused, "Why didn't she tell me?"

"Maybe she thought you'd judge her, you know, with the kind of family you come from and all," said Wanda. "Peachy keeps a lot to herself, always has. She's never been one to let you know what she really thinks or does. She always tries to act all happy and shit, but she's got a lot on her mind. Peaches is deeper than people give her credit for. They see happy-go-lucky, but that ain't the whole story."

"I feel so stupid," said Tish. "I never knew she was messing around. Do you think it's Vic Wooten?"

Wanda shook her head. "Naw, that brother isn't Peachy's type. I think I know who it is, but I'm not at liberty to say." She glanced at Tish's stricken face. "You take things too hard, girl. Peachy's gonna be fine. Her daddy'll throw a fit, and Miss Connie will cry, but they'll get over it. Don't tell anyone. She wants to finish her sophomore year, and if the school finds out, they'll kick her out."

Tish went on to class, out of sorts. When she later glimpsed Peachy laughing with Tina, she looked for obvious signs that Peachy was changed. What must such knowledge do to a girl?

"Hey, Tish," Peachy called out as if this were another ordinary day, and Tish said, "Hey, Peachy," back, and wondered if the flush rising in her face would give her away. It hurt her to think that Peachy had gone to the others and told, but not to her. And to think that Angela found out before she did! Only because Angela lived on the right side of town to know and care about such things and she, Tish, tucked away on the east side, consumed with her own worries, would always be the last to know.

For Tish the change in season also signaled being just that much closer to her sixteenth birthday, when she could legally drive, and the Rambler would be hers. At the last minute she began studying hard for exams and pulled mostly B's in all her classes, which didn't please her parents much, but which got them off her back. The girls' ensemble sang an end-of-the-year concert, and Tish thought she caught sight of

Goody at the back of the auditorium. There were senior graduation parties around town, including one for Holly's boyfriend, Taylor. Tish and Peachy and Dev all went together, first briefly to Taylor's, where a bunch of his hippie university friends showed up and made much over Peachy and Dev and Tish. Even as they laughed their way down Taylor's driveway (*Token Negro it-shay; do you think they were on acid?*), Tish wrestled with her desire to ask Peachy about the baby. It all felt so strange, Peachy now inhabiting a different world. Tish kept glancing at Peachy's middle, but Peachy had always been on the chunky side, and it was hard to say. Maybe it was a mistake. Maybe Peachy only thought she was pregnant, and there was no baby, and things could go on the way they had before.

Tish knew better than to count on running into Goody at Cintrilla Moore's graduation party (hadn't he mentioned he might have to drive down to Chillicothe with his mother for his cousin Phyllis's graduation, or was it his half-sister's, and then there was the sick aunt?), but she was still disappointed he wasn't there. She was so preoccupied with the chance he might show up that she almost missed what at the time seemed unremarkable. Reggie was amiably acting as host and deejay in the Moores' cramped living room, while Mr. and Mrs. Moore sat with other adults around a kitchen table playing whist and drinking Gallo in paper Dixie cups. Tish threaded her way through the house with Peachy and Dev, and then took up her post by the record player. Over the mantel a huge hand-painted banner said, "Congratulations to our graduate." Framed family photos were everywhere. It looked as if someone had been snapping pictures of the Moore family every second of their lives. More people began to arrive. Several white senior girls who had served on Cintrilla's homecoming court when she was chosen to be the first black queen showed up in party dresses and corsages, and Cintrilla's mother got up from the card table and made a point of being especially friendly and thanking them for coming. In the mix and stew of all the little scenes, Tish stood quietly, desperate for Goody, and munching potato chips. She was dying for a cigarette and wishing she had one. That's when the unremarkable thing happened.

Reggie, who had one moment been talking and gesturing with customary ardor, suddenly bent down and kissed Peachy on the mouth.

One hand went briefly to her waist. It was not a play brother kiss; it was an unexpected gesture of passion. It also signaled possession. And there was the utter absorption on Peachy's face that gave it all away. Even after Reggie had pulled back, her eyes stayed closed, holding on to the moment long after it was over. What had passed between them was so private that Tish felt embarrassed, as if she'd intruded. Then Reggie turned to greet more guests, and Peachy feigned casualness, made a point of getting Dev's attention. She whispered something and they began laughing together as if nothing had happened.

Tish busied herself by filling a paper plate with potato salad which she then wolfed down. Anxiously, she paced the edges of the cramped living room, thinking how nothing ever seemed to be what it was. She felt deceived, or blind, or both. How had she missed this? What else had Peachy kept from her? *Peachy and Reggie!* Surrounded by photos of the Moores, she followed the chronicle of their lives, births, birthdays, weddings, graduations, all carefully posed and framed, as if life were merely a series of static moments. Where was Goody? Even though she knew better, she prayed for him to walk in with his slightly sheepish grin, and surprise her. She wanted to hear Reggie say, "How you doin', man?" before turning to call out, "Tish, Goody's here." The ache developing inside her turned to full-blown panic. Nothing, not the lively chatter around her, and not the Temptations belting out "Ball of Confusion," felt right. Without saying a word to either Peachy or Dev, she walked straight out of the Moores' front door and down the driveway, fighting back tears. This wasn't the way things were supposed to be.

Mrs. Espy sat in the passenger seat of the Rambler. "You're getting to be quite the driver," she said with genuine pride. "How would you like the Rambler next year?"

"To use or own?" said Tish.

"Well, it will be mostly yours. I hope you'll let me use it once in a while if I need to." She smiled.

Tish smiled back. She felt an unexpected burst of camaraderie. At last she and her mother were connecting. True, the Rambler was a far cry from the yellow Mustang convertible Holly Penn's father was bestowing on her at the end of the year, but who cared? For a moment Tish just wanted to bask in her mother's generosity. It was an open acknowledgment that Tish was almost a grown-up. Maybe the last year had all been a misunderstanding, and next year would be different. In an impulsive moment of weakness she almost confessed the truth about Peachy, wanting so much for her mother to understand. But then she drew back, concentrating on maneuvering the turquoise and white car that would soon be hers. She drove into the center of town, where her mother had errands to run. Just as they pulled into an empty parking spot, Goody came sauntering out of Woolworth's. Her pulse quickened. He was alone. Each time she came upon him accidentally in the broad daylight like this, it was like seeing him for the first time.

"That's Marcus Goodman!" she announced to her mother, chest tightening with excitement.

Her mother was rooting in her bag for the shopping list.

Goody had paused and was now looking up and down the street, as if expecting someone. It was all Tish could do to keep from leaping out of the car. How surprised he'd be! She'd drag him over to meet her mother, and they would shake hands, and her mother would invite him to dinner. And maybe they'd go for a ride in the Rambler.

"Mom, there's Marcus Goodman," she repeated.

Mrs. Espy lifted her head and squinted through the windshield. "Who?" She paused. "Is *that* the boy you spend so much time on the phone with?"

A door had opened. Tish nodded. And now Goody was heading their way.

"He looks old," said Mrs. Espy tautly. "A lot older than you."

"Just a little bit," Tish said. "I'm almost sixteen, and he's barely eighteen."

It was an exaggeration. Goody would be nineteen in December, but her mother wouldn't know the difference. "Michael's two years older than Angela, and Wanda goes out with college guys."

She felt nervous springing her mother on Goody like this, but it was the most natural way to do it, so much better than a formal introduction in her living room, where the whole family would gather for their overly polite scrutiny and interrogation.

There was silence, then her mother cleared her throat. "How do you even know someone like that, Letitia?"

"I'd like to introduce you," Tish said. She began to lean out her window.

"Tish, don't," said her mother. She reached over and put her hand on Tish's arm.

Tish stopped. "What do you mean?" She turned.

"I don't want to meet him. He looks busy and I'm busy. We have errands to run." She shook her list in the air.

"But, Mom, he's right here." Goody was strolling by, not ten feet away, with the familiar little roll to his gait, his eyes squinting against the sun, arms swinging loosely in the warm air. He hadn't seen them, hadn't recognized the Rambler.

"He looks—well, rough," said her mother and turned her head.

"Rough!" said Tish.

"Yes, he looks like a ruffian."

"A ruffian?" Tish felt her mind jamming. She was totally unprepared for this. By now Goody had passed and was sauntering on down the street. Her mother's word had briefly rendered him unfamiliar. Tish felt the yank of outrage.

Just then, Reggie Moore came out of the bank, and both men stopped on the street and exchanged black-power handshakes. Her mother stiffened palpably beside her. A cold chill had entered the car.

Under her mother's hard stare, the two men seemed more like actors on a stage. They came apart in pieces: Reggie's do-rag, Goody's rangy natural, the way Reggie dipped and moved and threw back his head to laugh, the slow, easy grin crossing Goody's face. Two men—two black men—acknowledging and celebrating each other on the street, invisible to the white passersby who detoured around them.

"I like Goody a lot," Tish said, nervousness pouring through her. "I mean, he's kind of like my—my boyfriend." She tried out the words for the first time. Not "old man," as Wanda would have said, not "my heart," as Angela would have said, not "the dude I'm talking to." No, "boyfriend" was the kind of word Holly Penn would use, streamlined, inoffensive, and appropriately white. It was a word her mother wouldn't have to question, one she would find familiar, easy to swallow.

Mrs. Espy turned and stared Tish full in the face.

"What do you mean, boyfriend?"

"I mean I—I really care about him, Mom."

"What?" Mrs. Espy almost spat the word out. "What do you mean? *Him?* My God, you're a fifteen-year-old-girl, Letitia, highly impressionable and naive about the world. How can you say that man over there is your boyfriend? Don't be ridiculous. Look at him, Letitia."

"What's wrong with him?" Tish felt tears crowding her eyes.

"I won't even continue this absurd discussion," said Mrs. Espy. "What could you be thinking?"

How could Tish have miscalculated so dreadfully? And just when she thought she was getting a handle on things.

"What do you mean?" she said softly.

"I *mean,*" said her mother, "that you need to use your head more and not let your sympathies get in the way."

On the sidewalk, Goody had doubled over laughing and Reggie was laughing too. He had turned and was moving away from Goody, but his hand was outstretched in a lingering gesture. Tish heard him say, "Right on, man, later for you."

She watched helplessly as Goody leaned forward and gripped Reggie's hand at arm's length one more time before they turned and went their separate ways, Reggie crossing the street to the square, probably to drink a little wine, and Goody rounding the corner, the sunlight catching fire in his natural and lighting him up briefly as if in effigy before he disappeared.

The tight-lipped woman next to her opened the car door, gripping her errand list as if all you had to do to keep life under control was go down a list, checking off items. "Mom," Tish tried helplessly, ashamed of herself for her own cowardice. The Rambler, her love for Goody, her desire for freedom all hung in the balance. She watched as her mother, in no mood for further discussion, slammed the car door and strode purposefully across the same pavement Goody had just walked. Tish felt paralyzed. Her mother had made her point. Angela called it hypoc-risy. Was it bigotry? Without naming it, that was what Tish was left holding, along with the steering wheel of the Rambler, in her trembling hands.

XXVIII

But it *was* love. Her mother was wrong. Tish knew that in the same way she knew the air was there for her to breathe. And the love only grew, blooming in secret, like the flowers now filling her mother's garden with color. She wanted things to be easy, to walk through her front door with Goody, the way Angela walked through hers with Michael, and have her parents say, "How are you kids?" and her mother offer Goody some of his favorite bread pudding, and then all of them would sit around casually, no points to be proven, nothing to be accepted or understood. Just Tish and Goody holding hands on the sofa like any other couple in love. Why did the very thought fill her with such desperation?

"*. . . I didn't know just what was wrong with me/till your kiss helped me name it . . . You make me feel . . . you make me feel . . . you make me feel like a natural woman . . . Oh, baby, what you done to me . . .*"

It was the blood and guts of love, inexplicable and unexpressible, the deep-down, dusky intimacy that works its way through two people's hearts. It made her dizzy and clumsy. It was total distraction. *You make me feel like a natural woman.* What didn't Aretha know?

Tish was getting dressed for the noon shift at the Memorial Inn.

They'd called at the last minute, barely giving her time to iron the blue and yellow uniform. She checked herself in the mirror. She imagined running in to Goody. She imagined his coming to the restaurant and ordering a meal, and how she would serve him, and he would be impressed with her efficiency. Three hours later, on her way home from the inn, drenched in sweat, she would search each passing car for some sign of Goody. He must be out there. She stood for a moment on the pavement and closed her eyes, and lifted her face to the sun. It was warmth she craved. Warmth and tenderness. And possibility.

Love had something to do with those sticky-hot, lazy afternoons when everyone in her family had finally gone off to Curtis Pond to swim, and the airless house swelled up like a balloon. Outside the lawn seemed to sink in the heat and cicadas sizzled in the ivy crawling up the walls. From where she sprawled sweating on the sofa, legs and arms spread, she could measure her breathing by the tick-tock of her grandmother's red clock on the living room mantel and the swamp of heat rising inside her. It was unbearable, the beating of her own heart, longing mounting to a breaking point. And it wasn't appeased by the whirl of the box fans or the night breeze that would begin licking around the edges of her window. She tossed and turned in bed, wrapping her arms around herself, then hating what felt like mockery. It was Goody she wanted, and then she'd hate herself for her own desires.

Each time the quiet was broken by the hum of a distant motor, she thought she'd die. Every passing car raised her hopes as it slowed down at the corner. But then it would pass on down her street to another house—just somebody who had been out now going home. Someone like Holly Penn or Jeff Anderson. It was only when she heard the careful, muffled slam of a car door at the corner that the purest kind of excitement washed over her. It was then that the night exploded with promise, because as sometimes happened, Goody's shoes squished over the dewy lawn, making a soft sucking sound with each step in the lush grass below. Some nights—she'd never know which—long after she'd gotten off work at the restaurant, Goody appeared under her window, in the wee hours of the morning after he'd been out—probably over at Reggie Moore's smoking weed and listening to Miles and Coltrane. There was his soft whistle, the rustle of leaves at the end of the branch he reached up and shook. What was it that woke her? Chances were she hadn't been asleep at all, or if she had, she slept so lightly, expectation holding her on its razor's edge, that his presence was instantly known to her.

She rose up on her knees in her white gown, and moved to the window at the end of her bed. She could make out his silhouette below, his hair a furious halo against the night sky. She unhooked the screen and put her head out into the same night air, imagining her lips against his. So close . . . *You make me feel like a natural* . . . His voice urging her to come down—just for a minute. He would say in his teasing way, "Come on, girl, I just want to talk to you," but she knew from his smile he meant much more. How to stop the ache in her body. The longing that threatened never to cease. "Stop," she'd say, shivering from nerves. "I can't. You know I can't."

He'd make her laugh there in the dark, clowning under the tree, describing how all evening he'd seen nothing but a bunch of "hard ankles." Harmless diversion, just passing the time until he could hook up with a ride over to Woodland. *Gots to get my own ride,* he'd promise, and joke about how his uncle at Skin's needed to give him a raise. She whispered down to him about how busy work had been, with the annual socialist convention in town, serving hot meals to earnest, bearded men in socks and sandals who tipped poorly, and women who seemed fierce and smart. Wanda worked a couple shifts with her and made her laugh, talking in the back about customers, imitating them, the pompousness of the men with their precise diction.

But laughter couldn't stanch desire. It was finally the wanting part that stirred her into action, and several times she slipped down the back stairs into the yard to him, almost fainting at every creak in the floorboards and the explosive click of the back door lock.

It was scary enough meeting in the shadows on the side of her parents' house, in bare feet and gown, with Goody pulling her against him and touching her all over, but scarier yet parting from him and heading back in the house, changed and yet more herself than she knew, wondering if her empty bed had been discovered, and imagining what she'd say if it was. *I was looking at stars. That's all. I couldn't sleep.* What could her parents say to that?

There were places on her body she'd never known existed, all coming alive under Goody's hands. *R-E-S-P-E-C-T.* She took pleasure from his pleasure, amazed at her power to incite such feelings. She imagined what it would be like to be Goody, touching her. How the turn of her mouth or the soft sigh of her exhale had him murmuring "Baby, baby" in her ear. After a time he would get a little exasperated, step back, raise his head and chant *Damn, damn, damn* to the sky. But he was careful with her.

Now it was she who kept insisting, ready to lose herself, and he would be the one to say, "Not now, baby, not now," as if protecting her from herself. *Do-right woman, Do-right man . . .*

Pressed against the garage wall behind her house, the rough bark of her mother's garden mulch under her bare feet, she knew this was a chance she couldn't afford to take. She memorized the angle of his head and the slow axis of his shoulders when he went to turn around. She had claimed these things. They were hers. What felt like minutes stretched into hours. There was light along the far horizon. But she couldn't escape the facts of her body, and it was hard to separate where she ended and he began. It was the getting lost that she missed most when she was away from him, the forgetting of herself as she knew herself, and the transformation into the object of Goody's desire.

Once on her way back in, she heard the upstairs toilet flush, and someone's heavy footsteps padding between the rooms. Panicked, she hid herself in the darkness next to the kitchen sink, terrified of discovery. She waited, without breathing, until whoever it was had settled whatever pre-dawn business they'd had and returned to bed, before she crept up the stairs to her room. She lay in bed unable to sleep with the bulk of pillow pressed against herself, imagining it to be Goody. When she finally sat up and looked out the window again, the yard below was empty. Moonlight was fading into morning. Goody was gone, evaporated like the dew. The only proof that she hadn't dreamed it all was the thin gold ID bracelet on her wrist now catching the faint rays of early light.

Inside he'd engraved *My girl Red,* the date, followed by his initials. If her mother asked about it, which she surely would, Tish had already worked it out in her head that she would claim it as an early birthday present from Angela and then pray Angela didn't contradict.

Long after the sun was up she was slow to awaken and her mother, irritated, recommended she go to bed earlier if she wasn't getting enough sleep. As she moved like a somnambulist around the kitchen, still in her nightgown, taking the breakfast cereal back out of the cupboard, her mother's eye was on her, hard and suspicious. She felt a momentary clinch of pity for her mother's passionless life, mired in routine. Tish would never be so ordinary. She would always love Goody with the same intensity. In the hustle and bustle of family life, between Francis's tantrums and Ford's piano lessons, she sought a hiding place where she could sit and think, and imagine. It had become a regular habit, conjuring up Goody in her daydreams, imagining long conversations, her astute observations about books she'd read, their shared politics. She counted the hours until he phoned, praying for privacy, crouched in the stairwell, dragging the phone on its too-short cord into the hall closet. Oddly, her mother made no mention of the phone calls. It was as if she and Tish had reached an unspoken understanding; Marcus Goodman existed harmlessly on the periphery of Mrs. Espy's consciousness, reduced to little more than a disembodied voice on the telephone. Naturally she assumed when Tish wasn't waiting tables she was with her girlfriends, or otherwise occupying herself alone in her room. In the late evenings, walking home from the Memorial Inn, still in her uniform, Tish felt possibility swell like the humidity, her own yearnings flowering in the night air. She stopped on several occasions just to catch her breath. Tonight he might come. It was always a possibility. When her father invited her out to look at stars, she declined and went up to her room to wait. Everything she needed was right here on earth.

One afternoon, waiting for Goody's call, she settled down on the sofa, exhausted by love. A few feet from her Ford and square old Roger Lyons were playing speed chess on the floor. She closed her eyes, only faintly aware of the rhythmic *slap-slap* of the boys' hands on the chess clock button. In the humidity of the lazy afternoon she summoned up

Goody, like a magician's trick. Through the heat Goody's mouth moved like velvet across hers, his fingers tracing down her back. She thought she would lie there unable to move, until she died. She wondered if people really could die from love. In the distance the phone rang. . . . "Letitia, telephone!" This time it was her father intoning matter-of-factly. He handed her the phone, moved out of the way, and headed back to his study to work.

From the other end of the line Goody's voice oozed, tender and honeyed. It was as if he'd read her mind. She had conjured him up just like that, her yearning materializing in the resonance of his voice. *Oh, baby, what you done to me.* Then she heard the ominous click at the other end of someone hanging up and with a sharp jolt she suspected her mother had picked up the phone from upstairs and purposely listened in long enough to hear him call her "sugar." Any moment she expected her mother would sweep down the stairs and, with an accusing look, yank the phone from her hand. Why had he been so careless? Didn't he know better? She grew quiet, almost sullen, her muscles tightening in fear. Didn't he understand what was at stake?

"I'll be downtown later," he said casually, and she murmured, "Hmmm-mmmm." And then, as he often did, he casually mentioned a time, and she said, "Hmmm-mmmm" again, confused by her own secrecy, and hoping he hadn't misunderstood.

Finding a reason to leave the house after Goody called was a challenge. She played it cool, pretending she was going to do one thing, then having a last-minute switch of plans. She faked dialing Angela and parroted a quick conversation into the mouthpiece for her mother's benefit. She hung up. "Angela wants me to meet her at the square," she called out, hating herself for the lie. She didn't want it to be like this. But it was necessary. Goody under her parents' scrutiny would cease to be the man she loved, and turn shabby and second-rate through their eyes, someone she had to defend. She could picture it now, her parents' grim politeness, subjecting him to subtle interrogations, her mother's disapproval bordering on rudeness. His visit wouldn't be easy and light, the way such visits were at Peachy's or Angela's, where the presence of boys was natural and welcome. And where Tish saw a handsome, afroed, brown-skinned boy, clumsy and tender in love, her parents would see someone threatening and unfamiliar. They would of course make the false equation with Popeye and Gina that would drop like a template over Tish and Goody.

Escaping from the house, she practically ran all the way to the square. The excuse was simple, but she complicated it so as not to be pinned down. She was going downtown to meet Angela, who would be getting off work from the hardware store. They were going to pick up a culotte dress Angela had on layaway, Peachy might meet them for a soda at the Campus Restaurant; the falsehood spun its own course. Vagueness offered outs. *Might be, could be, maybe will* . . . no *for sure's.*

The bottoms of her sandals scraped the pavement. She desperately hoped her hair hadn't zigzagged out of control. On the way she smoked half a cigarette, her bowels cramping from nervousness.

When she arrived at the square, a few summer school students, mostly hippies, from the university were sprinkled around on the grass, books open. She leaned against the track, trying to appear casual, then decided she looked foolish, so obviously waiting. Where was Goody? Had she misunderstood? She crossed the street to Nickles' Bakery for a red cream soda. Jasmine's two girlfriends Maxine and Benita were at the counter buying ice cream cones. Tish ducked down one of the aisles until they had gone out. She didn't want people thinking the things people could think. "You know how sisters be sometimes," Peachy liked to say, shaking her head. And Tish knew exactly what she meant, but she also knew that once she and Goody were really together, the whole world would know and accept them.

The heat reflecting up from the pavement scorched her bare legs. She was sorry now she hadn't worn her flowered culottes; they gave shape to her calves. Walking around in the sun had given her more color, and even Wanda had remarked, "You trying to get black on us, girl?" and laughed about white girls and their tans.

Where was he? Precious minutes were ticking away.

She crossed back to the square and plunked herself down on the grass. If he wasn't there in two minutes . . . She glanced over at the hands of the bank clock. Okay, another five . . . She played with the fringe of her macramé belt. The grass made her legs itch. Everything inside her had gone all jumpy. A car honked. She didn't bother looking up at first, but when she did, there was Lamar's white Chevy Impala pulling alongside the curb. The passenger door opened, and Goody squeezed his long frame out of the backseat. Things slowed down. When he materialized, she felt an odd jolt of disappointment. Why hadn't she noticed the stringy patch of hair on his chin before? Was he growing a goatee? She hoped not. Inwardly she recoiled.

As if that weren't bad enough, Cindy Pavelka sat in the passenger seat of the Impala, bold as day, where Jasmine should have been. She stared out at Tish and smiled as if they had something in common. And there was Goody grinning his lazy, sloppy smile, the one that in their hidden moments had been just for her. He motioned Tish over. He'd left his shirt unbuttoned in the heat and she could make out the taut muscles of his bare torso. The sight of so much flesh embarrassed her, made her feel exposed, as if something very private had now gone public.

Car engine running, Lamar leaned across Cindy. "Come on, Red!"

It was Goody's private name for her, now turned taunt in Lamar's mouth. Goody began sauntering toward her. How fine he was in the sunlight with his beautiful hair and the bare skin of his muscled arms extending from the open shirt. She hadn't realized the different shapes and angles that made him up. And now that she saw him straight on, the goatee didn't bother her, it had just startled her.

"What's wrong, baby?" He held out his hand. She refused it. "We're thinkin' of goin' by Reggie's. Wanna come?"

"No," Tish snapped. "I don't want to sit over there and watch you all get high. And I'm definitely not going anywhere with *her.*"

He paused, puzzled, and spread his hands. "What's up?"

"First and foremost, I'm not getting in that car with that white bitch," she said. There, the words were out.

Goody rocked back on his heels in surprise and then burst out laughing. "Girl, you're somethin' else. You been hangin' with those hard-ass sisters too long. Next thing you'll be jumpin' sapphire on me." He pulled on his goatee with his long fingers. "Come on, Red, don't do me like this."

The nickname still made her uncomfortable. It was an intimacy he hadn't fully earned, one that seemed to refer to someone not herself. Tish yanked a fistful of leaves from one of the crab apple trees and concentrated on picking them apart. In biology last year they had been assigned cross sections, and she had learned the layers by heart: cuticle, upper epidermis, vascular bundle, spongy layer cells, lower epidermis—*oh, yeah*—and somewhere in there was the stoma, and something called "simple hair" that had made her and Angela laugh themselves sick. They started joking about good hair, bad hair, and simple hair.

"Baby, you're tripping," said Goody. It was obvious he was puzzled.

"I'm not playing," said Tish. She nodded toward the car. "I *know* you don't think I'm going anywhere with that ho."

Goody's expression turned into one of amusement. "Come on, Little Miss Thang."

Tish crossed her arms over her chest. Fragments of green leaves rained to the ground. "No," she said. "Jasmine's my girl and I'm not getting in Lamar's car with *her.*"

Goody sighed. "Oh, it's like that," he said. Lamar honked the horn and called out. Goody looked back and put his hands in the air, signaling he had a little problem.

"Tish, please, don't make me look stupid here. How about they just drop us off at the arboretum, okay? It's a nice day, we can take a walk. I know you don't have a lot of time and I was running late. Why are you trippin' so hard?"

Tish paused. Maybe it was harmless. Maybe she was overreacting. After all, she couldn't save Jasmine from Lamar. But she didn't want for a second to be seen in the company of Cindy or compared with a girl like that.

"Come on," Goody coaxed. He offered his hand. It was a sweet gesture, meant to soften her up. Reluctantly she took it, felt the soft, familiar pressure that signaled understanding. If only she could always be with him like this, alone, the two of them.

"They're just dropping us off, right?" she said.

Goody was pulling her along. Despite an uneasy feeling, Tish allowed him to help her squeeze behind Cindy. Goody plunked himself next to her and kissed her on the cheek.

"Hey, Tish," said Lamar, leaning around to grin.

"Hey, yourself," said Tish coldly. Arms still folded, she concentrated her stare out the window.

"You know Cindy, right?" Lamar said.

Tish barely nodded. She avoided looking at the back of the dyed-yellow cotton-candy head.

Cindy, oblivious, turned the radio up. Tish didn't know if it was Cindy's sense of entitlement or her sheer boldness, or both, that irritated. The song was "Grazin' in the Grass" by Hugh Masekela. "Ooooh, I love this," Cindy chirped, and began to dance jerkily in her seat. Her voice was so white and so squeaky. Like chalk on a chalkboard.

"We still headin' to Reggie's crib?" Lamar pantomimed smoking a joint.

Tish elbowed Goody hard. He began to concoct reasons why they couldn't. Tish relaxed. It was a short ride to the arboretum. She was thinking of Wanda and what Wanda would do or say right now. Being this close to Cindy in the car felt like betrayal. She wanted to say something, but she wasn't Wanda, and what would she look like calling Cindy out for being with Lamar?

Lamar maneuvered down by the railroad tracks and across the back of campus. He and Cindy were talking happily in the front seat. Cindy made some lame joke about "Lamar's permanent tan," sticking out her pale arm for contrast. Tish wanted to die right there in the backseat from embarrassment.

She was relieved when Lamar pulled up in the overgrown lot behind the arboretum, but stunned when he cut off the ignition, and Cindy grabbed her purse. She glanced over at Goody—hard—and he sort of shrugged. Cindy was laughing and then Lamar leaned over and tickled her and she giggled some more, and a moment later they too were getting out of the car, and Cindy was saying, "Oh, this is so beautiful out here. Let's walk with Goody and Tish before we go to Reggie's."

Tish was secretly cursing herself for having gotten in the car to begin with. They all began walking (Tish tried to drop back a little in case someone should come along and see them). Lamar seemed out of place in the woods with his shined shoes and tan slacks. Cindy, her big white legs extending from a skort, clutched his arm proprietarily.

Tish yanked Goody back a few feet. "What's going on?" she hissed. "I said, I don't want to be with them. Don't do this to me, Goody."

He grimaced. "I didn't know they were coming. I can't tell brother man he isn't welcome."

"I'm not going anywhere with them," Tish said. "You need to say something. Now."

Goody stopped. He pondered a moment, looked awkward.

"Hey, bro," he called out to Lamar. "We gonna take off, okay, man? Me and Tish got some business to take care of. Y'all go on ahead."

Lamar turned around. "What's up?"

"Tish here . . ." Goody paused. "We need to talk for a minute. You know how it is."

Lamar began to grin. Tish hated what was obviously running through his mind. "Yeah, man, I can dig it."

Cindy said, "You two have fun!" and she waved her hand as if she and Tish were equals with something in common. A thin silver charm bracelet jangled in the air. Tish didn't answer, just turned on her heel. She was desperate to get away.

Goody followed, but the mood was false. The trees and the smell of the damp earth on the floor of the forest were all wrong. Under other circumstances Tish would have pointed out the shagbark hickories and the signs of animal tracks leading back up toward the reservoir. She would have shown Goody what she knew, just the way she had pointed out stars to him, constellations, made connections between them and the world at large. Goody was behind her. "Why'd you go and cop an attitude?" he wanted to know. "What's wrong with you?"

Tish turned and put a hand on her hip. "Let's get something straight, Goody," she said. "I'm not like that."

"Like what?" he said.

"Don't act all innocent. You know exactly what I'm talking about. I told you I don't play that stuff."

"Damn!" Goody threw his head back. "You're crazy."

"Crazy?" said Tish. "No, I'm not crazy. And I'm not stupid either. I am not your little *white broad,* okay?" She felt the anger building. "Lamar and Cindy—I just don't want to have to be around them. I'm Jasmine's friend . . . you know who I run with. I'm sick of these white girls trying to go with black guys. . . ."

The words evaporated into the gray, humid air. Goody pondered this a moment. "Then what do you think about us?"

"I don't know," said Tish. "What do *you* think?"

"Well, I don't think of you as my little white broad, if that's what you mean."

"I'm not like Cindy," said Tish tersely.

"Hey, everything's cool," said Goody. "Lamar just wants to have some fun for a change. Things haven't been right between him and Jasmine for a long time."

"Haven't been right," repeated Tish. "I'll say they haven't been right, with Lamar always creeping around. Everyone knows how he messes around on Jasmine. I saw him with Cindy the night of Jasmine's party." She paused, because now the thread would lead back to mention of Sonya and her own jealousy that night. She didn't want Goody to know she'd even given any of that a second thought. Play it cool. That was the rule. You watch the right and left, but you keep walking straight ahead.

"Look," she said, "I saw Lamar and Cindy at the Boot Center having some kind of argument." She could see Goody was unmoved. She decided to pull out all stops. "Lamar . . . well, Lamar tried to hit on me too. He was writing me these childish secret admirer notes all year. It was stupid. They were stupid. Lamar was stupid. He just wanted to mess things up with him and Jasmine. He's doing it on purpose."

Goody shrugged. "I don't interfere in other people's business." He grinned. "You can't blame blood for trying."

Tish hated him for his cowardliness.

"I know you can't say you don't like to see black and white to-gether," he said, "because where does that leave us?"

Tish paused. She chose her words carefully. "I don't consider us like that. I don't even think about being white. I mean—" She realized how foolish she sounded to him, but she was desperate to make him understand. "Not in that way. It's not like that. Look, Goody, there's a reason I don't hang with white girls. I'm not hung up on black boys the way Cindy and some of these others are. It's an experiment to them. They think they're doing something to rebel, to prove a point."

"And what about you?"

"I'm not rebelling. I'm just being myself."

Goody shrugged again. He began to draw her to him, but she didn't want that. His touch was no longer reassuring.

"Look," said Tish, "I think I just need to go home, okay? You can go to Reggie's if you want." She felt headachey and angry. The heat was getting to her.

Goody sighed. "Man, you are one hardheaded woman." He shook his head. She began to walk away from him. Part of her wanted him to follow and acknowledge she was different, that he didn't think of her as white.

She walked on. Footsteps fell softly behind her.

"Tish, don't leave," Goody pleaded. "Why you got rocks in your jaw?"

She felt herself beginning to relent. Maybe she was being unfair, misjudging Goody. She turned around and put her arms out. He drew her close and stroked her hair, his fingers catching in the curls. He withdrew them gently, chuckling. "Tish, I really dig you. I haven't had a lot of women in my life. . . ."

"I don't think you understand me," she said, her cheek pressed against the slightly damp material of his open shirt.

"Not true, baby," he said. "I understand you better than you think." Under the shimmering green trees he held her close. "You're something else, Red," he said appreciatively. "You know that?" He kissed her cheek. "You bring me some more of your poems today, sweetheart? I love those poems."

"Next time," she said and let herself go weightless against him. It was her words that were connecting them, the stanzas on paper that he tucked away in his pocket and complimented her on later. She began to write in her head all the things he wanted to say. She caught herself just before the words "I love you" teetered off her tongue.

XXIX

Mrs. Stubbs's Fleetwood pulled into the Espys' drive—without Peachy—just as Tish was leaving for work at the inn. Mrs. Espy heard the engine first and walked out onto the porch with baby Francis toddling behind her, spaghetti sauce splattered on the front of his overalls. Mrs. Stubbs cut off the motor and got out of the car. She seemed tired, or sick, Tish wasn't sure which, and for the first time as she came up their walk, Tish noticed how sallow her complexion was and the slight limp in her left leg. Peachy had once mentioned her mother had a touch of arthritis.

"Well, hello," Mrs. Espy called out uncertainly. "I guess the girls are working the same shift tonight."

Mrs. Stubbs smiled politely and when she got to the bottom step, she stopped with a heavy sigh. Mrs. Espy urged her to come inside.

"No, I can't, thank you," said Mrs. Stubbs. As hot as it was, she wasn't even sweating. "I've just come by—in the hopes you might have seen or heard from Peaches."

"Well, no," said Mrs. Espy, and then she looked at Tish. "Have you?"

Tish shook her head. She had an odd feeling. What did Mrs. Stubbs know? What had Peachy done?

"I'm trying to find her before her father does." She paused, choosing her words carefully. "I was hoping she'd come here. She's not at Wanda's and she's not at Tina's. I went by there just a little bit ago."

"Please come in," urged Mrs. Espy.

"I can't. I need to go over to the campus and see if she's gone up there. I'm sorry to have bothered you."

She started to turn and walk away. Tish couldn't help herself. "Has something happened to Peachy?" she asked.

Mrs. Stubbs paused there on the walkway, the faint summer breeze ruffling the bottom edge of her flowered house dress. Her face, usually ageless, now showed signs of wear. Her voice was flat. "I thought you knew." She began to cry softly. "I thought everybody knew but me."

The truth was out. Mrs. Espy was talking now, but her words blurred in Tish's ears. It was obvious her mother didn't yet understand, and when Mrs. Stubbs uttered the word "pregnant," Mrs. Espy was quick with words of consolation. She was stumbling down a path she feared she might one day find herself on. Mrs. Stubbs was crying harder, and Mrs. Espy came down the steps and placed her arm around Mrs. Stubbs's shoulder, offering again to have her come inside and sit down.

Mrs. Stubbs looked up at Tish through tear-filled eyes. "If she calls you or you see her, please tell her to come home. We need to talk to her and straighten all this out." She turned and went back to her car. Tish looked at her mother. She didn't want to hear what she knew her mother was about to say. Instead she brushed past her. "I'm going to be late," she said.

"Letitia!" Her mother's voice rang out. Tish turned. "You really don't know anything about this?"

"No," said Tish stonily, "I don't know where Peachy is."

She couldn't stand the accusing look on her mother's face, as if it were she who had gotten pregnant and not Peachy. She went on down the driveway, carrying her waitress uniform folded up in a brown paper sack. The Rambler, freshly washed, was parked on the street. Soon, she thought, soon.

What with all the buzz about Peachy it was hard to concentrate on anything at work. Wanda was on the same shift, and she kept ordering Tish to "hurry your ass up." At break, they sneaked out on the loading dock and smoked a cigarette. Wanda shook her head and said the Stubbses should have seen this one coming. It was obvious Wanda knew more than she was letting on, and much more than Tish knew. Later, Angela called Tish to find out what she'd heard, and claimed to have "some more information" Edna had extracted from Wanda, but which she wasn't at liberty to share. This drove Tish wild, but she pretended not to care, and turned around and phoned Tina, who sighed and said Peachy's parents were tripping big time, and Peachy was refusing to name the father. That evening Mrs. Espy interrogated Tish in not so subtle ways, and Tish found herself defending Peachy without knowing the details. For a week things were a big mystery, and then Tish heard from Angela, who'd overheard her own mother talking to the Stubbses, that Peachy had been "located." Rumor had it she had caught the bus to Cleveland and was staying with her older sister Ann and her family.

Tish felt an unexplainable sadness, knowing she had been cut out of Peachy's personal life. Peachy had lied to her. Held up a front and pretended to be a virgin. Made a big deal about it, made a point of saying she would never let someone have sex with her until she was married. Simple, easygoing Peachy. Tish had underestimated her, presumed foolishly they were both virgins. *Black girls don't give it up like white girls do.* So while Tish so carefully guarded her own virginity, Peachy had gone ahead and left Tish behind. Tish felt tricked.

The next afternoon instead of eating during her break at the Memorial Inn, she used the pay phone to try calling Goody at home, desperate for consolation. The line was busy for some time. Then his mother answered on a half ring and tersely announced he was out. Where? Tish wondered, but didn't dare to ask. "Would you tell him Tish called, please?" The voice came back sharply. "Tish? Okay." The phone was hung up. It was as if Tish's name were unfamiliar to her. Or a name among many names. Tish had the odd sensation Goody's mother had no intention of passing along his messages, figuring girls had no business calling her son anyway. Sadness mounted. She thought about calling him at Skin's, but didn't want to have to explain to some stranger who she was. She could try Information for Reggie Moore's and track Goody down there, but he had never given her permission or even encouraged her. Suddenly she had a vision of how different things were for Angela and Michael, Michael accounting for every minute of his time, Angela privy to the details of his schedule, dropping by his house unannounced, Mrs. Thompson and Mrs. Brown getting together. How casually and naturally their lives intertwined. In contrast, she was struck by how little she knew about Goody, how easily she accepted speculation for truth, how she conceded to his vague explanations, and put so much weight on their cobbled-together rendezvous. The very day-to-day of Goody's life was foreign to her, existed only in her imagination, built from oblique references and anecdotes. She stood there holding the pay phone receiver in her hand, trying to think if there was anyone else she could call. The recording came on to remind her that the phone was off the hook. *If this is an emergency* . . . It took her a moment to remember what to do.

XXX

Over the weekend, when the air was at its most stifling, Tish rode with Angela and Michael in Michael's Cutlass out to Curtis Pond to swim. In the backseat she huddled, self-conscious in her secondhand one-piece bathing suit with the padded bra that didn't fit properly. Her stomach stuck out, her legs stretched thin, knees bony. She kept glancing at Angela in the front seat, the new afro blooming around her face. She looked all shapely in her two-piece (everyone was wearing two-pieces now) and the thin, net cover-up she'd borrowed from her mother. Tish prayed she wouldn't turn to her and make the starving Biafra baby joke again.

On the sand they spread their towels and Tish stretched out on her stomach. Angela retrieved a deck of Bicycle cards from her beach bag, and she and Tish played gin rummy while Michael napped in the sun, one brown arm flung over his eyes, his hairless, muscular torso exposed. There was black curly hair in his armpits. Tish studied him from the corner of her eye with curiosity. It was rare she was this close to a half-naked boy who was almost a grown man. He seemed so much less naked than the white boys spread around, their pale skin almost obscene in the glare of sunlight. Umbrellas mushroomed down the strip of beach. When the weather got this hot, everyone came out, black and white. Tish leaned back on her elbows and let the sun work on her skin. She was in the habit of looking around for Goody every place she went, but she knew he wouldn't be here. He didn't swim, for one thing. And for another, he was probably out of town again.

"You're getting all red," Angela remarked, slapping down another card. She herself turned a luscious, pancake gold in the sun.

Tish sat up straight and examined arms and legs. It was true. Her fair skin was getting blotchy. She helped herself to the Sea & Ski Angela offered. They began to talk about Peachy.

"Peachy was just plain old stupid," said Angela impatiently. "She should have known better." She glanced down at Michael, who was gently snoring. She lowered her voice to the depths of intimacy, the sun shimmering along the golden edges of her afro. She looked Tish dead in the eye. "You don't ever, ever let them put it all the way in."

Tish trusted what Angela, with all her experience, was saying. After all, how many times had she been tempted with Goody, with one of them pulling back at the last minute, just in time? Perhaps she had Angela to thank for her moments of caution. Or maybe it was her own resolve when Goody's failed.

"I miss Peachy" was all Tish said. She could only imagine how their friendship would change once Peachy had the baby. Peachy had left Tish behind.

"She'll be back," said Angela. She studied the cards in her hand, spreading them out before her like a fan. "She's not the first girl this happened to. In fact, she makes the fifth girl in our class this year, if you count that white girl Debbie who had that ugly-ass, pointy-head baby."

Tish didn't say anything. Angela picked up a card and lay down four jacks on her towel.

"By the way," she said, "I have something to tell you." She paused and looked right at Tish. "I'm not supposed to talk about it yet—my parents swore me to secrecy—but I heard them last week talking about moving to Pittsburgh. Then last night my mother told Monica and me that my dad is accepting a job there in management." Tish wasn't sure she was hearing correctly. "At first I thought my dad was going without us, and I thought maybe they were getting a divorce, but my mom said absolutely not, the whole family's going." Angela stopped and adjusted her cards. "I called Michael last night and we talked." She glanced over at his face, angelic and smooth in sleep, and Tish imagined it was grief that had made him drowsy. "Tish, you can't tell anybody, okay?"

Tish could hardly believe her ears. "You're going to move?"

Angela paused and pursed her lips. "Okay, here's the straight scoop. It's definite. My dad's even picked out a house." She sighed. "Look, I'm sad about leaving—you know, you and Michael, of course. But, Tish, it's going to be the best thing that ever happened for me. I can start all over and not have to struggle to fit in so much. My school will be all black and no one's going to think twice about me."

There was excitement in her voice.

"Pittsburgh!" Tish said, shocked.

"Yeah," said Angela. She curled her bottom lip in a gesture of determination. "By the end of the month this girl will be outa here. Pittsburgh's a tough city, honey. They got niggas for days."

Enviously, Tish imagined the all-black school, and the new friends Angela would make. She had the sinking feeling that Angela had few qualms about leaving. Right at the time when Tish needed Angela most, for validation. It was her connection to Angela that had given her a tenuous place at school.

"What about Michael?" Tish asked, when what she really wanted to say was, *How about me?*

Angela sighed and scratched her scalp. "Nothing's gonna change. He'll drive the Cutlass over on weekends. Mama said he could sleep on the sofa if we went out late. Things will change, but life goes on."

Her matter-of-factness chilled Tish to the bone.

"Does Edna know?" Tish asked. She couldn't help herself.

"No," said Angela, "I wanted to tell you first. After all . . ." she paused and then set her cards down. She reached out in an impulsive gesture to take both of Tish's hands in hers. "You're still my best friend."

"Yeah," said Tish, the tide of despair rising inside her. "I know."

"You've stuck by me," said Angela earnestly. "I see all the shit you take from those phony white bitches. You always have. Because you're yourself, Tish. You don't dance to their tune."

Tish thought guiltily of all the times she hadn't stuck by Angela, how she'd laughed behind Angela's back with Peachy and Wanda at how sadiddy Angela could be. How she'd covered up her own uncertainties with moments of disloyalty. How she wasn't really herself, because she didn't know who her self was, how the voices in her head all contradicted one another.

"I'll miss you, Tish," Angela was saying. "I hope you'll come visit me. I know I'll never have another friend like you."

Tish knew Angela meant more, that the time had come for them to go their separate ways. Their friendship had been a consolation for two misfits. They'd stuck it out together, wasn't that all it really was? The change started with Angela getting tight with girls like Edna, and now when she moved to Pittsburgh she'd meet more black girls, and she'd find the new beginning that Tish longed for. For Tish, it signaled the end. Without Angela, without Peachy, she was nobody. It would mean once again circling on the fringes of acceptance.

"I'm going in the water," she said, getting up. Sand stuck to her legs. Heat throbbed through the clouds, scorching her skin, making her head swim.

"When you come back," said Angela, grabbing hold of her ankle playfully, "would you braid my hair for me?"

"Sure," Tish said, uncertainly. And then, overcome by emotion, she took off running, gathering speed until her feet struck the water and she lost her balance and tumbled in. She held her breath and floated under the surface for as long as she could. In those few moments there was nothing but the weight of silence, and Tish could imagine briefly a world free of words.

XXXI

Two weeks had passed since Peachy disappeared to Cleveland. Tish pictured the escape: a bus ride among strangers, under the cover of darkness. She tried to imagine where she herself might run. Without a destination, there was no escape.

She threw herself into working every day at the inn. The socialists left, and the teachers' institute people replaced them. They were a cheerier lot, who wore white name tags pinned to their chests that said "Hello, I'm _____. Tish felt a certain annoyance for their careful scans of the menus, deliberating earnestly over the cottage cheese salad or the Jell-O mold. They left better tips than the socialists, but expected more. *My peas are cold. Miss, could you bring me more napkins? Do you have just the green Jell-O?* Wanda worked some of the same shifts, and when she did, she and Tish would meet out back for a smoke, and laugh about the customers. "Did you see the way that one old white man ordered me around?" Wanda said. "Kept calling me 'girl.' Do I look like somebody's damn girl?"

Goody called, claiming he was feeling under the weather and coughing as if to prove it, and then explaining he and his mother were driving down to Chillicothe to visit his aunt Baby, who was sick. "I miss you, Tish," he said and promised to surprise her at work one night, walk her home in the moonlight. Tish never thought to push farther. Goody was busy. She was busy. *Someday we'll be together,* she sang to herself.

Often their phone conversations were filled with silences Tish didn't know how to break. Yet sometimes it was enough just to hear his breath on the other end, to know he was there. In her mind she began to add up just how little time she and Goody had really spent together, amazed by how close they had managed to become simply through understanding. Pride stiffened her heart, made her unable to ask him for what she really wanted. If she acted too eager, came across as desperate, he would tire of her. After she hung up, she consoled herself with the fact that once she was sixteen and in possession of the Rambler, things would change between them. She could come to him. In just a couple weeks she would be free. She turned the ID bracelet around and around on her wrist. The weight of it reassured her. A circle closes on itself, allows for no intrusions. When she was lonely, she simply turned it over and read the inscription.

Oddly, her mother never asked about the bracelet. The omission was almost pointed. When Tish washed the lunch dishes, she liked the way the bracelet slid down her wrist, how the metal caught the light and sparkled through the soapsuds, casting a golden glow over her skin. She flicked the suds from her fingers and settled a plate in the drainer. Ford, passing by, gave her a sharp jab with his elbow. She wheeled around. "Stop, boy!" He smiled smugly and held up one hand. From his fingers dangled a wrinkled piece of paper, something that had clearly been ripped to pieces, but was now painstakingly Scotch-taped back together. For a moment Tish didn't get the point. Then she realized with horror that it was a mosaic of her own words. Something intimate she had written in private, then torn to tiny bits, and tossed in the trash. Ford, snooping, had retrieved and resurrected it. His discovery hung between them like a taunt.

Dearest Goody, you are the love of my life . . . I want to hold you. . . . Tish sprang forward like a cat. The words spoken in Ford's mocking voice sounded childish. She grabbed for the paper, but Ford had twisted away. He turned his back to her and crumpled the paper into his fist. Just out of reach he began to singsong, "Goody, I love you. Goody, make love to me. Baby, baby, baby. Goody, I want you, I need you. . . . I would give my life for you." Those were words she would never send. Words she was simply trying on like a hat or a coat. Words no one else had a right to read. Words that had burst so spontaneously from her mind like flames, consumed her with fire, left her breathless with the effort. When she was done, she had ripped the letter to bits, and sprinkled them like confetti into the trash.

Footsteps. The sound of Francis's and Fisher's voices. Her mother was coming. "Not now, boys, later. . . ." Ford was in stitches. "Oh, black man, do it to me, baby," he mocked. "Do it to me now," and he wiggled his hips. Tish stood burning with shame, her passion exposed and reduced to crude mimicry. The hours of ache had given way to the firestorm of words that Ford now held over her. She lunged. He made a dash for the doorway. For a moment Tish imagined herself revealed, torn apart and exposed for them all to see. Her mother sailed through the doorway. Ford squeezed past her and stood with the letter fanning out in his hand behind her back.

Mrs. Espy was carrying Francis on her hip. "Oh, hello, what are you two up to?" she asked cheerfully. Dismayed, Tish turned to Ford. Magically, the paper had disappeared.

"Nothing," he said, grinning, and vanished. A moment later his footsteps pounded up the stairs to the second floor.

"Tish, thank you for finishing up those dishes. That was very thoughtful." Mrs. Espy set Francis down. "Are you working at the inn this evening?"

Shaken, Tish imagined Ford slinking into his room, her precious, private words crushed between his fingers.

"No," said Tish. She turned back toward the dishes, panic fluttering in her stomach. "I was thinking of going to the library this afternoon, getting some new books."

Mrs. Espy flashed her a smile. "Well, that sounds like a fine idea, darling. You go right ahead."

The interior of the library was always cool and dark. The granite floors felt solid and smooth under her bare feet. Ever since she was little she had liked wandering among books, reading titles from the spines, pausing to browse opening words and release the scent of paper. The gold ID bracelet jingled on her arm, breaking the silence in the arched hallway. Ahead was the checkout desk. The librarian, who seemed to have been there forever, had awarded Tish and Angela each the best reader prize in the summer reading program back when they were just kids. The library had once been her sanctuary, but now it offered no relief.

She was out of squares and desperate for one. Through the open doors, sunlight sparkled down through the maple leaves on the terrace outside adult fiction. But Tish was in no mood for books. She turned and walked out the back door into the parking lot. Someone out there might have a Kool Long she could bum. Some stranger would surely be happy to reach into his pocket and share one of his cigarettes. Outside, the pavement was hot, the lot empty. A solitary car sat vacant on the edge. The sun beat down on her face. Tish remembered the cigarette machine over in the student union. She reached in the pocket of her cut-offs, feeling for change. Over the burning asphalt she padded in bare feet. The stinging on her soles came as odd relief, distracting her from the fear that her mother might at this moment be unfolding the intercepted letter, and discovering the daring words *I want to feel you inside me.*

A car pulled up alongside her. Tish was so deep in thought that its presence didn't register right away. A blast of horn startled her. She turned abruptly. It was Jasmine at the wheel of her father's black ninety-eight, her expression fierce. Benita and Maxine were with her.

"Hey, Tish." Jasmine said grimly. Fish-bowl earrings with plastic goldfish dangled from each ear.

Tish stepped to the curb. Jasmine leaned out. "Come on, get in," she ordered. "We're on our way to take care of a little business."

Tish slid in back next to Benita.

"Anyone got a square?" she asked. "I'm dying."

"I don't smoke," said Benita. No one else answered. There was tension in the car, and for a moment Tish thought it had something to do with her.

"What's up?" she said.

"A whole lotta mess," Maxine muttered from the front seat and turned her head to look out the window.

Jasmine nosed the car down College Street, past the west edge of campus. There were more cryptic, tight-lipped comments from the front seat.

"Where are y'all headed?" Tish asked, but no one was answering.

Jasmine cleared her throat from the front seat.

"I hope you're not in a hurry," was all she said.

Tish shrugged.

"When was the last time you talked to Goody?" Benita asked, with a sarcastic little laugh. A week maybe. Tish wasn't sure.

There were more murmurs in the car. Benita singsonged something incomprehensible and laughed again. Jasmine turned onto Eden Street, a neighborhood straddling the east and west sides, where lower-income black and white families lived among university students. The first thing Tish spotted was Lamar's Impala parked in front of a white duplex with peeling paint. Benita and Maxine were both talking at once: "Pull up there. Park here. Don't let him see."

"I knew it!" said Jasmine. "Goddamnit, I knew it."

Tish sighed. The continuing saga of Jasmine and Lamar. She wanted no part of this. Odd that Jasmine even wanted her along. Maybe she should just excuse herself and walk on back down to the union and bum a cigarette.

But Benita turned to her and said, almost as a challenge, "I hope you're with us on this." Her tone was strange. The air was so thick Tish thought if she didn't get a menthol cigarette fast to clear her lungs she would suffocate. The car pulled to the curb and stopped.

She followed the others as they emerged from the car, careful not to slam the doors, lowering their voices. Her back was sopping wet from where it had been pressed against the seat. Overhead the sky was beginning to cloud over. How quickly the weather changed. Rain had been threatening for several days. Way to the south loomed the dark edge of a thunderstorm. Ahead of her, Jasmine turned, her expression hard. She motioned for them to follow as she mounted the little porch that ran along the edge of the building. Music came from an open second-story window—jazz. Cannonball Adderley, maybe. A curtain was blowing outward, caught in a quick, sharp burst of air. Tish felt the stirring of anticipation. She patted down her hair, once again cork-screwing over her head.

Jasmine turned and paused again to let them all catch up. She was more beautiful than ever, her dark brown arms, shoulders, and back exposed in the halter top, her breasts carefully cradled in the flowered material. She had a gold cross around her neck with a tiny pearl on the tip. The opal ring, the one Lamar had given her, gleamed on her finger. "Girl," she said, to Tish, "I hope you're ready to go in there and kick some serious ass."

Tish said nothing, just stepped carefully over the toys littering the downstairs hall. Someone was cooking something greasy in the first-floor apartment. Tish could hear children's voices on the other side of the door. Up the carpeted, creaky steps. The music from behind the closed door grew louder. Tish heard laughter, then voices. Jasmine turned on the stairs and looked back down at the others.

"This is it," she said, eyes flaming. "The story ends right here."

What happened next happened in the way all impossible things do—in a blur of slow-motion, when space loses contour, and familiar shapes become unknowable. Someone must have opened the door, or maybe it was already opened, and they all just walked in. Afterward, Tish couldn't remember. They were inside a large, mostly empty room. The blinds were drawn, the room filled with dusky light. A record turned on the hi-fi. White fishnets dangled from the ceiling, and strange summer light infused the room with a glow. Two or three mattresses had been stacked on the floor next to a window seat where a tall, lean man lay stretched out smoking a joint and staring at the ceiling. The air was filled with the sweet, acrid smell of weed. On the coffee table sat a prismlike bottle of vodka catching the light. There were record albums scattered all over the floor like Frisbees. The four of them filled the room. From the corner, there were quick movements of two silhouettes separating, jumbled voices rising. One was moon-faced Cindy Pavelka scooching back on the mattress, her white legs sticking out, a joint in one hand, blond hair a tousled mess.

To the left Reggie was rising up out of a bean bag chair, demanding "What the hell?" But Tish still wasn't getting it. She heard Jasmine yell—it was almost a scream—a siren voice rising up and filling the room. And there was Cindy trying to get up off the mattress, and the familiar but unexpected shape of Goody materializing next to her, his face drawn in surprise. He was wearing only a pair of cut-off shorts. Sweat glistened on his bare, smooth chest. But there was some mistake, wasn't there? This should be Lamar. Cindy's blouse was unbuttoned. The flesh of her breasts swelled pearly-white from her brassiere. Her bare stomach shone smooth and white as a fish's belly. She was grinning—no, she wasn't grinning anymore. She was standing up. Confusion marked her face. Jasmine had pushed on past Cindy to a closed door, and the next thing Tish knew Lamar was emerging with nothing but a sheet wrapped around his waist, his hair mashed flat on one side of his head as if he'd been asleep. Behind him stood a white girl, one of Cindy's cheerleader friends, someone Tish knew only as Shirley, who lived out on Christ-Cripple Road in a trailer house. Everything seemed to be unfolding in one long scream that came from Jasmine as she raised both fists and began to pummel first Lamar, and then the girl.

Cindy, her face blanched with shock, was scrambling to pull her clothes together. And while Jasmine had hold of Shirley, and Lamar had hold of Jasmine, Tish found herself locked into the expression on Goody's face. He began gesturing with his hands, even protesting. He seemed to be saying something to her, but what came out was "Aw, man! Aw, shit!" And then he crumpled the empty can of Colt 45 he was holding in his hand and threw it on the floor. Tish heard her name, once, twice, three times, chiming like a bell, but she didn't recognize it. He said it again but she was having a hard time putting two and two together, unable to recall what came after the equal sign.

Reggie was saying, "Get her out of here," meaning Jasmine, who was pounding Shirley so hard the girl had fallen backward against the wall. Jasmine turned on him in fury and said, "You make me sick, Reggie, you and these goddamned hos you bring over here!"

Hos, sluts, and worse. White bitches. Honky trash. *Don't you niggas try to tell me shit!* Maxine pushed against Tish to get to Jasmine. She was saying, "Come on, girl, it ain't worth it. You've seen what you came to see. Now let's get out of here." But Jasmine pushed back. Shirley cowered behind Lamar, her nose bloody, eyes bugging. Jasmine stood staring at Lamar before she said, "You son of a bitch black bastard. I hope you fry in hell." Before anyone could stop her, she'd reached around and grabbed Shirley again by the hair and begun to swing her from side to side. Shirley was braying out for help, clutching at the air, and Lamar, seemingly helpless to do anything, backed away, trying to keep the sheet around him like a Roman toga.

Tish was beginning to understand. Why was it taking so long? she wondered. Why did she always have to have things spelled out? The ID bracelet had turned to fire on her wrist. The air was so thick she couldn't catch her breath.

Goody was trying to say something, but the words still made no sense, and Cindy now stood impudently, hand on her hip. Her lips were swollen and red from kissing Goody, her eyes slightly glazed with weed. Their bodies smelled of sweat and earth and wine and weed.

"Get out of my face, please," Cindy said to Tish. At the same time, Lamar was saying, "Jasmine . . ." and reaching for her, but she slapped his hand back, screaming out, "Don't you touch me!" as if his hands burned.

Reggie was trying to get everyone to leave. "This is *my* house, *my* crib, none o' y'all were invited, I want all y'all bitches out of here."

Cindy, combing her bangs with her fingers, said, "Tish, don't even try. If Goody were yours, he'd be with you and not me."

It was the insolence, the smug smile on her face, that pushed Tish over the line. She drew up her fist and pulled back her elbow as if stringing an arrow in a bow. At the moment her fist made contact with the side of Cindy's face, Reggie was already yanking her away.

Cindy stumbled back a few steps, her mouth drawing downward. She looked back in hatred. Jasmine was screaming, "You stupid honky bitch!" to Shirley.

Tish turned to face Cindy again. Even with Reggie pulling her toward the door, Tish knew there was only one place for her anger to go. "You ugly little white ho," Tish said, "you stupid, stupid bitch!"

Benita was trying to pull Reggie away from Tish. "Let her go," she said. And Reggie was saying, "All y'all need to leave. I don't want this in my house. You have no business . . ."

It was not the sheepish look on Goody's face that Tish remembered long after, or the way he shrank before her, turning smaller and shamed until he seemed to disappear. And it wasn't the open-mouthed fury of Cindy, who thought she was entitled to whatever she wanted. It was the look of stark rage on Jasmine's face as she turned to Lamar and slapped him straight across his head. The sound of her hand on his flesh resounded with a solid crack in the room.

Tish made one more lunge at Cindy. She managed to get a fistful of stiff, dyed yellow hair in her fingers. She twisted and pulled as hard as she could before Reggie pried her hand open and Cindy's head shot backward. He shoved Tish into the hallway and stood blocking the door, panting heavily. "Don't come back here," he said as if he'd never seen her before. Gone was the friendly grin, the quick flash of compliment.

Tish snapped, "I wouldn't come back if you paid me." She unhooked the bracelet from her wrist and in one smooth motion threw it back into the room. Jasmine pushed past her, and down the stairs, her body wracked with sobs and bent in the shape of heartache. A moment later Benita and Maxine followed. Benita murmured, "I told her she was asking for trouble. Girl is so stubborn."

Tish trailed after, but stopped when she got to the cracked sidewalk outside Reggie's duplex. An older black woman stuck her head out the window of the house next door and wanted to know what the hell was going on, she was calling the police.

"Tish!" It was Goody running to catch up, pulling on his shirt as he came. He was saying words that made no sense. *It was nothing. Baby, sorry, please, not what you think, Tish, wait, stop, let's talk.* It was like a bad poem, song lyrics minus the music.

Tish didn't answer. Instead, when he reached for her she yanked away and began to run. All she knew was the rhythm of her bare feet smacking against the hot pavement. How she hated them all. Start with Jasmine, who was a fool from way back. And then those stupid white girls, taking their little walk on the wild side, not caring who they went with so long as he was black.

Was this what she had been so careful for, guarding her body like some precious object, while Goody went off with girls like Cindy? Maybe he'd had Shirley too. Maybe they'd all sat up there day after day getting high and laughing behind her back, the slow tease of her desires the butt of Goody's grand joke.

She fled across the square, hoping she was no longer visible through the green jungle of trees. Past the library, past the Memorial Inn, where the socialists had talked about changing the world over fruit cocktail. To the east side, where the sky had grown so dark it looked like evening. She didn't slow down until she'd reached the bottom of Woodland. Only then, breathless, did she turn to see if anyone had followed. Only then, alone, did she begin to feel the substance of her own body again, one muscle at a time, and the ache of bone and ligament.

She turned away from home and cut across the empty lot next to the reservoir, where she and her father had fished and star-watched when she was little. Beyond that spread the arboretum, where she and Goody had walked.

Life loomed like an endless plague, an illness with no cure.

She was still winded by the time she reached the edge of the water, her breath high in her chest. She walked out on the little wooden dock and crouched down. She remembered the night her father brought her "moon fishing," and they had sat there together listening to the bullfrogs, dangling their lines in the dark water, and speculating about what lay below the inky surface. The moon and stars reflected in the water. Tish had wondered if what was above and what was below were mirror images, that you could just turn the world upside down.

In a tree behind her, a mockingbird called. No, someone was saying her name, and for a moment she panicked, thinking Goody had found her. But when she turned around, it was Holly Penn approaching from the gloomy line of trees. She was wearing ripped overalls and a tie-dyed T-shirt. She padded up, also in bare feet. She looked so different Tish almost didn't recognize her.

"I thought that was you. Not too many people with bright red hair like yours. How're you doing, Tish?"

"Fine," Tish murmured, feeling nothing.

Holly sighed and jammed her hands in her overalls pockets. "I'm so sick of summer. My parents are taking us all to Florida in three days. They have this time-share in Fort Lauderdale, with a pool and a sauna. It's so bourgeois I could puke, but they're making me go."

"Really," Tish said. Even the sight of a transformed Holly left her unmoved. *Goody's hands, Goody's mouth, Goody's eyes, Goody's beautiful smooth chest.* Once it had all been hers, or so she thought. The ache of losing him turned to a hunger unable to satisfy its own desire.

Holly was talking. ". . . because my father hates Taylor, and doesn't want me to see him anymore because Taylor said he'd go to Canada before he ever let himself get drafted."

Mr. Penn flew a huge American flag in the front yard of their house in French Woods. A bumper sticker on his Cadillac announced, "America—love it or leave it."

Tish stared out at the changing light over the water. She was only half listening.

"Taylor says my father's a fascist capitalist pig. I guess he is." She paused. "So, what are you up to these days?"

Tish shrugged. "Working," she said and kicked a pebble into the water with her toes.

"Oh, that's right," said Holly. "You have that job at the inn. I've been taking a drama course at the college. If I'm going to be an actress, I need to get serious." She didn't seem to notice Tish wasn't paying attention.

"You seeing anyone these days?" Holly went on. "You know, like a boyfriend?"

The timing of the question made Tish instantly suspect Holly of duplicity. But of course that wasn't possible. Holly would have no way of knowing anything.

"I was," Tish said guardedly. "It's over now." She felt crushed by the words. In the ensuing silence, their meaning spread, like the ripples from the pebble she kicked into the water.

For a moment she started to confide, but stopped herself in time.

Holly sighed. "My parents are threatening to send me away to private school in New Hampshire. Get me away from Taylor's influence."

"That's too bad," said Tish, thinking how lucky Holly was to get out of Brazil, even if it meant going off with a bunch of snotty, rich white girls who owned their own horses and wore floor-length gowns to dances. She tried to reconcile the barefooted Holly next to her with the girl she had known all these years.

"Looks like it's going to start pouring any second." The new Holly glanced up at the sky. "Guess I better get going. You walking home?"

Tish shook her head. "Nah, I'm gonna sit here for a little while," she said and plopped herself down. She stuck one foot in the water, still lukewarm from the heat of the day. Holly shrugged.

"See you, then." She paused. In the silence Tish felt the pressure of tears behind her eyes and knew there was nothing more to say.

She was relieved when Holly walked away, her hair glowing in the thickening dusk. Her retreating figure grew smaller until she disappeared among the trees on the other side of the reservoir.

Overhead, the sky was clotting, and thunderclouds began to boil. Far off along the horizon, thunder rolled. A raindrop plunked right onto Tish's scalp. It was cold and heavy. A few more fell in warning.

She got up and began to walk the two blocks home. From the front, her parents' house looked empty, the dark windows reflecting the black sky above. Tish crunched down the gravel driveway with a deep sense of foreboding. An odd yellow light smoldered in their backyard among the fir trees. It seemed to be slowly sucked back under, like a french inhale, then smothered by the rhododendrons, vibrant with their heavy dark green leaves and thick red flowers.

Tish entered through the back door just as a streak of lightning cut a thin gash in the sky. More thunder rolled.

Something delicious-smelling had recently been taken from the oven, and the kitchen was still thick with heat. Tish couldn't believe her mother had baked on such a hot day. She went straight to the freezer and opened the door for a blast of icy air.

There was a two-layer devil's food cake cooling on the counter, and Mrs. Espy was beating chocolate icing with a hand mixer. When she saw Tish, she clicked it off.

"Hello, honey. I glad you're home. There's a tornado watch. Quite amazing weather for Ford's birthday."

Birthday! Tish had completely forgotten. Of course, two weeks before her own, and she'd given it no thought. Why should she have the way he always bugged her to death? She retreated to the doorway and watched her mother, the strong, capable hands, the mouth curved in concentration. Next to her, the black wall phone hung quietly in its cradle. The house was silent the way it can be only before a storm. Then, Tish heard faintly the voices of Ford and a couple of his friends on the side porch.

"You want me to put the candles on or anything?" Tish asked meekly. She felt foolish and unworthy.

Mrs. Espy turned in one fluid motion. A soft, warm look flooded her face, a look Tish recalled from her childhood. She'd forgotten how much she missed that look. She resisted the urge to fall into her mother's arms and begin weeping, to confess everything, including her broken heart, and say she'd been a fool. She didn't deserve her mother's tenderness.

"Why, Tish," said her mother, "that's such a sweet offer, but every-thing's been pretty much taken care of. The boys are going to an early show at the movies. I thought I'd feed them first. You look hot and tired. Why don't you go relax? I'll let you know if I need anything."

Her compassion struck like a knife. They stood there for a moment, and Tish wondered what to say next. She came close to saying how much she needed her mother, but she didn't. Because there were things her mother could never understand.

"Looks as though we're in for a big storm," Mrs. Espy remarked with an eye on the sky beyond the window. "You want to check up-stairs and make sure the windows are closed?"

Tish counted the steps as she climbed to the second floor, even though she knew there were exactly eighteen. She had been counting them for years. There was comfort in habit. She went room to room checking the windows, her vision blurring with tears. Finally, she got to her own room, closed the door, and flung herself on the bed. She burst into a deep, quiet weeping that seemed to belong to someone else. She lay with her wet face in the soggy pillow and cried for a long time: for her own stupidity, for her rage toward Cindy, for her foolish love for Goody, and for the momentary glimmer of undeserved kindness from her mother. It was the last that was too much.

The storm broke overhead and the house was instantly awash with rain. Water streaked through her open window and onto the sill. Even-tually it ran down and pooled on the floor. She knew she should get up and close the window before the wood of the sill warped and the floor stained. But she couldn't move. She watched the puddle widen, imagining all the damage it could do. For a long time she lay very still, facedown, while rainwater gathered.

XXXII

Another heat wave. Every day the radio was warning old people to keep their fans on and stay inside. Tish's brothers were grouchy, and one night her father slept with Ford and Fisher on the roof so they could watch the stars (Mrs. Espy was terrified they'd all fall off and kept running up to check). Tish lay fatigued, but sleepless, in her airless room. No longer would Goody come to her as if in a dream across the lawn. It was her own disbelief that paralyzed her. He had phoned—she was sure of that—but she'd instructed her mother to say she wasn't home. "Say I'm on vacation," said Tish, willing herself far away. "Say I'm at work. Say I'm dead."

"Is this the Goodman boy? Tell him yourself. I don't like lying," said Mrs. Espy, uncertain what to make of Tish's lingering bad mood.

Angela's house was all packed up. Tish had dragged herself by to stand with her in the empty living room, eating take-out fried chicken on paper plates. It was depressing. "You'll come visit us in Pittsburgh now," Mrs. Thompson must have said twenty times. And Tish agreed she would, knowing she wouldn't.

Peachy returned to Brazil, already showing, but staying inside, away from the heat. Tish strolled over only once to drop off a friendship bracelet she'd made, and a copy of *The Bell Jar*. She tried imagining her own life following a similar fate. A *Gazette* headline: YOUNG PREGNANT GIRL POET LOSES MIND IN BRAZIL HEAT—SKETCHES OUT FINAL WORDS BEFORE DEATH. It was all so tragic she couldn't stand it.

Peachy talked matter-of-factly about having to wear those silly maternity clothes, and attending alternative school in the fall because pregnant girls were not allowed in public school. It was impossible to imagine Peachy hauling a baby around on her hip. "I don't want no ugly baby," Peachy joked. "Not like that white girl Debbie Walters—you see that pitiful thing she had?" Rumor had it that Missy King, a white junior, was pregnant by a black senior named Flip Wing. Hmmnhunh, the talk had gone among the black girls, we'll see if she keeps it or gives it up.

Seeing Peachy again was awkward because of Peachy's detachment, as if impending motherhood made it impossible for her to feel close to anyone but the child growing in her belly. Mrs. Stubbs's face looked slightly wan as she offered Tish something to eat. Then the phone rang, and it was obvious Peachy wanted to talk to whoever was on the other end and Tish left. "Thanks for coming by, Tish," Peachy said, leaning in the doorway, cupping the phone against her ear. She was smiling. On her wrist was the red, black, and green friendship bracelet ("Just the right size," she'd noted happily).

Going down the steps Tish heard the screen door behind her squeak open on its spring. Mrs. Stubbs poked her head out. "Thanks for coming by, sweetheart," she said. "You come back again, hear?" She was trying to make it all seem natural.

Tish nodded. She went on down the walk, scuffing her sandals along the pavement, overwhelmed by a terrible ache.

She named it loneliness, though the word wasn't right. It was partly that, but it was also wanting, and worrying, and yet no matter how she ran through the alphabet in her head, she couldn't locate the right word. She got stuck on the *l*'s with *loneliness, love, longing,* and it occurred to her later on in the thick night air wafting through her window that there simply were no words for what she felt. No language to explain the ferocity of that first attachment to Goody, and now the tearing away and closing down. She was finished with love. That was certain. Love brought pain, and even in its absence pointed to whatever was missing. She preferred silence, the escape into her own head. Even music was too painful.

"Your father's out back with his telescope," said her mother, appearing in the darkened doorway and appealing to the child Tish. "You want to go take a peek at the stars with him? I bet he'd love it if you did."

"No thanks," Tish said. It was mean and she knew it, but she couldn't bring herself to pretend.

"How's Peachy?" asked Mrs. Espy, lingering in the doorway as if they might actually have a conversation.

"Fine," said Tish, mildly touched.

Mrs. Espy paused, "It must be really hard," and Tish said, "Life goes on." Mrs. Espy tried again. "I'm sure your father would love to have you join him and the boys out back."

"I don't feel like it," said Tish and shifted on her bed. How could she explain she was too tired to get up, too worn out to even bother with a shower? The scent of the day clung to her, the mild pungency of her own sweat, the dust from the street. She reached up to scratch her scalp and when she withdrew her hand the oily scent of her own flesh clung to her fingertips. Let her family have the sky. She listened to her mother's retreating footsteps, ending in silence on the carpeted stairs.

Alone again, Tish fell back on her bed. The world went fuzzy along the edges. She lay quietly in the dark, listening to her own heartbeat through her sleeveless T-shirt. "Red," she murmured softly. "Red is dead."

During the days of that impossibly hot week Tish spent a lot of time sitting statue still on the front porch, drinking iced tea and staring out at the empty street. She left the house only to go to work in the late afternoons, and while she waited tables, she fixed her concentration firmly on the customers and their orders. It was easy and mindless if you knew the steps. Do this, do that. It suggested there was actually an order to the world.

Sometimes she worried that Goody would try to track her down at the Memorial Inn, and once she was sure she caught sight of him walking by. Startled, she eased back from the window and looked again, only to realize it was someone else. She didn't know if what she felt was disappointment or relief. It occurred to her he might have even left town. Gone down to Chillicothe to visit his sister or his aunt Baby with her mysterious illness. Was it possible he too was suffering?

Three days in a row Mrs. Espy took the younger kids swimming at Curtis Pond, and Tish declined the invitation to go along. She overheard her mother tell her father Tish was sulking again. She complained that Tish's mute presence was casting a pall over the whole house. Agitated with his own worries, Mr. Espy took Tish aside and asked her to please stop annoying her mother this way. He was trying to finish a book and needed peace and quiet. Couldn't Tish be more—well—cooperative? After all, this was a family. Tish half considered confiding in her father, but caught the distracted look in his eye. Had he even noticed she was growing up, that she wasn't the child who once so patiently studied the night sky with him? What did he know of passion and loss?

Sometimes in her silence she imagined herself and Peachy and the baby, with maybe Dev too, in the Rambler, leaving Brazil altogether. Tish would be at the wheel, Peachy in the passenger seat holding the baby in her lap. They would drive west and protect each other along the way, maybe even set up house and all raise the child. The four of them, living together in some place far away from Brazil, some place like San Francisco where they could join the revolution and change the world. In this new place no one would think of her as white, but simply a fact of herself, framed on either side by Dev and Peachy, where she could live safely in between, like a word held in place by parentheses. And then there would be the baby, not exactly her own, because that wasn't to happen for a long time, but a child she could partially claim, almost blood but not quite.

In seven days Tish would be sixteen. The Rambler sat in the driveway waiting for her. Her father had said they'd go together to the car wash and have it cleaned inside and out. She imagined what it would be like to climb behind the wheel and let the car take her wherever it was she needed to go.

"Come on down, Tish," Mr. Espy coaxed from the doorway of her bedroom. "Don't you want to see the miracle of the first man on the moon?"

Tish didn't. Days ago she'd decided it wasn't a miracle at all, just a mistake she wanted no part of. White people were never satisfied with what they had; they were always trying to conquer something. She had to laugh. That sounded like something Wanda would say. While black children starved to death in Mississippi, and Vietnamese children were dying from napalm, the government was spending money for a picnic on the moon. And why? Just to say they could do it.

"Letitia," her mother called up sharply from the dining room. "Don't be ridiculous. History is being made here."

It was pointless. Tish sighed and got off her bed and dragged herself downstairs. She heard her mother saying to her father, "Imagine what those two men must be feeling right now. To be way up in the middle of space like that, trusting on technology to help them breathe and move."

Ford sat at the table, reciting facts and figures about Neil Armstrong and Buzz Aldrin. "Did you know . . ." he kept saying until Tish wanted to shake him and scream out, "No, I didn't know and I don't want to." It was the wrong kind of knowledge, the testable fact that she never did get right in school.

She turned back into the living room and flung herself down on the sofa, inhaling the familiar musty smell of the cushion.

The rest of them out there, were traitors, assembled around the portable television in the dining room, mesmerized by a trick of light and angle that someone was calling "a walk on the moon." If they could walk on the moon, they could do anything, right? Then why was the world such a mess?

Tish could hear Fisher and Ford asking questions, the gasps of amazement. *Look, look, look!*

"Oh, my God," said Mrs. Espy. "I don't believe it. . . . It's wonderful—what magic."

Her naivete irritated Tish, who no longer believed in wonder or magic. She had no interest in witnessing a man encased in a protective suit, carrying his own oxygen, risking his life just to set foot on a mess of volcanic craters. It was almost funny, wasn't it? The moon, that distant mystery she had so often peered at through her father's telescope, was nothing more than a lie. Now some fool was clomping over it in big space boots, as if it were as ordinary as a football field.

"Letitia, get in here now!" This was her father's voice, sharpening ever so slightly. He was trying a range of tones with her, on the chance he'd land on one that worked.

"Look, look, there he goes! Oh, my great God, he's stepping down." Mrs. Espy's voice had gone all webby with incredulity. "Martin, please get Letitia in here—she's going to miss the whole thing."

That was when Mr. Espy popped up and stormed into the living room. Tish kept her head buried.

"Tish, I'm ordering you . . ." he said with just enough uncertainty in his tone to convince her he was only playing a part. And her role? That was easy. After all, she was the rebellious adolescent cliché they could do nothing with, who was tearing the family apart and making everyone miserable.

His voice mellowing, Mr. Espy pleaded, "Letitia, don't you think this drama has gone far enough?" He was giving her a chance, and extending his hand. For a moment she considered accepting, but that would be giving in. Her mother would see it as a triumph, a coming around, as if Tish were finally emerging from a long illness.

From the kitchen her mother's words were exaggerated for her benefit: "MissDifficultPrimaDonnaWhoDoesSheThinkSheIs." Then Ford's satisfied laugh. Mr. Espy stood a moment in clumsy silence. He's torn, Tish thought. But he can't pull back now.

In the next instant his voice dropped to a whisper, and she almost missed what he said. "You're impossible" hung in the air between them, as he turned back to the television.

In between the jumble of voices on the television, Tish made out fragments of what her parents were saying, a mosaic of "Don't let her spoil . . . let's just ignore . . . she's got a lot to learn. . . ."

They were strategizing, trying a different psychology as if that's all it would take to dislodge her. Just the right balance of threats and pleas, and she would straighten out, and then they would refer to this time as "that awful phase Letitia went through." It would be written into the family lore, something to be looked back on with humor once they had successfully reshaped her.

Weary, Tish pulled herself up from the sofa. With each step they cheered on the moon she felt something was being lost. It was as if a part of her were dying, but she didn't know why. She took herself stealthily back upstairs, avoiding the creakiest steps, so as not to call attention to herself.

In her room she felt no rush of relief, only the welcome habit of solitude. There was no joy left, no expectation. Once again she traced in her mind her own folly these last few months. She had overestimated her own powers, imagined her desires to be Goody's. Without him, she was empty and tired.

She considered the idea that she'd dreamed it all, or that she'd even misunderstood. On occasion she imagined confronting Goody and giving him a chance to explain. But what words could he have possibly used to change what she had seen?

She had spoken only once to Jasmine afterward, to learn that Jasmine "fired" Lamar for good, throwing the opal ring onto the hood of his Chevy. In a month she would be going off to college. Tish avoided mentioning Goody. There was nothing to say.

Outside the window, the cicadas made their racket. The silver maple glowed. A car engine hummed by. The air was thick and full of summer scent. She went to the closet and poked through a few leftover artifacts of childhood. She yanked out her old overnight case, the round powder-blue one with the blond teenage girl in a ponytail lounging next to a portable record player. With a pang, she recalled her excitement when at eight years of age she'd discovered it under the Christmas tree, a symbol of growing up. That's what it felt like at the time, having her own suitcase, as if overnight she had been elevated to the status of teenager, someone with the option to come and go as she pleased. It turned out Angela had gotten one too (their parents had consulted) and together they'd colored Angela's girl's face with brown crayon and darkened the hair to black. That year they spent practicing at being teenagers, packing and unpacking the cases for trips they never took.

Tish set the case back on the shelf, and pulled out her old knapsack, the one her mother had bought her the summer she attended a week of church camp with Angela. She began to consider what she would need: hairbrush, toothbrush, socks, a T-shirt, a pair of jeans, her jean jacket with the black-power fist on one sleeve and the cannabis leaf on the other. Into her bag went thirty dollars, a notebook, her *Black Fire* anthology and a book of poems by Nikki Giovanni, *Black Feeling, Black Talk,* as if the presence of these might arm her against the world. A movement in the mirror caught her eye. She looked up and caught herself, in motion. The purpose of her efforts had put extra color in her cheeks, and a sharp light in her eyes. She looked like an older version of herself. In a smooth gesture she snatched up her hair in one fist, drawing it away from her face and above her head, so the red curls cascaded like a waterfall toward her shoulders. She twisted the rubber band so tight her eyes teared. There, she thought, there I am, and regarded herself the way you would a stranger.

While her unsuspecting family celebrated the walk on the moon, Tish crept down the stairs and let herself out the back door. She entered the muggy street wearing cut-off jean shorts, sandals, and the dashiki Peachy had made for her, knapsack slung over one shoulder.

In the dusky silence the street felt unreal, like something imagined. There was the sensation of floating along in the early evening, past shapes that turned flat and receded in the twilight, the tree trunks foregrounded, rising up thick and dark. She got to the bottom of Woodland, where her feet slowed of their own accord. There was the odd sense she was being watched and followed. She stood and listened. In the distance, a power mower hummed against a chorus of cicadas chittering in the trees. Most likely everyone else would be inside watching the man on the moon.

She half expected to see her parents' Checker emerge from the shadows. She began to walk again, grateful for the solid weight of the knapsack, imagining herself to be fully prepared for anything. She could keep on walking and never look back.

In some better, distant place where she could start over, she conjured up the rattle and pull of people-filled streets, the slamming of car doors, the honking of horns, the tempest of excitement before a party, the strong beat of a good dance song, the heat of bodies swelling the room. A flood of voices filled her head—the fiery rhetoric of black militants and angry Vietnam protesters who were going to change the world—images of beatings and hosings and murders, countered by hope, free love, and flower power. She longed for whatever lay beyond Brazil.

She headed roughly west, crossing Division Street, without waiting for the light to change. Jeannie Lyons passed in a car with her parents. She was seated up front between them, the white porcelain face of Mrs. Lyons turned slightly down, and the ebony countenance of her father concentrating on the road. Tish turned up Division, following her feet. It didn't register until much later when she thought back on this strange, uncertain moment in her life that she automatically stopped at the square, lingering at the place where earth and sky were joined by a single length of railroad track. The square was empty. No one was out. Suddenly she felt very tired. She plunked down on the grass under the plaque to catch her breath, and watched the traffic light at the intersection go from green to yellow to red, and back to green. At about ten o'clock, the signal would change to blinking yellow, eliminating the red and green altogether.

Tish arranged herself on the grass and stretched out her legs. She had skipped dinner, and was now past the point of hunger. Nickles' Bakery had closed long ago. The shades of the Campus Restaurant were drawn. She settled into a pleasant numbness, as if physical need had conveniently ceased to exist. Several cars went by driven by people she didn't recognize. She imagined herself attached to each one heading out of Brazil, passing the fields on either side, heading north toward the lake.

Just about now her mother would stop thinking Tish had taken off on a walk without permission and begin to consider other, more serious possibilities. She had underestimated her daughter's stubbornness, her refusal to participate in the life of their family, to comply as a member. Instead, she was sliding away from them and now, in one impulsive moment, seemed to have vanished. Martha Espy would start by calling the Thompsons, only to discover their phone had already been disconnected. She would realize with a jolt she had misremembered the date and failed to say a formal good-bye to Linda. Already Angela was mounting the steps of her new house in a middle-class black neighborhood in Pittsburgh, wearing her IT'S A BLACK THANG T-shirt, and imagining how she would start off the school year with her giant afro. Mrs. Espy would turn to Tish's father, asking what punishment he thought they should inflict when Tish showed up, because in that way she could believe she still was in control.

At no one's request, just a need to take action, Martin Espy would leave to drive through the west side neighborhoods in the Rambler in search of his daughter. After an hour of aimless driving, he would return home, admitting to having no luck, and keeping up a brave front for Tish's mother, who was now distraught. Martha would secretly worry that Tish had gone off with a boy—there were those unspoken thoughts—someone black, older, and maybe even dangerous.

While Martha and Martin would not forego their excitement over the walk on the moon altogether, their attention would grow more and more earthbound, and they would once again question Ford, who would smirk and claim to know nothing. They would convene in Tish's room, awkward on the private turf of their daughter, searching for clues. Quietly they would look around, taking in Malcolm on the ceiling, Che on one wall, and Newton on the other. Martha Espy would finger the framed photo of Tish and Angela on the vanity table, lift it wordlessly and set it down. She and her husband would exchange glances and try to understand. They would speak philosophically of their daughter as "a product of our times," with equal measures of affection and anger, then one of them would remind the other, *Let's stop this. She's not dead. She'll be back. She's just trying to make a point.*

Of course they each would secretly wonder if she had run away, but neither would entertain the idea seriously. *We could try Wanda Beals's house. Oh, but someone would have called.* They would quickly dismiss the idea of phoning the police because of the trouble that could lead to, and Martin Espy's deep and abiding distrust of the law. Finally, Martha, remembering the appearance of Mrs. Stubbs on her own front walk, would telephone Peachy's house and get no answer because the Stubbses had taken their pregnant baby girl out to the all-you-can-eat fish fry by the lake and then an overnight to her sister's in Cleveland—a celebration because now they were back together and the forthcoming baby was a fact of life, and there was nothing else to do but make the best of things.

Back in Tish's room, she would watch Martin sink onto the India-print bedspread (he said he hadn't realized that the mattress sagged and suggested they get a new one), for the first time considering the room in all its detail: the portable record player, 45's stacked on the rack, the vanity table with the mirror tilting at just the right angle for him to catch a glimpse of his own distress. He would run his hand through his cropped brown hair. The corner of one of her school notebooks peeked out from under the bed. Martha would watch as he leaned over and lifted it onto his lap, pausing for a moment before opening it as if contemplating what he might find. It was just another helpless gesture, but as he began to leaf through, she would realize he might find explanations, things she hadn't understood. He would try to link the slanted, grown-up scrawl and anguished thoughts to the delighted child he used to hoist onto his shoulders for stargazing. There would be words he hadn't realized Tish even knew, language he hadn't considered her capable of. How little they actually knew of the person who had scribbled these pages. He would mention he felt shame at the intrusion, but it was justified, of course, under the circumstances. He would find sketches (not very good ones) mixed with poems, and scattered notes from classes. There would be pages filled with the initials "T.E. + M.G.," and strange equations in numbers and letters, added and compiled. It would be like reading an undecipherable code.

"Do you think she's with that Goodman boy?" Martha would want to know in a stricken voice. "And if she is, how do we find them?"

Martin would close the notebook, and lay it on the floor, where Tish would find it looking undisturbed when she returned. Because of course she would return. "This too will pass," he would say aloud by way of comfort. In this way husband and wife would keep returning to their missing daughter, who at that moment sat knees to chest in darkness, leaning against the track.

The grass beneath her felt comforting like the soft green bedding her mother used to hide the colored eggs in their Easter baskets when Tish was little. The ground still held the day's heat. Above, the air was striped with a strange mist, perceptible evidence of the disturbance made in the earth's atmosphere by the spaceship, she thought. Now she waited for the moon, which eventually began to rise as it always did, seemingly unfazed. She looked hard to see what if anything about it had changed. On the surface, it looked the same, but she knew better. In the perfect stillness, there came the faraway hooting of an owl.

Three winos showed up and sat on the stone benches in the middle of the square under one of the last elms to survive Dutch elm disease, their empty bottles of screw-top hitting the brick walkway with a crash of glass followed by their own buzzed laughter. A police car cruised by, circling the square, then another joined it. A truckload of Farmers slowed down. They shouted taunts at the winos and the winos yelled back. The Farmers finally drove off, "Sympathy for the Devil" blaring from the truck speakers. It was quiet again. Eventually the winos took off, bantering drunkenly down the street under the bank clock that was now striking eleven. One of them started across the street just as a passing car screeched to a halt. For a moment, Tish thought he had been hit. But the car stopped in time, and what she heard was the sound of slamming brakes. Excited voices rose up. A small commotion in the night. Someone in the car got out and pointed up at the traffic light, a blinking yellow eye as witness. There was a brief scuffle. The passenger from the car got out to make amends, and another one of the winos crossed over and pulled his buddy by the shoulders, and quickly peace was made. The car pulled off slowly through the blinking yellow light. Shortly after, two summer school students from the university showed up and made love in whispers in the bandshell. Tish could barely make out their silhouettes, but she could tell the boy had long hair, and the girl was wearing a granny dress. About midnight, Lamar Holiday's white Chevy sped by, toward the east side. He was alone in the driver's seat, undoubtedly on his way to meet a girl. Some things never changed. Tish stretched her arms over her head and leaned back, feeling the solid comfort of the track.

Eventually the moon rose higher, illuminating the sky. Off in the distance ground fog began to rise. She dug in her bag for her jean jacket, then took out the notebook she'd brought along, and set it on her thighs. She uncapped her ink pen, sucked the top, and tried to think. The pen felt solid and purposeful in her hand. She started with figures, adding up the money she'd made so far at the inn. Then she jotted columnar lists of words. Her mind knotted and unknotted. What she really wanted to write she couldn't, because words weren't enough. She tried to imagine herself back to an earlier time in her life, when things seemed so much simpler. Back when her parents could do no wrong, and her mother's capacity for warmth was endless. All she and Angela had cared about was who could swing higher. But even then, she knew the world was not an easy place. There was the time her little dark-skinned friend in grade school had cried because Tish chose to play instead with a light-skinned black girl named Renée. "You don't like me because I'm Negro," the dark child had wept accusingly, and Tish, shamefaced, denied it. The dark child had smelled bad, of poverty and despair, her nappy hair full of lint. Instinctively Tish had been drawn to the light-skinned girl's long curly hair, not so unlike her own—a mirror image of herself—and the way the girl could hang upside down on the monkey bars forever. The dark girl's accusation had stung because she had spoken a truth Tish hadn't realized was possible.

It was impossible to unknow what you know, the accumulation of intricate hurts that add up. How you totaled them was one of the main differences between white and black, Tish thought ironically. The way white people seemed to take their place in the world for granted—without ever questioning. Whiteness was a given. Wanda had once remarked how you could look right through white people, like mist, how there was nothing for the eye to hit up against. *Blackness stops you dead in your tracks*, she pronounced and added with characteristic irony, *Funny, ain't it, how black people are the ones they call spooks.*

Tish shifted positions on the grass, stretching out her stiff legs. No question that this year they'd grown longer, adding a good two inches to her height. No wonder nothing ever fit right. *When the revolution comes . . .* She imagined the pulse of change promised, the rhythm of upheaval, the world turned upside down, no longer organized around whiteness, sky and earth reversed, and not just because some white man was trudging across the moon. *When the revolution comes . . .*

She wondered how long she could sit there uninterrupted, in danger of becoming a ghost herself as the town went about its mundane business as usual. Who would notice or care? The seasons would change, and years would pass. She had a vision of her ghost self taking root right there in the square, like some tragic figure from Greek mythology, left to weather the chill of winter and the heat of summer.

The refrain came again with urgency: *When the revolution comes . . . black people will rise up . . .* The words took on a tangible quality. She wrote feverishly in her notebook, knowing herself to be on the edge of something important. Such knowledge would always separate her from the limits of whiteness, and save her from the deadening insularity of Brazil. The world as her parents imagined it would never be the same again.

For starters, Wanda would earn early admission to six Ivy League schools, but choose Howard because she was "sick of looking at all these goddam peckerwoods every day." Before leaving, she would give up her virginity to Grover in his dorm room in the name of the revolution, and go on to major in poli sci. A year later, Holly Penn, with Janis Joplin ringing in her head, would drop acid and drive her yellow Mustang on a rainbow all the way to Swarthmore where her first year would pass in a psychedelic blur. Peachy's daughter Kenya would be two by the time Mrs. Stubbs would retire from the college laundry to care for the grandchild she came possessively to think of as her own baby. Peachy would head down to Kent State for college just after four students were murdered by the National Guard. Eventually she dropped out and took a job in a bank in Columbus, saving her money so she could pack up and take her daughter to New York. Angela would write Tish from the University of Michigan, where she majored in French, preparing for a pilgrimage to the Mother Land. She would describe in detail the first time she tried cocaine with her jazz-musician boyfriend Ahmad, Michael Brown and his Cutlass just a faint shadow of the past. She would include a snapshot of herself and Ahmad, both with huge, symmetrical naturals, standing sternly under a red, black, and green flag in a dorm room, Angela's mouth firmly set in defiance, Ahmad's fist raised to the sky. Tina would briefly date Reggie Moore, then marry Tony Purify, have a baby, and take a job cashiering at Sparkle Market.

She turned to a new page in her notebook, smoothing the paper with the flat of her hand. In the faint moonlight, it was impossible to tell if there were words already written on the page or not. Not caring, Tish wrote over them, turned another page, and continued with the scrawl of her ballpoint. She imagined words gathering more words, old words bleeding through, transforming and then blending. Collecting energy, she filled page after page, urged on by instinct and the comforting motion of the pen. Momentum pushed her forward, built up speed. The miles began to pass beneath her as fast as she could write, flipping the pages of her notebook. She imagined herself in the Rambler traveling on words at the speed of light past cornfields and redneck towns, moving farther and farther away from the Midwest, until her voice joined the storm of voices all over the country chanting "Power to the people."

Later, when the sun rose, there would be plenty of light to read what she had written, if she chose. But for now there was no reason to pause to decipher anything. Only the motion of her hand mattered, the uncensored voices in her head exploding on the page.

The moon began its descent, the sky overhead dissolving slowly back into darkness. In a little while it would be dawn. She knew from feel that she was nearing the end. When she ran out of pages, she would close the book. There would be no room left to write. It wasn't long before the dew settling on her bare legs would evaporate in the warmth of early morning. She watched a rare white squirrel scamper across the square, pausing to forage in the grass. He was one of a dozen squirrels the university had imported from Asia as part of an experiment the year before, but by accident only males of the species had been shipped. Tish thought with irony how they had had no choice but to mate with the native squirrels, producing brown and white offspring. The spotted squirrels had been a joke among her friends, *lookin' just like you, Tina,* Peachy had signified. Tish smiled at the memory.

Humidity was already gathering in the air, signaling another hot day. Inhaling deeply, she got up and stretched into her new length. Foolishly she'd forgotten her cigarettes, and now she'd give anything for a smoke. It was too early for anyone to be out on the street, and the student union would still be closed. She bent over to retrieve her knapsack. There was the imprint of her body in the squashed grass, which, by midmorning, would smooth itself out as the green blades sprang back into place, leaving no evidence she had ever been there. Leisurely, she began to walk, knapsack slung over one shoulder, in a southerly direction down Division Street. She wondered if anyone was up yet at her house, and how her parents would react if she walked through the door. Shortly she would reach the intersection where the choice was to turn either east or west. At the curb, she would wait for the light to change, even though the street was empty of traffic. Even after the light turned green, she would stand a while longer. She would take in the brilliance of the morning, thinking with relief how she was one day closer to sixteen. That much closer to the future.

ACKNOWLEDGMENTS

I extend heartfelt gratitude to my agent, Nicole Aragi; my best friend/ life partner Stephen Powell; and fellow fiction writer and friend Lynna Williams for direct encouragement with this project. I gratefully acknowledge long-term indebtedness to my first editor, Charles East; my parents, Richard and Mary Miller; and the sanctuary of Olive House in Annapolis, California. Many thanks also to my editor, Peternelle van Arsdale, and her tireless assistant, Siobhan Adcock, at Doubleday. To my colleagues Tony Ardizzone and Susan Gubar, much appreciation for friendship and moral support through the long haul. Also, a final thanks to Indiana University for providing respectable employment.

PERMISSIONS